PENGUIN BOOKS

ENCHANTED GROUND

Sarah Woodhouse is the author of *A Season of Mists*, *The Indian Widow*, *The Daughter of the Sea*, *The Peacock's Feather*, which won the Romantic Novelists' Association Boots' Romantic Novel of the Year Award in 1989, and *The Native Air*, all historical novels. *Enchanted Ground* is her first novel to be set in the twentieth century. She lives on a farm in Norfolk and has two children.

D0200166

SARAH WOODHOUSE

———————

ENCHANTED GROUND

PENGUIN BOOKS

PENGUIN BOOKS

Published by the Penguin Group
Penguin Books Ltd, 27 Wrights Lane, London W8 5TZ, England
Penguin Books USA Inc., 375 Hudson Street, New York, New York 10014, USA
Penguin Books Australia Ltd, Ringwood, Victoria, Australia
Penguin Books Canada Ltd, 10 Alcorn Avenue, Toronto, Ontario, Canada M4V 3B2
Penguin Books (NZ) Ltd, 182–190 Wairau Road, Auckland 10, New Zealand

Penguin Books Ltd, Registered Offices: Harmondsworth, Middlesex, England

First published in Great Britain by Michael Joseph 1993
Published in Penguin Books 1994
1 3 5 7 9 10 8 6 4 2

Printed in England by Clays Ltd, St Ives plc

For Podge

Many people who have travelled, and many who have not, have some little corner of the earth which to them is enchanted ground.

Lilias Rider Haggard, *A Country Scrapbook*

BRETTON FAMILY TREE

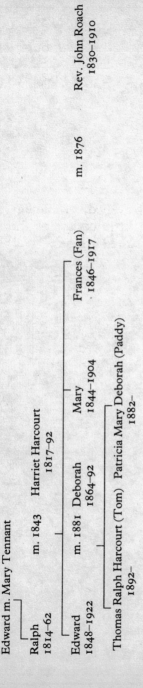

Edward m. Mary Tennant

Ralph
1814–62

m. 1843 Harriet Harcourt
1817–92

Edward
1848–1922

m. 1881 Deborah
1864–92

Mary
1844–1904

Frances (Fan)
1846–1917

m. 1876 Rev. John Roach
1830–1910

Thomas Ralph Harcourt (Tom)   Patricia Mary Deborah (Paddy)
1892–   1882–

CHANCE FAMILY TREE

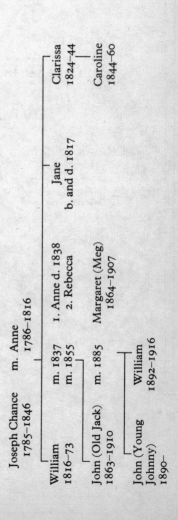

Joseph Chance   m. Anne
1785–1846   1786–1816

William
1816–73

m. 1837   1. Anne d. 1838
m. 1855   2. Rebecca

Jane
b. and d. 1817

Clarissa
1824–44

John (Old Jack)
1863–1910

m. 1885   Margaret (Meg)
1864–1907

Caroline
1844–60

John (Young
Johnny)
1890–

William
1892–1916

1

LAURA HALEY'S FIRST words on seeing the house were, apparently, 'How can an educated woman live without a bathroom?'

'Does she mean me – or herself?' asked Paddy Bretton afterwards, and then, suspiciously, 'Are you *sure* that was what she said?'

Curry was not sure but was affronted regardless. And what must Laura have thought of Curry, who was six feet tall and unspeakably haggard? Curry might repel a charge of archangels. Had she, however, repelled Laura Haley? Not very effectively perhaps. This unknown young woman had raced on, it seemed, to criticize everything her eye fell on: the absence of electric light, the long cold back passage by the gunroom, the huge dingy portraits on the landing. And she had refused to inspect the kitchen. What she had actually said was, 'Oh, I'm sure nothing's been changed since the house was built,' balking at the door to what Paget, the Bretton solicitor, referred to as 'domestic offices'. Instead she had returned for another look at the hall with its bold sweep of stairs.

She was wrong, of course. Paddy's grandmother Harriet had insisted on the great iron kitchener to replace the open hearth. The kitchener had been an advance equal to the coming of the railways. On the other hand, perhaps it was true little else had been altered or replaced since Bretton Hall was new in 1747 – only the lily pool and the rose garden, built in the 1880s, and the Piggery, built God knew when. The Piggery was a sort of butler's pantry – 'from the days when the Brettons might have owned to a butler,' said Paddy tartly – and was a mess of boots, old hats, hunting crops, watering cans, flower baskets and dog cushions. Paddy thought: If the Haleys rent the house I suppose I shall have to turn it out, turn out the debris of a hundred years. Damn. They ought not to have the house, they don't sound suitable. Then, more soberly: But we need the money.

'You could always sell the timber,' Paget had suggested once, but nervously, as a man might approach a cave of lions.

'We shall never sell the timber,' Paddy had replied in the steely tones of the hard-pressed.

'But when I last spoke to Mr Tom . . .'

'Oh, Tom would sell you the clothes off his back for a pound if you begged long enough.'

'There is always a demand for good timber,' Paget asserted. He felt it was his duty to underline the hard facts. Besides, he must also counteract Paddy's own assertiveness. She was too good at getting her own way. 'One day,' he continued stoutly, 'Mr Tom will inherit. We must be practical.'

There was nobody on earth more practical than Paddy. Without her Bretton would long ago have been sold up or demolished. Only during the war had she suffered it to be wrenched from her grasp and given over to 'convalescents' – 'Convalescents! They were *dying*!' she had cried. On her infrequent leaves from nursing in London she had raged at the wanton destruction, the acres of green paint. Her younger brother Tom had visited only once in all the four years. So far as she could tell he was unmoved. He had survived the

Somme but, as Paddy was to learn, there were degrees of survival. At the time, naively, she had thought it simply a matter of life and death. In London her ward smelled of boiled cabbage, disinfectant, gangrene. Though bombs fell and boys died holding her hand still she knew, when she was not too tired to think, that Tom's life at the Front would remain forever outside her experience. What he suffered she would never know.

Edward Bretton, her father, had been banished to the Lodge for the war years. The Lodge stood at the park gates and was inconvenient. Curry, who had been Bretton's housekeeper for nearly thirty years, remained in absolute charge of the Bretton kitchen, in spite of the Matron, the War Office, Army regulations and all attempts to evict her. In Bretton's drawing rooms, in the dining room, the ballroom, the library, the mangled amputations and the gas cases had their narrow iron beds. By the time peace was declared the house seemed irrecoverably ruined.

'Well, Home Farm's all right,' said Paget consolingly. 'Old Dack's a sound man. Not much wrong there.'

For a while prices were sound too, sound enough for them to start repairs, paint over the green. But now . . . Only four years since Tom had taken off his uniform, had said, 'This country's finished,' and had gone abroad to . . . To what? 'Heaven knows,' said Paddy. And here at Bretton everything still to do, Edward in his seventies and growing frail, prices falling fast, old Dack asking to retire. Tom should have come back and taken on Home Farm. But what had Tom known about farming? He would have sold all the timber to the next speculator who chanced through the gate and given up the fields on the Frilton road for houses.

'I'd rather sell the trees than the furniture,' he had said the last time he had been at Bretton, watching

3

Paddy label another consignment for auction. 'D'you know what you're doing, Pat? Does the old man agree?'

She knew what she was *trying* to do. 'Trying to save the roof over your head,' she might have said. But the roof he wanted was not Bretton.

'Why Italy?' she asked, exasperated.

'Why not? I like the climate. I like the people.'

He was tall and fair like all the Bretton men. He was only thirty yet it was sometimes difficult to remember he had ever been young. He was soft, mild, lazy, careless of his appearance and of other people's feelings. The world might go to pieces about him but he would never lift a finger. 'Not a fingernail, though the devil was at the door,' said Curry to Paddy. 'Your grandfather was just the same.'

'They're all the same,' cried Paddy furiously. Unworldly, incurious, hopeless with money – how else could she describe them? What strong emotion there was in the family was all Paddy's, more of it, as Curry often pointed out, than was good for her or for anyone else. But she had certainly protected Bretton, such as it still was. Tom could never have done that. He could do very little except shave himself and read the papers.

'I can't think how he managed in the Army,' said Paddy.

They would not sell the timber but they must do something.

'Let the house,' said Paget boldly. 'Move to the Lodge.'

His firm had served and survived several generations of Brettons and their wars, their crises, their perennial shortage of money. 'I like to think,' he said gently, 'that one day your father will have the means to pay my own bill, Miss Paddy.'

His wretched bill, one among so many, not computed for so long that the total must be astonishing.

'So do I,' said Paddy.

So began the delicate process of persuading Edward back to the Lodge. 'Only for a while,' lied Paddy brazenly. 'Think what we'll save not having to buy fuel for the kitchener.' But: 'Who are these people?' he demanded when the Haleys answered Paget's advertisement. 'Who are they? I won't have strangers in my house.'

They were extremely nice young people, Paget assured him, charming even. He was better at being persuasive than at being assertive and he knew, after so many years, exactly the degree of deference needed for Edward to remember he was an ally, professional adviser and humble servant together. There was nothing wrong with the Haleys, he declared, they were well known to Lady Somebody who was related to his wife's cousin. But to Paddy he said, 'You must let them have it, you know. If they offer anything near the rent we're asking you must let it go. If not, in six months . . .' He could not say to Edward: In six months we must sell. But Edward's daughter had kept the accounts since she was sixteen.

'Beggars have no choice, Miss Paddy,' he said.

The day the Haleys came to view was cold. The wind howled through the elms. Paddy thought how forsaken the place would look to strangers, half empty and freezing in this the worst blow yet of a cheerless, squally March. No, it would never do for a woman who feared life without a plumbed-in bath. The truth was that the house had been out of date before the turn of the century, perhaps before the turn of the previous century. Lack of money or lack of imagination had put paid to almost every improvement. The Haleys were bound to refuse it or refuse the rent being asked. 'It doesn't seem very much,' Paddy had said sadly to Paget, reading his advertisement. 'I mean, not for such a big house.'

'It's all we dare ask,' he had replied gently, seeing she was genuinely astonished. 'Nobody wants these great old houses any more, you know.' She knew. How she knew! But: 'Don't sell that horse for the price of one leg,' Jack Chance had warned her long ago during her first brazen attempt at horse-coping. 'Make it a third as much again,' she had commanded Paget, remembering, remembering Jack's voice, his gesture, the smell of his tweed coat. Years, years ago. Yet his voice was distinct in her ear, the movement of his big, long, capable hand. 'Make it a third as much again,' she said imperiously. 'We can always come down.'

But buying and selling horses was nothing, it seemed, to renting out vast inconvenient mansions miles from the amenities of modern life.

'I don't believe they were impressed,' said Paget unhappily.

'She wouldn't go down to the kitchen,' declared Curry, 'and she said . . . she said something about educated women not living without bathrooms.'

'Does she mean me – or herself?' asked Paddy.

Paddy had scarcely been educated. She had had a governess at the age of ten, the year Grandmother Harriet had died, the year Tom had been born, but drawing sticky-buds and sewing handkerchiefs and reciting 'The Lady of Shalott' was all she had been offered. 'So I learnt horse-coping,' said Paddy. She had been a keen pupil, Jack Chance an able tutor – a secret tutor. 'Everything had to be secret,' said Paddy, 'because he lived at Roman Hill, and Roman Hill was secret, was forbidden.'

Roman Hill was the farm in the valley beyond the palings of Bretton's park. 'Not paling, pale,' said Paddy, 'beyond the pale.' From the time she was a very little girl Paddy had known Roman Hill was out of bounds, was 'down there', was never to be visited. Nobody told her why. It was one of those things so familiar that there were long periods when it was unquestioned, as familiar and accepted as shutting all gates, not running from dogs, always walking up to a horse's shoulder. But Roman Hill was there and sometimes the questions bubbled, bubbled unspoken and unanswered. Jack Chance, the tenant, was the last tenant left the Brettons since the rest of the outlying land had been sold up, yet the Chances and the Brettons had had nothing to say to each other for fifty years. Rent was paid, accounts settled, legal form satisfied, but for the rest . . . For the rest they might have inhabited different continents. Then one day Paddy slipped out of the green garden door and ran down the hill – down Hobeys – and into a secret life.

Late that afternoon, the afternoon of the Haleys, Paddy walked from the Lodge up the drive to the gardens. The wind had died a little and dusk was falling. There was the smell of damp earth and air and rain. Half the daffodils were in tight bud, holding on for better times. The rhododendrons were storm-battered.

'Winter's last fling,' said Bushey morosely. He was digging by the asparagus bed with only his old red nose shining out of a smothering of scarves. All about him was the forlorn evidence of a great garden gone to ruin.

'Did you see the people who came to look over the house?'

'I did.'

'Were they interested in the gardens then?'

She had to turn aside suddenly to sneeze. She thought he said 'No' but perhaps he had simply grunted. She thought suddenly: He looks like a ferret. When she had been a child he had often kept one in his pocket and had always had about him their rank, unmistakable smell. He had come here in Harriet's time, a ten-year-old, 'gardener's boy'. Now he was all the gardener there was apart from Paddy.

Walking back through the flower garden she thought the house looked its worst. There were weeds on the terrace, weeds in the great urns by the steps. 'Turn your back,' Harriet had said long ago, 'and the wilderness flows in again.' Well, Paddy thought, we've turned our backs at last, we've retreated, bloodied, to the Lodge, and the wild things are closing in. She groped for her handkerchief and the house, her life's work, dissolved before her streaming eyes. But I never have colds, she thought. As the house returned to focus she examined it more critically, seeing it as a child might, growing up, see a parent for the first time as a separate and mysterious person. 'I hate it,' she could have said quite candidly. Yet she had fought, schemed, contrived, struggled, suffered for it. Why? What attached her to it? Habit? 'Cowardice' might have prompted the inner voice.

It was a huge house and well built. 'Solid,' said Harriet, who had loved it. Conceived by a distant Bretton who had been nothing more than a provincial lawyer overreaching himself, it had been a flight of fancy, an aberration – and the gods had obviously decided that for such an aberration, such presumption, the Brettons would be struck down. 'The truth is,' Paddy said, 'there's never been enough money since the day the first brick was laid.' It was lucky then that along with new linen, tea services and small fortunes, several Bretton wives brought cunning and the instinct for survival – and a head for figures. 'But *how* did they manage?' cried Paddy when it was her turn to wrestle with the accounts.

The Bretton men were neither clever nor ambitious. Alone they would have been reduced to living in a cottage and even then been thrown on the parish by their improvidence. They made silly investments, were easily influenced by rogues and nurtured deep passions for racehorses. But now and again they were lucky in a wife.

'They were lucky to get Harriet,' said Paddy, growing up, blessed with new insights.

'They were indeed,' said Curry, compressing her lips. She knew, because villages preserve memories of events fifty or a thousand years ago quite naturally, that there had been something hurried and shameful about Harriet's marriage to Ralph Bretton. The shame was not attached to Harriet but to her husband or to the circumstances, or perhaps, mysteriously, to Roman Hill. But: 'They were indeed,' she repeated fervently, 'and I'd give my eyes to see her walk in through that door this minute.'

Since Harriet could not take repossession of Bretton it was left to the Haleys to do for it what they could. They took it for a year and did not haggle over the rent. 'I find it quite amazing,' declared Paget. 'And to think I was so against increasing my original sum.' He remembered, belatedly, that Miss Paddy had been a more-than-capable horse dealer, that up until '14 and the outbreak of war she had kept Bretton afloat buying and selling. Penniless and desperate, at sixteen she had borrowed five pounds from Jack Chance to make her first purchase. She had paid him back and made ten shillings profit. 'I'll do better next time,' she had said boldly. He had lent her another five pounds and she had never looked back. 'You're the scourge of the county,' he had said later. 'I don't care,' Paddy had countered, 'as long as I make money.'

Since Hugh Haley had not challenged the rent he was either a gentleman or a fool, so said Paget privately to his wife. 'A quiet sort,' he described him to Edward Bretton at the Lodge. 'Resigned' was the word he used to himself. The wife had done all the talking. Indeed, all the conditions were Laura's own: that Paddy keep on the gardeners and that Curry, as housekeeper, find the appropriate staff for a place with eighteen rooms on each floor.

'Didn't you explain that Bushey and I are all the gardeners there are?' asked Paddy. 'And as for staff, there's none to be had in Stenton unless Babs Potter can be persuaded to come daily.'

The Potters had justified their existence for forty generations by being indispensible in times of crisis. There was a Potter for every eventuality, from rook scaring to rick thatching to keeping magistrates deep in the bogs of precedent and proof. If a cow needed digging from a ditch or a copse needed clearing a Potter would materialize stoat-like from the village under-growth. The current Mr Potter was doing hard labour but Mrs Potter was a competent laundrywoman. 'Well, I've never had cause to complain,' Curry often said in the tones of a woman who would certainly know how, adding, mysteriously, 'But all those babies.'

Several of the babies belonged to Babs, the eldest girl, but the fiction that they were Mrs Potter's own was never challenged. So 'It will have to be Babs and a parlourmaid,' Paddy said, 'and maybe Dack's boy to fetch and carry. They'll have to get a cook from an agency.'

'I don't care for it,' said Edward. 'Strangers in the house. My house. Does Tom approve? Have you written to Tom?'

'Of course I wrote to Tom, Father. I read you his replies. You know I did.'

Edward sat, skeletal and dignified, the teacup shaking a little in his long hand. 'He ought to come back. He ought to come back here to live.'

'What would he live on, Father?'

'Well, what do *we* live on?'

She could have said: Nothing. She had long ago given up showing him the figures, asking for advice. He had no advice, only to 'see Paget, that's what I pay him for,' unaware that Paget had not been paid since before the war. 'See Paget,' he said, or 'The rents will pay for the repairs.' 'There are no rents now,' she would retort. All the tenant farms had been sold off by Harriet to save Bretton from ruin in the seventies. But 'Nonsense!' Edward would cry, 'what about Roman Hill?' and yes, she had to admit there was still Roman Hill, still the Chances, though in the face of the repairs that rent was a spit in the wind, as Bushey might say.

'Father is seventy-four,' Paddy wrote to Tom in Italy, 'and really perfectly strong and alert, but he never pays attention when I talk about money. He pretends to be senile. He repeats "See Paget, see Paget" as if it was Paget who had run things all these years. He hates the Lodge, it's too small, too hot, too cold, too "public" – though hardly anything ever goes by on the Frilton road except on market days. Then I find him ordering things from Frilton and even London as if cost were no object.' As she wrote this she thought: And you are just like him. You'd do exactly the same.

'Tom Bretton's never been right since the war,' said the village, amazed anyone would voluntarily exchange Stenton for Italy – affronted too. Though the Brettons had never been called squires they had occupied that place at the top of the village pyramid. They ought to take their duties seriously. 'Tom does his duty when he can't do anything else,' said Paddy privately. But she knew he would never be happy at Bretton, getting to grips with country life. He had never seen himself in Edward's place. Mulish, disaffected, he had spent as much time as possible away, with schoolfriends, on walking tours, bicycling in France . . . And then the war had saved him from Bretton for ever.

Of course he resented being in uniform. There was a photograph Edward kept on his desk. It showed a sullen boy in a stiff collar who looked as if he had lockjaw. But then Tom had always been a mass of resentment. Nothing he was given, no part of the world he inhabited, was what he wanted. 'But what does he want?' asked Paddy.

'He ought to come home,' said Edward harshly, banging his stick on the floor.

'Father, please. What must Mrs Dye think? Tom will never come back. You know perfectly well he's quite happy where he is.'

'Doing what? And why Italy? Answer me that? Why Italy?'

'Why not?' asked Paddy. Over the teacups she caught Paget's sympathetic look. In the kitchen Mrs Dye's muted singing had stopped. In such a small place, thought Paddy, rows were village property in an instant.

'Why leave this country?' demanded Edward. 'What's wrong with this country?'

'Going to the dogs,' said Paget with a smile.

It occurred to Paddy, not for the first time, that it was Italy and not his son's disaffection which caused Edward distress. Did that mean her question might have an answer?

'Why not Italy, Father?'

Edward closed his eyes. The rage left him. 'This tea is cold,' he announced. 'Patricia, this tea is cold. Pour it away and tell that woman Dye to make another pot.'

'There used to be eight in and four out, not counting the gardeners,' remarked Bushey, carrying in another hod of coal for the kitchener.

'Well, there aren't now,' said Curry tartly, blowing on the embryo fire.

There was soot everywhere. 'A little goes a long way,' said Bushey, wiping his grimy forehead with a spotted handkerchief. Paddy wrenched open a window. For a moment she recalled the stream of servants passing through her childhood, servants always newly arrived or just on the point of departure. Only a few survived

Harriet's all-seeing eye and afterwards Curry's iron tyranny: Bragg the lady's maid, Webster the parlourmaid, Mrs Meikeljon the cook. Paddy's nurse Maudie had come back to take on the motherless Tom, but nurserymaids had come and gone by the dozen. 'Slovens!' cried Curry and out they went. In the gardens only Bushey lasted – and would last it out 'till doom' said Paddy. Bushey was gnomish, unpredictable and lazy. Paddy felt a brief stab of pity for the unknown Mrs Haley. What had Paget said? That she was charming? 'It shows a man is never too old to be fooled,' said Curry, who had her own opinion. But when questioned she said Mrs Haley was 'modern', whatever that meant.

The stove was being difficult. When had it been anything else? Only Curry could coax it to compliance. But then, thought Paddy, it must have terrorized the kitchen for years before Curry.

'I will have decently cooked food and plenty of hot water,' declared Harriet after spending a whole evening with ironmongers' catalogues and the account books. Within a month it was installed, a huge black menacing thing. The kitchenmaid quailed. The cook quailed. Only Harriet did not quail, standing with instruction book in hand, expounding on its capabilities. On paper its capabilities were legion, in reality it seemed only to have a capacity to annoy. It was temperamental, over-sensitive to wind and fuel. Harriet's meals were sometimes perfection and often disasters – and the water was not always hot.

Now, as the fire grew stronger and the warmth spread, Curry looked complacent. Paddy sat down, pushing her hair back from her forehead and leaving a dark smear. They uncorked the tea and sat amid the chaos drinking soberly to clear the soot from their throats. Rain drummed ceaselessly against the windows.

'The chimneys need sweeping,' said Curry.

'*All* the chimneys?' Paddy was outraged. 'I'm afraid

not. Unless you care to get a goose from the farm and use that.'

To Miss Hartley the following day she said, 'Have you ever tried to put a goose down a chimney? Or should it go up?'

Miss Hartley shrank back a little. 'Oh. Up, I should think,' was her tentative reply. Was Miss Bretton serious? Was Miss Bretton ever serious? It was so difficult to tell. In what she hoped was a diversion she said shyly, 'What a long way it seems to the Lodge, so much further than to the house. Quite silly, I know. It can't be more than a quarter of a mile.'

Momentarily Paddy's expression showed exactly how far a quarter of a mile might be. 'It was a distance travelled recently enough for her to still wince at the blisters incurred. The village, watching with incredulity, could not imagine how the old man would adapt, would humble himself. 'He won't,' Paddy could have said. 'He will be unreasonable and demanding and thoroughly miserable, even though he's warmer in the Lodge and has what's left of the good china and all the silver and his most precious odds and ends.'

'This war's done for a lot of people,' a Frilton shopkeeper had remarked to Paddy. 'Not only them as died.'

'Things are not what they were,' said Miss Hartley. She often walked up from the village for one of her charities and would depart with old clothes, cakes, jam, never money. 'There is no money at Bretton,' said the village. It was Bretton's back gate that gave on to the Stenton lane, the back gate deep in rhododendron thickets through which the village came for May frolics, fêtes, school treats. Perversely Bretton's front faced away towards Frilton, the market town. Now, to visit the Brettons, callers must cross the whole expanse of park. And: 'Things are not what they were,' said Miss Hartley.

Contrary to popular opinion she was not deaf. Once

she had heard Edward Bretton say, 'There's that old fright who writes shilling shockers.' But she was resilient. She still knocked at his door. 'I'm so glad there are tenants coming in,' she said to Paddy. 'So many houses are being shut up these days. And they're young too, I hear. How pleasant. And wealthy? They must be, else why take Bretton? Such an expense. But what will they do for servants? They could hardly bring their own, could they, not all the way from London? They are from London, aren't they? How different they'll find poor Bretton: oil lamps and candles and the quiet.'

Paddy, who was standing, turned round and looked at herself in the inadequate mirror over the fireplace. She saw a lined, strong, forty-year-old face, a mass of greying hair caught up in an old-fashioned bun.

'I expect they'll get used to it,' she said.

2

THE FIRST WEEK of April was still bitterly cold. On the Tuesday the Haleys moved into Bretton.

Paddy spent the entire morning doing the church flowers, wrestling with wet stems and savage chicken wire from the vestry cupboard. It was Bretton tradition that there were flowers in the church all week. 'It was Harriet,' said Paddy. 'She tried to turn the whole village into a sort of Bretton tradition.' In this she was doomed to be unsuccessful. What good she had ever done was cancelled cruelly by her sale of the tenant farms. The village did not tolerate change for change too often meant hardship. Harriet lost its respect and had never had its affection. Only the custom of the church flowers survived, a harmless eccentricity, and Paddy's only visible contribution now to village life.

She rode back to the Lodge on her bicycle. It had been Aunt Fan's, a relic of the early nineties, a scandal in its day. 'No daughter of mine is going about the village in bloomers,' Harriet had declared. But Fan had her way as usual. After all, she pointed out, she was forty-five and her husband was a clergyman – if he did not object, why should her mother? Paddy had no bloomers but she had a tight skirt, and the machine, like Aunt Fan herself, was heavy and headstrong. She took the slight hill in the village street with trepidation lest the thing run amok.

At Brook Court she was obliged to get off because Grace Paulley was near the gate, trowel in hand.

'My dear, you look exhausted. Why don't you come in?'

Paddy declined. Mrs Dye was preparing lunch and Edward was so rude to her. 'We can't afford to lose her,' Paddy said.

'Of course, Curry's always spoiled him,' said Grace. She did not say 'Curry's a treasure.' It would be absurd. They both knew Curry was the best housekeeper Bretton had ever had – and was a battleaxe.

The cold wind shivered the trees. Beyond the copper beech the large square house looked homely and complacent. Through that iron gate to the right was the walled garden, a miniature of the great walled garden at Bretton, where Philip Paulley had stolen strawberries for Paddy, crawling under the bird-netting. This should have been my home, she thought now.

'I won't have you engaged to a tenant's son,' Edward had shouted at that never-to-be-forgotten breakfast.

'Mr Paulley isn't your tenant. He never has been.' The young Paddy had gripped the table for support, gripped and gripped so that the blood left her fingers. 'Brook Court isn't ours any more. It hasn't been ours for twenty years. Grandmother sold it.'

'Be quiet. I will not have it, I tell you,' roared Edward.

'My dear,' said Grace, thinking how crushed and ugly Paddy's hat was, and then how crushed and ugly all Paddy's hats always were. 'My dear, what about the new people in the house? I must call.'

'They're very pleasant.' Always tell lies boldly, thought Paddy.

'But I hear Babs Potter is already grumbling about the amount of work.'

'Doesn't she always? Thank God the Haleys brought their cook with them and we managed to get a parlour-maid from Frilton. Ronnie Dack does all the heavy work and helps Bushey when he can.'

'Brought their cook,' said Grace. 'Good heavens! I wonder how she likes it?'

Perhaps, used to gas, tiled kitchens and a constant stream of tradesmen, she felt herself transported to abide with savages. 'I don't expect she likes it at all,' said Paddy. But she was not thinking of the London cook, she was thinking of Philip. What would marriage have been like? The bicycle leaned into her hip. Aunt Fan had married, had 'got away'. 'Your Aunt Fan always did what she wanted in the end,' Curry had said once. But Philip died, Paddy thought, he died. I would have got away too, but he died.

'That really is a terrible old bike,' said Grace.

At the Lodge Edward was banging his stick on the floor and calling for his food. Paddy threw her hat on the hallstand and marched in.

'There's no point in calling Curry. You know very well she's not here. And Mrs Dye will burn everything if you keep distracting her.'

'I tell you, Pat, we can't do without Curry. We've always had Curry. Those people ought to find their own housekeeper.'

Yes, they had always had Curry. She had come to Bretton as a barefoot twelve-year-old. Her mother had died and the cottage where they had lived at the foot of Hobeys had been cleared out. There had been bones and strange potions and mouldy old books. The parson might have told the village there was nothing harmful but the parson stayed away. In the night the cottage burned down and no more was said. Up at Bretton, however, Harriet raged over such superstition: she had opened her window to the smell of burning. 'Send for

Constance Murray,' she had commanded, and when they had hesitated: 'That is the child's name, isn't it? Constance?' And later: 'If she's clean she can start in the dairy.' It was not that she was dirty, they said, but they were afraid she would sour the milk, everyone knew the mother had been a witch. Even Harriet's fury broke impotently against such prejudice, but being Harriet she would not be entirely thwarted. 'Then set her to clean the floors,' she said.

Just how had Curry made herself indispensible? Perhaps by simply enduring. She had endured Harriet's stern regime while other servants broke and fled. She cost little. She was conscientious and competent. In some strange way she seemed to belong entirely to Bretton. The truth was she did not belong in the village – her mother had been the daughter of a Scottish drover as well as a witch – so must belong to Bretton or die.

Years later, of course, there was Deborah.

'Your mother,' said Curry to Paddy. 'I was very fond of your mother.' Between her and Harriet had been unshakable respect, but Bretton and Deborah between them had her heart. 'If your mother hadn't died . . .' she began once, but did not go on. And once: 'Those ten years were happy years considering.' Considering what? wondered Paddy. By the end of them Curry was housekeeper in impeccable black, the keys of Bretton firmly in her grasp. 'You won't leave?' pleaded the child Paddy after Deborah's funeral, hanging on to that strong hand. 'No,' said Curry firmly. 'I'll never leave.'

Edward, who had never liked her, who was afraid of her, came in his grief to depend on her entirely. When she came for the daily orders he would wave her away. 'You know what to do,' he would say, or, 'Do as you think fit.'

Since she had been obliged to blacklead it every morning at five thirty Curry had known how to deal with the kitchener, just as she knew how to deal with the routine of the house, with servants, flowers, meals, hot water cans. She could find her way about the larders, dairies, apple stores, cellars, in and out of the Piggery blindfold. 'There is nothing I haven't done for this house,' she said. After the war, with Paddy, she had painted over the hospital green – 'Four weeks of painting!' – and had torn down the flimsy partitions between 'wards'. They had painted in harmony, mostly in silence, breaking off only for cups of tea or to lean gasping from the windows clearing their lungs. Indispensible to Edward, Curry had become indispensible to Paddy.

'We began badly though,' said Paddy, remembering. She had thrown her breakfast boiled egg out of the nursery window. 'Little Miss Patricia in one of her moods again,' said Pinner the current nurserymaid to those agog in the kitchen. Curry had been on the terrace below when it had landed at her feet. 'I never liked boiled egg myself,' she told Paddy long afterwards, 'but I knew what it was to be hungry.' She had scooped up the revolting mess and made her way up, up, to the white door that separated Paddy from the adult world. Paddy, all glowering eyes and mutinous chin, had heard the swish of that housekeeper black, the chink of the great chatelaine. 'There are children in the village who would fight for what you throw away,' the chilling voice had said. 'Never let me hear of your wasting food again.'

Soon there was nothing at Bretton to waste. The cattle plague of the sixties that had helped bring them low and caused Harriet to sell the farms might long have passed over, but the nineties were not kind to farming either. There was water getting in the roof, damp in the back regions. 'If it doesn't come down it comes up,' said Curry grimly. Money leached away. 'Poured rather,' said Paddy, who was old enough to notice now. Deborah died in childbirth and left Tom, a plump demanding new person: 'a noise in a sailor suit,' said Deborah's unmarried sister Sarah who had come to live at Bretton temporarily to look after him. Aunt Fan wrote from her Devon rectory to ask if Paddy was to have a London season – or even a Frilton season – and Edward threw the letter on the fire and did not trouble to reply. At sixteen 'little Miss Patricia' had put up her hair and become mistress of Bretton, but she did not put off her 'moods', nor did she give up her secret life at Roman Hill. Instead she borrowed the five pounds from Jack Chance and embarked on her 'career'.

Edward, ignorant of the five pounds, Jack Chance and the frequent visits to the farm in the valley, pretended indifference to the horse dealing. If he was secretly pleased by Paddy's prowess he kept it to himself, and if he took any delight in seeing his crumbling stables occupied again he kept that to himself also. Now and again, for form's sake, he grumbled at her rubbing elbows with common horse copers in the hunting field – never let them disgrace the gravel at Bretton, he said, or he would put a stop to the whole business. But money came in. He met Sir Robert Jernham on the sacred gravel, come about a grey mare. He was told by men he respected that they would rather buy a horse from his daughter than from anyone. He did not like to think Paddy was keeping their bodies and souls together, Bretton and the Brettons, so he did not think of it. He existed apart, remote, removed. He might greet Sir Robert warmly but he would not let the conversation touch the grey mare.

Paddy was nineteen. She bought a new riding habit. Young William Jernham, helping her from a ditch on the hunting field, kissed her muddied hand. 'He won't stop at hands,' Jack Chance warned. But she had been young and in a 'mood'. She had galloped over several hearts that winter and sold three good horses into the bargain. In the spring new plants appeared in the garden.

'What are those?' asked Edward.

'Bushey and I are going to rescue the rose garden,' said Paddy.

'Frippery,' said Edward. He never entered the rose garden. It had been Deborah's.

'But we can't neglect the gardens for ever, Father,' Paddy told him firmly. Even then she was learning to be firm. But not firm enough. She bought the plants, pruned the roses, but she lost Philip Paulley. For the rest of her life she would think: If I had been determined to marry him, if I *had* married him, he wouldn't have died. He would not have gone away to Hereford and had the accident with the gun.

'But was it an accident?' asked the village.

'I *must* call on the Haleys tomorrow,' Paddy told Edward. 'I can't put it off. It looks so odd. I told Grace how pleasant they were as well. After all, we're only at the gate.'

'They don't use this gate. They go in and out of the back.' It was something Edward had garnered from Mrs Dye though he affected not to listen when she spoke to him.

'Probably because it's quicker to the station that way. We used the back gate more than this. You know that.'

Sooner or later they must meet her in the drive. Or the garden? They would find her splitting perennials, forking out bindweed. Before that happened, Paddy thought, she must turn up, spruce, welcoming, at the front door. Front door? How many years since we opened it? she wondered. We used the back, back door, back gate . . .

'Why is it always mutton at midday?' demanded Edward as a whiff reached them from the tiny kitchen.

'Always mutton. That woman doesn't know how to cook.'

'Don't be absurd, Father.'

'Why can't Mrs Salter come back?'

'Mrs Salter left to look after her son. He was blinded at Ypres. You must remember. And we had four cooks after Mrs Salter and you frightened them all away.'

'What a sharp old woman you've become.'

'I expect I have.'

'Comes of being forty probably. Women grow strange in middle age. Look at your Aunt Sarah.'

'Aunt Sarah did her best,' asserted Paddy. 'It wasn't easy for her.' Not easy coping with Maudie, so jealous of 'her' baby, with 'little Miss Patricia' and the 'moods', with Edward inarticulate with grief, with Curry who had been told she must do as she thought fit.

'Well, if you go up to the house tell them I don't get out much, I shan't walk up till the weather's warmer.'

'They know that. Paget will have told them. But think how embarrassing for them if they met me trowelling away in the garden.'

'Don't know why you have to do the garden. What about the men?'

'What men, Father?'

'Gardeners. Fowler. That skinny boy . . . Marsh?'

'They're gone, Father. They went years ago. Tom Marsh was killed on the Somme. There's only Bushey now.'

Edward knew this perfectly well, and she knew he knew it. But he resented her gardening and so, every few weeks, they must have this same conversation. His mother Harriet had always been gardening, and his wife. When he saw Paddy stooped over her beloved plants he saw them, the two women who had shaped him, stooped just so forty years before. The thought of the one stirred only faint and scarcely understood regret, but the memory of Deborah still consumed him.

23

Sometimes, looking at Paddy, he was surprised by Deborah looking back, for Paddy had Deborah's eyes: grey, candid, wide apart. He was only ever momentarily astonished however, for the rest of Paddy owed nothing to her mother. Where Deborah had been small and slight Paddy was tall and proud – 'Tall, proud and temperamental,' said Grace Paulley, who should have been her mother-in-law. Where Deborah had been brown, a tawny brown, Paddy was black. Yet still, seeing her bending in the borders, Edward saw not Paddy, but Deborah and Harriet superimposed.

The mutton came and went. Later, in the kitchen, Mrs Dye reported, 'Mr Bretton was difficult again this morning, madam.'

'I'm afraid he doesn't take kindly to the Lodge,' said Paddy.

'But what am I to do, Miss Bretton? I don't think I can manage much longer, not when he's so particular. I can't seem to please him. He wants to know where the cream Spode is, madam. I told him I don't know anything about any cream Spode, sir, perhaps you should ask Miss Bretton about it. He didn't believe me. He nearly called me a liar, madam, he very nearly did. And if he had, madam, then I would have had to give notice.'

Thus the sword of Damocles was set swinging again. 'If she goes there'll be chaos,' said Paddy. 'I can't cook. I won't cook. And there's no room for anyone to live in at the Lodge even if we could afford them.'

The rock of domestic routine had been the rock on which Paddy had been wrecked very early in life and on which she had only survived snarling with resentment. The daily round from bedroom to kitchen, to the Home Farm, to dairy, office, byre, barn and vegetable garden had sometimes seemed so immutable she could have thrown herself down in a tantrum. But there was no time for tantrums. She only mentally gambolled up and down the passages at Bretton smashing the vases and tearing the rugs asunder. Outwardly she appeared 'regal and shrewish' said Curry, who saw nothing odd in the combination having lived with it for forty years. She came down at six every morning with her long hair skewered up and her shabby respectable clothes smelling of the lavender and lad's love in the mahogany press. From six o'clock she was ready for anything. And some days anything happened: one of the stockmen gored by the bull, a baby born in the barn to a tinker, the farm horses escaped into the village trampling nasturtiums and small children, the partial collapse of the vegetable garden wall which meant builders and bills . . . And bills. Oh, there were domestic crises that would strain credulity.

'Mrs Dye, we could not do without you,' she said now with rare and totally disarming frankness. The red crumpled face of the other woman crumpled a little more as if, touched, she might even cry.

'Oh, madam, I hope I'd never leave you in a muddle,' she declared, and in the next breath, 'Will the cold rabbit do for supper? I know Mr Bretton isn't partial to cold rabbit.'

From rabbit Paddy passed to the cramped drawing room and: 'The Spode is sold, Father. Don't you remember?'

'No,' said Edward. 'Why was it sold?'

'To make money.'

'It was your mother's.' He never called her Deborah, always 'your mother'.

'No, it wasn't. I think it was Grandmother's. Grandmother Harriet.' 'Your mother' she wanted to retort.

'Grandmothers. Mothers.' He looked thoroughly ruffled, like an angry heron. 'Did you know there's a child up at the house?'

'Paget never mentioned a child.'

'Well, there is.' Had this too been gleaned from Mrs

Dye whom he so despised? He brooded a little, both hands on his stick. 'What a long time since there was a child at the house. Eh, Pat? What an age.'

'Thirty years,' said Paddy.

3

THE CHILD WAS crouched in the dirt under the great chestnut tree by the stableyard entrance, building pebbles into a small unstable house. The pigeons in the branches above took their two cows over and over and then abruptly hushed.

Paddy said, 'Hello. Who are you?'

'I'm Etta,' said the child. She had a squarish unformed face and very blue eyes. Under her felt hat her hair was brown and thick and straight.

'I'm Paddy,' said Paddy. 'Miss Bretton' she would say at the door when asked, but out here who could stand on ceremony? It was the first really warm day and she could smell wallflowers.

'I'm nine,' offered Etta. She brushed off her hands and stood up. 'Shall I show you the front door? You could go in this way but visitors aren't supposed to. I don't know why really. It's much quicker.'

'I know,' said Paddy. 'I used to live here.'

At the front door Lily Foster, the new parlourmaid, let her in, announced her. Etta smiled shyly and was gone.

'Miss Bretton.'

'Thank you, Foster,' said a cool young voice, the voice of the unknown Mrs Haley who was, it might be supposed, learning to manage Curry, the disgruntled

London cook, slovenly Babs Potter, contrary old Bushey. 'Miss Bretton' rang about the room somehow as Paddy stepped forward, a stranger in her own house. It was the same drawing room, yellow and cream again now, where once eight beds had been crammed in down the window side and the Sister had cried, bearing down on Paddy, 'No one unauthorized is allowed in the wards. May I ask what you're doing here?'

'Miss Bretton,' said Laura Haley, 'How good of you to call.'

She was small, slender, vivacious. Flirtatious? Her close cap of shining dark hair was the very latest thing. 'Well?' Paddy had asked. 'She's modern,' Curry had replied. And so she was, young, modern, delightful.

'I met your daughter in the drive,' Paddy remarked.

'Henrietta? I'm afraid she runs rather wild. She had to have an operation at the end of last summer and she's been so delicate since. I spent weeks and weeks in the most desolate seaside places all the doctors recommended and they did nothing for her and even less for me. Of course, she ought to have a governess. Perhaps when we've settled in, in a month or two . . .'

A stocky, pleasant-looking man appeared on the threshold. He seemed remarkably uncertain of his reception. Until the sleek little dark head turned in his direction he did not move.

'Oh Hugh. Miss Bretton, this is my husband Hugh.'

His handshake was firm. Any hesitancy, any shyness, was connected with the lovely Laura then, thought Paddy. He seemed to have, though not for his wife, a rueful and charming smile.

Lily Foster brought tea. She was a plump cheerful girl, very 'country' said Laura. Her whole round smiling face was freckled like a good egg. And how infinitely strange, thought Paddy, to be served tea at Bretton, to see Laura lift the silver pot, to know the Spode was sold. 'Nearly everything's sold,' Tom had grumbled.

Had he seen his Italian idyll ending because there was nothing left to sell?

'This is such a beautiful place,' Hugh Haley was saying. He sounded as if he meant it. 'I hate it,' Paddy might have said to anyone who asked, yet to hear Bretton criticized raised her black hackles. He was standing by one of the long windows looking out. She knew exactly what he could see: the terrace steps leading down to the lily pool her father had made for his bride, a shy tawny girl who had lived most of her life in Italy and pined for gardens full of the sound of water and the shade of cypresses. 'That was the best I could do,' Edward had said. 'And she was touched. I believe she liked it better than anything else I gave her.'

'I'm afraid the gardens have gone to ruin,' Paddy said.

'I'm not surprised.' Laura was reaching to ring the bell for Lily. 'Two gardeners can hardly be expected to manage.'

'There were never enough. My grandmother and my mother spent most of their time out there fighting the weeds but it was really no use. Then during the war it was practically abandoned. Since then, with only the two of us . . .'

'Two of you?'

'Fred Bushey and myself.'

'Mr Paget,' said Laura firmly, 'led us to believe it was Bushey and . . .' Hugh had turned, interested. She glanced across at him as if he, along with Paget, had been caught out in a falsehood. 'Bushey and a boy.'

'Well, I'm the boy,' said Paddy.

Hugh came over for his tea, smiling. 'You don't mean we might stumble on you in the garden, digging potatoes?'

'No,' said Paddy, 'not potatoes. I would never dare lay a finger on the vegetable garden. It's Bushey's kingdom.'

The door opened. Lily bobbed towards Laura.

'I thought there were to be scones, Foster?'

'Mrs Prince has had trouble with the range again, mum.'

To the Haleys' surprise their dignified guest broke into sudden laughter.

'And was transformed,' said Hugh afterwards, still astounded.

'An eccentric old biddy,' said Laura.

What else had Edward given Deborah apart from the lily pool? The rose garden with its fountain, a social position she hated, a son. Entertaining adults had terrified her, she was happiest at children's parties, and charity committees – 'Why *must* we be involved?' – drove her to a frenzy. 'Surely they can have their coal allowance in cash?' she had cried, stirred at last to open protest. When it was suggested the village poor might spend this meagre sum on beer she stormed, 'Why not?' and left the meeting in disarray. But the storm was brief. Sweet and kind, she had no nerve for a fight. 'Don't let them bully you,' said Harriet, who never let anyone bully her, but the parson and committee won: it was coals not cash. And: 'I suppose that's what they really wanted after all,' said Deborah with a sigh.

She did not 'fit in'. Harriet had not fitted in either, at least not into the conventional mould Ralph had prepared for her, but Harriet had not cared. Harriet was made of stronger stuff. Deborah, more and more, felt guilty. Such a load of guilt all her married life. How she hated calling on her neighbours, organizing fêtes, the school treats, the workhouse Christmas gifts. She only wanted to live quietly at Bretton with her daughter, her mother-in-law and her garden. She did not like the cold little parish church, all puritan whitewash and naked altar. She liked statues, candles, the blue mist of incense. 'Mrs Bretton was seduced by Rome when she was a girl,' Wenlow the parson told his churchwardens. He hated Rome though his knowledge was pitiful. He made no effort to welcome Deborah in spite of his hope the Brettons might find a little spare cash for the church roof. When Paddy was born she was baptised privately and by a clergyman so High Church that the Pope might have mistaken him for one of his own. Years of silent animosity went by and then Tom was born. 'She died of blood poisoning,' said Curry. 'That slut of a midwife and that old fool of a doctor killed your mother between them.' Tom lived, Deborah died. A priest came for the last rites. Had that been a spiritual need, Paddy wondered, or simply a reminder of Deborah's girlhood in Umbria? But then, after what the village called the 'arvy-palarvy', the priest and bells and holy smoke, old Wenlow had to perform the burial service.

Edward had insisted on it. 'She was not a Roman, you prejudiced old fool. She has a right to lie in this church with my family.' The row blazed across the county to the ears of the bishop and back. Wenlow capitulated. Deborah was buried in Stenton, but not in the church after all, outside between the great yew and the churchyard wall. 'She would have preferred it anyway,' said Curry. 'It would be more like the garden.'

Wenlow, still humbled, baptized Tom. 'I remember that,' Paddy was always to say. 'It rained. And he screamed and screamed. And I wore black.' Scratchy funeral black, not like Curry's smooth housekeeper's black. Curry had been thirty-two when Deborah died. Thirty-two sounded young, but had Curry ever been properly young? She had been twelve when she had walked up to Bretton from the burnt cottage, yet even then could she have been called a child?

'Your Grandmother Harriet sent me a message.'

'And you came,' said the young Paddy, who always liked to hear the story.

'I came the very same day.'

'Where had you slept?'

'In the hedge.'

'Because the cottage had burned down? But how did they know where to bring the message?'

It had been hardly a cottage, just a one-room hovel tucked away in the flank of Hobeys by the beck where they used to wash the sheep. Jack Chance's father, William, used to ride by on his way home to Roman Hill and say it should be pulled down. 'If Ralph Bretton ever stirred his lazy carcase outside his own gates for anything other than a race meeting he'd have it razed to the ground.'

' 'T ain't Ralph Bretton's land,' the witch would reply, the baby Constance on her hip.

'Oh yes it is, my dear. And even if 'twas mine, I'd rout you out into a cleaner sty than this.'

When the witch died the call to Bretton had come down to the sheep-splash before the inevitable summons to Roman Hill. Curry had washed her face in the beck and had set out, up through Lower Bit, Upper Bit, Hobeys. She had crossed the lane that led from the Frilton road to Home Farm and had gone in through the green door in the walled garden.

'I hurried,' she said.

'In case Mr Chance was looking for you? But you might have liked it better at Roman Hill,' said Paddy, who was always to like it better there herself.

Curry did not explain she had always seen Bretton as her destiny. Skinny twelve-year-olds, illegitimate, outcast, have nothing to do with destiny. Besides, there were interesting women at Bretton, the terrible Harriet and the 'aunts', Fan and Mary – though they were not aunts then, there would be no Paddy for another ten years – and there were maids, a housekeeper, the cook. Roman Hill was only a farm and Curry knew all about farms. She knew nothing about grand houses, the flowers in every room, the baize aprons, oyster patties, celery sauce. 'I wanted to know,' said Constance Murray, stopping just inside the green door and bobbing behind a box hedge to pull the hole in her black stocking further round and out of sight. And so, in time, she became Curry and 'indispensible' said Harriet and Fan and Mary and Deborah and Paddy in turn.

'And of course,' Curry said, 'I was a bit afraid of Mr William Chance. His temper grew very bad in his old age.'

There were no women at Roman Hill in those days, no proper women, only old Aggie who was William's housekeeper and sometimes managed to secure a village girl to run about with a duster. Mrs William had left with her young son to go home to her mother. Well, she was years younger than her husband, a second wife, a little spoiled, daughter of a doctor over by Ashton. She would have been silly to expect to keep a great lusty Chance at her side exclusively but there you were, said the village, some will stomach it and some won't. But he would never have dared touch Curry, Paddy thought years later, would he? He must have been in his fifties then, still physically fit. He had been six foot three and fair, not the usual Chance red. He had given Curry a penny once, reaching down from his tall horse, and he might have been a god reaching from Olympus.

'He was not a bad man,' said Curry, 'but it had to be Bretton. I knew it had to be Bretton when the time came.'

The following year, 1873, William broke his neck at the Frilton horse fair. The horse slipped on the cobbles, they told Harriet, it was an unlucky fall. Harriet said yes, it was a terrible accident and had word been sent to Rebecca and the young son over at Ashton? Afterwards, as she often did towards dusk, she went out alone to walk. This time she was gone so many hours that there was talk of a search party. Darkness had fallen by the time they heard her step in the hall. 'Madam, we were so worried,' said Bragg, laying out the dinner dress. Harriet, scoured by the March wind – red cheeks, red eyes, red nose – said she had walked too far for her age, she would not come down to dinner, put the dress away.

Rebecca Chance, absent for seven years, returned to manage Roman Hill until ten-year-old Jack was strong enough to cope alone. 'So,' said Harriet, opening the great ledger, 'a third generation of Chances at Roman Hill.' Joseph, William, Jack. 'I can manage,' Rebecca had said, stepping from the market cart driven by her son to cross the gravel and climb the steps and be admitted through Bretton's great front door. There had been challenge in the lift of her head, the hard stare. Does she know? wondered Harriet. Can she guess the secrets of the past?

That there had been secrets Paddy knew, but by the time she asked why and how and when Rebecca was dead and Harriet grown old and severe. 'You must never go to Roman Hill,' Harriet said.

I must never go to Roman Hill, thought Paddy, peering through the elm leaves at its red chimneys. She slipped further down the hill. Now she could see crooked casements open to the sun, a curtain blowing.

'Who are you?' demanded a strong male voice. There was a man by the elder bushes watching her. He was tall and his hair was red. She particularly noticed his hair because he wore no hat.

'My name is Patricia Mary Deborah Bretton.'

'You're never a Bretton!' and the man laughed and moved out of the shadow, coming towards her.

'I am!'

'No, you're a changeling.'

'I'm not!'

He laughed again, an easy good-natured laugh. He seemed very large and very old to her though afterwards she knew he had only been twenty-seven and not as tall as his father. The red wiry hair fascinated her.

'How old are you?' he asked.

'I'm eight.'

'Well,' and he looked her up and down, considering. 'You're certainly no Bretton. And your mother . . .' He smiled a little, as if at some memory. 'Your mother's a beauty.'

'Please,' said Paddy, putting the end of her pigtail in her mouth as she did when she was anxious. 'Please may I see the farm?'

And so began her secret life at Roman Hill. Why did it have to be secret? 'Because of all the other secrets, I suppose,' said Paddy. Nobody would tell her, not even Curry. 'There's always been bad blood,' was all Curry would say. 'What's bad blood?' Paddy asked Jack Chance. 'And why has it always been here?' But even he would not, could not answer her. 'Old stories,' he said. 'Old feuds.'

Paddy was nine, ten, thirteen, fourteen. Up and down Hobeys she went, slipping in and out of the elm shadows like a weasel. 'I learnt how to be careful,' she said. For twenty years she was careful, nearly twenty years. No one at Bretton must know she knew Jack Chance. Of course the village knew. The men in the fields went home to tell their wives: little Paddy Bretton riding in the crook of Jack's arm, running at his coat tails, favoured above his sons. 'I'd like a daughter, Pat,' he had said. 'A tough little vixen like you.'

Years later she sold him a roan pony, one she had bred herself, a wicked beast who could trot fifteen miles an hour and keep it up all day. 'He's a rogue,' said Jack cheerfully, 'but I'll have him if it means you get a new dress.'

'The stables need a new roof first.'

'Blast it, then. I won't buy.' But he did, and added five guineas over the price and a note: 'Don't be proud. Go to the dressmaker.'

35

Paddy burnt the note, her hand trembling. She *was* too proud. He was her father's tenant and he had more money than her family had owned in a century. He dared send her five paltry guineas for clothes! It was too much to bear.

Jack said, 'It's life. Take what you can and be thankful.'

'You humiliate me.'

'Well, I can't help it if you take it like that. All I know is that you go without while that young Tom gets all he wants. If a gift of five guineas rubs you up so much you'd better give it back.'

She faced him, chin up. She knew him so well by now, his explosive temper counterbalanced by his extraordinary patience with animals, his hard-headed business sense, his disgust at sentimentality. 'No,' she said. 'I won't give it back.'

He laughed. 'That's my Paddy Bretton,' he said.

Joseph Chance had come to Roman Hill in 1805. In 1911 Young John, Jack's son, paid the rent on quarter day and his name went down in the great book. '*Another* generation,' said Curry with a portentous pursing of the lips. 'They'll own that farm afore they're done,' was the general opinion as Johnny Chance swept through the village behind the old roan pony at his heart-stopping pace. 'And Bretton too,' was a more private suggestion behind the women's skirts at the pump.

Paddy had had nothing to do with Young John, had only caught brief glimpses of him: a child at Roman Hill, a boy at village gatherings, once at the sheep-washing. After Jack died she did not look for him, afraid the red head and Chance features might unnerve her. Then Edward was ill on rent day.

'He isn't anything like his father,' Paddy said afterwards to Curry, who raised an eyebrow, saying in her opinion he was very like: tall, brown-eyed. As yet perhaps he did not have his father's breadth. 'He hev his manner,' said Bushey. 'Hinsolent.'

Then war. Johnny and his brother Will went to France. Nearly all the young men went to France. 'What are we left with?' asked Paddy. They were left with women, boys, the aged and the infirm. Still, they managed.

'Your place is here,' Edward stormed the day Paddy put on her nurse's uniform. 'How can we keep going without you?' He was furious at the seizure of his house, furious at having to live in the Lodge, furious at everything.

'I shall come back for harvest,' said Paddy calmly.

'And how will she do that, the varmint?' demanded Bushey.

But she did.

Will Chance's name appeared on the ever-lengthening casualty lists the day they celebrated harvest home. He was the twelfth from the village.

'God works in mysterious ways,' said Grace Paulley bitterly, seeing Paddy off at the station.

It was a dusty gold evening, swallows skimming the empty platform. The small engine hissed and chinked, the driver leaning out to talk to the porter, an elderly, stooped figure. The two women kissed, the one in nursing uniform, the one in sober grey with the un-fashionable hat. They might have been mother and daughter. Above and around and through the summer gold was the faint smell of autumn.

Nothing will ever be the same again, thought Paddy.

'There was something I meant to ask you,' said Laura, meeting Paddy in the rose garden. 'We've bought a pony trap and are looking out for a pony. Hugh thought it would be just the thing for me to get about the village.' She looked as if she disagreed and had done so at length quite recently. 'Do you know anyone local who might have a quiet pony of the right sort?'

37

'It all depends . . .' began Paddy.

'We've been told about a Mr Chance. Apparently he often has a pony or two.'

'Yes, I believe he does.'

'A farmer?'

'He also owns the mill in Frilton, and the gravel workings.'

'Would you recommend him?'

'I don't know how you kept a straight face,' said Curry, calling at the Lodge that evening with a basket of eggs. 'Did you mention she'd need a long spoon to sup with the devil?'

'But he might have just the thing. There's always a pony to spare at Roman Hill.'

'I told you he's just like his father.'

'And I still don't think so.'

'He'd sell a horse to anyone who came by. Just like a Chance.'

'And he farms well and looks after his men and he pays the rent,' said Paddy. 'That's more than we can do.'

Curry drew herself up. 'Let's hope he doesn't sell Mrs Haley a rogue. I doubt she knows which end kicks and which end bites.'

4

The Haleys had been at Bretton for a month.

Perhaps Laura had intended, on first stepping through the front door and gazing up at the beautiful sweep of stairs, to fill the house with the chatter and laughter of endless parties. She had pointed out the overgrown tennis court with enthusiasm, hanging on Hugh's arm. But her friends did not seem to care for this distant rural hideout. Those few who had ventured here so far had sighed for hot water, for the interesting food, the conveniences of the city. 'Where can you go to dance?' they asked. Laura hoped summer might bring a change of heart. What was more delightful than the country in summer? And she would have her own dance, dancing every week, in Bretton's abandoned ballroom.

She had taken Etta, fresh from her bath and in her dressing-gown, to see the ballroom.

'There,' she had said, swinging wide the door.

The evening sunlight fell through the windows from which she had wrestled the tall shutters. The ceiling had garlands of flowers and fruit.

'Oh,' breathed Etta.

Laura's shoes tap-tapped across the polished boards – and left footprints: there was dust everywhere. The pink walls were greying. They had escaped the hospital

green because Matron had found the ballroom impossible to heat. Robust young men would have thought
nothing of it, but she had none of those. Reluctantly she
turned the key and Harriet's sugar-pink was reprieved.

'Oh,' said Etta again. She was not like Laura, needing
constant company. She had learned to be alone. She
liked to be alone. But this large echoing splendid space
excited her. She heard music, saw whirling couples . . .
'When will it be?' she cried. 'When will it happen?'

But: 'Where have you been all day?' Laura asked.

'Oh. At the farm.'

'Again? What can you find to do there?'

'Lots of things.'

'What things?'

Etta knew serious explanations were not required.
Sometimes, though, Laura was fickle. It was as well to
know how to deflect her sudden curiosity.

'Oh, just things. Feeding the hens. You know.'

Laura's interest waned. She was only glad the child
had found something to keep her occupied, seemed so
easy to please. It had not been the case in Kensington.
And how much easier to please than Hugh, or her
friends, or the man she had once hoped would be her
lover. She looked up and down the long, lovely room.
Like Etta she pictured it alive with sound and movement. She must have sound and movement, and this
great old house . . . She was beginning to think it was
like a tomb.

Etta looked stumpy and solid. Her dressing-gown
had a duck on the pocket. Her hair, plaited for bed,
gave her a grandmotherly assurance. 'Is Father coming
home tomorrow?' she asked.

'I really couldn't say. I suppose so. Doesn't he usually
come Friday night? Have you had your milk?'

'Lily's making it.'

'Then say goodnight and run along.'

But they walked back to the hall together. The

thought of bringing musicians, flowers, a buffet supper . . . Yes, yes, it must be done formally just once, as it might have been done in the old days. The thought of a ball had filled Laura with delight. She smiled. She felt light and happy. Her hand touched the shoulder of the duck-embroidered dressing-gown.

'You really ought to have a nanny,' she said, quite tenderly.

Etta let this pass. She knew her mother had had a nanny in the long ago when *she* had needed one – when, presumably, she had been that remarkable child in the photograph on the dressing table, masses of dark hair spilled romantically over bare shoulders. 'You ought to have a nanny, or maybe a governess, but your father says nonsense, you should go to school,' was what Laura often said, and sometimes reminisced about happy days with Nanny Bloom. Etta, who had detected the false note long ago, was not impressed.

Laura went into the yellow drawing room. She liked it. She liked its colour. In such a setting her pale modern sofas looked at home. She sat and reached for a cigarette, leaning back to watch the smoke rise. Good God, there was plaster fruit and leaves – some sort of leaves – on this ceiling too and she had never noticed.

'Mother . . .'

'Are you still here?' She looked more closely. 'Henrietta, why have you got such a peculiar fringe?'

'Lily said you were going to take me to London for a haircut.'

'Was I?' and a cloud of smoke wreathed between them. '*Was* I? To London?' No doubt she had mentioned it. How irritatingly children recalled such casual remarks.

'You said so to Lily.'

After an effort of memory Laura said, 'So I did.' And Lily Foster had said, she was sure of it, 'Miss Bretton goes to Frilton, mum.'

'I swear she'd know where everyone within five miles goes for meat, cigars and calling cards. One only has to sneeze and every cottage knows about it within the hour,' Laura had protested to Hugh. But: 'Well, I can't see why Etta shouldn't have her hair cut in Frilton,' said Hugh mildly.

Etta's hair was thick strong determined hair. Like the child herself, thought Laura, who was sometimes frightened by it. She felt that Etta judged her. It had not occurred to her until recently that such a thing was possible. 'What a lumpish child she is,' she said to Hugh: a lumpish, quite tractable child, in general happy with her own company. Yet there were times, more frequently now, when Etta was 'difficult'.

'How "difficult"?' asked Hugh.

'She wants to know why all the time. And contradicts.'

'Well, she's a person too. She must have her own opinions.'

'At nine?'

'Why not at nine?'

Hugh often defended his daughter although he saw so little of her that she was nothing much more than a name and shape. He was aware only that the shape grew, that it spoke now more clearly and matter-of-factly – 'as if she were a hundred at least.' In reality he knew nothing about her, nothing about any child, and was too miserable to find out.

Laura had walked to look at her face in the mirror over the fireplace.

'You do look pretty,' declared Etta impulsively.

'Thank you, darling,' said Laura, smiling at her dim reflection. How different the child was, she thought, when she behaved like a child instead of being so . . . challenging? Instead of thinking so much perhaps.

'Henrietta is a great thinker,' Laura told her friends. But what did she think *about*? What did she think of her mother?

42

'Thank you, darling,' said Laura again, turning to retrieve her cigarette.

She was beginning to sense how troublesome daughters might become.

The milk had not arrived in the nursery and sunlight still chequered the floor. Etta ran down and let herself out of the side door, making stealthy headway through the shrubbery. Then she was away across the grass under the cedars with their dry resiny smell, down past the tennis court, skirting the rose garden, running on and on between the yew hedges. Beyond the vegetables was the green door that opened on to the lane to Home Farm, the green door through which Curry had come to Bretton in 1872 and through which Paddy had escaped from Bretton until Jack Chance died of a heart attack.

And Harriet?

There had been a time, in blinding snow, when Harriet had pressed her palms and her forehead to that door, trying to draw breath and stem her tears in the same moment. 'Ridiculous! Melodramatic!' she had exclaimed, remembering it years later. But the feel of the cold smooth wood against her brow and the terrible sensation of choking never left her.

The green door was simply a door to Etta, who loved the worlds on either side equally and with whom no ghosts passed in or out. She ran up the lane between the burgeoning nettles and the crowding burdock to where, on the right, was the gate into Hobeys. It had been known as Hobeys for generations. Bushey had replied to her enquiry that old Hobey had been hung on the gibbet over to Ellum Cross 'as a warnin' to all them others as fancied poachin' Bretton deer'.

'What's poachin'?' asked Etta.

'Takin' what in't your'n.'

'But there are no deer,' puzzled Etta.

'There were deer once,' Paddy had explained. 'The

43

park was full of deer. And before them there were vineyards and a villa, a Roman villa.'

'But that was *ages* ago,' said Etta, amazed.

'The ford through the beck at the foot of the hill is paved with Roman stones.'

'Are you *sure*?' asked Etta.

The pasture in Hobeys was strong and 'herbical' said Bushey. The marks of the medieval ploughmen could sometimes be seen when the sun was westering, and here and there signs of ancient terracing that made running down the field so exciting. Etta, careering from slope to slope, flung out her arms and laughed aloud.

Hobeys, she knew, belonged to Bretton but was rented by the red-headed man from the farm at the foot of the hill. That meant, Bushey had explained patiently, he paid money to use it for his own. 'But it's still Bretton,' Etta said. 'I can go in there?'

'You can go where you please,' Bushey assured her, 'long as you shut ivry gate behind you.'

Hobeys was where the young cart colts were put after they were cut, or sometimes the young cattle who would skitter up and down its steep places with their tails whirling and great clods of ancient turf thrown up behind. They were all in charge of Bonniman, the Chance head stockman, who was tall and broad and quiet – 'and deep' said Curry. It was Bonniman who broke the colts and the fractious fillies and castrated the pigs. He was the acknowledged superior in animal command. But then, said Curry darkly, he had the power of the bones.

'What bones?' asked Etta.

She had met him here once and had found him good company, confident though inarticulate. 'He doesn't talk at me,' said Etta gratefully. She had shared his strong cheese and ironhard bread in the lee of the bramble hedge that separated Hobeys from Upper Bit. Upper Bit and Lower Bit were the lower fields where the land began to level out by the farm buildings. Etta had learnt all the field names, reciting them on her forays beyond the green door: Home Acre, Cuckoolands, Pond Field, Scaldy Field, Upper Bit, Lower Bit, Hobeys. 'I like Hobeys best,' she said. It was like standing on the top of the world.

Now, running through the wet cold grass, her dressing gown clutched up, she glanced about anxiously. It was late, the bats were out. The sun had vanished behind the elms, leaving only a pink edge to the gathering clouds. What if the young carthorse were lurking in the shadows?

'You didn't oughta be afeard of an old hoss,' said Pen Potter scornfully.

'I'm not,' said Etta, but she was. She knew he was big. They were all big; and they rattled their chains and swung their great heads terrifyingly close and they could move quickly and suddenly if they chose.

'You didn't oughta hev nothin' to do with them Potters,' said Bushey.

'But why not? Babs works in the house. And Mrs Potter does the laundry. Pen's ten. Did you know? She' a year older than me.'

'Hmmmph,' said Bushey.

Was there time to go down to Roman Hill? She had reached the elms, the bramble hedge by Upper Bit. It was dark under the trees. No, she couldn't go to Roman Hill. She had her dressing gown on and Lily would be carrying her milk up the back stairs at Bretton, puffing and humming. Besides, what would Johnny Chance say if she burst in on his dinner? She wondered if he would laugh. She would hate him to laugh at her, because of the dressing gown, because of her tremendous ignorance of country things, because Pen Potter had told him she, Etta, was afraid of the horses ... But Pen Potter rarely went to Roman Hill and never into the house. The house, Etta knew, was magical. Rambling, low-ceilinged, still in some places wearing its medieval livery of red and blue, it smelled of woodsmoke, pipesmoke and wet dogs. There were lots of pictures, mostly of animals, but one of a small fair woman with a lapful of roses and another of two children in pantaloons and bonnets. There were books about stock-breeding or horse ailments, and a square piano with a china shepherd and shepherdess on it, she concerned for the pinkish lamb at her feet, he insouciant and smiling, propped against an ivied tree trunk. 'They belonged to my grandmother,' Johnny Chance had said.

In sudden panic Etta turned and ran upwards, leaping from tussock to tussock. There was no terrible horse, no cattle, but there would be retribution if she were found out of doors at bedtime. On the summit, just before the gate, she paused, heaving in air, pressing the stitch in her side. It was late, late. It was nearly dark. She was out alone.

She never felt alone in Hobeys.

Was it the medieval peasants, the Romans tending their vines, or old Hobey himself who accompanied her? Or Old Jack inspecting his summering hunters, Paddy beside him? Or Jack's father William climbing steadily towards Bretton, drawn by desire? Or Philip Paulley in the hollow under the elms waiting for the girl he was sure he was going to marry? Or Harriet surrendering, grass stains on her silk dress?

Only at the back door, in the lozenge of light, did Etta realize how dark it really was. She blinked. The back stairs were steep and twisting and they creaked. Above Lily's voice, rising and rising in desperation: 'Etta! Ettaaa!'

'Here I am.'

'You young vixen. Where you been? You've got wet feet. And look at this!' She plucked disparagingly at the dressing-gown hem, soaked through.

'I've been out.'

'Well, you didn't ought've been. Not in the dark. The bats'll get you.'

'It's not dark outside. Not properly dark.'

'But it's not allowed.'

'Pen Potter goes out in the dark. She told me. She has a brother who catches moths,' said Etta through the folds of the clean dry nightdress Lily had thrust over her head.

'That little madam. I've heard she's got brothers who catch more than moths. Pheasants. And trout.' 'And girls in haystacks' in an undertone. 'Now, quick. Brush your hair and get into bed.'

'What about prayers?'

'Say them in bed. I should be downstairs dishing . . . That's it. And God bless everyone . . .' Lily closed the sash, adjusted the curtains and then bent to peck Etta's cheek. She was only twenty, stout, red, ignorant and kind, the youngest of eight. She had often lacked a pair of shoes but never the generous affection of a close family. You wasn't wanted, she thought, gazing down. And you the only one!

'Lily. Can Curry come up and see me?'

'You know she can't. She's seeing to dinner. And she's Mrs Murray to you, don't you forget it.'

Lily blew out the candle and the thick dark of Bretton lapped round.

'I do hope Mr Chance has a pony,' said Etta as the door closed.

47

5

JOHNNY CHANCE HAD a pony but Laura could not manage it. It ran away in Stenton and tried to roll in the watersplash. 'Why can't she manage it?' demanded Johnny when Etta ran down to Roman Hill to tell him. In a fit of exasperation and curiosity he walked up to Bretton to find out for himself.

Bushey saw him come in through the green door in the wall. 'Blast,' he said afterwards to Curry. 'I near dropped my spade, I did. A Chance at Bretton after all these years. He come through the door as if he owned the place, lookin' all about him.'

He had looked all about him because he did not know his way. He had hoped, by going through the gardens, to arrive at the stables unremarked, but the high yew hedges cut off his view. He lost his bearings on the stableyard bell tower – a painted wood cupola in which hung the fire bell – and found himself far from the house at the end of the long border where Paddy was on her hands and knees pushing in an extra bit of something. 'The whole garden's bits of things pushed in over the years,' she had said once. She looked up and he looked down, mutually astonished.

'I'm lost,' he confessed disarmingly.

'In general,' she rebuked gently, 'visitors use the front avenue and ring the bell.'

48

He pushed his hands deeper into his pockets. 'I'm not dressed for the front avenue,' he said.

Paddy sat back on her heels and pushed a stray strand of hair behind her ear. 'Then I take it you want the stables?'

'I had word the pony I sent up has been misbehaving.'

'Has it? It seemed a quiet enough little thing.'

His grin was unexpected. 'Not like the hothead you sold my father.'

'He goes well enough for you. I've seen him.' She paused, examining her earthy fingers. 'He must be all of twenty now. I forget. The years go so quickly.'

'I'm not complaining. I'll never own another the like of him.'

It occurred to Paddy that however stilted this conversation was it was still a most extraordinary one, for she had lived within half a mile of this man all her life and never spoken more than a dozen words to him. And he stood there at ease, looking up and down her border as if he might even be interested in plants.

'Perhaps you could lead me to the front door then,' he said after a while. 'It might look better after all.'

He helped Paddy to her feet. She brushed stalks and crumbled earth off her knees. Her old tweed skirt was baggy from so much kneeling, from 'pushing in the bits'. The dark hair with its streaks of grey blew gently round her face, a plain strong face, nothing like a Bretton.

'I'm afraid . . .' she began.

'It is *your* door.'

'At the moment it is very much the Haleys' door. In any case, it could never be mine, it's my father's.'

Only because of you, he wanted to say. Though the village was quick to criticize the village was quite sure of one thing: no one could have worked harder than Paddy Bretton to keep the great house going. 'If the old

49

man has two farthings to his name it's Miss Paddy's doing,' was the unanimous verdict. Even at Roman Hill, isolated on the village fringe, such things were reported down the years. Right from the beginning, always Miss Paddy . . . Overseeing Home Farm, selling her horses, attacking the weeds. Johnny Chance had heard all about the roan pony from his father, though not about the five guineas and the stable roof.

'Well, will you take me up to the house?' he asked.

They came up under the cedars to the front lawn. 'How disreputable we look,' said Paddy. 'I really don't think I should come any further.'

'What? Miss Bretton driven to knock at the kitchens? I thought you'd be too proud. Come on. We'll ring the bell like Christians and take the consequences.'

'I've never seen anyone hang on a bell with more determination,' said Paddy afterwards. 'You'd have thought there was a fire. And along came Lily Foster in a silly little apron and a frilly starched cap and showed us both into the drawing room without blinking an eye and there were at least two hundred people in there taking tea . . .'

'Twenty,' said Curry.

'Two hundred including the parson who to the best of my knowledge had never set foot in the place before. You know how Father's been against parsons ever since Wenlow refused to bury Mother. And there we stood on the threshold in old tweeds and muddy shoes picking the twigs from our hair. The silence was deafening.'

'Good God, that young jackanapes!' exclaimed Frank Paulley as the hubbub resumed. He was addressing Grace but several near neighbours nodded sympathetically. The young jackanapes was brazening it out like a true Chance of course but Paddy – Paddy! – was at his side. The last time she had appeared in public with a Chance she had been eighteen and dressed in virginal white. She and Old Jack had waltzed up and down a long room ablaze with candles. *That* was another world, thought Paddy, catching sight of Laura's charming bobbed head. She glanced up at Johnny's face suddenly as if . . . As if by so doing she might surprise his father there. The shape of the skull, the tanned skin, even the nose, these were familiar, but Johnny's was a thoughtful face and the eyes full of humour. 'Well might he grin,' said Curry. 'I never thought I'd live to see a Chance at Bretton taking tea like a gentleman.'

Long long ago when the Chances had first lighted on Roman Hill and Joseph's name had first been entered in the Bretton rent book they had been frequent visitors. The country was still at war with Napoleon, there were invasion scares, there were the Volunteers. There was also a sprightly Mrs Bretton who did not give a toss for social divisions. But as the years passed a new order came about. The Chances prospered, bought the Frilton mill, then the Ashton one, bred the best sheep and some of the best horses in the county, but the decree had gone out: they were not gentry. Harriet came as Ralph's bride, bred in a family that held farmers in contempt. 'Though *I* was one in the end,' she said. 'The bitter end.' Ralph too would have nothing to do with them. In his case, perhaps, there were darker reasons. 'I suppose mine were dark too,' said Harriet, 'in later years.'

'The Chances go everywhere in riding boots,' declared the village, 'even to dine with the Lord Lieutenant.' Had they ever dined with the Lord Lieutenant? They had certainly sold him horses. 'They are tenant farmers,' said Ralph and considered he had said it all – but they were also mill owners, three by the seventies, and had property in Frilton. 'They have money,' said Harriet, who never seemed to have any worth counting. She knew, though she never asked and never listened to gossip, almost to a guinea what they asked for their horses, riding horses, trotting horses . . . 'They're rogues!' she cried when Ralph suggested William Chance might find a pair of carriage horses if the deal were negotiated by a third party. She went herself to London and bought them there at London prices, one of her only extravagances in nearly fifty years.

'Why can we never talk about the Chances?' asked her younger daughter Frances, intractable Aunt Fan.

'Because,' replied Harriet, and walked away.

But: 'How very nice of you to come,' was Laura Haley's greeting to this latest Chance arrival. She had no idea who he was, old Dack had gone after the pony, but she could see he was young, thirty-two or three perhaps, and was certainly striking. She was tired of old men and dowdy women in country clothes.

'We didn't mean to intrude. It's all a mistake,' said Paddy. She looked as if she thought nothing of intruding, or of intruding in garden clothes.

'It really doesn't matter. I'm sure you know everybody. Far better than we do, I expect. You must have some tea now you're here.'

Johnny Chance said into Paddy's ear, 'Shouldn't you have been invited anyway?'

'Perhaps they thought I'd be embarrassed – or be an embarrassment.'

'So you are. You've got mud on your chin.'

She groped in the deep pockets of her jacket. 'This was my grandmother's coat,' she murmured. 'I can find anything you like, string, seed packets, labels . . . but no handkerchief.'

He handed her his. 'Left side. Low down. I can see why the pony misbehaves. She'd lose her temper. Fatal to lose your temper.'

'Who *is* that?' asked the parson, Maycroft, who was installed on a sofa at the far end of the room. It was a large room and extra chairs had been brought in so that he was, in effect, beached well beyond the tide line.

'Young John Chance,' said Miss Hartley, craning to see.

'I hardly thought to see a Chance at Bretton. Are you sure?'

Who could mistake that red head? 'It's certainly Mr Chance. I think he's dressed for riding though.'

Etta was conscious of behaving properly, speaking when spoken to, handing cake, but she felt uncomfortable, the only child in the room. She saw Paddy at once, saw too that she also was an oddity, so shabbily dressed, man's handkerchief in one hand, a cup of tea in the other. She drew near, warm with inexplicable relief. Quietly she tucked herself in behind. In front Frank Paulley loomed, a big-nosed, big-voiced man. 'Patricia, how are you, my dear? You look charming. Always do.' He was fired with guilty joy. He took her hand, the hand with the handkerchief, and crushed it happily in his own. How glad he was his son Philip had not lived to marry her. She was plain, opinionated, old-fashioned. Well, she would be old-fashioned, she was middle-aged. She was always old-fashioned, an inner voice suggested, never quite of her own time and place. And all her opinions had always been strong and unusual. 'Unexpected,' Grace said more kindly.

Laura was talking to Johnny Chance. 'Who else?' asked Curry with a crack of protesting whalebone. They made a striking pair. They might be the hero and heroine in one of Miss Hartley's novels. Miss Hartley's novels were always required to have such a couple and after many tribulations there was always a happy ending.

'I suppose he's explaining about the pony,' Paddy said to Frank Paulley.

'It ran away with us. It's not really suitable,' put in Etta from behind Paddy's skirts. The dregs of adult conversations had been sprinkled on her head from babyhood and sometimes she liked to repeat the phrases, savouring their strangeness. 'It's not really suitable at all.'

'It needs a good wallop,' said Frank, stroking his moustache.

'Henrietta. Oh, Henrietta,' and Laura was there, begging their pardon, slipping a hand under Etta's rounded little elbow. 'Run out and tell Mrs Murray we need more cakes.'

The house beyond the drawing-room door was dim and cool; there were windows open to the vigorous spring blow. Etta paused to listen. Sometimes there seemed to be voices. But whose?

'I shall marry him, Mother.'

'Brook Court isn't ours any more. It hasn't been ours for twenty years.'

'You are insolent, disobedient and a liar.'

Fan, Paddy, Edward. It was not that Etta could hear the words, but she knew the air was charged.

'More cakes?' said Mrs Prince, the London cook, scowling at the kitchener.

'There are no more cakes,' said Curry firmly. 'This is afternoon tea not a parish outing.' She smoothed her black hair in which there was less grey than Paddy's, settled her bodice more comfortably over her flat chest, and strode forth.

'Mrs Murray is a tower of strength,' announced Mrs Prince with a sigh of gratitude.

The hall was full of the noise of departure. By the door Grace Paulley was saying an affectionate goodbye to Paddy. Was it only Etta who noticed Paddy shrinking inwardly from the attention? Perhaps Mrs Paulley was always especially kind because Paddy had once been going to marry her son Philip. She had only had one son, Etta knew, but he had died. Why had he died? In the war? Pen Potter said no one ever talked about it,

54

there had been an accident, something to do with a gun. But when? And why?

'Do stop asking why all the time,' Laura had exclaimed at some point during that dreadful time in seaside hotels, plagued by boredom, doctors, arctic winds. Now in the hall at Bretton she came forward to see Paddy out and compared with that experienced and sardonic older woman she looked innocence personified, young, pure and true.

They shook hands.

It would have been hard to say who was the hostess, who the guest. 'You may not have any money but you've got style,' said an admiring Johnny Chance ages after.

'Bare-faced effrontery, you mean,' said Paddy. 'I learnt it in my cradle.'

'I think you might have left one day at least free for us to be alone,' complained Hugh, looking out of the window at the shaven lawn, the lily pool, the dark of the yew hedge that hid the tennis court.

'But how was I to know you'd be here till Tuesday? You always go back to town Sunday night. If you'd said anything, of course, I could have arranged . . .'

How reasonable she sounded, how pained under the reasonableness! And it was difficult to believe, after all, that she had organized things deliberately to annoy him. She had simply said that some people were coming on Monday to play tennis.

'Well, at least we'll have dinner in peace,' he said.

She looked across at him, judging his mood. But his mood was just irritation at never being sure of anything: the domestic arrangements, social obligations, his wife. He stood very still, all his natural cheerfulness quenched. He had often been cheerful once, and eager, pursuing Laura against great odds. Now that he saw the struggle had been for nothing he was reluctant to show enthusiasm at all.

Etta accepted this reticence, this fading into the background. She felt him to be dependable, a solid object around which, dragged in the wake of the unstable Laura, she thankfully revolved. But she felt he possessed no humour and no cunning. With a child's impeccable instinct she knew he was not cunning. And he was not. He never entirely believed Laura's many explanations yet he could not out-talk her, out-wit her or out-manoeuvre her. He hated the house being invaded – he called it an 'invasion' – yet he would dutifully put up with these people on Monday, would dutifully talk, eat and even play tennis, which he hated. 'That nice young Mr Haley,' said Miss Hartley contentedly, for he appeared so like several of her gentler heroes it was quite gratifying: gratifying to think such people could actually exist in the flesh. The village as a whole was sceptical. Why did he work in London? London was fifty miles away. It was unnatural. Miss Hartley explained, 'The little girl had to have an operation and no amount of sea air afterwards seemed to help, so they thought renting a place in the country for a year might do the trick.' But Etta was well-nourished, sturdy, energetic. And what about all the country air much nearer London than Stenton? There must be a thousand houses to rent from which Hugh Haley might drive daily to his office instead of being put to the expense of rooms. Grace Paulley said thoughtfully, '*I* wouldn't care to leave that woman alone all week with nothing to occupy her.'

'I don't know why you're making a fuss,' said Laura, crossing her ankles and looking down at them. Her ankles were slender and shapely, so were her legs. Would skirts get shorter? Hugh had turned from the window to look at her and he followed the direction of her glance. But it would not profit him much to think about Laura's legs.

'And has it never occurred to you,' he said, as if they had been talking about this other thing all the time, 'that it can't be good for Etta to spend all her time at Home Farm? What does she do all day? Mrs Paulley warned me at your tea party about some girl called Potter.'

'Babs Potter's sister.'

'You mean *the* Babs?'

'The very one.'

'Then it's hardly suitable, is it?' Ordinarily he might not have minded, but he found Babs both provocative and not particular about dirt, qualities undesirable in a housemaid. He had also heard the incredible but disquieting story of Babs' three babies, all apparently fathered by different men and all brought up as Mrs Potter's own. I wonder why I should be making moral distinctions? he thought. He looked at Laura for a moment with that sad helpless look that had become habitual.

'I don't think she sees very much of this girl,' Laura was saying. 'Heaven knows, there aren't any other companions for her.'

'Then why shouldn't we send her to school?'

'You know perfectly well old Bridges said she must have the year off, no strict routine, no lessons, nothing. She was so terribly ill after the operation.'

'I don't believe there was ever anything wrong with her appendix at all. She was so young. How could they tell? It wasn't as if she could even describe the symptoms.'

'Well, I'm sticking to Bridges' advice. He's the only doctor who made any sense.'

'She could have a governess.' But could she? He was not sure he could stretch to the expense, not unless Laura curbed her extravagance. He swung about again to stare moodily into the garden. One of the only advantages he had seen in this terrible great house had been its setting, the romantic neglected gardens stretching away beyond the cedars. He was beginning to feel, however, that they did not compensate for the house itself, in which he always seemed to come to quarrels with his wife.

'So who are these people coming on Monday?'

'Madge Talbot's house party, mostly young cousins. They're motoring up,' and seeing his frown, knowing how much he disliked them all, 'Larter House is barely twenty-five miles away the other side of Frilton. Why shouldn't they come? Madge is my oldest friend.'

Silence.

'Then I thought,' she continued, on a higher, more brittle note, 'why not a few people from the village? That Baxter girl's all right. And the Freeborns from the Grange.'

'And Miss Bretton?'

'Good God! She's old as the hills. Besides, she terrifies people. She's a witch, like her Mrs Murray. Did you see the way she practically took over the tea party?'

'I thought she behaved very well. She must have felt strange, poor woman, dressed like that.'

'Perhaps she did it on purpose. I can't think why Foster showed her in. Well, yes, I suppose I can. She still behaves as if this were her house. You like her, do you?'

'Not as much as you like that fellow Chance. Will *he* be coming on Monday?'

'Of course not.'

'Didn't he have anything interesting to say?'

'I don't remember.'

'I would have thought,' said Hugh, taking refuge again in gazing at the lily pool, 'he would have played tennis rather well.'

'Mother is quarrelling with Father,' said Etta to Lily, who was going through the bedtime ritual of adjusting the sash – 'so them wicked bats don't get in' – and tucking in.

'No,' said Lily firmly. ''Course they're not quarrel-ling.'

'Do you think Mr and Mrs Paulley quarrel?'

'Lord, what a question! No. No, I shouldn't think so for a minute.' Lily whipped the sheet in, anxious to be gone. It occurred to her that because the Haleys were at odds she would have to serve dinner in that prickly silence which made her so hopelessly clumsy.

'Goodnight, Lily.'

'Goodnight.'

Laura never climbed the nursery stairs to kiss her daughter. She only came at all if she were upstairs already dressing to go out. In Kensington she would drift in smelling of freesias, something pinned in her hair, gold bracelets on her fragile wrists. 'Goodnight, darling,' she would say from the foot of the bed, blowing kisses.

As soon as Lily's heavy tread had died away Etta flew out of bed and perched on the window sill. The night was cool and still. Soon it would be true summer, the nights hardly dark, the cedars throwing immense and inky shadows on the lawns. From below, far below, came the occasional clink of china from the dining room, sometimes a subdued voice, for that window too was open in anticipation of the summer to come.

'She ought to have *some* lessons,' Hugh said.

'She's having lessons in life.'

'No doubt, with that Potter girl as a friend.'

'She's growing inches taller running about in the fresh air.'

'She'd grow anyway. All children grow.'

'She didn't grow last year moping and freezing in those terrible hotels. Convalescence! There were old men in invalid chairs and young men with no legs.'

'And you had no social life for weeks.'

'How absurd you are. Of course I hated it. Henrietta hated it. She lost weight. She looked like a little wax doll. Now she's healthy and happy and almost recovered. D'you want all that fuss of doctors over again? What does it matter if she plays at the farm? She can't come to much harm. I've met the Dacks. They're dreadfully old-fashioned, quite ancient, but they won't let her be silly.'

Etta leaned right out, her hands clutching the bottom of the raised sash. She thought, though it was impossible, that she heard her name. She was always afraid when she heard her name bandied between her parents. She felt her father did not really like her. Perhaps he wished she were a boy. He rarely took any proper notice of her and all last year, between hospital and seaside, she had scarcely seen him. Though she was glad of him as a fixed point he worried her. Once or twice she had thought, with sudden fright, with a huge inner shrinking, that he did not often remember she was there.

She wished she could run away down Hobeys and hammer at the door of Roman Hill. 'Just come,' Johnny had said, laughing. 'Any time. The door's usually open.' Or perhaps she could go to the Lodge. Paddy would let her in. But then Paddy was a stickler for duty. She might send her back. And there was old Mr Bretton, bony and fierce. 'He doesn't like little girls,' Curry had told her. 'But he had one of his own,' said Etta.

There was a faint crash from below. A glass smashed? Lily being nervous? Etta thought her parents might still be quarrelling. Over her? They often quarrelled wordlessly, Laura electric, Hugh cold. Please not over her. Not wanting to hear any more she pulled down the stiff sash and sprinted to the bed and got right in, dragging up the covers. Whatever happened they mustn't stop her going to the farm, or Hobeys, or Roman Hill – did they guess she had found her way to Roman Hill? – or to Paddy at the Lodge.

Mother and Father. She spoke under the warm heaviness of the bedclothes: 'Mother and Father.' It sounded odd. Yet that was what she called them to their faces, what she called them to Lily and Curry, Paddy and Johnny Chance, to Pen Potter and old Mr Dack. But inside herself she did not call them anything and always thought of them with anxiety.

'We should have taken a house nearer London,' Laura was saying downstairs. 'Have you ever thought I might be lonely?'

'But it was you who wanted this house. It's big enough for anything, you said. We could have twenty people for the weekend.'

'So we could. If they'd come.'

'Why shouldn't they? Madge is coming.'

'Probably out of curiosity.'

'You say she's your best friend.'

'But I didn't realize how remote it is. And how can we manage any entertaining with so few servants?'

Hugh pushed away his plate. He was tired. He tried to return to what he had felt was important. 'But what are we going to do about Etta?'

'I really don't think I care,' and Laura got up suddenly, walking to the door. 'You decide. You don't normally take the least interest in her. But you were the one who wanted her.'

'Yes. And I would have liked more children.' He sounded a little surprised, as if he could not remember why.

'Perhaps you would. I wouldn't.'

The door closed behind her.

And: 'There's trouble to come,' said Mrs Prince who was sitting with Lily at the kitchen table reading the tea leaves.

6

THE SUN WAS hot and the shadows were black under the young green of the trees. Etta was down the Long Pasture with Bushey, attacking docks.

'It doesn't take much to put Bushey off his stroke,' Paddy had complained for years. She meant his stroke in the vegetable garden. She had known him slip through the green door many a time. Now she came slowly down the track between the budding sprays of elder flowers and saw them there, the dark stumpy figure and the smaller one bent together over the devilish weeds. She paused and looked along the hedge to the hump of Hobeys where it glittered green through the trees. When I was Etta's age, she thought suddenly, Hobeys was my favourite place.

And afterwards?

'Marry me! What does it matter about anyone else?' she had cried in Hobeys, propped on one elbow to look down at Philip.

'But it does matter.'

Blue sky, the tickling grass, buttercups, joy, frustration: 'Why should it? Why must it?' Then, because he did not answer: 'I'm twenty-one. I'm not a child. I don't even have to ask their permission any more.'

How many years since Philip had died? The cattle were in Hobeys now as they had been every spring, frolicsome young things. 'Varminty buggers,' said Bushey. To Etta he said, 'Missus look crabbed. Here she come. Do you hand me that dibber. And keep your head down.'

'Etta,' said Paddy, striding down the grass. 'Etta, Lily's just run over to fetch you. She says you have to go back to the house. There are guests.'

'It's only a tennis party,' protested Etta, pushing her straw hat up and looking flushed and defiant.

'I don't know what it is, but you're to go at once.'

Etta hesitated. 'I don't want to go home,' was what she said most often though always silently, always like this: set mouth, poked-out little chin. 'I don't want to go but I shall,' said that pugnacious chin. She was a dutiful child. She would drag back through the green door, across the gardens and up to the nursery, miserable but obedient to the hour. Or nearly the hour. 'Where've you been?' Lily would squawk, seizing water jug and flannel. 'As if I need to ask.'

'Come on, Etta,' said Paddy gently, reaching for her shoulder.

Side by side they went back up the field to the gate into the green lane, the cart track that wound to the farm. Here was shadowy cool and the rank smell of elder and masses of sweet sneezy cow parsley. Where the lane ran out to take a swing round the stackyard the shade was deeper, danker. There was an old unused pond decaying beneath the sloping alders and young self-seeded ash.

'Do I have to go?' Etta tried.

'Yes. Lily says you were told at breakfast . . .' but she stopped. Etta's small face was deathly white. It was a trick of the light here under the trees. Paddy knew it was simply a trick of the light, but there was no denying the pinched unhappy look.

Lily was at the green door, peering anxiously for them. She had been harried mercilessly all morning,

63

bringing in armfuls of flowers for the house that Bushey had disobligingly left in the ruinous hothouses; polishing the dining table twice; rearranging every rug in the house; and still she had failed to please Laura, who was in a state of unbearable tension.

'Oh, where've you been?' she wailed at Etta, taking in the earthy knees, the stained pinafore, the jammy mouth.

'Jabbing docks,' said Etta truthfully. She thought it better to say nothing about the jam sandwich Bushey had produced from a deep and savoury inside pocket.

'Oh!' cried Lily. 'Oh!'

Etta's feet hardly touched the ground between the green door and the kitchen. 'Don't you dawdle,' moaned Lily, 'do I shall get wrong again.' Up the backstairs, Lily behind now with a can of water snatched from Mrs Prince's floury hands. It would take a week with a scrubbing brush to get them knees clean, said Lily, but the best blue dress would just cover them, and stockings . . . 'Oh, not my best blue dress,' said Etta. 'It itches.' But in ten minutes she was in it, buttoned up firmly, all the elder leaves brushed from her hair with merciless vigour. A distant and compelling voice yelled, 'Lily!' up the stair. Lily yelped, drew Etta's hair back into a rebellious tail and struggled to confine it with a large blue bow. 'Downstairs. Quick!' she panted.

Etta crept down the grand staircase. She loved its satisfying curve but it was not her territory. Like the front door it was usually forbidden her. The flagstones looked far down like a grey sea. Where was she supposed to go?

'Well, you're the lucky one,' said a voice. 'I wasn't even invited.' It was Johnny Chance. He had been hesitating in the cool shadow below. 'No Chance ever hesitates,' Harriet would have said. 'They go straight in and take what they want.'

'I came for the pony,' Johnny said to a thin young

man in tennis flannels emerging from the drawing room.

'Pony?'

'There was nobody in the yard. A driving pony.'

'Laura couldn't drive a rabbit.'

Johnny smiled, turning away. 'I can see I've blundered in again. I'd better go.'

Etta ran down the last few stairs. He must stay, she thought. He would talk to her, he would make her laugh. Those others ... Mother's friends ... They would simply comment on her. Mrs Talbot would be there, Mrs Talbot with the fingernails and the thin arms and predatory eyes.

'Wait!' called Etta. 'Wait for me!'

He had reached the side door, the door through which he had, avoiding the bell, entered the house with such an air of Chance confidence. And suddenly there was Laura, running in from the tennis court to pour forgotten instructions on Mrs Prince's head. Slender and full of life she poised there, breathing quickly. Like a dragonfly, thought Etta. Johnny thought: Does she look at every man like that? He stood aside to let her pass, but before she could speak he walked off in the direction of the stables.

So what were the implications, he wondered, of making love to a married woman in a small village guaranteed to know everything?

Footsteps behind, quick and light. He turned to find that stiff little figure in blue, thick brown hair already coming adrift.

'I hate grown-up parties,' said Etta. And then, irrelevantly: 'Lily didn't have time to plait my hair.'

'Good. I like it like that. But the bow's slipped.'

'Mother will be cross.'

He took her limp, hot little hand. 'She'll be too busy playing tennis to be cross. Come on. Show me where the pony is.'

'Those Chances,' said Curry, 'would charm the eyes out of your head.'

'He made the pony kneel down,' Etta told her. It had seemed an awesome thing.

'Oh, that's a trick. All their animals do tricks.'

'But he just tapped him on the leg and he kneeled down.'

There was straw on the blue dress and the bow was off, dangling from her fingers. A vast shining satisfaction glowed in her wondering face. 'He kneeled down,' she repeated, more to herself than to Curry.

'These are grand stables,' Johnny had said, looking round.

'But you've seen them before.'

'Only once.'

'But you only live down the hill.' Etta could hardly believe it, just as she could hardly believe the pony had got down at a touch.

'My father fell out with Mr Bretton. It was to do with broken promises. And then with your Miss Paddy. You don't break promises, do you, Hettyetta?'

'No,' and she stood staunch and square, glad she could be positive. But: 'I don't have anyone to make promises to. Except Lily. And Pen.'

She longed to ask what Paddy had had to do with Roman Hill. She knew she never went there just as this man, this adorable man, seemed never to have come to Bretton.

But the pony, piqued at being ignored, pushed at her chest and slobbered down the best dress.

'And Mr Chance was there,' said Etta, biting off a piece of crust.

'Don't make crumbs. Where are your manners? What was a rascally Chance doing at a tennis party?' asked Edward, poking the child with the end of his stick. That pretty Mrs Haley, that's what, he thought. No Chance could ever keep away from a pretty woman.

66

The Lodge was abnormally quiet. Etta had come to tell Paddy about the tennis, about the kneeling pony, but Paddy was doing the church flowers, Mrs Dye had not yet arrived to prepare supper, and Edward was alone and in a good mood. 'Thank God that woman isn't here,' he had said. 'She sings all the time. Like a damn owl. I can't read. I can't sleep. Who does she think she is?' He was used to Bretton where the kitchens were 'a hundred miles from anywhere' said Paddy, and he divined in Mrs Dye's grudging solicitude a patronizing compassion for the afflicted. What must she report in the village? The old man reduced to the one room and that all full of books? How could she dust? Everything here and there and him banging his stick and calling for the Spode. 'How am I supposed to clean?' she asked Paddy. 'Never mind. I'll clean,' said Paddy. But she never did. Paddy had never been one for housework. Hard work yes, but housework no. 'Let it be, Mrs Dye,' she would say, sweeping up in one of her passions. 'Father will pick it all up later.' Instead he just sat and gave orders: fetch this, bang, fetch that, bang, find out where Miss Bretton's gone.

'Do you sing?' Edward asked Etta, whom he had found on the doorstep and had ushered in, indifferent to her nervous shrinking.

'No,' she replied, puzzled.

'Good.'

Somehow, in ten minutes or so, they were sitting down together and eating the new bread. It was a loaf that had been sent down from Bretton, part of the spoils of Mrs Prince's baking day. 'Mrs Prince says she knows how to get the better of the oven now,' said Etta. The oven in question was the great bread oven in the 'back' kitchen, the bread kitchen. It was as old as the house and had a tall chimney built on 'scientific principles' said Harriet, who had been fascinated by it. But then Harriet had never had to knead the dough or rake out the bundles of brushwood. The whole process to her was just a weekly ritual carried out by her kitchen staff. But she often went to watch, and the bread was always excellent.

Edward broke off a piece of the latest offering and chewed it slowly. It was soft and warm. The child, crouched on the footstool near by, had made scandalous inroads at the other end.

'We'll be scolded,' he said. He saw Etta's sudden anxious look, as if she thought Curry might arrive any moment astride a broomstick. He added, smiling, 'Oh, I expect we'll be forgiven. Tell me about the tennis party.'

'It wasn't very nice,' she said in a small voice. 'At least . . . it wasn't very nice at first.'

'Why?'

'Because I had to wear my blue dress and it itches.'

'And then?'

'And then Mr Chance took me to see the pony kneel down.'

'All their animals did tricks,' said Edward.

'That's what Curry said.'

Edward mopped the crumbs off his chin. They might have invited Pat, he thought, she's good at tennis. Comes of playing with Tom. He might not be good for much but he always hit a ball a fair whack. Tennis, cricket, rounders . . . There had been rounders under the cedars on Pat's ninth birthday, Deborah with her skirts held up and her face red, running.

'I don't think I'm a dignified sort of woman,' Deborah had replied when Edward had said, 'Do you think it's very dignified to rush about like this?' Her back hair was coming down. There were beads of perspiration on her smooth brow. Children shrieked round her calling 'Mrs Bretton! Mrs Bretton!' and balls were coming hard and fast.

'What a violent game,' said Edward to his mother.

'Exciting,' said Harriet, who was enjoying every minute.

Two of the visiting nannies, scandalized, agreed they would never have expected such behaviour. Old Mrs Bretton was a law unto herself, but young Mrs Bretton . . . She had always been the perfect lady.

The village agreed on this. Deborah Bretton was a perfect lady. 'But what *is* a perfect lady?' demanded Etta in her own time when admonished by Lily for some caper. It seemed the definition was vague – and malleable. Still, Deborah was perfect, pale and quiet and 'beautiful' said Curry. The local doctor – Dr Ward in those days – detected searing unhappiness doughtily hidden. But she would never unburden herself to him, even when he walked for an hour at a time through her beloved gardens, delighted in her company. He was a young man, and personable, and he did not care much for Edward. Edward was possessive. '*Opp*ressive,' said young Dr Ward, helplessly in love. 'He keeps her at Bretton as if it were a prison.' And once, stricken in a muddle of hopeless desire, professional caution and plain jealousy: 'I don't believe he trusts her out of his sight.' Except in the gardens, perhaps, which were peculiarly her own.

Of course he did not trust her. 'But I never lied,' said Deborah to Harriet. 'Ah,' said Harriet, 'you never told the truth either, not until you had to.'

'Would you? In my position, would you?'

'No,' said Harriet.

Harriet, Deborah, Pat . . . Etta. Edward chewed his new bread reflectively, looking down at the brown head. What a serious, shy child! She was sitting obediently on her stool but she looked tired. Those Haleys never had time for her, he remembered Mrs Dye saying. Why, even he had been washed and brushed and brought to Harriet once a day, and she had taught him his prayers and how to write, holding his unwilling little fist. Seventy years ago. He leaned back in his chair. The new bread had made him feel queer. Indigestion? *That* had been a boy's tomfoolery, eating the yeasty crust. His mother would have punished him for it. He closed his eyes. Harriet . . . A large woman in a black dress, dark eyes, fine hands . . .

'He played tennis with me,' said Etta.

'Who did?' How many young men had played tennis with Deborah? 'You have no reason to be jealous,' she had said. 'Oh, none at all.'

'Mr Chance.'

'But I thought he called to take away the pony? D'you mean your mother invited him, invited that fellow to Bretton?'

'Oh no. He wasn't invited. We . . . we played while everyone was at tea.'

The grass had been warm and scuffed, the net sagging a little after such combat. The quiet was no longer pierced by shrieks and laughter and the hurry of feet. There were pigeons crooning in the cedars. Johnny removed his jacket. 'I warn you. I haven't played for years, not since before the war.'

It was easy to imagine him a boy again, at school, playing tennis. For all his size and authority he seemed boyish still. Etta knew he must have climbed trees and made catapults and fished the beck. And he must have known Paddy all his life. But: 'No,' said Johnny, choosing two racquets from the pile left so casually by the deckchairs. 'No, I never knew Paddy. I only saw her in the distance.'

'Didn't you ever speak?'

'Not that I can remember.'

He sent a ball lobbed high and crooked. It landed at her feet. 'Well, hit it,' said Johnny.

A game developed, a game of sorts, somewhat slow and jerky and punctuated by laughter and small squeaks.

Etta's hair had flown out of its ribbon twice and Johnny hit himself across the chest and doubled up, gasping.

'Mother found us and was cross,' said Etta.

'I expect she was,' said Edward soberly. His own daughter had behaved foolishly with a Chance. Jack Chance. He let her ride his horses, thought Edward, he danced with her. Had it only been the once, waltzing up that long room at Frilton Hall? Or had there been other times, other times no one at Bretton ever knew about? Damn Jack Chance. He had been a blackguard.

'Mother said I was to go in at once and straight to the nursery. And Mr Chance said it was his fault, not mine. He thought I'd been missing out on the fun, and the tea, and . . . and everything. Then he put down his racquet and he thanked me for being his partner and he walked away.'

'Damn insolence,' said Edward. 'They were all like that.' He closed his eyes. He felt tired, much more tired than usual.

'I like Mr Chance,' said Etta.

But Edward was asleep.

'They were both asleep,' Paddy told Curry. 'Father in his chair and Etta on the floor with her head on the footstool.'

'That child,' said Curry, 'sometimes cries in the night.'

'Well, it must be lonely in the nursery. Why can't she have a room on the first floor? It isn't as if there were five children and a clutch of nursemaids.'

Even in Harriet's day there had never been as many as five children in the nursery. Harriet's mother Sophie tactlessly said two girls were all very well but she could quite understand Ralph wanting a son, then after Edward was born she said surely he might have a little brother? No, said Harriet, though like Etta she said it to herself and set her jaw. It was not as if she had not struggled with her marriage. If only I knew what was wanted of me, she had thought in the beginning. Rather too soon she found Ralph wanted no more than an amiable self-effacing handmaid. 'I could never be that,' declared Harriet. Because she was practical she turned to Bretton as her salvation. She learnt how the farm was run, how much rent the tenants paid and how well they husbanded their acres. Until Curry, whom she trusted absolutely, she went over the household accounts every week with the house-keeper – the succession of housekeepers. It was rumoured that she even knew what the servants did on their pitifully few days off. She curbed Ralph's extravagances, paid off most of his debts, put him right with the bank – but she could not make him love her. 'He never loved me,' she said to Deborah, long after.

Whatever else, she did her duty. She had been brought up to it. On her wedding morning, anxious for advice, she had been fobbed off with 'You must do your duty' and was told her husband's happiness was to be everything to her. 'But what about mine?' said the young Harriet. But that was later. Perhaps she said it after Edward was born and she locked her door at night. 'I've done my duty. I've finished with it,' she said to herself. Only Deborah was ever to know of that locked door and that was because Harriet told her, as she told her so many things. At the time not even her maid was aware of it – 'And servants know everything,' said Harriet. The village was surprised there were no more children but who knew what strange ideas the gentry harboured. Besides, who would care to get into a bed with Mrs Bretton? She could be formidable. And there had never been many children in Bretton's nurs-ery. In Paddy's day there would only be two and only one getting any attention. She too had cried in the night, but the young Paddy was made of steelier stuff than the young Etta and her tears had often been of rage.

★

'It's really too bad,' said Laura. 'First she's late and looks positively untidy, then she plays about in the stables and runs round the tennis court in her best dress giggling and shouting with that man Chance, and now she turns up at the Lodge fast asleep.' And she sent Lily to fetch her.

'That one should never have been a mother,' remarked Mrs Dye confidentially.

'It takes all sorts,' said Lily.

'But fancy her and the old man eating the new loaf. Well, I never. He was never one for children, I'm sure he never was.'

'I want to stay here,' moaned Etta when Lily woke her.

'She's not come to, poor lamb,' said Lily.

'Is Mother still cross?'

''Course not. She's been worrying about you.'

'Don't tell me she ran away?' asked Mrs Dye in a low voice.

'All I know,' said Lily sharply, 'is that she was told to stay in the nursery and she didn't.'

'Poor little thing. And nobody looked to make sure?'

'We were all so busy,' said Lily.

7

ALL MY LIFE I have worried about that house, thought Paddy, looking at it critically across the front lawns. The signs of neglect were not so apparent at this distance and the mellow brick was undeniably attractive. Below the terrace was the sudden gleam of water: the lily pool.

'It was a sort of peace-offering,' Deborah told Harriet. 'And I *was* grateful. Oh, I was.'

It needs clearing out, thought Paddy, for the lilies were thick across the surface and the irises even thicker at the margin. There ought to be fish in it. There *had* been fish in it. Long ago Tom, who generally was not a naughty child, felt rebellion bubbling like yeast and took a net from the Piggery and scooped the poor gasping things out on to the lawn. For that he had been beaten, the only beating of his charmed life. If he had broken a window deliberately Edward might have been lenient but animals were sacred at Bretton: horses, dogs, even the fish. Or perhaps the fish were doubly precious in a way no one except Edward understood, for they lived in the lily pool that had been made, romantically, for a much-loved young wife.

Paddy saw only that the pool needed cleaning out and replanting.

'There's Miss Bretton in the garden,' said Hugh,

74

looking out of his dressing-room window and speaking over his shoulder to Laura, who sat in bed with a tray and a book. 'She's in those awful shapeless old clothes and she's carrying . . .' He craned to see, at the same time anxious not to be seen. 'She's got a trowel.'

'That seems natural enough if she's gardening,' said Laura calmly. 'But I wish she wouldn't wander about near the house so early. I'll have to tell her not to come the days we have people here for tennis.'

'You could always invite her to play.'

'But everyone would think she was the hostess. Besides, I don't imagine she has any proper clothes to play in. She might not have tried to hit a ball in twenty years. Did you hear that funny little man Paget refer to her as "Miss Paddy"? Always Miss Paddy this and Miss Paddy that. As if she was Henrietta's age.'

Hugh watched Paddy's queenly progress towards the lily pool. If she looked up now she would surely see him. 'It must be difficult with strangers in the house.'

'I believe you do like her.'

'Perhaps I do.'

'I can't think why. She walks well, I suppose, but her clothes . . . And how much better she'd look with short hair.'

'I think I like long hair on a woman,' said Hugh. It was the first challenge he had offered in years but Laura, whose book was more interesting than Paddy Bretton, did not hear him.

After a while: 'Let's have a dance,' she said, looking up.

'Here?'

'Well of course here. Where else? There's a ballroom, isn't there?'

'It's been shut up for years. Since this place was a hospital.'

'But they must have had dances in the old days.'

'It would be expensive,' said Hugh cautiously. Laura

75

had made him so very very cautious over the ten years of their marriage. He had once been only ordinarily shy and awkward, a gentle, polite young man. Now he was extraordinarily wary, like an old horse who knows what it is to hit a fence and has no faith in his rider.

'Hugh darling, it would be a dream!' cried Laura, flinging the book away and moving to sit on the edge of the bed. 'Think. We could fill the place with flowers, have an orchestra.'

Hugh watched Paddy stand, apparently scowling, at the very edge of the lily pool. Then she turned abruptly and strode away. When he looked in at Laura he saw her silk top had slipped to reveal her slender shoulders and felt at once the old frustrated desire. At first, when he had been stubborn about something or other, she had bartered herself for compliance, but gradually disillusion had made him less susceptible. Now she usually rejected him, always with plausible excuses, and only when as he grew restless would make a gift of herself. 'A man ought to know when a woman is lying,' Harriet had said, 'but he seldom does.' After Edward was born she turned Ralph away with surprising firmness – 'And I wasn't as firm then as I became later on,' she said. Weeks ran to months and then the door was locked. She had done her duty. She never asked if Ralph went elsewhere and to his credit he was remarkably discreet.

Hugh Haley found he did not, after all, want to make love to his wife. He wanted to dress and go downstairs and out into the May morning. He wanted to ask 'Miss Paddy' to show him round the gardens. Why had he never thought of it before?

'Hugh, are you listening? If we had it in June . . . Roses, masses of roses . . .'

There had certainly been balls at Bretton in the dim past, but not all of them had been successful and one or two had brought 'ruin' said Harriet, taking her last jewels to be sold. The one Edward had planned had never taken place. 'When the baby's born we'll invite the whole county,' he had said. 'As soon as you're up and about.'

'Suppose it's a girl?' asked Deborah.

'It's a boy. It's a boy for Bretton.'

They never cared for Bretton but they cared for sons to inherit it. 'Did Edward ever care for me?' wondered Deborah. Could his suffocating passion really be anything to do with love? But the baby *was* a boy, a true Bretton. 'A boy!' shouted Paddy, infected by the excitement. 'Yes, you have a little brother,' said old Dr Broughton. Had he really said that, coming down the cold front stairs and finding her at the bottom, flushed and anxious, wondering if she dare go up? He must have done. He would hardly have said, 'You have a brother but in a few days you'll be motherless.'

'He drank,' said Curry, and once: 'He never washed his hands.'

It should have been young antiseptic Dr Ward instead of this careless, incompetent old man. 'Why wasn't it?' howled Paddy. Of course it should have been Dr Ward with his thin hair and baby face, but he had been on holiday and the baby was early. 'Too early' said the pessimistic midwife, though he was whole and adequately pink. The whole pregnancy had been a trial, joyless, uncomfortable. But: 'That was *my* duty,' Deborah might have told Harriet had she still been alive. 'I owed Bretton an heir.'

How Edward had raged, left with an heir and no wife! His grief was one long rage that upheld him through the grim days before the funeral and the grim days after. For the service itself he ordered what Deborah would have liked: flowers, candles, singing. The old parson Wenlow was appalled. Afterwards, after the battle and his victory, Edward said, 'This is the last time I shall set foot in this church.' Later he had gone out into the garden to stand by the lily pool and he had stood there so long that Jackson, the second parlour-maid, had begun to think he had rooted. Every time she looked out of the window he was there, immobile, staring at the water. Half an hour, three quarters ... 'An hour at least,' she reported to the kitchens. It was autumn and the evenings were cool. 'He must come in,' said Curry as darkness fell, but only she had the nerve to go out and confront him, carrying his coat.

'We ought to have a go at the pool,' Paddy said to Bushey who had appeared with the shears under his arm.

'Always jobs want doin',' he retorted. 'Dirty one that. It'll keep till next year.'

'I suppose it will have to,' said Paddy.

Etta crouched among the gooseberries.

She lay on her stomach with the hard baked earth digging in all over and listened to the murmur of voices beyond the asparagus bed where Paddy and Bushey had paused on their weekly inspection. Wireworm, bullaces, the errant sweet rocket – why rampant in the potato patch? – were subjects bandied back and forth. The air was warm and still between the high walls. Etta could see Paddy's white blouse between the gooseberry branches, hear her crisp voice, Bushey's mild, considered replies. This was another of the rituals that drew her to Bretton, this weekly consultation peppered with mysterious terms, this stately circumambulation by the woman in the white blouse and the old man with the Gladstonian whiskers. There were daily rituals too: the arrival of the butcher's cart, the impatient swish of Babs Potter sweeping the back steps at seven thirty, Lily clanking hot water up the backstairs on the stroke of eight. There were days for scrubbing the bricks in the back passages, days for laundry, Mrs Potter with her sleeves rolled up and her face mottled puce vanishing in the steam pouring forth from the great coppers. There were days for baking fragrant with pastry and hot bread and wood ash. And 'Why?' asked Etta, or 'How does it work?'

'That child ought to have a governess,' said Mrs Prince, whose daily battles with Harriet's kitchener often left her short of sympathy.

'I don't run wild, do I?' Etta asked Paddy.

'Who says so?'

'Babs. I accidentally walked on her wet floor.'

'I don't think you do.'

There had been no question about Paddy: she had run wild as soon as Deborah died. 'As soon as Mother died I was neglected,' she said. 'Aunt Sarah was too busy with Tom.' Lacking the two women who had meant everything to her, lacking affection, lacking super-vision, what more natural than that she should escape to Roman Hill where her welcome was always sure? 'They used to think I was in the schoolroom reading or was down in the village at the Paulleys'.' No one ever knew where she really was. No one ever asked. Her first day's hunting had been on a pony borrowed from Roman Hill, a rough just-broken bang-tailed cob. At fifteen she had cunning and determination. At fifteen Deborah had still been a child, sheltered by class and parental con-cern. But Paddy's childhood ended with Deborah's death and Bretton was socially isolated, Edward uninter-ested. He only cared for Tom, was only proud of Tom. Tom was bought a pony and was taught to ride while Paddy, who had begun on the carthorses at Home Farm, was mounted occasionally by the Paulleys on donkeys. Then there was Roman Hill and the 'real thing' said Paddy, taught to sit straight and nurture nerves of steel on a succession of miscreants. For years she crept out at dawn and ran down Hobeys in the faint first light, to consult Jack, to do business, sometimes to borrow a mount when hers were lame or unsuitable. If she sold one of Jack's on the hunting field she was paid commission. 'You're a hard-headed piece, aren't you?' he said. 'Someone has to be,' she replied, 'or what would happen to Bretton?'

It had only ended when Tom had traded her secret to avoid his father's wrath.

'What was he angry about?' demanded Paddy.

'Oh, probably the usual. But he was terrible fierce, Pat.' Tom had a baby language all his own when he wished to be ingratiating. 'And I said before I could stop myself, it's Pat you ought to be shouting at, she's the one who breaks all the rules.'

She was twenty-six then. She had got away with it for twelve years. 'You had a good innings really,' was Tom's nonchalant remark. He was mad about cricket that summer. But: 'Twenty-six,' said Paddy furiously, 'and he shouted at me as if I were ten.'

'Even though you'd never cost him a penny in horse-flesh,' said Jack Chance. 'You bought your own or borrowed mine. But then he always was a blinkered fool.'

It salved her sore spirit to hear her father described so cavalierly but it did nothing for her trembling conscience. 'I thought he was going to have a heart attack,' she said.

'Not him. He'll live for ever. You mind what I say, Paddy my dear, and leave before it's too late. You'll be waiting on him hand and foot till you're an old, old woman.'

'I tried to leave before.'

'Then try harder.'

Edward had said, 'You are insolent, disobedient and a liar. But then, it's no more than I'd expect. You have always wanted your own way. As to your relationship with Chance . . .'

'You can't think . . .' began Paddy.

'As to your relationship, I would rather know nothing.

80

You will never refer to the matter again.' To Paget he said, 'Get that man Chance out of my farm.'

'I believe,' Paget replied in a low, dismal voice, 'it would be wise to proceed cautiously. That business over disputed valuations . . . and then those repairs the year before last. You were contractually responsible for . . .'

'Damn you! Damn them! If I can't get them out of Roman Hill may they rot in it.'

The village watched with interest. Sympathy for Paddy was tempered by a twelve-year knowledge that she had it coming. The social rules had been broken – elastic as social rules had always been at Bretton – and everyone knew what little good ever came of that. There had been an almighty row over Philip Paulley, raised voices, defiance, Miss Paddy refusing to eat. Would this last as long?

But: 'If he'd wanted a lady he should have brought her up as one,' was the verdict at the pump.

Paddy suddenly stooped. 'Etta!' and hooked out the stumpy body. 'Come out. Just look at you.'

Etta stood up. Her pinafore was smeared with earth and was torn. Paddy could have said, 'You look like a Potter,' but she pressed her lips together to stop herself smiling.

'What about the cucumbers?' she said to Bushey.

'They do nicely. But I doubt we'll have a good summer for cucums. Not like last year.' He wrinkled up his face, gazing at the sky, as if he could see July's clouds already on the horizon. How irritating you can be, thought Paddy, you and Father together: too much rain, too much sun, too cold, too hot. And never enough money. She had settled Edward in his chair in the garden before she came out and nothing had been right for him. He had said he felt strange. He said it was the weather, these soft spring days. He said he could not stand Mrs Dye singing hymns all morning. 'I'll speak to her,' Paddy had promised.

'The cucumbers'll be all right,' she snapped at Bushey. Yes, the cucumbers would do, snug in their pots in the old hothouses, and the weather would hold for the church fête – but would it hold for the hay or for harvest?

She walked to the green door in the wall. It had dropped on its hinges and needed lifting. Etta followed at a respectful distance. One did not cling to Paddy, one did not touch. She moved with queenly certainty, bonily splendid, and when she glanced back her grey eyes might have been earth dark under their positive brows.

'May I come too?' asked Etta.

The lane to Home Farm had once been a muddied track but Harriet had ordered it to be made up with hardcore and kept in reasonable repair. 'You over-ordered,' she told Dack with her customary bluntness, and she sold the extra stones to Sir George Brocket at Frilton Hall for a profit.

'What's a profit?' asked Etta when told this story.

'If you bought a sherbet dab for a farthing and sold it to Pen Potter for a halfpenny you'd make a farthing profit. See?' said Curry.

'I think so. But Pen wouldn't be so silly as to pay a halfpenny for a farthing dab.'

Sir George, however, was silly enough to pay too much for Harriet's hoggin. Of course, it was all conducted by third parties for the principals could not be seen haggling over a heap of stones. 'There's money in the bank from it, that's what counts,' said Harriet, 'though it won't last. It never lasts.' Not a pessimist by nature she was feeling her age and also, for the first time in thirty years, a sort of aimlessness. Bretton was practically solvent, Fan had run off to her Devon parson, Mary was companion to an elderly cousin in

Brighton. And William Chance was dead. The pleasure at getting the better of the Brockets faded; she scowled at the stones every time – every weekday afternoon – she walked on them to Home Farm.

Paddy and Etta walked on them with something of her briskness. There was no time to admire flowers in the hedges or the view from the gate into Hobeys. Etta was forced to keep up a jog-trot and she grew hot. At last: 'My freckles will explode,' she said, and Paddy laughed and slowed down.

The farm seemed deserted when they reached it, but there were fifteen or twenty young steers bawling their heads off in the stockyard.

'Where did they come from?' asked Etta.

'I think they must have broken out of Hobeys.'

'That they did,' said old Dack. 'Before I knew it half on 'em went by over the garden. I shouted to young Eddie and we druv them on in and shut them up.'

Paddy made sympathetic noises over the wrecked garden. She knew he was fond of it. She said, 'Has Eddie gone down to Roman Hill?'

'Well . . .' the old man began, in what quite clearly was the prelude to an involved excuse. 'Well . . . he were on his way to the mill for middlings. I told him he didn't oughta stop. And he . . .'

'Is there anybody else?'

'Well, not . . .'

'Then I'll go down,' said Paddy.

'*You* will, Miss Bretton?'

Not since all that drama fourteen years ago had a Bretton gone down to Roman Hill.

'I will,' she repeated.

'And I'll come too,' said Etta.

They walked down Hobeys through the rich young grass, Paddy with her swinging step, Etta veering away now and then to sprint across the rolling slopes. The sun smote down. Paddy's cheap Frilton hat was like a bee skep. 'How ugly fashions are now,' Grace Paulley had said with a sigh.

'I can almost fly,' called Etta and she ran on again, flapping her arms.

'What nonsense!' Laura would have said if she had seen her, for of all children Etta was peculiarly earthbound, a creature of solid form and undoubted wind resistance.

'Wait for me,' cried Paddy.

The small figure had already been precipitated into the shade of the elms. In that shade twenty years ago Philip had stood, had often said, 'Wait for me,' to Paddy who, after another verbal tussle about their marriage, would begin the long climb to the summit and Bretton not caring if she left him in mid-sentence. 'Wait for me' and he would run after her, half adoring, half hating her. Too passionate to suffer injustice lightly, too energetic to argue without movement, she must walk or dissolve. Willowy, tireless, physically strong, she could not cope with what she called, cruelly he thought, this 'amorous inertia'. Secret meetings, a few kisses – how much longer must these be enough?

Etta climbed the stile into Upper Bit. She looked hot.

'We're over half-way down,' she said.

They walked together now, almost sedately. In Lower Bit Paddy settled her hat more firmly as if by shading her face she could defend her heart. They crossed the beck by the narrow plank bridge next to the ford with its Roman stones and went on through the orchard.

Paddy faltered.

'Don't you know the way?' asked Etta. 'I do.'

They came round to the front of the house that faced the yard across a small patch of grass with its sentinel chestnut tree. It's fourteen years, thought Paddy. She had endured fourteen years' exile from this ancient house with its smells of woodsmoke, brick, old rugs, damp, from the clean level yard where the poultry scratched, from the garden with its old roses and its great mulberry. On hunting mornings Jack's wife Meg had given her tea and biscuits. At any moment she might appear, unsentimental, comfortable. She had never seemed to grudge – or judge. And so Paddy had gravitated to Roman Hill as water to a deep and sheltering hollow.

When Meg had died she had gone to the funeral. 'You've an exaggerated sense of duty,' said the fifteen-year-old Tom. But someone from Bretton ought to go, she told Edward, it was only common decency. He did not know how much she owed to that quiet, self-effacing woman. He gave his permission grudgingly and told her she looked like a scarecrow in black.

'There's no one in,' said Etta.

'There must be,' said Paddy. She walked into the dim familiar interior. There were coats, whips, hats all over the mahogany hallstand opposite the door. Nothing's changed, she thought, with a sudden shock.

'Lord!' exclaimed Mrs Blessing, Johnny's housekeeper, appearing at the end of the passage in an aura of baking. 'Miss Bretton!'

'Are any of the men about?' Paddy asked. 'I've all Mr Chance's young cattle up at Home Farm.'

'They're all over to Frilton,' the woman said cautiously, as if afraid she might be required to fetch them herself.

'But isn't anyone here? Bonniman? Frank Crowe?'

'I'm sorry, Miss Bretton. It's the sheep fair.'

'And Mr Chance?'

'Now that I wouldn't rightly know. He's about the farm but I can't tell you better than that.'

Paddy took Etta's hand. They made for the buildings. Implement sheds, corn barn, the depleted stack yard . . . 'He isn't here,' said Etta, disappointed. They leaned on a gate and scanned the nearer fields.

'I haven't time to tramp,' said Paddy. She meant tramp round five hundred acres.

'Does it all belong to Bretton really?' demanded Etta, still grappling with concepts of ownership.

'The house and two hundred acres belong to Bretton. The rest is Mr Chance's own.'

They passed into Lower Bit and began to climb. Now they struggled, growing breathless. Along the margins the grass was lush and the parsley head-high. Paddy's dark grey skirt was freckled with pollen. 'It must be nice to be tall,' remarked Etta, sneezing. 'You can see where we are.'

But Paddy did not need to see in Hobeys. Hobeys had known her in winter dusks and summer dawns, had seen her playing pirates and sneaking by in riding habits and kissing her young man. Hobeys had known her picnicking, panicking, loving. It was to Hobeys she had taken her grief when Harriet died, when Deborah died, when Philip was killed, when Jack Chance was found sprawled and cold on Longman Field. Away up the steepest flush of green she walked, treading in her own past footsteps. It was very hot. There was a background hum of bees and the swallows rose and fell over the ruined terraces. Then, coming in sight of the gate to the lane, they saw a tall man with two spaniels.

'The cattle are at Home Farm,' said Paddy.

'Are they indeed?' replied Johnny Chance, calling the dogs in as they bounded lovingly towards Etta. 'Is Bushey about? Or Dack? Perhaps they could help me drive the young fools back. All my men are away in Frilton.'

'I know. We've just been down to the farm.'

He digested this amazing information. His gaze swept from her sensible footwear to her awful hat. Beneath the brim her eyes burned with defiance. Of him? Of all Chances? Of old Edward? Of the past? But Paddy was thinking how cruel it was that he should be so like Jack

86

and so unlike him. 'I defied the world – my world, anyway – to go to your mother's funeral,' she could have told him, 'and how long ago it seems. Perhaps it was a pointless gesture after all. They would all have known why I couldn't be there. But she was kind to me. Not motherly, just kind.'

'Keep your chin up,' Jack had said. 'Keep fighting.'

'I'm tired of fighting,' Paddy had wailed, battered half to death by the storm over her proposed marriage.

'You've got to keep fighting or you'll go under. You'll be a slave all your life. Not even a slave – a slave has more consideration.'

She would have liked to howl into his tweed shoulder but there was no such intimacy between them. Instead, as always, she drew her strength from his brutal encouragement, his blunt opinions.

'Run away,' he said. 'You may not be happy but you can always come back.'

'They wouldn't have me back.'

'Of course they would. Try it.'

His voice, so gentle with his horses, had a note of harsh command when he spoke to her of Bretton. Once or twice she was almost resolved to do as he said. Whatever crisis pulled her down he offered no sympathy but set her on her feet and insisted she keep fighting. But: 'You're too soft,' he told her despairingly. 'I thought I'd taught you how to harden your heart? You'll let them ruin your life for want of halfpenny-worth of nerve.'

Looking at the back of Jack's son Paddy thought: It's a long time since I followed a Chance in Hobeys. At the gate he stopped and unhooked it for her. His eyes glinted as she passed through. With amusement?

They were all clever and energetic and occasionally devious, the Chances. 'I know what I want,' they said, generation after generation, and by and large they got it, whatever it was. They were not known to cheat but no opportunity passed them by. 'What harm if we profit by other men's folly?' said William, buying a hundred acres in Stenton and then the Ashton mill. 'By the time he died he could have bought Roman Hill twice over,' said Curry to Paddy during their times of pondering on Bretton's history. 'But your father wouldn't have sold an acre if he'd begged on his knees.' 'He will own the freehold of the whole village soon,' cried Harriet at her darkest hour, plagued by legal papers, poor corn prices and arthritis. He could have built himself a fine house, a gentleman's house, but instead he clung to the tenancy of Roman Hill.

'I can't think why,' Edward was to say over and over. 'Why stay as tenant when he must have enough to buy up Charlesworth Place and Frilton Hall and almost anywhere else he had a mind for? It isn't as if he lacks ambition. There's talk he's taking a fifty-per-cent share in another two mills.'

But: 'Yes,' Joseph Chance had said in 1805, climbing to the top of Hobeys and gazing out across the county. 'Yes, this will do.' And William his son, and Old Jack and Young Johnny had stood there in turn and had, so to speak, taken seisin.

'You will never get the Chances out of Roman Hill,' Paget had said bluntly to Edward, just as his own father had told Ralph fifty years before.

'What is it that keeps you here?' Paddy wanted to ask. Instead, in the yard of Home Farm, the spaniels fawning around her, she said, 'Dack will help you drive the cattle.' As she spoke she was extricating Fan's bicycle from where it leaned in the nettles by the wood store. She rode away conscious of Johnny's eyes on her as if he too was remembering, and was thinking perhaps how unlike the bold young girl he had known was this desiccated old maid.

Etta said, slipping her hand in his, 'I wish I had a bicycle.'

8

THE NEXT DAY the heat was more intense. Paddy worked on the accounts at the farm, and wrote up the farm diary. 'Wednesday,' she put, 'Clear sky, tremendous heat. Two heifers sold at Frilton for . . .' She groped across the desk to find the auction slip, forgetting the price. The page of her strong, elegant writing, marshalled in days, looked solid and important. 'There's been nothing of real importance to write since the end of the war,' she said to herself.

She had just found what the heifers had fetched when Curry arrived.

'It was right Mrs Murray should break the news,' said the village.

'But she didn't even ask by-your-leave,' complained Laura. 'She just vanished.'

'The doctor's car was in the drive ten minutes,' said Babs Potter who had knocked off her cap trying to put her head out of the window to see it. The doctor's car was a small Ford that usually got along in a series of leaps like a kangaroo. 'The throttle sticks,' he would say. He said it every time he arrived and every time he left. But not today. 'I must speak to Mrs Murray at once,' was what he said today, formal and authoritative as never before.

'He didn't even say what he wanted her for,' Laura

was to tell Hugh. 'You'd think he'd have the courtesy to do that. He came in the front and walked straight through to the back with Foster and nobody told me anything about it till afterwards.'

'Where has Mrs Murray gone?' demanded Laura, making a rare appearance in the kitchen.

'To the Lodge, madam. I think Mr Bretton's took bad,' Mrs Prince told her.

Curry, having visited the Lodge, walked to the farm. She walked up the front drive and through the gardens and out of the green door into the lane. Her severe face was more severe than ever. Bushey, picking gooseberries, saw her go by at a distance and straightened, touched by premonition.

In the outhouse used as the farm office Curry said, 'My dear . . .', she who never used petnames or made familiar gestures.

For a moment, looking up, Paddy saw only the blaze of sun round the strange thin figure in the doorway. Then she heard words, several words that presumably made up a sentence. She supposed they did, though for a long time they did not make any sense.

'My dear, Mr Bretton has died.'

Paddy scraped back her chair. 'Father?'

'In his sleep. In his chair in the garden. Mrs Dye went out with his coffee and found him.' She did not add anything to this. She did not say: he felt nothing. Who was to say what he had felt?

'We must call Dr Hawker,' said Paddy in a cool, distant voice. Her face was pale. 'She never cried in public,' Curry said.

'It was Dr Hawker who fetched me from the house,' she said.

Paddy closed the ledger, the diary. 'Clear sky,' she saw. 'Tremendous heat.' She put away the pen. 'Then I'd better come at once,' she said. 'I'll leave this . . . I'll leave it for now.'

Together they went back, up the lane, through the gardens. They moved silently along the drive between the rhododendrons with their mass of flowers, two tall women, old-fashioned even at a distance. As they came in sight of the Lodge there was the gleam of a car, two cars through the leaves.

'I hope it's not the parson,' said Paddy. 'Father always told me he wanted to be buried in the park.'

Even in death Edward Bretton had not done with the constant and exaggerated care of his household.

'He should be lying up at the house,' was Mrs Dye's opinion, 'instead of in this poky place.' But it was improbable the Haleys would welcome a dead body in the drawing room.

'We have no right to the house for anything,' said Paddy firmly. All day she had been tactful, but firm. Dr Hawker thought she was indifferent. He had always felt too much of life was wasted on superfluous emotion but this self-containment was unnatural. She has not wept, he thought unsympathetically, and it did not occur to him she might be suffering shock.

'He died of old age,' he said. 'It's all straightforward. I've been treating him for the last six months. His heart was weak. We knew that.'

'*I* shall lay him out,' said Curry, fixing him with her most venomous eye. 'You've no need to send for the nurse.'

Hawker hurried away to his car. 'I hope that throttle sticks on him good and proper,' said Mrs Dye, wiping her hands on her apron. 'He's very free with words of comfort, I'm sure.'

When Mrs Dye had departed to spread the news about the village, cycling more quickly through the park than usual and vanishing rapidly among the rhododendrons, Paddy sat down at the kitchen table.

'Tea,' said Curry.

'I must send a telegram to Tom at once.'

'There's time for a cup of tea.'

'Mrs Haley must be wondering where you are.'

'She knows where I am. Mrs Prince or Babs or Lily will have told her.'

There was a scuffle outside the door and the latch lifted. A small face poked in. It did not smile, for its owner was a creature of instinct still and had already divined the change in atmosphere.

'May I come in?' asked Etta.

It was Laura herself who came down an hour later to fetch her daughter. She found the Lodge shrouded, the blinds drawn, the ticking of a clock unnaturally loud. Paddy was out so she had to deal with Curry instead, of whom she knew herself to be unreasonably afraid. As in the case of nervous dogs fright made her savage. She snapped at Curry and hauled Etta bodily over the kitchen step, further inflamed at having to remove her from what she considered the servants' domain. She had dressed soberly for the occasion but somehow the effect was lost in having to use the back door. Curry's manner, on the contrary, was definitely that of the grand lady. 'And I learnt how from Mrs Harriet,' Curry could have said. There could have been no finer teacher.

In a rage Laura propelled Etta back to Bretton, only on the threshold breaking the smouldering silence to say, 'What *did* you think you were doing, going there when old Mr Bretton had died? I shall forbid you to leave the garden in future.'

'But I didn't know he'd died,' said Etta, adding unwisely, 'and the Lodge is in the garden really, isn't it?' At which she was sent up to the nursery in disgrace.

It was at times like these Laura felt confounded by motherhood. She had not wanted a child and, having one, often wondered where the pleasure was to be found in it. She would have liked to show Etta off as she had when she was a baby but Etta in company tended to sit mute. If she were dressed prettily she looked wrong. If she misbehaved she took her punishment stoically, and righteous anger ran off her like rain from feathers. 'And as she gets older it gets worse,' Laura was frequently moved to tell Hugh.

Harriet loved her children passionately but the passion was so carefully contained that no one might have known it. Though her character was totally opposed to Edward's in every particular she found him more biddable than the girls. The girls were difficult. 'I suppose girls are,' said Harriet who found herself worrying more and more about their future. Mary was the quiet one – 'quietly determined' said Harriet – and Fan the rebel. 'There's no doing anything with her,' was the constant complaint. 'She argues, she answers back, she says no. And she bursts out in company, she has opinions.' And this was the 1860s.

Fan's mutinous looks were nothing to Etta's. Etta did not have to hide hers from anyone. The house was no longer full of servants and siblings. Etta could go up to the nursery and be quite alone, staring stonily out at the topmost branches of the cedars, as cross and ugly as she cared to be. By the time Hugh came home on Friday evening a whole catalogue of crimes had been laid at her door: rudeness, smacking the kitchen cat, refusing to eat her greens, sulking.

'We all sulk sometimes,' said Hugh, moved on Etta's behalf. She looked so pale and 'inward' he thought. 'Exhausted with being naughty,' said Mrs Prince.

'I told her to stay in the garden. The funeral's to-morrow.'

'You should have made that rule in the beginning, it's a shame to make it now. And anyway,' he looked innocently across the room, 'isn't the Lodge, strictly speaking, part of the garden?'

93

Laura took a cigarette and tapped it angrily on the outside of the box. 'No, it isn't. It's in the grounds. When I say garden I mean the garden near the house. But the point is, I never know where she is. On the day the old man died I found her in the kitchen of that dreadful eccentric little place while the body was across the passage. I had to go down myself. There was no Mrs Murray. I couldn't send Lily Foster . . .'

Hugh walked, as was his custom, to stand and look out at the garden. He did not listen to why she could not have sent Lily. He said, 'I wonder what they'll do with this place?'

'Oh, there's a younger brother somewhere. Italy, I think.' Laura did not take offence at his lapse because she was interested in the younger brother. 'Still, I expect "Miss Paddy" will go on as before. She's given the only orders that count, no doubt, for years and years.'

'Perhaps the brother will turn her out. Where would she go?'

For a moment a childish pleasure stirred in Laura at the thought of Paddy Bretton with nowhere to lay her proud head but it was, to her credit, a very brief moment.

'I can't imagine where she would go,' she said. 'Perhaps there are other relatives. No, I can't imagine it. This place has been her life.'

Edward Bretton had been a tyrant as a spoiled child is a tyrant, always desiring to be the centre of attention and behaving badly when he is not. He did not care for Bretton, only for his own comfort. He had grieved for its loss to the Haleys because he had been happy there and it accorded with his view of himself as squire. He wanted to see Tom living in the house, bringing up another generation, because that too flattered his self-importance.

I am free now, Paddy thought at his bedside, looking down at his thin white hands. There will be a little money, enough to live on, and the rest of my life with which to do what I like. The treacherous inner voice added: If Tom comes back. If Tom marries. If Tom lets you go. 'I'm going anyway,' she said aloud. She could not bear to look at Edward any more and turned away. All her life, it seemed, she had lived on hope, the hope of escape.

'She isn't in black,' whispered Miss Hartley to Grace Paulley.

'Her skirt is black,' returned Grace loyally. But the crisp white blouse destroyed any illusion of mourning.

'I will do all the right things to a point,' declared Paddy. No one ever knew where the point was, its size or variability. In this case she felt obscurely the necessity of avoiding black all over 'like a Spanish widow'. She did not care if she were misunderstood or thought eccentric. If she was suffering at all it was not obvious, nor was the fact she could not wait to be alone. She needed to be alone simply to draw breath, she thought, to get a new grip on life, the old one having been prised away so abruptly. The men, Bushey, Dack, Paget, who needed to speak to her about the routine of garden, farm and house, found her subdued but still competent, marking the ledgers, paying the wages, accepting condolences. Between themselves they said they doubted there had been much love lost between father and daughter since the row over Master Philip and the more terrible one over Jack Chance. Besides, the old man had had a long life and an easy one and it was only natural he should be gathered to his fathers.

The parson Maycroft had thought out what he might say on the matter with some care, but when he called about the burial he found the Lodge apparently deserted. Being a nosy man he entered anyway and walked in to look at the body, but he found the inner door locked and Curry keeping guard.

'I was hoping to see Miss Bretton,' he said defensively.

'She's at the farm.'

'The farm? Oh, I see. I had supposed . . .' He was not sure what he had supposed. He remembered how once, long ago when he had first come to Stenton, he had kissed Paddy Bretton's cheek under the mistletoe at the vicarage door – oh, yes, long ago before the war – and that cheek had been ice-cold, as ice-cold as her eyes when he came to look into them. It was rash to suppose anything where Paddy Bretton was concerned. He could have sworn she would be a passionate sort of woman under that spinsterish dignity.

'Please tell Miss Bretton I called to make the arrangements,' he said to Curry. 'I really need to see her as soon as possible.'

Grace Paulley called not five minutes after he had left and sat on the hard sofa for some time before concluding Paddy was making a morning of it. 'I can't wait,' she said to Curry, poking her large hat round the kitchen door. 'I have two more calls and Mrs Haley . . . Tell Paddy I waited. I'll see her later, poor dear.' She never stood on ceremony with Curry. She admired Curry. 'She's given that family the whole of her life,' she was fond of saying in admiring tones. Now she skewered at her hat with her usual vigour, though there had been no need to alter the angle of the pins, and gathered her bag to her breast as she stepped outside again into the sunshine. She was unaccountably nervous. She walked away quickly and even with relief, putting distance between herself and wherever Paddy might be. 'I'm glad she was out, keeping busy,' she said to herself as she came to the village.

At her own gate she paused, taking stock. The large red brick house was separated from its stables by a high

96

wall smothered in roses. All this should be Paddy's, she thought. If Philip had lived. She had always been fond of Paddy, but rather as she had been fond of Philip's hunters, violent, unpredictable animals. Their dash and beauty stirred her soul but she was always conscious of danger. Of course Paddy, though dashing, had never been beautiful. 'She had ... something,' Grace said doubtfully. 'She glowed.' Neglected, she had somehow found her way to Brook Court as a child. 'But then, perhaps I invited her,' Grace said, struggling to remember. 'It might have been Philip's birthday.' Philip had said, enchanted, 'She's really like a boy. She dares anything.'

She climbed trees, risked her neck on the backs of the half-broken cart colts, caught fish in her hands. 'I've never seen anyone as clever at it as Pat,' Philip said, and, watching her, he had seen the water run silver up her bare arms and the heavy black hair fall to one side as she had looked round at him, laughing in triumph.

'I'm quite ordinary,' he confided to Grace. 'Pat isn't.' He was a plain, stocky boy, brown-skinned, brown-haired. He also had a conscience. 'You ought not to do that, Pat,' he said a hundred times. He might have been dull but there was always a certain engaging stubbornness; he knew his own mind.

'He wants to marry her,' said Grace to her husband.

'It might not be a bad thing.' He had not sounded unequivocally enthusiastic. 'There might be some money there after all.'

'Phil doesn't need money,' Grace said seriously. 'He needs a good wife.' By this she meant, as many mothers do, an amiable conventional girl who would not dream of giving any trouble.

'She has spirit,' said Philip, recounting Paddy's first brush with Edward over the intended marriage. It had been a minor skirmish, mostly, though he did not know it, because Edward had not taken it seriously. For the moment the future still seemed bright.

Perhaps she has too much 'spirit', thought Grace, remembering the horses. She felt anxious. She did not want to put thorn bushes in the path of true love, but she felt anxious. All mothers worry, she told herself.

'I'm going to see the old man tomorrow,' said Philip. 'A formal interview with the Bretton ogre.' He laughed, young and certain, though a little nervous of muffing the ritual, as a man might be who has never entered a church before. But afterwards, shattered: 'He wasn't even civil. He said no daughter of his would marry a small farmer.' He had never thought of his father as a small farmer. Three hundred acres and a modest private income combined to set him on a different level – level enough, surely, to look the Brettons in the eye. The Paulleys were always welcome at Frilton Hall. Frank's mother had been the Honourable Miss Fane.

'It isn't anything to do with all that,' Paddy said. 'I think he just wants to keep me at home.' Certainly she felt that in saying no to Philip Edward had said no effectively to any man who asked.

'We can run away,' declared Philip, electrified by his experience. He was amazed at himself for feeling so angry. He had never felt so angry before.

'Cut and run,' said Jack Chance, finding Paddy in Hobeys, red-eyed but fighting fierce.

Only: 'Don't marry that girl in any hole-in-the-corner way,' Frank Paulley told his son.

And: 'Your place is where you're needed most,' Edward informed his daughter.

Duty, convention, upbringing were the snares set about them.

'But we love each other!' protested Paddy. She was more volatile than ever although she had to find the energy to run Bretton, run the farm, buy and sell her horses, oppose Edward – *and* love and suffer. She had opposed Edward violently at first but now she resisted doggedly, biding her time.

She still believed Philip would take her away.

'Paddy's only just twenty,' said Frank, sounding infinitely reasonable. 'Why not wait another year? Bretton will come round when she's of age. He won't risk a family rift.' In a year, he was thinking, this violent young passion will have burnt itself out.

By the time Paddy was twenty-one Edward had showed himself indifferent whether he caused a rift or not. He would not agree to any marriage.

'Then we'll *have* to elope,' said Paddy.

But Philip had grown 'cool' said Curry, who was helping keep Bretton afloat in the storm. He went to see Dale, the new young curate, approachable and theologically unsound. 'He said we really mustn't think about running away,' Philip confessed to Paddy in the fastness of Hobeys, the rain dripping through the elm leaves and running down her cold face. 'He says he'll speak to your father.'

'He won't be allowed past the door,' said Paddy, a shell of misery. 'Why did you go to him? Why? It's private. It's our business, not his.' It was theirs to sort out, she felt, she was tired of advice. Adults always advised caution, having faced crises and knowing they pass. 'Well, everything passes,' said Paddy. 'You could spend your whole life ducking decisions and still survive. But would you have been happy?'

'Nothing's private,' Philip argued. 'There's my family, and yours . . .' He could not tell her he suspected his own of secretly hoping there would never be a wedding. Without their support he doubted he could persevere. Edward would remain intransigent, he knew. That meant he had to marry Paddy and be damned, or give her up.

Ask me, ask me to run away with you, she implored, kissing him in Hobeys. 'Pat. Darling Pat . . .' he said, but it was the agony of indecision, not subdued desire. She knew this. A new and cruel discernment was hers these days. 'It will come to nothing,' she said aloud one morning, disturbed by dreams and opening her eyes on the chill pre-dawn darkness.

'I should have seduced him,' she said afterwards to Jack. He was the only person she could say such things to, admit such – for her – outrageous propositions.

'What do you know about seduction? A few chaste kisses and a grope in the long grass? And would that have solved the problem?'

'He would have felt he had to marry me, having done . . . that.'

'But was that what you wanted?'

I think I only wanted to be loved, thought Paddy twenty years later.

9

THE FUNERAL TEA was a solemn matter and it was held at Bretton.

'Really Laura, I can't see your objection,' said Hugh. 'It's the least we can do.' And it was as well Laura capitulated, for the Lodge would not have held a twentieth of the people who came.

The long table in the dining room was spread with the bleached cloths and laid with the best china. 'He would have liked that,' said Mrs Dye. Half the village was there to see it and to sample the cakes and delicate sandwiches. The other half was outside in the yard consuming its own quota under the chestnut trees and washing it down with home-brewed ale.

'Why isn't the brother here?' Maycroft asked Miss Hartley, whom he often found under his wing as she was, besides a writer of romance, the church organist. 'Surely he could get here in time?' If he had he might have put a stop to this unseemly nonsense of a burial in the park.

'Oh, I don't know.' Miss Hartley had a soft spot for Tom, whose rather vacuously handsome Bretton face had always seemed full of tragic potential. 'Mr Bretton died on Wednesday and this is only Saturday.'

Was it only Saturday? thought Maycroft. He seemed to have been battling with Paddy for weeks.

'If you won't take the service I'll find someone who will,' she had threatened.

'But it's not hallowed ground,' he had hazarded, desperate for solid rock from which to make a stand.

'I don't think Father believed in hallowed ground,' had been the prompt and cutting reply.

'No reply to the telegrams, not one,' Grace was saying to Laura, who was suffering from not being hostess in what she considered her own house.

'Telegrams?'

'To Italy. Just like Tom. He was always . . . difficult.' She meant sulky. She hated sulkiness. And he was slow to act. 'Determined to do nothing,' Curry had said. 'I did enough in the war,' Tom might have countered such criticism.

Laura took a bite of Curry's fruit cake. 'Funeral cake,' said Curry, letting Etta dip her finger in the bowl. The recipe, written in a spidery hand, had been hallowed by use: funeral cakes, wedding cakes, christening cakes for a hundred years.

'Perhaps young Mr Bretton won't come at all?' said Laura. She hoped he did. She was intrigued.

'But he'll have to sooner or later. Bretton is his now. I must say,' and Grace gazed round brightly, 'you'd never know it had been a hospital. It was green in here. Pea green.' Her eyes grew vacant. 'All those poor boys. They were dying mostly.' Several times during the war she had thanked God Philip was already dead. It seemed a terrible thing to be thankful for. But after the experience of Bretton, which had carried the war into her orderly and sheltered life, she felt nothing but relief he would never have to risk being amongst those ranks of grotesque, disfigured young men. Dead or alive but not maimed would have been her prayer if he had survived that long-ago exile to Hereford.

'Of course,' Laura was saying. 'Old Mr B. might have left it all to Miss B.'

'Paddy?' Grace was amazed. Then she remembered Laura was unaware of Paddy's history. 'Oh my dear, I don't think that's likely. He was terribly old-fashioned. Tom was always the heir.'

She is dispossessed, thought Maycroft, still smarting from having to conduct the funeral in a pagan glade. If Tom Bretton marries ... She will never be in charge here again. He watched her cross the room. He felt deceived and disillusioned. 'Hot blood,' said the village. 'She was harum-scarum when she was a girl.' But he had seen no evidence of it and was disappointed, disappointed in his scarcely formulated intentions to make Paddy Bretton a parson's wife. He had enjoyed the thought of marrying into the big house, of a wild thing tamed, of a woman passionate in good works and sexual adventure. Well, that had been years ago, before that cold kiss under the mistletoe and his growing disbelief in her warm past.

As from a long way off he heard someone say in a confidential voice, 'I still say it's odd to be buried in the park.'

It is perverse, thought the Reverend Maycroft, accepting his share of the funeral cake with suitable humility.

'And what are *you* doing here?' asked Curry, re-entering the kitchen with the empty water jugs.

'I came down,' said Etta, as if stating the obvious would excuse it. 'Can't I sit here? No one would know.'

'*May* I sit here,' corrected Curry automatically. She passed into the echoing back regions and there came the wheeze and clank of the pump handle. 'Water, water, tea, tea,' cried Mrs Prince, bearing in another tray of sandwiches. 'Gabble, gabble, gossip, gossip.'

'Is that what funerals are like?' asked Etta.

'And weddings. And christenings.'

Curry put the kettle on the hob and lifted its twin, already simmering there. 'It's been a good many years since there was a christening in this house.'

'How long?' demanded Etta. 'Was it P— Miss Bretton?'

'No, it was not. Mind, you'll be scalded. It was Mr Tom.'

The door opened. 'Forgive me,' said Paget, mopping his cheeks. 'Strong tea brings on my palpitations. May I trouble you for a glass of water, Mrs Murray?'

'You should have rung, sir,' said Curry.

'To be honest, I was glad to escape. It is quite a wake, is it not?' He peered through his delicate round spectacles at his company. 'Quite a turnout.'

'What is a wake?' asked Etta.

'Well, Miss Henrietta,' said Paget genially. 'How are you, my dear?'

The door opened and Hugh stood there. For a moment he did not speak. They all looked towards him expectantly. He was the master. It would have taken a fire at least, Curry thought, to have induced Edward to cross the kitchen threshold.

'Mrs Haley has been ringing the bell,' he told them, having got over his initial hesitancy. 'Didn't you hear, Mrs Murray?'

'I don't think any bell's rung these fifteen minutes,' said Mrs Prince in her low, measured tones. 'What was it Mrs Haley wanted, sir?'

'But I rang it myself,' he said.

'I expect it's off its wire,' said Paget helpfully. 'Mrs Salter, who used to be cook here, used to disconnect it at the bell board quite often, I believe. Old Mr Edward used to ring it rather a lot and the poor maid was always scampering up and down stairs.'

Hugh grinned. He could believe this of Edward, whom he had only ever met once. But he wondered what sort of woman Mrs Salter might have been who

104

would dare tamper with the bell board under Curry's baleful eye.

'Etta, should you be here?' he asked.

'No, Father.'

'Where should you be?' He had no idea.

'In the nursery, Father.'

The child was in a grey dress and her hair was loose. She looked remarkably at home sitting at the great scrubbed table by Paget and his glass of water. It was this unexpectedly domesticated scene that had startled Hugh when he had pushed open the door.

'I think perhaps you'd better go back up,' he said gently. 'You might be in the way.'

Babs flew in, retying her small white apron as she called, 'Where's the new pot? Quick, Mrs Prince, do I shall fall wrong of Mrs H.' A moment later she noticed Hugh, whom she had naturally not expected in the kitchen and therefore had not seen. She shrank a little, but self-consciously, glancing at him sideways. He was nice looking, she thought, but a bit of a dull stick. She wondered if he had been wounded in the war which would account for his apparent stiffness, like a man careful of exacerbating pain.

'*I'll* look at the bell,' he said to Curry. 'Come on, Etta.'

They passed through to the back passage.

'I never knew there were so many bells,' Hugh said, staring at the double row. 'There must be rooms I've never been in.' He reached and fingered a thin bent wire, smiling, and twisted its end into place. 'There. That will keep Lily and Babs going for another half hour,' he said.

'Will they be gone then? All the people, I mean?' asked Etta.

'I hope so. Miss Bretton is beginning to look a little corpselike herself,' and then, aware this was not a suitable thing to say to a child he added quickly, 'Look, I'll take you upstairs if you promise to stay put. When's nursery tea? Lily will be up the moment they start leaving.'

He did not know where the backstairs were. Etta led the way growing warm with self-importance. She had never imagined he would one day depend on her superior knowledge.

'Where are we?' he asked on the first landing.

'We're not there yet.'

They climbed again. The white door was shut. Etta flung it open on her domain and ushered him in. 'This is the schoolroom,' said Etta, 'and there's three bedrooms and a sort of bathroom but it hasn't a bath in it, we bath by the fire in here, and there's a sitting room for the nanny.'

Hugh allowed himself to be drawn through this set of rooms while trying to recall why he had never seen them before. Laura, presumably, had inspected them and passed them fit. But did Etta sleep up here alone? Her spartan little bed had been Paddy's once, and on it sat a tired-looking bear-like creature. 'Oh no,' corrected Etta, 'it's a donkey. I found him in a cupboard. There are lots of things in the cupboards. Books, toys . . .'

Hugh thought: If there was a fire who would ever come up here to carry her down? He looked out of the barred window and saw the dark upper branches of the cedars.

'You do like it, don't you?' asked Etta anxiously.

'Yes, I do.'

He spoke sincerely for his own nursery had been much like this, though more crammed with colour and furniture and reassuring human presence. But he wanted to ask: Aren't you lonely? It shamed him such a thing had never occurred to him before. He had only worried about Laura's attitude, Laura's irregular affection.

'I must go down,' he said.

Etta felt disappointment sink through her. She wondered why he frowned so but adults were so often struck by mysterious troubles. Then suddenly, as if, after all, she could read his mind, 'Lily sleeps in here. I didn't show you because I don't go in. It's her room. You didn't think I was up here by myself?' asked Etta.

Black suits her, thought Grace, but she looks older. 'I will only wear it for the funeral,' Paddy had declared, and had pinned Harriet's cornelians at her throat to totally ruin the effect. Dark, how dark she is . . . Grace was lost in reflection. Deborah was never as dark. Warm brown, reddish brown, and grey eyes . . . She has Deborah's eyes, that's all. Didn't Jack Chance always say Paddy was a changeling? Thank God, thank God Philip didn't marry her. They would never have been happy.

'My dear,' she said, touching Paddy's arm, 'how glad you will be when it's all over.'

The village would have been quite prepared to accept that Paddy was a changeling. The only person she remotely resembled was Harriet but Harriet had not been tempestuous, nor had her hair been black. Paddy's hair was always coming down, sprung from its bands and pins by accident and shock. Out hunting she took more than her share of falls. How she was never discovered, creeping back into Bretton with her habit mud from neck to hem and wet black tresses rammed under her bowler, she never knew. 'How romantic, Miss,' said the new housemaid Annie when she heard how Mr Fulton had rescued Paddy from the ditch. The umpteenth ditch. But it was not at all romantic. Mud, steaming wet horse, frozen hands, scratches, torn skirts, torn veil – how were these romantic? In any case Fulton was married with four daughters and was practically in his grave.

'Sir William stuck like a limpet,' said Paddy to Jack

Chance after a day of pace and glory. 'He said he'd never seen a woman ride so well. When I left for home he kissed my hand.'

'I believe a young fool is worse than an old one after all.'

'He's engaged to that Hatherton girl, the one with teeth.'

'I hope she has teeth, the poor dear. Well, he could be unengaged. Is that what you want, young William Jernham?'

'I wish you wouldn't keep asking me what I want. Anyway, he's charming. Only a little silly. He asked if he could escort me home.'

'And did you let him?'

'Of course not. I caught up with Mrs Fox and behaved perfectly.'

'All I can say is,' said Jack, 'mind you don't come neck over crop. You're too busy looking through your lashes at a gaggle of half-fledged boys to see where you're going.'

Wherever she was going it was a perilous business. When she rode a horse of her own Morris, the Bretton groom, would ride with her, but if she hunted one of Jack's she went alone, defying convention and common sense together. Never, in all those years, did he accompany her. '*That*,' said Paddy, 'would certainly have been a scandal.'

It was an age of small waists and whalebone. 'No one sits straighter on a horse,' boasted Philip the year he and Paddy fell in love.

'I'm not surprised,' she said. 'I couldn't bend if I tried.'

But even hooked and tied she was impossible to contain, too tall, too vigorous, too 'bursting' said Annie. The elongated fashions of the early part of the century might have suited her but she wore them with a carelessness that only seemed untidy. Besides, the same costume had to be reworked several times due to the ever-difficult financial situation and eventually, 'You can't make ten purses out of one sow's ear,' said Curry. On top of that, she had a terrible taste in hats. Hats to Paddy were unbearable and restricting things, only endured because of necessity. She was happiest in a bowler though she wore out several of those falling on her head.

'Harum-scarum,' said the village.

She took her village duties seriously enough but the church flowers were not arranged, they were thrust all together in pots just as she had brought them from the Bretton garden. Sometimes she would visit a cottage and ride her horse up the path. She was always direct, unaffected. 'Outspoken' said the county, to whose social events she seldom went.

And: 'I don't like the way all the other men want to dance with you,' complained Philip on his birthday. In the candlelight his hair looked sandy, like the coat of his old retriever.

She was a little drunk: on attention, silly flattery, the late hour, the music, champagne.

'I do,' she said.

'If the brother inherits Bretton what does Miss Bretton inherit?' asked Hugh the evening of the funeral, walking into Laura's bedroom and finding her in a chair with a magazine.

'I've no idea. Mrs Paulley – dreadful chattering woman – mentioned some cottage over near Frilton. Did you know they used to own all the land this side of Frilton? There's not much left now apparently.'

'What kind of cottage?' There were several kinds, he knew, ranging from Miss Hartley's scrupulously clean and painstakingly prettified one to the ruin crumbling about the heads of the Potters at Dobby's Hole.

'How should I know? A sort of dower cottage, I suppose.'

'But he's not married, is he, this brother? Won't he need her here?'

'Hugh, really. How should I know?'

She lit a cigarette, bending her boyish cropped head. Hugh thought of Paddy at the funeral. She had looked almost bored beside the grave, sometimes staring up at the oaks, sometimes away across the shining grass. Hugh had been there because he felt it a necessary sign of respect: he was, after all, a tenant. Laura had thought it macabre. 'There will be no one there except you and our "Miss Paddy" and all the old retainers. It will look so odd.' But in the event the village had been there, plodding self-consciously through the park in groups.

'I don't understand why he had to be buried in the park,' said Laura, who found it distasteful. 'Why not with all the other Brettons in the church? It isn't as if there was a mausoleum or anything. What was wrong with a decent Christian burial at Stenton?'

'I'm not sure he qualified as a Christian. There was a row or something. Some parson refused to bury his wife.'

'How these village squabbles carry on.' Laura gave a small laugh and then drew on the cigarette. 'Can you imagine what a drama it must have been? You know what these country people are like.'

He did not know, he thought. They seemed to him, a city creature, reticent and out-of-date. He had no idea what might move them to riot and defection.

'Well, I can't see Miss Bretton in a cottage,' he said. Had she been bored, or trying not to weep? Had she, under that iron exterior, been amused her father should, at the last, have confounded both the parson and the officious gentlemen concerned for public health?

'Are you going to bed?' asked Laura. She had closed her magazine.

'I thought . . .' He hated to be supplicatory. He felt belittled. He reached out a hand and touched her hair.

'I have to be up so early tomorrow. Surely you haven't forgotten? I'm going up to town.'

'I had forgotten.'

'Madge and I are going to make a day of it. And a night. I told you we're staying with Edith Blackmore.'

'You could have stayed with me.'

'In a bachelor apartment ten-feet square? And where would Madge sleep?'

'With this Edith woman as arranged.'

'Blackmore. Don't be ridiculous. The whole point is that we're three women together, no domestic bother, no children, no husbands. Just gossip and shopping.'

Hugh stooped reluctantly to kiss the top of her head and went out, closing the door quietly behind him. Downstairs he was equally careful with the side door to the garden, the convenient door that gave on to the path to the shrubbery.

The gardens at night were strange. Hugh walked slowly, keeping to the grass. The sky was clear and the moon three quarters full. There was the smell of earth and of flowers he could not recognize. He hardly knew the name of a flower, he thought. Beyond the gardens lay the park.

It was not a bad place to be buried, he thought. He lit a cigarette and smoked it, leaning on the fence. It was so quiet. He could only hear the faint wind in the leaves and occasionally something moving in the grass. Not long ago he had thought the world would never be quiet again, that even if he died the noise might go on. He must not think of it, he decided. He regretted his small outburst to the parson, who had confided in him that he did not think it fitting to bury a man in a field.

'I wish I could have buried my men in your "field",' Hugh had retorted.

'I'm so sorry,' Maycroft had murmured. 'Of course, it's *Major* Haley, isn't it?'

'I don't use it as a title,' said Hugh.

He walked back right round the house, past the sunken garden, past the peculiar raised piece of lawn where Harriet's peony border had been. He knew nothing of Harriet. He could not have identified a peony.

The side door was still open.

'Do you never lock it?' Hugh asked Curry who was crossing the hall.

'No, sir.'

'But anybody could walk in,' he said, astounded.

'It was always left open for Miss Bretton.'

'But Miss Bretton doesn't use it any more.'

'No, sir. Would you like me to lock it?'

Her eyes were black and strangely without light. He had always found her unfailingly efficient – but he wondered if she could cast spells.

'I think I'd feel safer, Mrs Murray.'

He could hear the key turning in the stiff lock as he climbed the stairs.

10

PAGET FUSSED WITH his briefcase. 'I really don't know how to put this,' he said. He stood up and walked to the window, looking down on the market-day crowds.

'I do wish you'd get on with it,' said Paddy. 'What is it? A mortgage I don't know about? More debts?'

He looked fragile, an elderly man not in the best of health. Edward's sudden death had come as a shock to him. He had thought they had reached safe ground at last, a plateau perhaps: Bretton let, Paddy able to concentrate on Home Farm, a little money trickling in. Now he saw a precipice.

'Your father's will . . .' he began. He felt suddenly both his advancing age and the cruelty of duty.

'Yes?' said Paddy.

'Your father changed his will. The new will is dated 1 December 1908.' He paused, wondering if she already saw the significance of the date. 'It was to do with that business of Roman Hill, with your friendship with Mr Chance.'

'Yes, I guessed that,' said Paddy. It was all right, she thought, she knew what was coming. She sat stiffly in the old oak chair. 'I don't expect to be comfortable in a solicitor's office,' she had once said to Curry. She sat quietly, her hands folded. She was still in black – 'partly in black' – and looked her most austere.

Paget returned from the window and sat down. He snatched up the offending document, smoothed it in his hands, discarded it. He took off his spectacles. 'I never thought I'd be the bearer of such news. I thought I'd be retired before . . .' And then, with sudden decision: 'Edward Bretton was not your father, Miss Paddy.'

So she had not known what was coming after all.

'Of course he was my father.' Her voice was strong and positive. To be deprived of Bretton was enough, surely. Must she also be deprived of her identity?

'I'm afraid not. It seems your father was an Italian whom your mother had known from childhood, a friend of her family. You know, of course, that your father met your mother in Italy?'

'She'd lived there since she was five. Her father had bought a house in the hills. It was for her mother's health.'

'Yes, quite.'

'My mother and father were married there.'

'Indeed. And legally, I must stress, you are a child of the marriage. There is no evidence to suggest otherwise in any case. I do not even know how your . . . how Mr Bretton found out. He simply told me that he knew, that your mother confirmed it, and that he had been prepared to bring you up as his own to avoid scandal. And I must say,' and Paget leaned forward, his pale eyes sympathetic, 'I know he loved your mother very much.'

'Yes,' said Paddy flatly.

'Up until 1908 you were to be left a small income along with the moneys held in trust since your mother died. Then there was the row over Roman Hill. It was a terrible time, Miss Paddy.'

'Yes.'

'In the new will you are left nothing at all. Shall I read it? I feel I should.'

'No, please don't bother.'

'The estate goes to Mr Tom absolutely.'

'I never thought it wouldn't.'

'Your mother's money left in the trusts having been paid over when you were thirty, there's . . .' He felt he had expressed himself badly, had failed to cushion the shock for her. He put on his spectacles again and picked up the will. 'There is nothing for you, Miss Paddy. Nothing.'

The sound of Paget's secretary, a large-eared young man with a shock of red hair and the latest in trousers, could be heard through the closed door. He was singing and rattling tea spoons. The roar of the market square seemed strangely muted, though the window was open a little.

Paddy did not speak.

'I'm sure Mr Tom will make more than adequate provision as soon as he understands the situation,' said Paget.

'Have you heard from him? I've only had the one message saying he couldn't come to the funeral – and that arrived yesterday.'

How like him, they both thought, looking at each other across the desk.

'He must come home and make arrangements.'

'Bretton was never home to Tom.'

'But he has inherited it. It is his responsibility.'

Tea would be coming in soon, he thought. He had given strict instructions for the stroke of eleven. He had thought half an hour enough time to cope with this devilish business. On second thoughts, should he give her a glass of sherry? Was it his imagination or did she look pale?

The bleating of sheep and the patter of hooves passed beneath the window.

'I think,' said Paddy, 'that the most appropriate person to inherit Bretton would be Curry.'

★

115

'You will not go to Roman Hill,' said Harriet to Paddy, whose ardent nature struck her as too much like her own. 'Your father would not like you to.'

'Why not?'

'Because it is forbidden.'

'Why is it forbidden?' Paddy asked Jack Chance, flitting secretly down Hobeys to his doorstep.

'Old loves, old hates, old foolery,' said Jack to the nine-year-old Paddy. 'There was a quarrel long ago over one of my aunts. Water under the bridge.'

But the water still flowed with bad feeling, with 'division and distrust' said the older Paddy. 'Jack, what was it all about?'

'It was fifty years ago. What does it matter?'

'But it's still with us. Coming between.'

Harriet had said, 'I'm always the last to know. *I* have to find out.' Finding out was a painful process and took 'a lifetime' she told Deborah. She had arrived at Bretton thinking herself in love. At twenty-five she had seen two younger sisters married and mothers, had expected to be the one who stayed to nurse her parents in old age. Ralph's frantic courtship, her mother's unexpected enthusiasm, the turmoil of decision, preparation, achievement, had left her dizzy. She looked forward to her new home. She was determined to do well, to be a good and gentle influence: on Ralph, on her servants, on the village.

Instead: 'I became a tyrant,' she said.

In the year of her marriage, 1843, Bretton showed signs of financial uncertainty. 'Financial ruin,' said Harriet. Though she had brought a great deal of money to the marriage Ralph seemed indifferent and what was worse, lacked imagination. 'What if . . .' Harriet found herself saying over and over. What if they did repairs, redecorated the two drawing rooms, employed another man in the garden? Ralph said, 'Do what you like,' and went to Newmarket, riding a new horse.

'He gambled away thousands,' Harriet told Deborah. 'I don't know how long it took me to see he was spending all my money on horses. On worse.'

Her eyes had been opened to other facts, however, one being that he did not love her, that he had never loved her. His visits to her bed were perfunctory. He made no allowances for her timidity.

Since she was ignorant and he callous, 'There was no hope for us,' said Harriet. But being Harriet, she soon learnt not to be afraid of him.

There had been a day that first year when she had fallen for the brown mare at the Frilton horse sale. She was not an intrepid horsewoman but had ridden, had even hunted, because she felt Ralph would like her to, would appreciate a wife who shared at least this among his distractions. Until now she had allowed herself to be mounted on one of his thoroughbreds and had been terrified several times and nearly killed once. Here at last she sensed she had found an animal more suited to her modest capabilities. But: 'Out of the question,' said Ralph. 'I warned you to stay at home, didn't I? This is no place for ladies.'

'Why is it out of the question?' demanded Harriet in a voice Stenton would later come to know well. 'Why?'

'She's a Chance mare.'

'From Roman Hill?'

He had nodded. He did not want a scene in front of his land agent and a crowd of lesser mortals jostling for a view.

'But what's wrong with that?' cried Harriet. She could see he was embarrassed and ignored it. She had learned by now he was not the strong loving character she had hoped for and because she was Harriet, 'and not meek' she said, she grew impatient with him – 'and hard' said Curry a generation later. She received his lecture on why there being everything wrong with a Bretton buying a horse from his own tenant in a public market, all of which was nonsense, with commendable calm, then gave him one on how suitable the mare was, how obviously genuine and how sensibly priced. What more, she asked, could be wanted?

Ralph sent the Bretton carriage home, and Harriet in it.

In the morning she went down to Roman Hill.

She went alone and secretly – and she bought the brown mare. 'I had the devil in me,' she told Deborah. Ralph allowed her so much a quarter from her money, 'my poor dowry' said Harriet, and it was this she took with her to pay Joseph Chance. He could not have been more gracious or more understanding. At no time did she fear he would tell Ralph of the transaction.

'She is bold and honest,' said Joseph when she had gone. 'And she knows nothing.'

'You shouldn't have done business with her,' said his son William.

The mare was a success and Ralph, hoodwinked, did not recognize her when she cantered under his nose. But: 'What is it about the Chances?' Harriet asked. 'Why is there this . . . coldness?' At tenants' suppers, harvest homes, rent days, church, they passed at a distance, silent. '*What* is it?' demanded Harriet, increasingly frustrated in her marriage and more and more ready to challenge. 'What happened?' For something had 'happened', she was sure of it. At any rate, she must avoid Roman Hill until she knew. 'Which meant there was never a time I didn't avoid it until I was an old woman,' she said.

She felt in those years that she could not allow herself to be fond of anyone. She was so desperate to love and be loved she was afraid she might crush the recipient with the force of her emotion. She was careful with the two girls, Mary and Fan, careful with Edward. But Edward was a true Bretton, not a spark of Harriet in him anywhere – 'But there *must* be. Or isn't he mine at all?' she had been moved to ask once. He responded to affection by demanding treats and toys. He disliked human contact. He screamed when he was cuddled and he had no sense of humour.

So that left Bretton itself.

'I have saved your inheritance,' Harriet said grandly to Edward before she died, and she could be forgiven her satisfaction. It had been a difficult job well done.

'An impossible job. I don't know how she managed,' said Paget. 'She kept the estate together as long as she could and even then salvaged a good part of the wreck.'

The tenant farms, the outlying land, were part of the wreck. All except Roman Hill. 'It's the best,' she said when Edward protested. 'We would be fools to lose it.' He did not know it but she went from this interview to stand at the gate into Hobeys, gazing down on the disputed ground.

'Enchanted ground,' said Harriet.

She had gone this way to pay old Joseph for the brown mare, the brown mare whose years of faithful service were recorded now on the new mounting block in the stableyard at Bretton. She would go this way now to tell Jack Chance that, contrary to village rumour, she would not sacrifice Roman Hill to any agricultural depression, ill-intentioned government or sly stroke of fate.

He was still a boy, his mother at his elbow. Harriet sensed his latent energy and zest for life and felt herself respond to it. He is like William, she thought, and her heart contracted. She remembered William in Hobeys, walking up to rouse the haymakers, the soft aftermath brushing underfoot. 'Good day, Mrs Bretton,' and he had inclined that fair head. Not red, William, but a Chance all through. But why had Harriet been there by the gate? She had been thirty-five and handsome in her own way. 'My overbearing way,' she said. She had worn a pale dress and a small fashionable hat on her dark coiled hair, and she had carried a sunshade.

'Good day,' she had said to William, wondering what his kiss might be like, his hands. How we all want what we don't have, she thought later, ashamed.

And years later to Paddy she said truthfully, 'There are lots of reasons why Brettons don't go down to Roman Hill.'

Fan was the impulsive one, the physical one. She would fling her arms round grief to make it better and round happiness to share in delight. Whatever she was thinking showed in her face. 'You have no sense of proportion,' Harriet told her. But 'Oh, Mother!' would be Fan's reply. Mary, who grew 'more and more like Ralph' said Harriet, called her sister undignified, and was bitterly upset it was Fan who received all the valentines and who found partners for tennis. 'No one will marry her though,' she said with sour satisfaction. 'She talks too much and always thinks she's right.'

Mediating between her daughters, struggling to interest her son in the estate, Harriet led a useful and a lonely life. Wryly, she thought: All my kisses are women's kisses. 'Dutiful pecks,' she said to Fan, who responded with a warning 'Mother!', astonished and dismayed Harriet might care for more. Soon all kisses were for Deborah and Paddy. Harriet would scoop up the baby and laugh into the soft black fuzz of her hair, and soon the baby too would laugh, reaching up her fat hands to pull Harriet's garden hat. 'It doesn't work for me,' complained Deborah, who never got to grips with Paddy's moods.

Paddy had a cup of tea in one of Frilton's poky tea shops and sat looking out. There were cattle in the road on their way to the market place, and netted carts full of pigs. The clop of hooves punctuated by the constant tooting of horns never ceased.

'Is everything all right? Would you care for a cake?' asked the girl, smiling down.

'No, thank you.'

'You wouldn't like a cake?'

'No.'

Paget's news had made her inarticulate. She was not sure how she had ever got out of his office, refusing his tea, his sherry, his clumsy sympathy. She thought she had said something about being alone, needing to think, but such phrases seemed more fitting for one of Miss Hartley's works of fiction. Surely in real life people found more sensible and original excuses for lapses in behaviour? I hurt his feelings, she thought. Poor old Paget. He means well. He so wanted to ply me with strong tea and tell me Tom would put everything right.

There were two women discussing strawberry jam at the next table. Everywhere was the clink of cutlery on china, the low eager murmur of conversation, the faint aroma of livestock.

He was not my father, thought Paddy.

She felt suddenly detached from solid earth, floating, remote. She could not hear properly. When she picked up the spoon in her saucer and stirred her sugarless tea she saw her hand from a great distance as if it were not her own at all.

I'm going to faint, she thought.

The tea was as strong as Paget's would have been and, without his anxious sympathy, it was more bracing. She looked up and out of the window again seeing, now she was recovered, the grubbiness of the glass, the animal and human chaos of the street.

He was not my father. The thought rose again and this time she faced it, breathing normally, sipping the tea. She saw that Edward not being her father might explain a great deal. She had wondered, in the past, if he had neglected her because he did not like women much, or conversely that he did not care to be reminded through her of her mother, his beloved Deborah. He went mad with grief when she died, Paddy remembered. He shut himself up for days on end. What then had he done when discovering Deborah's daughter was not his?

There is so much we don't know, Paddy thought. She wondered if Curry knew. Yes, Curry must know.

'Shall I bring another pot?' The girl's smile was both cunning and perfunctory. She hoped Paddy would leave so she could seat two of the weary shoppers waiting for a table, but she also hoped for a tip.

'No, thank you. Could I have the bill?'

While she waited Paddy listened to the conversation on strawberry jam veer away to comfortable shoes and mustard plasters. The bell jingled as the door opened and a new waft of pig entered with a woman in a headscarf.

'Here you are, madam,' said the girl, returning. 'It's turning out a funny day. Drizzle now.'

Paddy paid, stepped out into the damp.

She thought: How strange! I turned out to be a changeling after all.

11

A WEEK PASSED and still no Tom.
'He'm a varminty bugger too,' said Bushey to the
young cattle as he stopped up yet another gap. The sun
was so strong now he wore his 'summer' hat, an ancient
felt with an undulating brim. Beyond the seeding grasses
the woods were intensely green, their shade darker than
at any other time of year. At noon no birds sang, and
only the pigeons flapped among the leaves. 'As hot as
Italy, surely,' said Grace, fanning herself with a discarded laundry list as she sat on a hard chair in the
living room at the Lodge.

'He'll have to come back eventually,' said Paddy.

'He never did do what was expected.'

'Tom? No, not often.'

'But now your father's dead . . .' Grace stopped, conscious of being on shifting ground. She thought: I
ought to mince my words. I ought to say 'passed on'
perhaps. I ought to sound grave and sympathetic, not
brisk and ordinary.

'Now Father's dead,' said Paddy bluntly, 'he has no
excuse.'

Now his father's dead things will be different, Harriet
had thought, watching the fifteen-year-old Edward
stride away into the garden. But nothing was different
except, perhaps, that he took even less notice of his

mother, less interest in the estate. 'I envy women who are close to their sons,' Harriet said to Curry when she was an old woman. 'I never was to mine.' He is too much a Bretton, she could have added, too inherently careless. With what? Money? Time? Other people's emotions? 'They live cut off,' said Harriet. 'Because they feel so little themselves they think everyone else is the same.' And once, behind the locked door, about Ralph: 'Indifference is more cruel than hatred.'

'My dear, he must come back. Mr Paget ought to send furious letters by every post,' said Grace.

'I'm sure he does,' said Paddy.

'But who is to pay the bills?'

'It's more than bills. Tax. Debts.' Paddy was wondering: Why do I still call him Father when I speak of him? 'Something will have to be done.'

Grace tried to look worldly. 'Sell Roman Hill?'

'Or Bretton.'

It was unthinkable, Grace decided, though she knew other houses abandoned or blown up. She glanced quickly at Paddy. How proud and fierce she looked these days. It was like sharing a perfectly ordinary room with an eagle, unexpected and discomfiting. She seemed thinner, all her bones more prominent, and she wore her hair twisted low down on her neck.

'My dear, wouldn't it be better to sell Roman Hill to Johnny Chance? You could ask a good price. The Chances have been besotted with that place for a century.'

'That's for Tom to decide.'

'Well, if you intend to wait for Tom you'll be waiting in vain,' Grace was moved to exclaim. 'He'll expect you to sort it all out. He always has in the past.'

Paddy ignored this. She said: 'Paget suggests selling that light land along the Frilton road for houses.'

'I don't like the sound of that.'

'Or sell the timber. He's tried for years to get me to

agree to that. I expect Tom will be much easier to persuade.'

Grace could find nothing to say to this. Bretton shorn of its trees would be absurd. In her mind's eye she saw a vast expanse of naked park, and the cedars gone.

'Oh my dear, surely not?' was all she could muster after a long long moment and then thought she sounded foolish and followed it with: 'I do hope your father is to have a stone. Or is . . .' She found she could not continue, 'Is the grave to be anonymous, to be just another patch of grass in the park?'

'I hope so. Old Trenchard is supposed to be carving one. It will be flat.' Paddy sounded matter-of-fact. 'Well, flattish. I think it will have just the name and dates.'

Grace thought this appropriate and said so. She felt a strange ambiguity when thinking about Edward Bretton, for she was grateful to him for preventing Paddy's marriage and yet had disliked him from the moment he had done so. He had been a difficult man to know, she thought unhappily. The only certain thing had been that he had loved his wife.

'I'm still surprised,' said Grace, looking out of the open window at the park with its endangered oaks, 'that he didn't want to be buried with your mother.'

She had been thinking aloud. She turned apologetically. But Paddy was not there.

'I haven't seen you for ages,' said Etta, cheerfully and politely. One did not take liberties with Paddy.

'I've been very busy.' Paddy was in the lane beyond the green door.

'Where are you going?' Paddy had stopped at the gate into Hobeys. The young cattle were all down under the elms, switching at flies and dozing. 'Down to Roman Hill? May I come? Please may I come?'

As they descended, briskly at first and then less so,

growing pink, Etta added: 'It's because of the bullocks. I daren't come in here now. I have to go round by the lane and it's miles and miles.'

'Do you go often?'

'Oh yes.'

'So did I when I was young.'

Etta could not imagine Paddy young. Some people, she had decided, must arrive fully grown. She stumped on, swinging her arms and humming to herself. Paddy followed, looking out from under her straw hat at the familiar fall of land. Now she could see the chimneys of the house, the different green that marked the line of alders by the beck. A voice, Harriet's voice, said to her: 'There are lots of reasons why Brettons don't go down to Roman Hill.'

Harriet, thought Paddy. Harriet was not my grandmother.

The enormity of the loss struck her but could not be assimilated. To lose Edward, to lose completely her sense of who she was and why she was, all that was bad enough, but to lose Harriet . . .

'Oh, I'm not by myself,' she heard Etta's voice floating back across the orchard. 'Miss Bretton's coming.'

The door stood open, for only in the worst of weather was it ever closed. Johnny stood with one hand stretched out to tweak affectionately at Etta's pigtail.

'Miss Bretton,' and he looked up. 'Come in, won't you?'

She hesitated. She was still grappling with her loss, the loss of someone who had remained, even long after her death, a fixed and shining point in life, a reference point.

'I think you should come in,' said Johnny gently. She was distracted, he thought. The strain of holding herself together had been too much. Today she could not manage the stony face, the tight lips. He stood automatically to one side and added: 'You know the way.'

But she let him lead her. He felt, though he did not look behind, that she hung back. 'My mother's room,' he said, opening the door. Did he mean to imply it was neutral ground? He was not sure himself, but he remembered her at his mother's funeral and with maturity had come an appreciation of how difficult that must have been for her. He knew, of course, that before Meg had appropriated it, the room had been his father's office, and before William, Joseph's snug, but he did not guess this would be of significance. He saw that she held herself stiffly and that her eyes seemed glazed. The battered nature of her straw hat was embarrassingly evident and her grey skirt had dust in a rime round the hem.

'Has your brother come home?' he asked. He was sure that was why she had come down.

'No, I'm afraid not. Things are no further forward. I thought you ought to know.' The village is full of speculation, she might have added. There are even rumours that you covet Home Farm. He was a Chance and his instinct, she thought, was for acquisition. 'They get what they want,' said Curry. 'They get more than they ought to have,' said Harriet grimly, remembering the green door and the hard wood and the cold.

'Is Mr Tom all right?' asked Johnny.

For a moment she could not think what he meant and then understood slowly and with indignation. The war had left a great many young men not quite 'all right'.

'Why ever should you think he wasn't?' she demanded foolishly.

Johnny replied, with reason: 'He doesn't seem to be behaving normally, does he? It's nearly three weeks since the funeral.'

Paddy felt the effort of being indignant on Tom's behalf too much, and too absurd. She capitulated. 'I don't know what he's doing,' she said. 'I don't know if he's "all right". I don't know if he ever means to come back. Arthur Paget is talking about taking a trip to Italy. The whole world . . .' and she stopped, as if afraid of growing hysterical, and moved her hand in a helpless gesture and walked to look out of the window.

In the yard Etta was coming out of the byre, closing the door behind her with exaggerated care. 'What you find closed you close behind you,' Bonniman had told her.

Tom is my half-brother, she thought. Her world was still tilting. Among the debris of altered circumstance she supposed she might eventually get a foothold. She repeated: Tom is my half-brother, and waited for her own reaction.

'I hate him! He does what he likes and no one ever minds,' she had protested to Jack Chance once, deeply hurt over some trifle, one of the myriad petty injustices. 'My brother goes his own way,' she had told Paget icily when Tom had squandered his twenty-first birth-day inheritance in a matter of months. 'It was almost all the money there was, Miss Paddy,' wailed Paget, aghast. But Tom had always gone his own way. He was not emotional, not given to temper or outbursts, he was simply tenacious. If he wanted something he kept after it: a spaniel puppy, ferrets, new top boots, a different school, Italy. He fixed his mind, Paddy thought, and could not be turned till he had achieved that goal and fixed it on something else. He was the stuff of martyrs, he had made an art of determination. 'Of pig-headedness,' said Curry. 'All martyrs were pig-headed,' retorted Paddy. 'Some were sliced in pieces and never gave an inch.' And never giving an inch paid off: Tom got the puppy, the ferrets, the boots, was removed from one school and sent to another, and wrung enough out of the estate – 'There was nothing there but he squeezed something,' said Paget – to settle in Italy.

Etta put her head in at the door. 'There are some

lovely calves. I think they're hungry.' Then wistfully: 'So am I.'

'What about a picnic?' asked Johnny.

Etta face burned with joy. 'Oh yes. Oh yes please.'

Hobeys fell in its long steep curve from the tangled copse on its summit – 'Where the villa stood fifteen hundred years ago,' said Paddy – to the lower fields. Etta climbed stolidly, swinging the hazel stick she had picked from the hedge, and her hot face was creased with serious intent: she had to choose a suitable place for the picnic. The gravity of the task overwhelmed her, for these were people she loved: she must make everything perfect for them.

Behind, the adults came on in prickly silence, Paddy not sure why she had acquiesced to this folly. The sun was fierce when they stepped from under the trees and Etta was a long way ahead and waving her arms.

'Surely this will do?' asked Paddy, but still they climbed.

'Is this all right?' Etta was scarlet from exertion and anxiety.

'The best place,' said Johnny cheerfully.

Etta had chosen it because from here the red chimneys of the farm were just visible and so, in the other direction, was the gate into the lane, the way home to Bretton. This then was the perfect place, pitched between two worlds she adored.

'Why do we always have to meet here?' Philip had grumbled. 'It's too near the farm. That fellow Chance might see us.'

'What if he does?' challenged the young Paddy, reckless, in love.

'Why use my meadow for your courting?' asked Jack inevitably.

'Because no one would look for us here,' Paddy replied.

'Does your father know?'

'Of course not.'

Jack had looked down his beaked nose. 'Well, if I were your father I'd whip you.'

She could not tell if he was serious.

Twenty years later his son put down the basket he was carrying, looked round and said quietly, 'We camped in a place like this somewhere near Ypres when I first went out. Not such a hill, of course. You could hear the birds singing and the sound of guns seemed far off and unimportant.'

'I'm sorry about Will,' said Paddy. It might have been better not to let his thoughts turn inexorably towards the war but she had wanted to say it. She remembered Will only as a boisterous, lanky boy, but she did remember him. In a way I was a sister, thought Paddy. 'If I had a daughter,' Jack had said, 'I'd want one like you.'

Etta had thrown herself on the grass and was burrowing into it, enjoying the world from another angle. When she rolled over on to her back the deep blue bowl of the sky was a shock, so vast was it after the miniature world between the grass stems. Chaffinches chinked down the hedge and there was the faintest breeze through the elm leaves. 'I like it here,' she declared, rolling over again in an excess of happiness and squashing her wide-brimmed hat. And then, catching sight of the contents of the basket: 'Chicken!'

'And elderflower wine,' said Johnny.

'And gooseberry pie and lemonade,' said Paddy.

Etta sat up. Her hat tipped off and her hair sprung from its plait. 'Always a mess. What will your Ma say?' was Lily's daily lament. The sun was hot on her face. Chicken, gooseberry pie, Paddy, Johnny Chance, Hobeys . . .

'I wonder where you'll be when you're grown up,' said Johnny.

'I'll be here.' Her reply was immediate, her certainty

unshakeable. 'I shall live here.' Her fingers dug into the grass stems as if she feared at any moment to be snatched away. She must cling on as long as possible, to Bretton, to the present, to this patch of field. Sooner or later Laura would grow restless and prise husband and daughter away. 'Like plants,' the grown-up Etta was to say. 'We were always being dug up and moved around. But you can only do that so many times. You have to be careful. Or the plant dies.'

The world was all trembling green, the birdsong fading with the intense heat of noon. Johnny had sunk on one elbow and was steadying his mug of wine.

'May I go down and paddle in the beck?' asked Etta.

'I don't see why not.'

'I wonder why they neglect her so?' said Paddy, watching the small figure climbing the stile. She lifted her head, shading her eyes, and so the whole tidy concoction of her hair came loose in an instant, strained by the eccentric angle of her beehive hat. 'I wish she had a friend.'

'She has you,' and when there was no response: 'Pen Potter?'

'Don't mock. She needs . . .'

'She needs a mother.'

'She has one of those.'

'Now who's mocking?'

He watched her remove her hat and try to pin up her hair. She was unselfconscious, and graceful. Into his mind, from under layers of memory, rose the vision of a young woman bending to twist up her hair, sitting on the edge of the water trough in the yard at Roman Hill. As it rose so it sank away. It might have been this woman beside him. It might have been his mother.

A bee flew past Paddy's nose and she brushed at it, knocking over her wine. 'What a waste,' she said.

'Think of it as an oblation,' Johnny told her, 'for the gods of Hobeys. If there aren't gods there are ghosts.'

For a moment they both contemplated their own ghosts in silence. Paddy would have been astonished to learn she was one for Johnny Chance. The first time he had ever seen her she had been up here, standing by his father's side looking at the new foals. She had had black pigtails to her waist.

'I'd better go and see what Etta's up to,' she said now, rising. The grass was slippery underfoot, the light blinding. In Lower Bit she stopped to listen but could hear nothing except the rustle of leaves and the faint splash of water.

'She's by the ford,' said Johnny.

This was where Paddy had paddled as a child, holding up her much longer skirts and feeling the silt ooze between her toes. Here she had first felt the delicious terror of small fishes swimming against her bare skin, had first eaten watercress, first seen the kingfisher.

'Etta, what have you done with your stockings?'

'They're in the tree.'

'And do pull your hat on properly. If it falls in it will be out of shape for ever.'

Johnny removed his boots and socks. 'Don't be so stuffy. You aren't addressing a parish council meeting. Why don't you paddle too?'

'Don't be so ridiculous.'

But she envied them. She felt she had forgotten how to be young and careless, how to be happy. She knew she had once spent blissful hours here and that the Paddy who had been lonely and resentful up at the big house became a different creature in this magical water. The stones of the ford had been slippery under the soles of her thin white feet. She had sung to herself, and smiled.

'You look remarkably disapproving,' said Johnny.

'I'd have thought you were too old to splash around like a fool.'

'I'm afraid not. Anyway, I'd rather make a fool of myself in here than on the bank.'

Paddy found she wanted to laugh.

Etta, finding some object, held it up. 'Look.' The light dappled on the moving water, the swirling weed, the cress bed where the ripples broke in sunshine. There were long trails of mud stirred up by two pairs of careless feet.

'Oh. I've trodden on something. Something hard,' cried Etta, plunging. Johnny steadied her, laughing. 'It hurts. It hurts.'

He picked her up and staggered to the bank. 'You weigh as much as a calf. Let's look at the damage.' There was none. 'You trod on a branch,' he said. 'Or an eel. I never thought you'd make a fuss. Not you.'

In order not to disappoint him she brushed at the threatening tears. She's gritting her teeth, thought Paddy, amused.

'You'd better run up to the top of the hill to dry off,' she told her. 'You'll never get stockings on wet legs.'

'Do I have to wear them?'

'Certainly you have to. What would your mother think if you went home barefoot, covered in mud and slime?'

Etta ducked away and ran out into the blazing heat. Paddy followed slowly, the stockings twisted in her hand and Etta's boots dangling.

'She ought to be in sandals,' said Johnny.

'They don't seem to notice what she wears. Only when there are guests.'

'You notice.'

Paddy gave him 'a Miss Bretton look' he said. Presumably it meant 'keep your distance'. He had heard old Dack say once, 'She hev an eye could quench a fire, our missus.' He was not intimidated though. And like his father, he stood on no ceremonies.

'You're fond of her,' he said.

In answer she strode away from him, one hand raised to keep hat and hair together.

He caught her up. 'How many times did you paddle down there when you were a child?'

'Hundreds.'

She had seen him once, a sturdy five-year-old, peering through the trees. His had been the only face intruding on her solitary playtimes in the beck. God send somebody for me, she had prayed, but God never had. There was no one. She had nobody to laugh with, not even the girls she sometimes shared lessons with at the Grange. They seemed only to laugh at other things. She had nobody on whom to lavish the accumulation of years of frustrated affection.

'My God,' said Johnny suddenly, 'you punished those horses. D'you remember? Hacking ten miles to the meet, hunting all day, hacking home across half the county.'

'You never came out. Why not? I don't . . .' Yes, she was sure of it. 'I hardly ever saw you.'

'Oh, I hid from you,' he replied disconcertingly.

'From me?'

'I thought you were proud. And Father adored you. I resented that. You rode better than I did and he never let me forget it. He admired your airs and graces. He admired your nerve.'

'Did I have any airs and graces?' Paddy was astounded.

He had sulked about the yard on those hunting mornings, waiting for her to ride away. In the unsatisfactory light of stable lanterns he had seen her indistinctly, a tall bowler-hatted girl. The way she sat a horse meant business. Sometimes he had heard her clear imperious voice. But once he had heard her laugh, a low pleasant sound. Like an ordinary human being, he thought. And as time went on a wretchedly grudging admiration smothered his resentment, though he was away from Roman Hill more and more, seldom saw her and then at a distance, never spoke. He heard from the village about her foolhardy exploits, from his father of how she kept to her secret life with a shocking tenacity. 'Well, they won't let me have a life of my own that isn't secret,' she said. He heard how she got herself home come what may: kicks, bruises, cuts, lameness, fog, wind, sheer stupid exhaustion. 'It's my only pleasure,' she said to Jack the day she came back with a dent in the bowler and blood all down her face. 'Perhaps it is, but should I encourage you in it?' he had asked, shaken at the sight of her.

'But you have done for years.'

'Better to come to my senses late than not at all.'

'I'll only ride my own horses then.' She was schooling two youngsters to sell on at the time, bought cheaply at Frilton.

Jack's eyes glinted. 'My conscience couldn't stand that,' he said. 'They're not safe out of the yard.'

Etta was climbing the gate. They had a glimpse of white drawers.

'I'm sorry about the airs and graces,' said Paddy. 'I had no right.'

'You haven't got over your father's death. How could you? I shouldn't have teased you at the beck.'

She looked into his face. His likeness to his father was, as she had always known, only superficial. He was finer stuff, kinder, more gently humorous, more civilized. His charming smile was his mother's. She felt she ought to be comforted by this, by the thought that weeks of unseemly wrangling in Paget's office over the sale of Roman Hill would be made easier by it. Yet she longed for Jack, her Jack, for the harsh deep voice commanding her courage, steadying her nerves.

She smiled bleakly, holding out her hand.

'I must go after Etta,' she said.

'Mr Haley,' and Curry came forth, hearing his step in the hall. 'Mrs Haley has gone up to bed early.'

'Is she unwell?'

'She said she felt tired. She asked me to serve dinner as soon as you arrived.'

'Very well,' said Hugh. Laura was always tired when she was bored, he thought. He went to the dining room and found it laid for one. What state for a solitary diner! He smiled, thinking how stupid it was, eating alone in such grandeur, living in this great echoing house. He lingered a moment by the window, looking out into the garden.

I like the garden, he thought. I must get out into it more. I must get to know a hoe from a mattock, a peony from a carnation.

'I shan't change,' he said to Curry. 'Can you serve at once? I want to walk round the garden before it grows too dark.'

12

SHOCK RECEDED. Violent anger took Paddy over.
'She do burn about the place these days,' said
Bushey, recruited from stopping gaps in Hobeys to
helping in the harvest field. They were short-handed, as
they had been since the war, and one memorable afternoon
she burned among them to take charge of the sail reaper. 'I
can still drive a horse in a straight line, I hope,' she said.
But she drove too fast, her electrical impulses conveyed to
the old mare, and something jammed.

'She hev a short way with words,' remarked old
Norris at the day's end.

The weather held in spite of everything, the corn was
gathered. Grace Paulley, walking up on parish business,
was forced to tramp across twenty acres to where Paddy
bent, tanned and sweaty, over yet another line of shocks.
'You'll kill yourself,' she was tempted to say but re-
frained, seeing Paddy's reddened eyes and the unnatural
intensity of her concentration. She recalled the worst
summer of the war when there had scarcely been able
bodies enough in Stenton to get in any harvest, in spite
of some Land Army women and a dozen public school-
boys all fingers and thumbs. Old Dack had been driven
to his bed by his exertions and Paddy had been left to
carry on without him, out in the fields dawn till dark,
one eye always on the sky. It had been the first time

since Philip died that Grace had seen what Paddy might have meant to Brook Court. Even so, admiration mingled with doubt. She might have been the making of poor Phil, Grace thought – or might, quite easily, have destroyed him. Who knew what demands Paddy might have made, someone of her own to love at last?

Now they were beginning on the wheat. Each load lightened Paddy's heart. Another year, another harvest, another small heap of money to stave off ruin.

'Come home,' she wrote to Tom, and the words scored into the paper with a fury she had never felt before. 'Come home or I shall come to Italy to fetch you.' 'Or kill you,' she might have truthfully added. And on the day the last of the wheat went into the stack, at Home Farm he did come, leaving the station trap in the village and walking over the fields, hands in pockets. He strolled down the stubble to watch his sister leading up the spare horses, surrounded by the cottage children who had been beating for rabbits.

He recognized her only too well, in spite of the corduroy trousers, the shirt, the man's cap.

'Hello, Pat.'

She stopped the horses. The crowd of children began to melt away. Only one, with thick lank brown hair, crept closer to Paddy and stared with unblinking ferocity.

'This place was mortgaged to the chimneys to pay for Italy,' she said.

'I knew things were bad.' He had not expected a direct assault so soon. She did not offer to kiss him before she began, or take his hand, or pay lip service to any sisterly affection.

'Did you know about me?' she asked.

'About . . . Oh, that. Yes, I knew.'

'It never occurred to you to tell me about it?'

'I thought it would be kinder . . . He never made any

138

fuss, did he? He brought you up. You need never have known.'

'Until he died.'

He walked uneasily beside her as she started the horses again, gave her a guilty look. Damn her, she always made him feel conscience-stricken. His pale blue eyes were anxious. 'You need never have known,' he repeated. 'It's been forty years a secret. Why should you learn about it now? I don't understand why Paget mentioned it, the old fool. It had nothing to do with your being cut out.' He was aware the unknown child kept pace with them, still regarded him with unabated hostility. 'That was because of Jack Chance, all that old row. You know that.'

'Paget told me because there was a letter with the will asking him to do so.'

They were leaving the fields and coming to the yard.

'Why didn't you tell me?' Paddy demanded. 'It might have helped explain so much.'

'He only told me just before I left for Italy. What was the point of telling you then?'

He had been back fifteen minutes, he thought, and already they were at odds. 'I don't understand you,' he had cried once. 'Why do you take things so seriously?' Even now he could not comprehend how seriously she might take being divested of her very self. She was Patricia Bretton, had always been Patricia Bretton, and would continue to be Patricia Bretton. He did not see she had lost anything but a small share of a bankrupt estate. He followed the horses slowly and with mild irritation saw them stop by the horse pond.

'You might let the men see to the animals,' he said. 'I've had a long journey.'

Paddy looked round. The horses raised mild, tired heads, whiskers dripping. 'Mrs Dye is at the Lodge. There'll be a cold supper. You'd better go up straight away.'

He could only say, bemused, 'But where's Curry?'

'At the house looking after the Haleys.'

Tom frowned. There was nothing appealing in the Lodge. He felt that being confined with Paddy in so small a space might be too much for his constitution.

But: 'I'll wait for you,' he said. 'I'll go and talk to the men.'

He had not wanted to come back. He had put it off as long as he could, longer than was decent. He had been safe in his cypress-ringed villa with the doves in the courtyard and Marco and Gabriella to attend him. He had been happy with his convivial, idle life, his gallery of Tuscan landscapes, his few undemanding books. He had not wanted to be reminded of obligation, responsibility or the past, in which his father's expectations and the horror of his soldiering figured hugely. He had hated Bretton. He had hated the extreme cold of winters in the great old house, the breaking of the ice in his water jug before he could shave, the plain cooking – 'economical cooking,' said Paddy – the country society. 'It's your duty to go,' Edward had told him when he refused to attend some local entertainment. 'It's your duty,' said Paget, 'to behave responsibly.'

'I don't want to be responsible,' said Tom. 'I don't want to be responsible for anything.'

Walking to the Lodge – 'Of course you can't visit the house without an invitation,' said Paddy – he could smell both horse and the sweet dusty flour of the grain coming from Paddy's clothes. That brown-haired child had turned out to be the offspring of his tenants. *His* tenants. He savoured the thought a little, wondering why he disliked it so. They would soon be someone else's tenants after all. He had rehearsed in the train what he would say to Paget: 'I don't want Bretton. I don't want a bloody brick of it. I don't want it tenanted or untenanted, solvent or bust. Sell it. Pull it down. Give it to Pat.'

'You aren't going to contest the will?' he asked suddenly.

'Of course not.'

'You don't think I'd leave you without anything?' He wondered as he spoke how much would be left to give her.

'I haven't thought about it.' And it was true, she had not considered the future. She had spent these last weeks trying to make sense of the past.

'Not thought about it?' Surely she had thought of nothing else?

She looked at him. He looked well. As far as she knew the only anxiety in his face was that which she had put there this last hour. He wore a suit, good shoes, a stylish panama. Everything about him told her how far behind he hoped to have left Bretton and everything connected with it.

'You've no idea how I really feel, have you?' she said softly.

The most terrible thing, Harriet had thought, is that he has no idea how I feel. And if I told him, in words of one syllable, over and over, he would still not understand. He would be as totally at a loss as if I were speaking gibberish. 'You have your children,' Ralph had replied on one of the occasions she had raised the subject. 'You have a fine house. Why can't you be content?'

If content were so easy how merry life would be, thought Harriet, and subsequently took out her frustration on the village and the servants, keeping herself busy at their expense. 'You don't love me,' she said to Ralph. 'I accept that. But pay me some attention or I shan't answer for what I might do.'

'I don't know what you're talking about.'

'You do. You must.'

But instead: 'Why can't you be content?' he continued to ask.

141

Perhaps even the flowers in the church were a cry for help: Look what I do for you, God. Do something for me. For a while she tried to cling to faith but she knew she had none; it had dwindled away in the disillusion of her marriage. All I do now is keep up appearances, she thought. Her attendance record, her dignity, her hats were formidable, and yet in church, where she might have expected peace and solace, her inner conflict was only heightened. Kneeling, praying for God's love, she thought of the weeks she had prayed for Ralph's. 'He was a weak man and a liar,' she said to Deborah and felt eased, saying the words. 'I found it out two months after we were married. Two months and a few days perhaps. He had never cared for me. He married me for my money and because he needed a wife badly. He needed a wife in order to avoid his obligations to another woman. I was convenient,' said Harriet.

She had been convenient as the servants were convenient, each fulfilling their allotted role. Harriet's role was to grace Bretton as its mistress, to allow Ralph the use of her fortune, and to raise legitimate children. No more than the servants was she to receive companionship, conversation or tenderness.

'I thought, in the beginning, I would go mad,' said Harriet.

Paddy left Tom breakfasting at the Lodge under Mrs Dye's indulgent eye and answered the call for help from Bretton.

For some reason Harriet was on her mind.

She was not my grandmother, she thought, sorting the sheets and putting them away in the press, Lily at her elbow. She had grown used to the thought but not its implications. She felt as bereft as if she had been snatched, screaming, from Harriet's living arms. That light-headed sense of unreality gripped her again. Who was she? What was she? Not Patricia Mary Deborah Bretton, that was for sure. Then who?

'Miss Bretton, I'd no idea you were here,' said Laura, with a brave attempt at not accentuating 'you'. She stood on the back landing in a silk wrapper, her hair in a bandeau. She had just endured a bath in the hip bath in the dressing room.

'I had a message from Mrs Murray that Babs was ill,' – 'And we know what *that* is,' Curry had said resignedly – 'and that Mrs Prince has been called away. I hoped I could be of some help.'

'We were at sixes and sevens this morning, mum,' struck in Lily.

'Then that was very kind,' Laura said firmly before her tongue might run away with something less gracious. The absurdly antiquated ritual of the bath had made her both hot and irritable. 'Baths,' she had complained to Hugh the last time, 'should make one feel refreshed.' She knew that her wanting one this morning had added to the burden of her household. Indeed, Lily had purposely announced Bab's absence and Mrs Prince's imminent defection the moment she had drawn the curtains in order to give Laura the chance to cancel her 'splash'. 'Splash' was Bab's own word, stemming from 'Every time she want her splash we hev to work time and a half.' Certainly the 'splash' involved copious cans of hot water and buckets of cold and much heaving and sweating and misery. Laura had ignored Lily's hopeful tone but had found the water lukewarm and then had met Ronnie Dack lumbering up the corridor to remove it on huge muffled feet. He had been as horrified to see her as she to see him but Lily, learning of his encounter with the silk wrapper, thought Laura well paid out for such lack of consideration.

'Mrs Prince will be back tomorrow,' Laura told Paddy. 'I don't believe her sister is very ill at all.'

Paddy did not reply. Lily continued to hand across

the sheets. Laura was conscious of interrupting an old ritual. For decades each worn and precious piece of linen had been seen royally to its shelf in the cedarwood interior. Some of the sheets were monogrammed: D, C, H – Bretton wives who had brought them in their marriage chests. H was Harriet of course, a flamboyant and romantic H as if belonging to an entirely different Harriet altogether. Paddy smoothed it out with her strong brown hand – a gardener's hand, the nails short and a little dirty – and once again felt the terrible ache of loss.

Laura wondered what she must do to be taken proper notice of on her own landing. She thought: What did Hugh say about the lease? Something to do with curtailment, death of one or other party, reasonable notice. She had not listened. Dislocated words floated back but meant nothing. She had been disappointed in Bretton, bored, impatient, but now: This is *our* house, she thought. She was lit by a flame of possessiveness.

But she dare not rage at Paddy.

'Where is Mrs Murray?' she asked Lily.

'In the kitchen, mum.'

Laura turned. Her neat rounded buttocks were quite visible through the thin silk of the wrapper, just as her nipples were and the slight curve of her belly. No wonder Ronnie Dack had bolted.

'I'd better go down and discuss the menu then,' she said over her shoulder.

'This one's nearly done for,' Lily remarked. The linen had worn so thin that it was almost transparent. In the corner was another H.

Paddy took it without a word and transferred it carefully to the waiting shelf.

'I suppose we shall have to call her *Mrs* Murray,' said Edward the day Harriet gave the keys of Bretton to Curry.

'It is customary.'

'Well, I think you're making a mistake, Mother.'

'Do you? Well, I'm quite certain I'm not.'

'And I really feel it's for Deborah to appoint a house-keeper.'

'Deborah agrees with me, Constance is the obvious choice.'

Once Edward had suspected his shy and gentle wife was no match for his overbearing mother. Now he suspected instead that they were aligned against him in a mysterious feminine alliance. Logically it was absurd; they were not only dissimilar in character, they were rivals. He knew Harriet had never allowed Deborah to be anything but titular mistress of Bretton. And yet . . .

'Of course Constance Murray must be housekeeper,' said Deborah. 'I can't imagine anyone better suited.'

'She's far too young,' protested Edward feebly.

She was young and she was handsome in a dark gipsy fashion, but her height was intimidating, her reticence, her eyes. 'That woman smoulders,' said a college friend of Edward's uneasily, but it was not the warm smoulder of a sexual fire. 'Would you like to marry?' Harriet had dared to ask once, and afterwards: 'Would you like children?' But by that time Curry had a child: Deborah. Shortly afterwards she had Paddy. 'Bretton, Deborah and Paddy,' said Harriet. 'Those are her children. And in that order.'

'What can I do?' Edward cried three years later, his mother and his wife both dead and a new young son howling in the nursery.

'I will see to everything,' said Curry with a quiet authority that was like balm. How had he ever disliked her? Why had he ever been frightened of her? 'Remember,' Harriet had told him, 'Mrs Murray keeps the lar and penates. Trust her.' Edward did not *quite* trust her yet, he thought her hard and ambitious, but he put himself in her hands. What else was he to do? It was Curry who arranged for Deborah's unmarried sister to move to Bretton while Tom was small. Sarah turned out to be 'starchy' said Edward, disappointed; 'strict' said Paddy, furious. 'She stands no nonsense, she is plain and good,' said Curry, judging that this was what they needed.

It was Curry who ran the house, who did the books at the farm. 'I don't know about sowing and reaping,' she said to Dack, 'but I know about money, about profit and loss.' When Paddy was old enough she took her in hand and taught her all she knew. 'We have to keep the place going,' she said. 'You and I now. You in the future.'

'If you sell up,' Paddy told Tom, 'Curry will die. I mean it. She'll die.'

'Don't be so melodramatic. People don't just die. I know she's given her life to the place but it can't be helped.'

'It can be helped. You needn't sell. There are other ways to survive.'

'Not for me.'

Etta asked, 'Is Mr Bretton going to sell the house?' She had overheard things in the kitchen.

'Him?' cried Pen Potter with a scornful flick of her greasy hair. 'Not him. My Ma says he has to do what Miss B tells him.'

'Sell?' grunted Bushey, pausing to sharpen his hook. 'Sell? Why should he sell? There've allus been Brettons at Bretton.'

But Etta had met Tom walking in the far reaches of the park and had, instinctively, recognized his shrinking. From what? 'All things Brettonian,' Paddy might have said sharply. He shrank from the Englishness of it all, the shabby grandeur, the repairs never accomplished, the beauty, the responsibility – most of all from the responsibility. 'I gave enough orders in France,' he said when challenged by Paddy. 'I'm not giving any more.' In the disproportionately large and draughty pew reserved for the Brettons he momentarily looked the part of the squire but his spirit was far away. 'Among the cypresses,' said Paddy.

'He might sell,' continued Etta seriously. 'Then we'd have to move again. I heard Mother say so.' She spoke these things aloud because she needed them to be denied. She wanted to be reassured that Bretton was for ever. 'There used to be Romans here,' she went on. 'Miss Bretton told me.'

'Allus pokin' into old books, she were.'

'Well, the Romans aren't here any more,' Etta persevered remorselessly. 'They only stayed a bit and then went somewhere else.'

Bushey sliced the nettles with venom. 'You talks too much,' he said.

Etta came through the green door and saw Paddy bent over a row of greenstuff. The garden was secret and warm, the great walls shutting them in, shutting out the world. Hours, minutes, meant nothing here, only the passing of seasons. There was a sense of extraordinary permanence in the ancient trees, the ranks of vegetables, the flowers, the dry box hedges, even the weeds. 'Like a nunnery garden,' Hugh had said the day he had seen it for the first time.

'You aren't going away, are you?' Etta asked anxiously.

'Away? No, I haven't planned to.'

'Someone said . . . Someone said Mr Bretton would sell our house.'

'Oh, people talk,' replied Paddy cheerfully. 'You mustn't take any notice. It doesn't mean they think at the same time.'

'Promise you won't go away.'

There was a silence during which the annoyed

chirping of a bird in the fruit trees and the repetitive hooing of the pigeons sounded very loud. 'I can't promise,' said Paddy. 'It may not be for me to decide in the end.'

So solid ground had, after all, only been solid ice – and the ice was moving. Etta hung back, brushing her hand across the top of the box hedges and watching a dozen ladybirds drop away. She had been so certain Paddy would never break a promise that it had never occurred to her Paddy might not make one.

She looked up and saw Tom coming towards them.

He wore a straw hat and was swinging a cane, gazing about with those oddly stricken blue eyes. For a moment, dwarfing the hedges, he looked like his father, lean, fair and shambling.

'The place is a ruin,' he said to Paddy as he reached her.

'Not quite yet, surely?'

'But all this . . .' and his bewildered gaze swept over the whole garden. 'When we were children . . .'

They had never been children together. Their shared memories were almost solely of Edward, his inflexibility, his aloofness, his refusal to acknowledge either of them as individuals in need of knowledge and stimulation he could not provide. Tom's face hardened. He was looking at the old hothouses with their broken panes and patched guttering but he was seeing Edward, Edward sitting in his garden chair on the terrace, flailing his cane at the gravel, crying in a strong, frightening voice, 'Italy? What d'you mean Italy? Why should you want to remove yourself to Italy, sir?'

The brown-haired child, the child of his tenants, was staring at him, he realized. He supposed he should smile at her, but a smile in the face of such hostility seemed trivial. He thought of the lovely elfin woman up at the house and her diffident, boorish husband. Was this lumpen, solid creature really theirs?

'It's a lovely garden,' she declared abruptly, 'and Miss Bretton works very hard in it.'

'That *was* a rebuke,' said Tom as he watched the child dive through the green door and out of sight. 'I get the impression she would rather I went away again.'

Paddy pulled out a weed and threw it aside carelessly as if whether it rooted somewhere else was no longer any concern of hers. 'And when are you going away again?'

'As soon as all the legal ends are tied up.' He looked rather dampened, like a small boy who has suddenly perceived that the adults want to be left alone. 'Are you tired of me already?'

She straightened, stepped over the hedge on to the path beside him and took his arm. 'No,' she said.

'And you're not angry any more?'

'No,' she said. 'I'm over that.' She did not add: There are other things I shall be angry about by and by.

'And all that old nonsense about your not being Father's. We don't even know if it's true.'

'You don't think it matters, do you?'

'No. Not in the least.'

She was steering him towards the gate. He remembered the unrelenting grip of her fingers. She had never held him gently, coaxed him over his fears. She had taken his hand like a steel trap and hauled him bodily willy-nilly. At fifteen she had towered above his five. 'Whatever he wants, he gets,' she had complained to Maudie while they sat by the nursery fire. 'Well, poor mite,' Maudie had replied in her tired, kindly voice. 'Knick-knacks don't make up for much.'

They were walking between the yew hedges.

'It will all come right in the end,' he said lightly. She recognized one of Maudie's sayings. Where she had had Harriet and Deborah for ten years, he had had Maudie and Sarah for six.

'I suppose so.' She did not believe things came right, only that they came different, and that sometimes this was a solution and sometimes not.

In fragile and unexpected harmony Tom and Paddy skirted the house, keeping under the trees where they would not be seen. They knew all the sheltering trunks, the helpful laurels, the hollowed rhododendrons, the corners where one could wait, trembling but invisible.

'God knows, we've had a lot of practice,' said Tom.

I wish he'd go away. I hate him! I hate him! thought Etta. How she ran, plunging through the rose garden, tearing down Paddy's borders, skimming under the cedars!

She burst at last through the back door and into the kitchen.

'Mind the floor!' cried Curry, poised on the edge of what seemed an acre of scrubbed brick.

'I'll take my sandals off. My feet are clean,' announced Etta, and imprinted the mark of ten plump toes from door to door across the damp wasteland. Curry's look was stern but then Curry's look was always stern. 'I don't have any nonsense in my house,' she had told Mrs Prince right at the beginning, and Babs, and Lily, as she had told every other cook, housemaid, parlourmaid and knife boy since she had received into her hands the keys of Bretton. My house, my kitchen, she said, and who would contradict her? Paddy held sway in the gardens but Bretton was Curry's, brick, mortar, furniture, servants and all. She had come naturally to it, 'starting with the flagstones and the range' she could have said. She had not schemed for it nor appeared ambitious, she had simply known that one day, as of right, she would receive the keys.

'I am where I should be,' she might have said the day she crossed the threshold. Since then she had been too busy to think of other needs: men, children, possessions.

She possessed Bretton and it was enough. 'She is a treasure,' declared Sarah, who had never found anyone before about whom she could say this and mean it. 'She's a witch,' retorted Edward. 'They say in the village she can cast spells.' He had never lost the last vestiges of his fear of her. And yet, whenever times were bad, he leaned on her without compunction, looking with relief for her grave face, her strong, low, respectful voice. Only sometimes, just sometimes, he received the full force of her eyes, sloe-black, electrifying, and all the old uneasiness flooded back.

He did not notice it but she stood firmly between him and Paddy. 'Somebody has to,' she said. The occasions he took notice of his daughter would have been terrifying ordeals but for Curry's intervention. Paddy had been thin and supple, bones sticking through layers of clothes – what layers of clothes they had worn in those days – and with great pleading eyes. Pleading for what? Love? Of course love. Everyone desires to be loved. But perhaps even less than love in this case: recognition. 'He ignores Patricia and dotes on the boy,' reported an indignant young Mrs Paulley to her husband. 'And I always thought him a fair man, intelligent.' She found, as time went on, she was a little afraid of him; he so disliked social contact, growing more reclusive every year since Deborah's death. Still, she braved him about Philip's marriage, about the desperate young people whose hearts he was breaking. 'I must do it,' she said to Frank, though she looked all nose and stubborn chin in her fright. 'If Paddy is what Philip wants, then I must try to help get her for him.'

'I really cannot deal with hysterical women,' Edward had told her. Grace, who had thought she was being coherent and reasonable, went home to weep on Frank's shoulder. 'He's as hard as rock,' she said. 'He won't even listen.' She no longer thought him fair or intelligent. 'Brettons never listen if anyone else is talking,'

Paddy told her, 'and they never notice another person's pain.'

Ralph had been like that too. 'Some families have big noses,' said Paddy, 'the Brettons have no hearts.' In the past they had turned men off for momentary lapses, remained implacable in the face of starving children, ailing wives. 'Let them go on the Parish,' they said, and then grumbled at their dinner table about the parish rate. There was always this undercurrent of indignation at Bretton, for the world outside the gate was always harsher and more critical than they would have liked.

'I don't like Mr Bretton,' Etta said. 'He wants to sell the house and the farm and . . . and everything.' She had paused at the far door and was looking back, her sandals still in her hand. The expression on Curry's face had not changed and yet: I have another child, she was thinking. The thought altered subtly all her angular rigidity, though nobody could have seen it but Paddy – and Etta.

Etta ran back on chilled bare feet.

'I love you,' she said, embracing whalebone.

'Well!' exclaimed Curry, to whom this had never been said before. She folded her arms briefly, tightly about the sturdy young body.

She said, 'Now get upstairs before you catch cold.'

'Look,' said Tom, 'I don't want to live in it. What are the chances of selling?'

He was tired of bantering pleasantries and drinking sherry in a cramped and musty office still furnished in the style of the 1860s.

'Sell? Not a good idea. Not the house. There are a dozen places in the country in the same predicament. The land is another matter.'

'And the trees?'

'Well yes, and the trees. But I suggest our first move is to offer Roman Hill to young John Chance.'

Death duties, debts, mortgages . . . Tom listened and nodded, standing looking down at the market square. He turned the sherry glass in his hand. He thought of the lurch and sway of his father's high dogcart, the countrywomen snatching their baskets and their children from its path. 'Get ready to jump down and get hold of his head,' Edward had said, and Tom had stared at the horse's laid-back ears, at the stiffened neck. Please don't let him have to do it. Please. He was afraid, knowing the horse would not stand quiet for him as it would for Paddy. It would rear, upset by the crowds, the jostling cattle, the loose pigs. Please, please, he prayed. Another fifty yards and they would have reached the inn, someone experienced and sympathetic would reach for the bridle and make the animal stand while they got out.

Edward had always driven fast, smart horses. 'He's no horseman,' said Harriet. 'He likes to make a show.' In his hands the safest old nag grew restive, he was always coming to grief with these blood horses. Besides, he seldom drove further than Frilton and fifty miles would have suited them better, fifty miles at a good round pace.

'I take it you intend to remain in Italy?' Paget asked. 'In that case there is . . .'

'Where else?' Tom turned from the window. 'Where else do you suggest? Look at the state this country's in. And Bretton's done, you know that. Life'll never be the same as it was before the war. It ought to be pulled down. It's history.'

'There's Miss Paddy to consider.'

'Pat? Oh, Pat'll be all right. She can share a cottage with that . . . What's that odd woman's name? Hartley? . . . and keep bees and chickens and write a history of Stenton. I'll see she has enough to be comfortable if the government leaves me anything at all.'

'Have you talked to her about it?'

Tom fingered his tie. 'All she keeps saying is it's going to break old Curry's heart or something. Sentimental rubbish. And Pat was never sentimental. Nor was Curry, come to that. I thought you might explain everything better than I could – about the money side, land prices, the trees . . . She was always against selling the trees.'

'Yes, indeed,' said Paget. 'Indeed she always was.'

'So that's settled then,' said Tom.

13

PADDY WENT DOWN to Hobeys.

This was where she had always come, to think, to be alone, to be with Philip, to meet Jack, to be comforted. She sat down by the hedge, out of sight of the gate. She knew she would get dirt and grass stains on her formal suit. I don't care, she thought. How different everything was from down here, seen from Etta's viewpoint, from the viewpoint of the Paddy who had existed long ago before loss, disappointment, quarrels, duties, age.

'So you see,' Paget had said apologetically, 'you see how it is. I'm so sorry, Miss Paddy, but what can I do?'

'Nothing.'

'We may talk him round a little. About the trees especially.'

They both knew Tom was never amenable to being 'talked round'. They were simply trying, with false optimism, to accustom themselves to catastrophe. In her suit and plain hat Paddy looked formidable, as formidable as Mrs Harriet, thought Paget. In spite of it he sensed her sympathy. She knew he had always done his best within his limits, which is all anyone can do. Besides, there was his bill, the still unpaid bill. A great number of the trees might go towards paying that.

In front of them on the desk had been the map of the estate, an old map, much thumbed, fragile along the fold lines. The red boundary that enclosed Bretton land had once curved arrogantly to the edge of Frilton, taking in the whole of Stenton and seven farms. Now the red was 'contracted' said Paget diplomatically, squinting through his spectacles, and was reduced almost to nothing once he had tentatively drawn in pencil round the acres the council might purchase for housing development, all of Home Farm and the rest of Roman Hill. Hobeys was called the Vineyards, further down Upper and Lower Bit, no hedge between, were labelled Sweetfields. It's true, Paddy thought, they have the best grass. She felt she ought to be comforted by this evidence of ancient change, but was not.

'We will sell that and that,' Harriet had said, stabbing her finger down, 'and perhaps that.'

'And Roman Hill?' The Paget of Harriet's day had been called Shipley, a mournful man with heavy whiskers.

'No, not Roman Hill. It's the best of the land. Its borders march with Home Farm. We'll keep Roman Hill.'

Shipley put a pencil cross by three other farms. 'It's a sad time, Mrs Bretton. A sad time.'

'I shall see all the tenants myself,' she told him. Under her summer hat her face was strong and deeply lined. 'Fanatical' thought Shipley, though what he meant by this he could not say. He had always found her magnificent, dictatorial, terrifying. She was tall and full-breasted – 'Large,' she had complained to her mother long ago. 'Just large.' It was a firm rounded largeness and with maturity had come stateliness. I could almost look William Chance in the eye, she had once thought, but not any more. She tried not to think about William. William was dead. His son Jack was there to fill his place, confident that he could. 'They think a lot of themselves,' said the village. 'All eyes and insolence every one.'

As the Chances prospered so the social hierarchy tottered. They stirred their tea with silver spoons and were invited to gentlemen's dances. They were quarry-owners, mill-owners, horse breeders. The farm was prosperous where many failed. 'Well, we work for what we have,' said William, sweating it out with his own reapers, driving fifty miles to market and back, making himself a name. Nearly all the money went back into the land and the business: new gear, new stock, new markets. 'You can't stand still,' said William, gazing over Home Farm's untidy acres. Jack was sent away to school but this only meant, as the village pointed out, that he learnt a bit of poetry with which to wheedle girls under the hedges. 'He did all right when he didn't know any poetry,' said the young Curry. By the standards of the day he could not aspire to be a gentleman yet yeoman farmer did not adequately describe him. In the year of his death the local trade directory named him 'landowner', one line under Edward Bretton who was 'principal landowner'.

The silver-topped canes, the teaspoons, the veneer of education were as nothing compared with their passion for Roman Hill. Practical, earthy men who scorned sentiment, they had a love of that house and fields and especially the steep secret hill behind it that defied logic. 'Love always defies logic,' said Harriet. The farm-house was never enlarged or altered but around it grew up a whole village of agricultural enterprise: new cart-sheds and implement houses for the latest in horse hoes and drills, another barn for the oats the horses consumed, another row of stalls.

'Those were the days,' said Jack to Paddy not long before he died.

'Those were terrible days,' Harriet told Deborah. 'As Bretton shrank so Roman Hill grew.' They were the days of the cattle plague, failed harvests, Ralph's death. Edward was fourteen when Ralph died and 'quite happy

157

doing nothing' said Harriet. Sometimes she did not know how she had survived those years, wracked with anxiety: for Bretton, for her children, for herself. Ten years, ten whole years of struggle culminating in the sale of the farms. 'One by one, then three together,' Harriet told her daughter-in-law. What she did not tell her was how she had felt, ordering, arranging, signing the papers, meeting her tenants in their cold parlours hastily dusted and aired for her reception. She did not need to say. Deborah understood. They had a growing affection for each other, these two Mrs Brettons, already shared the subtle, informal intimacy of loving friends. And all after such an unpromising start.

It was bound to be unpromising. For one thing Harriet had never trusted Edward's judgement. 'When one is prepared for the worst,' she said, 'the best comes as a shock.' Deborah was slender, shy, touchingly young – but she could laugh. 'You have a childish sense of humour,' grumbled Edward, who had none at all. 'A sense of fun,' was what Curry called it, speaking to Paddy. Harriet felt that anyway it was too late for her to share it, she had grown into an old tartar. 'I wouldn't want to be a young bride in the house with *that* old tartar,' said the village. 'The housekeeper has the keys and I leave well alone,' Harriet said tartly – and untruthfully – when Edward brought his bride back from Italy. It was certainly a challenge, though not unkindly meant. Harriet had no malice in her. It was simply her instinctive groping after the measure of this girl, this eighteen-year-old beauty. How had he found her? And where? Pisa? Ravenna? Perugia? 'I would like to go to those places,' said Harriet, who had always longed passionately for new horizons. She had not been asked to the wedding. 'How would they manage at Bretton without you?' Edward had written. In any case, by the time she received his second letter it was all over, the marriage had taken place. 'Well,' said Mrs Meikeljon to the kitchen, 'that was a health cure, that was. Go away for congestion of the lungs and come back with a wife.'

'The housekeeper has the keys,' said Harriet provokingly. 'Then we'll let her keep the house,' replied Deborah. 'I was never afraid of you, even in the beginning,' she told Harriet. 'I was so lonely I think I recognized your loneliness immediately and felt comforted.' Instead of the house she showed interest in the garden. 'The garden's the best place for you,' said Harriet. She loved to show off her plants like children. Since Deborah had lived almost all her life in Italy and in surroundings of formal greenery, stone paths and running water, she had a great deal to learn. Soon they were together every day, bent over some growing sprig. Already Deborah was obviously with child. Edward was displeased though he accepted it stoically. He could do nothing else. Still incandescent with sexual desire he found pregnancy baffling and distasteful. Though the baby was not yet a reality to him he was conscious of change and irritated by her asking him to be careful. It would never have occurred to him she might be asking for herself, not the child. Six months married, lonely, unhappy – 'living a lie,' said Deborah afterwards – she had gravitated to Harriet and the garden.

Harriet was sixty-five when the baby was born. She had driven herself to Frilton in the dogcart as it was market day and she had come home weary – 'Growing old, I suppose' – to find the midwife in residence and the servants running about like fools. 'The whole house turned upside down for nothing,' she complained. With her grand and implacable authority she rescued her daughter-in-law from the gaggle about her bed, put her into a bed-wrapper and propelled her into the garden. 'We may as well look at the border,' she said firmly, her arm round Deborah's shoulders. 'The worst thing,' she declared as they turned back towards the house an hour later, 'is to lie frightened on a bed waiting for the pains.' 'Did you do that?' 'Yes,' said Harriet, and then added with her rare smile, 'But only the first time.'

Three hours later the midwife hurried out to lay Paddy in Harriet's arms. 'She isn't a Bretton, not one inch of her,' was Harriet's reaction. Edward was only concerned with his wife and scarcely gave the baby a second glance. He was not overwhelmed by fatherhood. He vaguely supposed that in time the nursery floor would be noisy with his sons and daughters and though he cared nothing for children – beyond an heir for Bretton – it did not occur to him that anything might be done to prevent it. He simply assumed it would be so while at the same time being resentful that repeated pregnancies would seriously interfere with his enjoyment of his wife. So he only looked quickly at Paddy when she was held out for his inspection and was relieved when she was sent upstairs – 'banished' said Paddy – where no father could be expected to visit her. Harriet, however, plucked her down again at every opportunity and Deborah took her into the garden every fine day. 'You're always tired,' complained Edward. 'You really shouldn't dig about in the garden yourself. Ask the gardeners to do whatever it is you want.'

'But I like gardening,' said Deborah, and the sight of her pale oval face beneath her summer hat confused him, he thought it so lovely and so secret. It was if he had taken charge of some fairy woman, created from stardust, infinitely precious.

'Why did you marry him?' Harriet would ask.

'Because I was young and afraid. Because he was perfectly ordinary, an ordinary sort of Englishman like my father. He called every day, he was attentive, protective. I knew he would marry me at once.'

He had never met anyone like her. 'Botticelli might have used her as a model,' he said. He believed he had found perfection. He saw her as a creature of grace and light, almost a holy virgin. He was enchanted. He was . . . touched.

'Touched in the head,' said Mrs Meikeljon, watching Edward by the lily pool ten years later, petrified by grief.

'Listen,' said Tom, 'I don't want anything to do with the place. I can't think why you care about it so.'

'Because I'm not a Bretton, you mean?'

'I don't mean any such thing. Of course you're a Bretton. It never crossed my mind you weren't.' And perhaps it never had, he was indifferent to her feelings except when they affected himself.

'But I'm not, am I? I don't know who I am.'

'I suppose you might find out, if it worried you.'

They were walking up the lane from Home Farm and Tom was knocking stones out of the way with his walking stick.

'The past doesn't mean anything to you, does it?' Paddy asked.

'No. Not much. Why should it?'

It was inconceivable to her that he might not have been happy here, that all his life he had felt compelled to run away. He had had everything: attention, material wealth. Every penny the poor dwindling estate had produced went to him, at school, at college, even in the Army.

They walked on in silence. The weather must break soon, thought Paddy. There would be a great storm. Beside her in the hedge that was the boundary of Hobeys there was a rustling and fluttering of small birds. Tom took off his hat to bang it against his knee and half a dozen of them burst up out of the tangle of hawthorn and hazel with a chatter of alarm. From Roman Hill, far down in the valley, came the sudden mournful lowing of a cow.

'Nothing's changed,' said Tom. 'That's part of the trouble. Nothing changes.'

'How can you say that? Father ... Your father's dead. The house is let. The farm is going to ruin. There are new houses in the village, hardly any able-bodied men for miles, and we're all old and tired. Is that "no change"?'

'But all this,' and he looked in despair at the dusty lane between the overgrown hedge and the great garden wall. 'It's all the same as when I was a boy.'

How could it be otherwise, she wanted to ask, when he had taken every penny that might have been spent to change it? She said sourly, 'Has much changed at the Villa Ardolfo in the last hundred years? An old house on a hill between two medieval cities, you said. If it's progress you want, why choose to live in such a place?'

It was not that he had no answer to this but that he could not frame one, or not sensibly enough to deflect her scorn. He took refuge in looking sulky. In any case, he was sure Edward had suffered a crisis of will, not of cash. There had been no real reason not to improve, modernize, rebuild.

'Since Mother died ...' he began, thinking aloud. But he stopped, gazing across the park. There were the great trees he had often climbed – but not climbed as well as Paddy who once, when quite a grown-up seventeen, had pushed him out of one she said was her favourite and exclusive territory. He could not remember which it was, but the shock of hitting the hard rooty ground, the white dazzle in front of his eyes, the terrible frightening inability to draw breath – all that was as clear as if it had just happened. 'I might have broken my neck,' he said aloud.

'What?'

'Nothing's changed,' he said again. He saw no virtue in changelessness if it was the changelessness of Bretton.

162

'The Haleys might buy it,' Paddy suggested. She did not believe they would entertain such an idea for a moment.

'Oh, them,' said Tom. He was touchy on the subject of the Haleys. He had found them pleasant but still he resented them, not because they occupied his house but simply because they were living proof of Paddy's economies. Also he failed to understand how such a beautiful young woman could put up with such a self-effacing nondescript husband. Barely affected by people he had been affected instantly by Laura. He liked most women only at a distance, had no longing to possess. 'Thank God I never knew the old harridan,' he said of Harriet. There had been too many women in his childhood trying to civilize him without adding his grandmother to the misery. He had found Aunt Sarah an unsettling combination of the firm and the indulgent, while Curry had been 'cast in adamant' he said and Paddy mercurial. He had been frightened of Paddy in her pyrotechnic moods. 'Only Father ever listens to me,' he complained again and again. 'Father spoils you,' Paddy had retorted. It was true Edward spoiled and fussed and took a great deal of notice: dogs, ponies, school, fishing rods, clothes. 'But he didn't care for me any more than he cared for you,' Tom told Paddy. 'The only difference was that I was the heir to Bretton.'

'And, of course, you were his child,' said Paddy, full of new, disturbing knowledge.

They stood side by side looking over the park to the disputed house. Paddy had taken off her hat. Whenever Tom thought of her at all he thought of her hatless: up the tree, going to Frilton Hall for a dance, swooping round under the cedars like a maenad, her hair loose and flying, her bare feet leaving deep prints in the dew.

'You'd better ask the Haleys,' he said. 'Otherwise it can go brick by brick for all I care. It can be turned into a sanitorium. Or a school.'

163

Paddy thought: Why should it matter to me so much? I've spent thirty years longing to escape, haven't I? On the other hand, like being called Paddy Bretton, she was used to the house, the grounds, the daily struggle. It was like a long and unromantic marriage which nevertheless survives on shared memories and custom.

We love the things we are used to more than we know, thought Paddy.

Disappointment unsteadied Edward. Though he had dreaded the effects of pregnancy and childbirth he had not imagined Paddy would be an only child. After five years the wait for a son seemed unnaturally long and he grew suspicious. He wondered if bearing her daughter had in some way damaged Deborah, had caused some gynaecological fault.

He consulted his mother.

'I don't know,' said Harriet.

It had shaken Edward's composure to speak of such things. He did not pursue them. Besides, he thought that if indeed something was wrong, it would be Harriet who told him; Deborah was too shy.

'I would like a boy,' he said, thinking the expression of such a natural masculine ambition would excuse this sudden interest in women's internal arrangements.

'But if you don't have one,' Harriet said gently, 'you have Patricia.'

Up until now he had taken no notice of Paddy. She had been paraded regularly for his inspection but he had seen only a small dark unformed thing. Being jealous of her hold over Deborah he found it best to ignore her. He knew she had a temper for some days the atmosphere in the house was heightened by it, and he knew she could laugh immoderately because he had heard her in the garden with Harriet. He had been surprised. He did not think he had ever heard his own mother laugh before.

Another year went by and he still had no son nor any sign of one. He urged Deborah, through Harriet, to visit a specialist. He's becoming obsessed, thought Harriet, and grew a little afraid remembering Ralph and his obsession with Roman Hill. For the sake of quiet Deborah submitted herself to investigation but the result was 'nothing' said Harriet anxiously. It was as if she had a premonition of where all this might be leading. 'It ought not to lead anywhere,' she told herself. The doctors, finding nothing abnormal, earned their fees by giving confused opinions. Paddy, they said, had been premature. It had not been a difficult birth but then such cases were so prone to variable factors: the woman's age, constitution, anatomical capacity. Edward shrank. In horror he fastened on the only word that had made instant impact: he had not realized Paddy had been premature.

'Eight months babies are common enough,' Harriet said with conviction.

It was true no one had questioned it at the time. He saw Harriet puzzling why he should question it now. And why should he? But 'suspicion is a poison' said Harriet afterwards. Slow and insidious, it began its work in Edward. Small things, submerged in memory, rose to torment him, intimate things, things he could not talk about – and dates: over and over he worked out the dates.

He looked at Paddy, so unlike him, so unlike anyone. 'She's like me,' said Harriet staunchly. He felt suffocated by his monstrous suspicion. It was not possible, he thought: Deborah was not capable of such duplicity. He remembered the first time he had seen her in the garden of the villa she had made her home after her parents had died. Her black mourning clothes had seemed wicked on one so young.

'Do you ever think of San Gennaro?' he asked her one evening.

'No, I don't believe I ever do. The old Signora Borletti died. You knew that.'

'They were kind, taking you in.'

'Yes, they were always kind. Anyway, they knew I'd have to come back to England sooner or later. Sarah had offered me a home.'

'But you married me.'

'Yes, I married you.'

Then another evening he came to her late. At dinner he had been accused by Harriet of 'extravagance'. 'Things aren't as bad as all that,' he had told her. 'They're worse than ever or I'd never have spoken out,' said Harriet. After a difficult half hour he had shut himself in the library and drunk himself truculent and touchy. Was he always to be under his mother's thumb? He was almost forty. He forgot how convenient it was to leave everything to Harriet. Damn her parsimony. He would show her what extravagance was. When he finally went to bed he said, 'We ought to winter in Italy this year. You'd like that. You're too much at Bretton.'

She had been pretending to be asleep. Such subterfuge did not usually save her. Tonight he reached for her slender hunched shoulders at once, as if arguing with Harriet had given him a sense of urgency. Instead of being able to turn her to him, he found her curling tighter on herself. He could not move her. It was the first time she had refused him. It had always been her nature to surrender rather than resist.

'Deborah? What is it?'

For a long time she said nothing. Then: 'I would rather not go to Italy.'

'But you love Italy. It was your home.'

'I would rather not.'

Her voice, like her limbs, was inflexible. He grew angry.

'But why not? Why not? Is there something about Italy you'd rather forget?'

'I don't know what you mean?'

'Don't you?'

Such drama is foolish, Deborah thought afterwards, and so easily gets out of hand. Even at the time it seemed absurd, Edward shouting – or had he been simply speaking loudly? His mouth had been close to her ear, his hand still clamped to her shoulder – and the words jumbled and incoherent, dashed off, as it were, in a frenzy. The old suspicions, pushed down out of sight, rose and enraged him. She heard him say, 'She might not even be my child.' She felt strangely empty, strangely weightless. Though she lay rigid in the bed, her arms round her knees, she might have been outside, flying between the cedars. It has come, she thought. She had always known this moment must come.

'Well, is she?' demanded Edward.

'No,' said Deborah.

She could not remember how they spent the rest of the night. At one point she was sitting up in the chair, a quilt wrapped round her but conscious of freezing feet. She knew she had cried, but they had been slow, relentless tears, squeezing between her lids, running down her cheeks and falling away into her nightgown, into the quilt.

'Whose child is she?' Edward had cried. His cry, so loud that the servants might have heard, still lingered on the air at Bretton.

'Nobody you ever met. It doesn't matter,' was Deborah's weary answer.

'It doesn't matter!'

'I was very young, my parents had just died, he was my friend. I went for comfort, only comfort.'

'Comfort!' He was so enraged that he had trouble with the word, it sounded unfamiliar. He repeated it twice more under his breath, trying to come to terms with it, with what it meant. It meant that she had been possessed before. The virgin he had taken with blind triumphant satisfaction, the deepest joy he had ever felt, had not only been already used but already carrying another man's child.

'But I was seeing you every day,' he protested. 'You knew how I felt. Every day. And you were running to this . . . to this "friend" as soon as I left you.'

'No,' said Deborah. 'It wasn't like that.'

'Then what was it like? Why didn't *he* marry you?'

Her face had been drained of colour, of life. The grey eyes had been darkened by resignation, the lids reddened by tears.

'He was already married.'

'He had a wife and three children,' Deborah told Harriet. 'I'd loved him since I was a child. He was my father's godson. I was so lost, left alone for the first time. I didn't know how to pay bills, how to fill in the forms, how to talk to lawyers. The Borlettis were kind but they could only comfort me by saying I'd soon be with Sarah, that I'd soon be going "home". Only Alessandro gave me courage, made me laugh again. I thought I ought not to laugh but he said that was foolish, *they* would have wanted me to be happy. Of course he wanted me, even inexperienced girls know when a man wants them, but I don't think he would ever have . . . ever. But I wanted it too. I wanted to be in his arms, safe, desired. I wanted him to kiss me and kiss me.'

In her innocence she had supposed kisses to be everything. 'Kisses get the babies under the gooseberry bushes,' Lily told Etta when challenged. 'Just kisses?' frowned Etta.

'I didn't know I was carrying Paddy when I accepted Edward,' said Deborah. 'I thought I was ill. Nobody had ever told me anything. And it was only the first month. Edward had asked and asked, came with flowers every day, was so impatient, insistent. I thought he could give me a new life where I'd be happy again.' She had hoped for a new life far away from the guilt and confusion, the shameless longing. 'He made me happy to be shameless,' she said to Harriet. 'It was only when I left him, when I went back to the Borlettis, ate my supper, made up some story about where I had walked, what I had seen or sketched or done – it was then that I hated it all, thought of his wife and children, thought of . . . myself. It was then that I accepted Edward. I felt I had to. I felt I must get away or . . . or something terrible would happen.'

And then we grow up, she could have added, and sometimes grow wiser. In a year she realized what she had done. She had an inconsolable longing for Alessandro, a marriage to a possessive man who often frightened her, and Paddy, her dark tempestuous proof of sin. 'I didn't know what love was until she was born,' said Deborah to Harriet and her face softened at the memory, the moment she had first seen the tiny rounded face, the puckered mouth. She's mine, I made her, she had told herself in a triumph of creation. The soft gold October afternoons at San Gennaro were pushed far far down, were locked away. Paddy was something she had achieved entirely alone.

Unfortunately she still achieved nothing with Edward's help. Though the sight of her still roused his possessiveness and so his passion, as if the sexual act were positive confirmation of ownership, no child followed these now infrequent but stormy encounters. He accused her of 'taking measures', whatever they might be. He scarcely knew himself. 'What do you mean?' asked Deborah. He said he thought Mrs Murray might have 'arranged' something. Girls had crept down to the hovel by the sheepsplash for things to be 'arranged' long ago.

'What do you think I am?' cried Deborah. 'How could you even think it?' But he no longer knew what he thought she was, except that she was beautiful and elusive and false, and that he could not give her up. And she, without the steely core that both Harriet and Paddy possessed, would see him standing by the lily pool, dejected, remote, and would think of his disappointment, the shock of which still drove him to such bitter statements and other, minor brutalities. Dissolved in guilt she would go to him, try to make peace.

There was no real peace but at last there was Tom.

'We'll have a ball,' Edward said.

'It may not be a boy after all.'

'It will be a boy.'

He willed it. It would be a boy and legitimate. In his mind he no longer saw Paddy as legitimate nor even as his responsibility, but he would not court scandal by repudiating her.

Ill and desperate, Deborah willed it too. 'Harriet, Harriet,' she cried when the pain went on and on. 'Harriet, I need you.'

'Poor dear,' said the midwife. It was a bad sign, calling on the dead.

'You have a little brother,' said the doctor to Paddy whom he found at the foot of the stairs. She had run wild all day, ignored, forgotten.

'May I see? May I go up and see?'

'Not now. In the morning.'

In the morning Deborah had still been in a stupor of weariness. She seemed so thin that she was nothing but delicate bones overlaid by white skin. She did not hold the baby as Paddy had been expecting. He lay in his crib by the window, a snuffling downy crumpled thing.

'His name is Thomas Ralph Harcourt Bretton,' said the midwife. Such a mouthful it seemed for such a sorry scrap. She smiled encouragingly at Paddy but the child hung back from the cradle. In another moment she was by the bed, her face pushed into the crook of

Deborah's arm, her long black plait flung over Deborah's breast.

It was the last time she was to see Deborah alive.

14

THE WEATHER CHANGED. Great swathes of summer rain hid the woods in mist. The unthatched ricks were covered with tarpaulins. The young cattle, sobering with maturity, steamed at the gate to Hobeys.

Laura cancelled a tennis party.

'That's the second time,' she told Hugh. 'There's nothing for it. I shall have to go and stay with Madge.'

'Why?' asked Hugh. 'Does she have better weather?'

'Not at Larter House. In France. She asked me down any time. Remember?'

He did not remember. He knew he scarcely heard a word Madge said. Should he perhaps have listened more attentively? He said quietly, 'But you don't want to go to France, do you? There's Henrietta. And besides, think of the expense.'

'It won't be any more expensive than a week in Brighton. Madge doesn't charge her friends to stay.'

The tone of her voice stung him, but he was stung so often that he bore it patiently, 'like an old donkey' he thought when he cared to be analytical.

'How long would you be gone?'

'Until the end of September? I don't know.'

'And what about Etta?'

Afterwards, as usual, he took refuge in the garden.

Under the cedars the rain was only a faint whispering.

He stood a while in their resiny damp shelter, smoking a cigarette. The path through the old iron gate to the rose garden caught his eye. He felt drawn there irresistibly. He felt it was a secret place and, like the secret places of his childhood, held the possibility of consolation. He pushed open the gate, brushing past the lavender hedges and coming to the round basin and the fountain that never played.

'That never has run,' Bushey had replied to his question the first day he had explored this lost corner.

'But it must have once. Look, the water runs out of the faun's mouth and there must be some device for draining it into the channel.' He had parted the fern fronds and the weeds. 'Where does it go?'

Bushey had said nothing.

'I'd like to see it working again,' said Hugh. 'It must have been pleasant sitting here listening to the water.'

A week later: 'Any progress?'

'I didn't know for sure you wanted it touched,' said Bushey.

A man with no cunning may sometimes recognize cunning in another. 'I asked you to look into it,' Hugh said sternly.

'Oh, I *looked*.'

'And can it be mended?'

'I wouldn't like to say.'

Hugh had fetched a spade and investigated for himself. There was, after all, nothing complicated about it. The fountain had simply been disconnected from the spring-fed stream that supplied it – which Bushey must have known. 'Well, I did it, didn't I?' Bushey might have told him.

'Stop the damn thing running,' Edward had commanded. 'Stop it. Now. Today.' In the weeks following Deborah's death he had been unrelievedly passionate – 'unstable' said Paget – and every action, statement, even movement was imbued with this passion. 'How long can a man go on being in a temper?' asked Mrs Meikeljon, suffering the rejection of dish after dish.

'It wouldn't take more than an hour or two to reconnect it,' Hugh told Bushey. 'The pipe's bent though. See,' and he showed Bushey Bushey's own handiwork as if explaining a technicality to Man Friday. 'It looks as if,' he finished, after a great deal about rate of flow and diameters, 'someone intended to make sure it never worked again.'

'Yes,' said Bushey enigmatically.

The pipe still waited to be bent true. Blast the old rogue, thought Hugh. Hadn't he been given clear enough orders? He watched the rain falling into the basin. This was a magical place. He could sit here with Laura in the long evenings if . . . But he was never sure of Laura.

He was aware of getting wet. He left the rose garden and walked on, coming out by the curved end of Paddy's border where the old seat was half-smothered in its arbour by the dripping honeysuckle. The smell of wet earth and grass and leaves came to him. He dug his hands in his pockets, feeling the water running on his chin, and went on between the yew hedges. In front was the gate to the vegetable garden, Bushey's kingdom. He hesitated. It was Sunday. Bushey would not be there. He went in.

If it had not been for Bushey, whose devious procrastination he had met in men under his command in the trenches, he would have come here more often. He enjoyed its other-worldliness, its separateness. The house was an eighteenth-century house looking out across an eighteenth-century park while behind was a nineteenth-century garden, bold and romantically intimate by turns. But this place, sealed in by its high walls, could have been the physic garden of a medieval monastery. Now, in the rain, he felt obscurely that he was on a valedictory visit, that here was something he would shortly have to give up – and he found he did not want to give it up. He recognized the first vague internal shrinking that was the forerunner of grief, the realization of loss.

'Why don't you come in the hothouse?' came Paddy's voice as he wandered distractedly along the wall beside the figs and apricots. 'You can steam dry, if that's not a contradiction in terms.'

She was in an old raincoat, a man's coat, and a sou'wester. Rain dripped off her nose. In one hand was a trowel, in the other a pair of scissors. He followed her into the ruinous glasshouses reluctantly. As the peculiar sour warmth engulfed him he wondered why he had never ventured here before. How much more of Bretton had he missed?

'Grapes,' he said, astounded. There was a whole wall of grapes.

'Grapes, melons, more figs, tomatoes,' said Paddy. He might have seen for himself if he kept walking and looked about, but he stood perfectly still and his eyes seemed glazed. 'Like a sleepwalker' Paddy told Curry. The rain hushed against the glass and blew away and then, falling more furiously, drummed down on them. Some came triumphantly through the broken panes. Paddy swiped off the sou'wester and shook it.

'You shouldn't have come out without a coat,' she said.

'I didn't think about it.' He glanced down at the wet sleeves of his jacket. 'I'd forgotten it was raining.'

'Weather means nothing to townspeople,' Mrs Prince had asserted, initiating Babs Potter into the mysteries of cream caramel, a task akin to Sisyphus's with the stone. Paddy thought that Hugh would not be wandering in the garden in the rain if his mind had not been on other things. On Laura? Several Sundays she had seen him strolling about, gloomy and preoccupied. 'It isn't natural,' was Lily's opinion in the kitchen. 'Living here, working there, leaving Mrs H alone so much.' 'And no more children,' added Mrs Prince. 'Children are a great steadier.'

Hugh watched the rain running down the glass. What could he find to say to this odd woman?

'I had a letter from Mr Paget yesterday,' he said at last. 'He says your brother is definitely going to sell up.'

'Yes.'

He turned slightly. She looked pale and tired, he thought. What had been the truth about the old man's will? Again the shadow of loss to come fell on him, but this time the loss was Paddy's as well as his own.

'I'll be sorry to leave.'

'Don't worry. I'm sure Tom won't want to wrestle with your tenancy agreement. There are only a few months to run and he could never sell the house before the winter.'

Will he ever sell it at all? Hugh wondered. 'If I were a wealthy man . . .' he began. He felt he ought to have said, 'If I didn't have an expensive wife . . .' But why would he want Bretton? What had put it into his head to even consider it?

'I mean . . .' he tried again.

'You meant to be consoling. You meant me to think: Who knows, there may still be a happy ending. Well, I doubt it.' She put up the hand with the trowel to dash the raindrops from her nose. 'I thought I hated this place. All my life I've ached to be free of it. And now . . . now when I find I don't even belong here . . .'

The rain fell with more urgency. The glass had steamed over. Hugh suddenly took Paddy's elbow and led her to the ancient seat under the vine on the wall. Several of its wooden slats were missing. They sat side by side, uncomfortably, waiting for the downpour to be over.

'How could you not belong?' he asked.

She told him.

He felt burdened by her secret. He felt helpless. Brought up to be polite and attentive to women but always to keep his distance, he could offer no real comfort. He looked at her long dirtied hands lying in her lap and wondered, if he covered them with his own, if she would misconstrue his intention.

'Is that Etta?' Paddy asked, peering out through the streaming panes to where a small shape was flitting beyond the hedges.

'She shouldn't be out in this,' said Hugh.

There was the scrape of small running feet on the gravel. Etta reached the shelter of the hothouse with a last breathless spurt and burst in before she had properly seen who was there. She had expected Paddy and Bushey, Paddy and Tom Bretton, even Paddy and Johnny Chance, but not Paddy and her own father in a companionable fug between the vine leaves. On the grating stood a basket of figs and eggs, eccentrically mingled. 'I love fig trees,' said Paddy. Like yews and olives, even the great cedars, they promised renewal, eternal life. 'But not even trees live for ever,' insisted the pragmatic Etta.

Now, gazing at the basket, she said, 'I did so want to feed the hens. I ran all the way to the farm but you weren't there.'

'Etta, you're all wet,' interrupted Hugh unnecessarily.

'Well, it's raining.'

'But you shouldn't be running about in it.'

He has no idea, Paddy thought, what to say to his own child. In a moment he would ask if Lily knew where she was and Etta would say no and that would complete a pointless and banal conversation. Yet how alike they were. For the first time she noticed that his face, which she had thought tanned, was massively freckled like his daughter's. They shared too the same trick of considering some problem with their heads tilted slightly, their lips puckered up. Etta's sturdiness was Hugh's, and probably her practical, sensitive nature. Paddy wondered why she had told him about Deborah and Edward. 'Such old secrets,' Paget had said encouragingly. 'After so long they should be left decently covered. There's no need for anyone to know, my dear, no need at all.'

'You know,' Hugh was saying, 'your old rogue Bushey hasn't the least intention of tackling the fountain.'

'Tackling the fountain?'

'The fountain in the rose garden. I want it mended.' It was the voice of the Hugh Haley who had sent all those poor devils out to cut the wire or whatever was necessary. Like Sergeant Tuffnel Paddy had the wit to recognize someone living on his nerves.

'How enterprising of you! Nobody else has ever thought of touching it in thirty years. Etta, your father's never been in here before. Why don't you show him the lemon trees?'

She watched them go, side by side but carefully separated, like strangers, to where the lemons hung like Christmas tree decorations amid the dark foliage.

Johnny Chance rode by on the new young chestnut mare just as Paddy had reached the Lodge. On seeing her, the animal gave a spectacular series of bucks, and it was some minutes before she could be calmed and induced to stand still.

'She does it whenever she sees something she doesn't care for,' said Johnny nonchalantly. 'She hopes to buck me off and make a run for home.'

'She's not up to your weight.'

'She's a lady's horse.'

'With those manners?'

'Ah, she'll be cured of all that in no time.'

The mare chewed angrily at her bit. The hair on her neck was curled with sweat.

'If anyone asks me about her,' said Paddy, 'I shall keep a diplomatic silence.'

The rain, which had left huge sheets of water in the road and battered down the last of the standing corn, had blown away to only a few drops. Paddy looked damp and slightly disreputable in her old clothes. Had he ever glimpsed her in anything fashionable or new? Only as a girl in the newest of safety habits, boots polished, hair immaculately confined.

'Would you ride her for me if I put up a lady's saddle?' he asked suddenly, leaning down towards her. 'I'd value your opinion.'

'I'm too old for such risks.'

'When I've finished with her she'll be suitable for an invalid.'

His grin was a challenge. The mare flung up her head and tried to sidle.

'She looks as if she'd make invalids, not carry them.'

Johnny said, 'I never thought you were a coward.'

She smiled up at him and it was a wide, mischievous smile.

'I hope I'm not,' she said. 'I'll ride your mare. But if she bucks once you can pay me five guineas.'

'Done,' said Johnny Chance.

In 1843 Bretton was not in the back of beyond. Very little of England was anything other than remote. 'Remote from what?' asked Etta when she was older and had travelled a little. 'How do you know Bretton isn't the centre of the universe?' In the summer of 1843 it was certainly the centre of attention. The Harcourts spoke of it at every meal and inbetween.

'Harriet could hardly have done better unless she'd married a title,' said an unmarried aunt.

'Such a fine house. And the railway is promised in

Frilton,' said Sophie, thinking of all the advantages this might bring to Harriet.

'On the other hand, it is all a little sudden. Why, three months ago Harriet had never heard of Mr Bretton.'

'There is really nothing to wait for,' said Sophie, and added as an afterthought, 'Young people these days like to hurry.'

Harriet, even in a daze, poked and pulled into her half-made wedding dress, poked and pulled out of it, measured, remeasured, harried, hounded, showered with breathless good wishes, felt that Ralph was not much given to hurrying, that there was something . . . He was irresistibly ardent – 'all day and every day' remembered Harriet. He kissed her fingers, her palms, he stroked her hair. She forgot herself in his urgency, gave herself up to his passion. 'No one had kissed me before,' she said, 'only on the cheek.' She was twenty-five, tall, angular, slow-maturing. In all her wedding finery she had a regal bearing. 'But I was really just young and afraid,' said Harriet.

The photograph of Ralph that stood on Harriet's desk to the end of her life showed a handsome man of forty-five. 'He *was* handsome. He had the Bretton looks,' said Harriet. He was tall and had the Bretton bony face, deeply sculptured, and the thick fair hair. It was Fan who inherited the hair but Mary who received the temperament, sulky and easily dissatisfied. Sometimes, on her way past to some trifling duty, Harriet would pause by her desk and stare at the picture – but she never smiled at it.

'Did the bells ring at your wedding, Mama?' Mary had asked once when she was quite little.

'Yes, of course they did,' said Harriet. She would never forget that first step out into the sunshine on Ralph's arm, the clash of the bells above. At long last it seemed she came to the surface after a strange, prolonged immersion, and with her, above the family hysteria, the welter of preparations, the letters, the gifts, the clamouring of her own heart, came the question she had been trying to ask herself for days. What have I done? she thought. What have I done?

15

~~~~

LAURA'S DINNER PARTY was not a success. 'I never thought it would be,' she said afterwards. By then she was aware she had asked all the wrong people, had ignored Hugh's gentle warnings to her own disadvantage, and knew that Johnny Chance had no intention of making love to her.

'You shouldn't have asked him,' Hugh said. 'I told you, there was some trouble between Bretton and Roman Hill.'

'What trouble?'

'I've no idea.'

'Must they feud for generations in the country?' sighed Laura.

For all that Hugh was grateful Johnny had been there. He found him easy to talk to, cheerful, informed. He was aware that he too had shared the horrors of the war, that he too had been irritated when the parson had gone on and on about the hardships faced by civilians, the food shortages, the fear of Zeppelins.

Paddy had worn dark green. 'The colour of life,' said Lily to Etta as she brushed out her hair before bed. 'I thought green was unlucky,' said Etta dubiously. But it could never be unlucky if Paddy wore it; it must be magical: the colour of the trees. Yes, the colour of life. The dress itself was plain, cut down from one Paddy had had before the war. The before-the-war version had touched the floor and had a high neck and sleeves. This one, transformed by Miss Squires' painstaking hand, had a scoop neck and no sleeves and ended just above the ankle. Etta, who had peeped through the banisters, had never seen Paddy so revealed before. 'Bare,' said Etta. 'Like Mother.' But in reality it was a very suitable dinner dress for a middle-aged spinster, even a little conservative. 'I may be many things,' said Paddy, 'but I hope I'm not conservative.' So though the dress was decent she wore it tonight with a sort of defiance, as if it were not. Maycroft, who had never seen her collarbones or the warm bare skin of her back until tonight, remembered the much younger Paddy under the mistletoe and all his crushed hopes, his half-formulated desires. There was no comparison with Laura Haley of course. Even in youth Paddy had never been ethereal. 'Or charming' said Maycroft. Still, unlike Laura Paddy was even now, theoretically, obtainable. Despite their rancorous exchanges over the old man's burial, he could see her as somehow vulnerable, a difficult woman and unpredictable but perhaps open to offers. She would not, however, make much of a parson's wife.

'Paddy's in a mood,' Grace Paulley whispered to her husband. What kind of mood, God only knew. Had it to do with the fact that the Paulleys had not dined at Bretton since before the 'engagement'? Did Paddy, as well as they, see Philip sitting at the long table where he had sat so often in the years before he became a suitor – and therefore 'unsuitable' said Paddy? He had been everything Paddy was not: stable, gentle and yes, conservative. 'We were complementary,' Paddy told Grace.

'A woman shouldn't bully a man as you bully that poor boy,' said Jack Chance under the elms in Hobeys.

'I don't. I don't bully him. That's absurd. I love him.'

'You bully, he bends the knee. He's not strong enough for you.'

'But I love him.'

'You do now. But will you next week, or next year?'

No, it would never have done, thought Grace. Across the room she saw Paddy apparently listening intently to something Elinor Barnes was saying. Her mass of hair was very carelessly pinned up. She had about her an air of wildness, as if she were tethered by only the frailest strings of convention. 'Well, she *is* wild,' Grace had often said. 'There are two Paddys, one sober and efficient, one drunk and disorderly.'

'I'm a difficult character,' Paddy had told Philip in the long grass of Hobeys. 'That's what Aunt Sarah used to say. And Mrs Meikeljon always insisted the stars were in collision when I was born, or in opposition, or shooting backwards or something.'

'I thought you believed we made our own fate?' He was tracing the long curve of her neck, her smooth young shoulder. He would have liked to do this with his lips but was afraid to.

'We do. Of course we do. But perhaps . . .'

'Don't start being profound,' said Philip. 'It's too nice a day.'

We were never profound, thought Paddy afterwards. We lived from touch to touch, from kiss to kiss. Sometimes we hardly spoke. The whole world took on different colours.

'How dare you say it isn't love!' she accused Jack, inspecting his young hunters in the cool of the early morning.

'I never said it wasn't love. I only said be careful.'

'We *shall* be married. If we have to wait till I'm twenty-one.' As the grey dipped his head to lip at her fingers she saw Jack's face, closed and critical – 'doubting' she remembered when it was all over. 'You don't like him much, do you?' she asked in a subdued voice, like a small child.

'Of course I like him. He's a decent boy. He's just not . . .'

'What isn't he?' Her temper was rising again. He had turned to pull gently at the ears of the bay colt and did not answer. 'Love endures,' she continued. 'Love finds a way. Phil will find a way.' Her stock of poetry had until now been mostly martial or equine but she had read, 'Love endures vicissitude and season as the grass.' 'Yes,' she said approvingly, 'there's nothing tougher than grass.' It grew again where the cattle churned the gateway and where the hunters scored the gaps and narrow headlands. But later, to herself, she said wearily, 'There were too many vicissitudes after all. Or else it wasn't love.' It was love, she thought as year followed year, but love can't solve all the problems. Even if it endures like grass it can't do that. And now I shall never know if anything would have survived, anything at all.

Mrs Barnes said, 'Oh, it was wicked to make it into a hospital.'

'I can't imagine what it must have been like,' said Laura thankfully.

'It was painted pea green,' Maycroft told her.

'And brown, I bet,' said Hugh. 'It was supposed to be resistant to attack by army boots.'

'There was a sister . . .' began Maycroft, reminded. 'She almost hated the patients, they dirtied the ward, looked untidy. If she had had her way she would have swept them up with a dustpan and brush and just had empty beds with clean starched linen. Do you remember?' and he turned appealingly to Paddy.

'Yes,' said Paddy. 'I remember.'

'That woman should be murdered in her sleep,' an infantry captain had whispered to a nurse as she bent over his dressings. For a while the whole ward was mutinous; there was a real chance someone might do it – not all the men were confined to bed. And then came the day Paddy returned, eyes like slate under the brim of a terrible old hat. She had not seen the pea green until this moment but she had just come from the Lodge where her father had informed her of untold vandalism.

'No visitors are allowed,' said the Sister, bearing down.

'I'm not a visitor,' said Paddy. 'I'm Miss Bretton.'

'Do I have to repeat myself?'

'Not unless you want to look foolish. I'm Miss Bretton. I live here.'

The voice was crisp. The hat, instead of being dowdy and out of shape, might have been a knight's casque. The Sister fell back.

'Routed,' said the captain with gratitude. 'The enemy in retreat. Long live Miss Bretton.'

I can hear Father, thought Etta, silently descending the stairs on her bottom, her face pressed momentarily between each rail. And that's Mother laughing. And Mr Paulley rumbling. The drawing-room door was open a little. If she stayed seven stairs up and waited . . . she could see . . . a green shape: Paddy? A bangled arm: Laura? Silver lace: Mrs Barnes. She thought: I wonder what they all talk about?

Curry came from the kitchen with a coffee pot. Her beady eye turned upward. 'Why aren't you in bed?'

'I wanted to see.'

'There isn't anything to see.' She delivered the coffee, came out, closed the door. 'Go straight up,' she said, 'or I'll send Lily after you with the carpet beater.'

Etta curled her cold toes, still sitting on the seventh stair.

'Hello Hettyetta.' Johnny Chance had come into the hall. In evening clothes he was 'transformed' said Grace. Etta only saw he was different from the boyish Johnny of the tennis court, the horse-leather-cigarette-open-air-smelling Johnny of the farm and stables, the Johnny who could make ponies kneel down at a touch.

'Can't you sleep?'

'I wanted to . . . see. I wanted to see Miss Bretton's dress.'

'It's green. It's very nice.'

The light fell on his red head. Etta looked down between the rails at the wiry hair, waving and thick. She was always noticing things about him, intimate things: the way the hairs grew into his nape, the freckles on his hands, on his high nose. She would have been able to describe him more accurately than her own father. 'He has white teeth,' she had informed Laura. 'Good heavens,' Laura had protested. 'Why should you be interested in such things?'

He came to sit on the bottom stair, gazing up at her. 'You look rather sad,' he said.

'Yes.'

'Is it something you can talk about?'

She hesitated. 'I don't want to go away,' she said.

'Darling,' cried Laura, hurrying into the hall. 'You should be asleep. Run up, there's a good girl. I'll ring for Lily.' She tried to keep the irritation from her voice. This was just the sort of dinner party, she thought, to be interrupted by children in nightgowns. Conversation was prickly, the food had been far from Mrs Prince's best. 'And I asked the wrong people,' she admitted. Only Mrs Barnes and her leggy, rather belligerent young daughter Amelia, invited to make up the numbers, could be said to be an unqualified success.

And Tom Bretton.

'I do so like your brother,' Laura told Paddy.

'Oh, Tom Bretton's perfectly charming in his own way. Perhaps not very interested in women.' Laura glanced at Hugh's shadowy face behind her own in the mirror. 'What do you think?'

'About Bretton? Not much.'

'But as for that man Chance, d'you know what he was doing? He was talking to Etta on the stairs. She had her nightdress on and her hair all over her face.'

'I didn't know Etta had come down. It was rather late, wasn't it?'

'Lily had put her to bed once.'

'I expect she wanted to see the house lit up. It has a certain atmosphere when all the candelabra are brought out.'

'Candles!' exclaimed Laura. 'And I suppose you think oil lamps are romantic too.' She was as indignant as if she had to clean them herself. 'Hugh, this is such a primitive place. What about . . .' She smoothed cream on her face. Was he mellow tonight, or defensive? He had seemed to enjoy the dinner. 'Hugh, what about moving back to London?'

He had been standing just inside the door, having come to say his usual distant goodnight. If she had looked more closely in the mirror she would have seen how his face grew suddenly closed and pinched.

'It's all right for you,' she continued. 'You're only here at weekends. You see it at its best. You miss all the dramas.'

'What dramas?'

'Oh, that wretched stove for one thing. Day in, day out, there's always a problem. Look at the meal tonight. And then there's that dreadful Potter girl. Mrs Murray thinks she's expecting a baby. Besides . . . besides, we really are miles from anywhere.'

'But you wanted to be miles from anywhere. You knew it was – what did you call it? – primitive. You knew there were candles and a fifty-year-old range. Anyway, there's Frilton. Isn't that somewhere?'

'You know it isn't. It's a wretched little country town. The shops sell pig troughs and knitted under-wear.' She bit her lips. 'Oh Hugh, it's just . . .' She rose, came towards him. He saw her breasts outlined by the light, the despised candlelight. Four years ago, three, he might have put out a tentative hand. Now he stood waiting. 'I get so bored,' she said. 'I thought people would come and visit.'

The evening had disappointed her. She had expected too much of 'conservative rustics' she said to Hugh. The parson had told humourless clerical stories, Frank Paulley had talked bulls, and while the men drank their port the women had worried the subjects of jazz, hemlines and farmworkers' wages. Through all this Paddy Bretton had remained aloof, tall, straight and slender. 'Like a cypress,' said Laura in disgust. 'And about as much use.' Johnny Chance too had failed miserably to live up to her expectations. He had not avoided her eye but met it with icy imperturbability. As the evening had progressed she had grown cold and quiet, leaving Hugh to play the amiable host, something he often did well if she let him. At some point she had been shocked by a chilling insight: only among her own friends could she really shine.

'Hugh, I need to get away for a while. I can't have Dot and Beatrice and the rest up here as often as I'd like. They swore they'd come but now they insist it's too far, oh, any excuse . . . And then Madge in France. If we're staying here till next year I really do think I'll have to go and spend a week or two with Madge.'

'You were only saying the other day Bretton was *our* house and you were tired of Paddy Bretton coming and going as if she still lived here.'

'Well, of course. It *is* our house.'

'But you don't want it any more.'

'It's not . . . It's just not what I hoped it might be.'

Five months, thought Hugh. Five short months and she's already tired of it. It had happened so often before that he was not surprised but this time he did not feel resigned. This time he knew what he wanted and it was to stay, to stay at Bretton and give up his London job. I shall be buried in the park, he thought, beside the old man.

He smiled at the thought.

'Are you all right?' asked Laura.

'Perfectly. Look,' he said, 'do what you think best. Go to France if you must.' He leaned forward and kissed her forehead. 'Goodnight.'

Then he turned and went out.

Paddy was at the end of the long border. Her face looked bleached in the moonlight.

'Tom, don't sell out to speculators. Anything but that.'

They had been on their way back to the Lodge but had somehow drifted through the gardens instead.

'Why not?' he asked. 'Why not sell to speculators?'

'You could wait until the spring.'

'I'm going back to Italy at the end of this week.'

'I know, but that doesn't mean things have to be done in a hurry.'

They moved over the grass, he in front, she far behind. He could hear the faint whisper of her dress. He did not remember the original from before the war though tonight, on the way to dinner, she had joked about its age. He only knew it was her colour – green.

'You beast. You ... you pagan beast,' he had cried when she had pushed him out of the tree and he had looked up and seen her oval face with its frame of heavy black hair peering through the leaves at him. Pagan had been a new word and he liked it but after he had applied it to Paddy he rarely used it again, it reminded him of her elemental fury, her long, strong, pushing hands.

'Can you tell me where I'm to live?' she asked suddenly.

'Live?' He had not thought of it. 'In the Lodge, I

suppose. Why not? Afterwards you'll have enough to buy a cottage in the village. Anything. Whatever you like.'

'I don't know what I'd like. I don't even know who I am.'

'Don't talk rot, Pat. You're my sister.'

The green dress looked black in the moonlight. 'I ought to be in mourning still,' she had said earlier in the evening.

'All that mourning nonsense. Take no notice of it.'

'I don't.'

'But you said . . .'

'I just meant they will all stare and think: green. Green! And then they'll shake their heads and tell themselves that I always was headstrong and contrary. And Grace will be glad all over again that I didn't marry Philip.'

Reaching the drive and the rhododendrons Tom said, 'You know what you said about Grace Paulley. About Philip. You didn't really mean it, did you?'

'Well, do you think I should have married him?'

'Yes, of course I do. I always did. But I was eight at the time, nine – I don't remember. I didn't have a say.'

'Well, nobody else was in favour.'

Tom gave an uneasy laugh. 'Philip must have been.'

'Not even Philip in the end,' said Paddy, 'though I was too selfish to see it. And he, poor Phil, he didn't have the courage to tell me.'

16

THE HALEYS DID not quarrel over Laura's decision to go to France. Laura was ready for a fight but Hugh took himself off to mend the fountain in the rose garden. His indifference was so marked that for once she was briefly distracted from her preoccupation with self. 'Henrietta,' she asked, 'where is your father?' She brooded a little, wondering, but after all she did not bother to go down across the lawn and through the gate to confront him. She ordered Lily to help her pack.

Hugh cut his hand and came to be bandaged. It was Curry who sat him down and bound him up as if he had been a small child. He was charmingly grateful, nursing the injury while she made a cup of tea. 'But in the kitchen!' murmured an affronted Mrs Prince to Bushey on the back step. 'Really, he ought to stay out of my kitchen.'

'I'll get it working again somehow,' said Hugh.

Curry put down the large willow cup and saucer. It was strong dark tea, kitchen tea. 'Old Mr Bretton ordered it to be broken.'

His blue eyes lifted, startled. 'Why?'

'He had it built for his wife. When she died . . .'

'I see.'

No, you don't, thought Curry. 'Curry, what's Father having done to the fountain?' Paddy had asked. 'Bushey won't tell.'

'It reminds him.'

'But Mother loved it. She would have hated it all spoiled.'

Paddy was as stunned by grief as Edward was enraged. She grew thin, she grew silent, she grew 'awkward' said Sarah. For years she avoided the rose garden. Only when she became head gardener – 'Who else was there?' asked Paddy – did she venture to open its gate at last.

'Well,' said Hugh, looking deep into his overpowering tea. 'You can't go on breaking things for ever. Now and then you have to mend them.'

'Sentimental nonsense!' said Curry afterwards to the piled rubbish in the Piggery. 'Thank God I was never sentimental.'

The Piggery was a ferment of disturbed objects. 'What's this awful object?' was Lily's constant cry as she hauled yet another oddity from the mass. Hugh had given orders that the Piggery should be cleared. It would make an excellent room for coats, boots, dogs. He had an idea at the back of his mind, scarcely acknowledged, that he might go shooting. And in any case 'The Brettons will want it cleared before the sale,' he said airily to Curry, who pursed up her lips and made no reply – no audible reply.

In the end, of course, that same day Laura was packing and Hugh cut his hand, Paddy had to be called from the Lodge to pass sentence.

'I'm sorry,' said Hugh. 'I never realized there was so much . . . well, family stuff. I thought it was just old tennis nets and broken croquet sticks.'

They gazed bleakly at the heaps. 'It's all right,' Paddy said consolingly, 'there's nothing important.'

An hour later she was still sitting on the bricks reading a dance card of 1870 – Fan's, before she 'escaped' – and surrounded by odd gloves, letters and bills of sale. In the same box as the card was a photograph, very early, horribly faded, of Harriet on the brown mare she had bought from Joseph Chance. For a moment Paddy did not recognize her and then the faint resemblance to the oil portrait over the fireplace in the blue drawing room struck her, that wedding portrait of Harriet: oval-faced, modest, roses in her lap. Had the older Harriet looked at that younger self with a wry smile? Or had the young Harriet smiled wryly too but been severely rebuked by the artist and smoothed – in paint, at least – into conventional and demure sweetness? Here on the brown mare she was the real Harriet, determined even if uncertain. They would not take risks but they would finish the hunt together and having followed their own line, the mare blowing and Harriet pink-cheeked with exertion and relief.

'I gave up hunting when I had the children,' she said, but she still pottered about the lanes on the brown mare, young Johnnie Dack the groom in attendance. Once, at the watersplash in the village, the mare had behaved abominably, trying to lie down. Johnnie's powerful encouragement to 'Hit her, mum. Hit her!' brought all the village women to their doors. Harriet, vanishing in a welter of spray, furious squawking ducks, pig-headed horseflesh, was lost to dignity and control. Her hair was coming down – the peril of the horsewoman with a fashionable hat – and to crown everything she could feel her saddle slipping.

Another horse entered the ford. A voice said, 'Keep her head up, the temperamental madam,' and then a hand reached for the bridle above the bit and led them out.

It was the most difficult thank you of her life, Harriet remembered. Her hair had fallen down her back, her habit was soaked, her hands were trembling. She was sitting crookedly because of the saddle and had dropped her whip. The village was enchanted. It was the first time they had seen her discomfited and it would be, though they had no means of knowing it, the last. All in all she had managed quite famously: there was nothing so cantankerous as a quiet horse set on mischief.

'If you don't mind,' said William Chance, 'I shall ride with you to your gate.'

She did not mind. She did not look round to see if Johnnie minded. He should have rescued her himself. On the long mile to Bretton she scarcely spoke. She replied automatically to William's polite enquiries: her husband, her children, the harvest. He was not interested in any of them, she thought afterwards. Was she mistaken in thinking he was interested in her? She recalled her walk down Hobeys at the haymaking, his curt good day, his look. Now they ambled along the dusty lane side by side, the wind fretting all the loose strands of her hastily twisted-up hair and drying out her habit. The mare was tranquil and resigned. There was nothing they said to each other which could not have been overheard by Johnnie, three lengths behind, or even Ralph.

The girl with the sweet smile and the roses would not have tempted any Chance; they judged their women as they did their horses and required honesty and courage, a bold heart. But Harriet losing her temper in the watersplash had been a revelation. 'You're very alike, you and the mare,' William could have told her. 'Quiet and contained, only occasionally rebellious, but unstoppable once your blood is up.' Perhaps he remembered her counting down the guineas on his father's table.

'I miss her,' said Paddy, and put down the photograph.

She pulled out a broken tennis racquet: Fan's. Had Fan missed her mother, tucked away in her Devon rectory? 'I loved my children,' said Harriet, but severity had been the custom of the day. She had not been thought strange in keeping her distance. 'But I loved them,' she said. So deeply did she love them when they were little, her two adorable girls, that she was afraid lest she spoil them or, possessive, keep them in unnatural bondage. 'You see, I had nothing else to love,' she said. With that brown mareish determination she bent her energies on Bretton, the village, the farm. 'You never played with us,' Fan protested, grown up but still stung by old omissions. 'You never had the time.'

'Parents didn't "play" with their children in those days,' Harriet replied. 'You had your nurse, your governess.'

How she ached to play with them, hold them, read to them. She read them the Bible for a while, an accepted 'recreation', but gave up, longing instead to read Robin Hood and nursery rhymes. She sent books up to the nursery time after time, all the books she wished they might listen to sitting on her knee, but when she saw them she was remote and magisterial, gravely inspecting their small nails and neatly brushed heads and asking them their abc 'like a text-book' she said.

Fan had broken the racquet playing with Augustus Cummings. Being Fan, with all her mother's temper but none of her self-containment, she threw it on the lawn and refused to borrow another and continue. She was tired of tennis, and of Augustus, whom her mother was apparently encouraging. 'Well, *I* won't encourage him,' said Fan, and instead persecuted him quite abominably, escaping his company when she could and involving him in dreary domestic routine when she could not: 'You can take these vases to the vestry for me, can't you, Mr Cummings?' To make matters worse she and Mary had once, as small children, had a dog called Augustus, a woolly unappealing dog whose rule in the nursery had been brief. This was the source of many private jokes between the sisters which poor Cummings suspected but could not comprehend.

Under the racquet was a stiff old bag full of cricket stumps and misshapen balls. There was also a tin box, very small, with . . . 'Wedding cake!' said Paddy, astonished. 'A piece of wedding cake.' It had not so much gone mouldy as been mummified. 'But why in a tin?' asked Paddy. 'Why hidden away?'

'Why not eaten?' asked Curry, coming in and going away again.

'We must give them our congratulations,' said Harriet. 'It would look so odd not to. This everlasting animosity is childish.'

'Then you must do as you like. I shan't set foot in that house,' said Ralph.

Harriet had herself driven down in the carriage. She would have preferred to walk down Hobeys in order to 'be ready' she said, but this ordeal had to be endured by the book. She carried no present, she had told Paget to allow William Chance a suitable sum off the rent as a gift, and she carried herself with a rigidity that owed almost nothing to her corsets and everything to grief. There is no point in grieving, she told herself, for something that could never have been mine.

They were already eating when she arrived, a great crowd of people tucking into a wedding breakfast as elaborate as her own had been. There were small children running about in the yard and a great many dogs, and carts and gigs by the dozen. She stepped through the open door of Roman Hill into a smell of boot polish and trifle, perfume, bread and flowers.

'Mrs Bretton,' and there was consternation, a silence, then a subdued resumption of eating and talk. She said her congratulations stiffly, kissed the bride, a shy young thing, and gave her hand to William. This was his second wife; his first had died in childbirth before Harriet had come to Bretton. He acknowledged he was a lucky man. Playing the great lady Harriet was unsurpassable, and by now she was thirty-eight, elegant, statuesque. A single movement of her head could be gracious or condescending. It was the only way she could touch his outstretched hand and keep her expression unchanged.

As she left they gave her a piece of the bride cake. She held it in her hand all the way back to Bretton. She thought: If I throw it out Johnnie won't see, he has his back to me. But she held it, wrapped in its paper, in her long gloved hand.

'I wonder whose wedding?' said Paddy, looking at the fragments years later. There had been several weddings: Fan's, Deborah's, a nurse during the war. There was a trunk in the attic full of veils, wax bridal wreaths, even a wedding dress.

'I think it's time it was thrown away, whosever it was,' said Paddy, and then, gazing round: 'We shall have to have a bonfire.'

The scouring of the Piggery took two days. The debris of at least six generations was piled in its corners. Occasionally Hugh penetrated the dark kitchen passages and found Paddy still at work there, usually sitting, usually reading: a letter, a scrap of newspaper, a list. Now and then he met Curry or Bushey or Ronnie Dack carrying sacks to the back door. And in the corner Etta crouched, unseen, listening and waiting.

'There was Aunt Fan,' she told Lily at bedtime. 'She was the pretty one in the photograph with the umbrellas. Her hair was fair and fluffy. She ran away to marry a Mr Roach who was a vicar. And there was Aunt Mary. She was tall and strict. She didn't marry anyone but went to live with an old cousin when she was thirty-five.'

'My goodness! And who's been telling you all this?'

'Paddy.'

'Miss Bretton to you. How many more times?'

'But everyone calls her Paddy in the village.'

'They call her "Miss Paddy" and that's no call for you to do the same.'

Hugh said, 'I suppose the tennis racquets had better

go in the hall cupboard.' The tennis net was full of holes. 'A hedgehog got in it once and we had to cut the net to rescue him,' said Paddy. Hugh, unravelling foot after foot, thought there must have been a great many hedgehogs to cause such devastation. 'Next year,' he said thoughtfully, 'we must buy a new one.'

Next year, Paddy wanted to tell him, this place will be empty. There will be no trees in the park or the Great Plantation, the gates will be off their hinges, the gardens jungle, the hothouses collapsed. She looked up from where she sat surrounded by hats: bowlers, toppers, Harriet's fashionable curly-brimmed riding hat. Her eyes met Hugh's.

A small voice behind them said, 'Please let's stay here. Please.'

It occurred to Hugh, not for the first time lately, that he did not know the first thing about children. With great difficulty he tried to remember being one himself but nothing, until now, had shown him the way back. Now Etta's words stirred something deep down. He had surely heard them before. He had said them himself when he was Etta's age, sent away to boarding school, forlorn on the platform with his trunk and Miss Peterson who had been given notice. 'Please let's stay here, Nanny. Please.'

'I try not to be sentimental,' he would have defended himself to Curry, but he had always been easily moved. He had been moved so easily by Laura the moment he first saw her; he had been cast down, lost, waving from space. He had wanted her. And above and between and under the physical desire so strong it was a physical pain was the desire to worship and protect. His mother, who had led a tiresomely lonely life, had steeped him in romance and chivalry from the cradle. In Laura he recognized the romantic ideal. Small, dark and fragile, she was the charming antithesis of his dull and kindly nature.

Etta's hand touched his arm. 'Please, Father.'

This was Laura's child, he thought. Laura's and his. He might have doubted she was his but her square chin and level eyes were his own. 'It isn't really up to me, Hetty.'

'I like it here,' she insisted in a small voice.

Hugh thought of his bank account, of his mother's legacy kept safe for Etta. He thought of his resolution to be buried in the park.

He thought he must be more of a fool than he had supposed.

Laura did not kiss Etta goodbye. 'Darling, you'll crush my hat. Look, give me my bag,' and she extracted mirror and rouge and did something imperceptible to her face.

'Will it be hot in France?' asked Etta.

'I'm sure it will.'

'As hot as here?'

The pigeons in the cedars ceased their take-two-cows suddenly and the heavy late summer silence was only broken by the faint chirping of the sparrows and the hum of bees in the roses on the wall below the open window. Etta hung out, looking down at the lawns, the deep shadows under the trees.

'Oh, hotter. Ring for Lily, Henrietta, will you.'

Lily toiled down with the cases. There was a taxi ordered from Frilton, that outpost of civilization. The front door stood open waiting but the drive was empty. Laura walked impatiently to the front steps and then back to the foot of the stairs.

'Don't sit up there, Henrietta. Come down.'

She came. She had a stuffed toy under one arm, a gangling rabbit she had found in the nursery.

'Henrietta, what is that?' Laura could be sharp when she was feeling guilty. She was feeling guilty this morning because Hugh had not spoken at breakfast, Curry

200

had not spoken when she had opened the great front door, and Etta too seemed oddly reluctant to communicate. It was a terrible weight of silent accusation. 'I'm only going for a holiday,' she wanted to say, but Hugh's extraordinary withdrawal had made her anxious. Could it be that he did not expect her to come back? She thought: But I always come back.

'This?' Etta held it out. 'This is Rabbit.'

'Where did you get it?'

Etta restored the rabbit to his place under her arm and stared with . . . hostility, thought Laura, shocked. What a strange unattractive old-fashioned child and how like Hugh she was! It amazed Laura suddenly that she should actually have borne Hugh a child, Hugh of all men.

'The taxi's coming, mum,' announced Lily from the front step. A vehicle had vanished temporarily among the rhododendrons and emerged jerkily, the driver peering about.

'Hugh!' cried Laura. 'Hugh.'

'Father's in the garden,' said Etta. Her face was rather white under the freckles. She held on to Rabbit with both hands. 'I always knew she wasn't permanent,' she said years afterwards. 'She wasn't a permanent person at all. But she was my mother. I thought mothers should stay with their children. She'd been away and come back so many times that I ought to have been used to it but that morning . . . Perhaps I had a premonition.'

'Darling, kiss me,' said Laura unexpectedly.

'Goodbye, Mother,' said Etta, complying. She smelled Laura's face powder. Her cheek was cool.

And there was the taxi, trembling at the foot of the steps, and Curry was helping Lily with the baggage. The man was strangely helpless, looking first at Bretton and then at Laura as if he had never seen anything like them. 'Gawping,' said Babs Potter, who was dusting the porch bedroom and happened to look out.

'Where is Hugh?' Laura demanded.

'Here he is,' said Etta.

He was in corduroys and shirt sleeves. He wore his old army boots. His hands were covered with earth and bramble scratches. He looked 'content' thought Laura. She was thinking a great deal this morning and feeling very little. A numbness had crept over her. She assumed it was relief, relief to be leaving Bretton and her unexciting marriage. But if it were relief it was a dull heavy sensation and she had known nothing like it before.

'Darling, I'll write.' She had to reach up to kiss him. There were eyes watching, critical eyes: Lily at the top of the steps, Curry at the bottom, Etta, the driver even. Hugh's smile was not encouraging. It was slow and sad.

He's saying goodbye to something he regrets is finished, thought Laura. She had seen him smile like that once or twice looking out of the window at the garden. He seemed to be fond of the garden. It was only halfway down the drive, plunged into the gloom of the rhododendrons, that she realized he had been saying goodbye to her. Then what had finished?

She looked back out of the tiny rear window. Hugh and Etta stood side by side on the gravel, diminishing with every moment. They looked rather shabby and ordinary in front of the big house as if they had strayed there by mistake.

At the Lodge the taxi turned right on to the Frilton road and she sat back again, thinking of Madge and France.

'Mother's like a butterfly,' said Etta.

'I suppose she is,' said Hugh.

'May I come and watch you mend the fountain?'

'If you don't make a noise.'

'Why should I make a noise?' asked Etta.

For a while, Hugh thought, ordinary plain mortals

can be charmed by butterflies but they flutter away and
are forgotten. Only the memory of their colour remains
and of the little breathtaking dazzle as they move.

17

~

THE PIGGERY WAS CLEARED. Sack after sack had been carried away and put on the bonfire Bushey stoked for two days in the walled garden. Etta watched Babs Potter scrub the brick floor.

'I liked it better when it was a muddle,' she said.

'And what's this then?' challenged Babs, wiping her hair out of her eyes and reaching for something lodged between the bricks. 'Someone's been careless.'

'It's a key,' cried Etta. 'It's a little key.'

It did not belong to Curry's large bunch. 'I've never seen it before,' said Curry, but even as she spoke she knew she had.

'It could open anything,' said Paddy, turning it on her long hard palm. 'You may keep it if you like.'

The key was in the third drawer of the desk, the writing desk that had belonged to Ralph's mother and stood in his dressing room.

'What key is this?' Harriet had asked the housekeeper, laying it on the oak table in the library.

The woman had picked it up and turned it over anxiously. Then she glanced down at the great bunch of keys at her waist. 'I don't know, madam.'

Sunlight fell across the table. Generations had sat at it, polished it, abused it. The housekeeper put down the key and for a moment Harriet saw two keys, one a misty reflection of the other. It had been a trying morning, she was tired, and twice, going to and fro turning out drawers and cupboards and the desk, she had caught sight of herself in mirrors and thought: This woman is some other Harriet. And once, looking down at herself: I shall not wear black for ever.

She made a label and tied it on the key but she wrote nothing on the label. There was nothing to write. She put the key in her own desk and closed the drawer on it and went on with life, Bretton life 'that never lets up' she said afterwards to Deborah. Then, when Paddy was five, she found something else. 'Only an old letter pushed into a book,' said the housemaid to the kitchen, 'but she turned quite white and had to sit down.' 'Small things change lives as irrevocably as big ones,' said Harriet. She had spent the morning with an inventory of the library's books in one hand, sorting out the ones underlined by Paget in consultation with a rare-book dealer. 'They're never read,' she had told him. 'They must help earn Bretton's keep.' In an hour she had two respectable piles. Then out of a Latin grammar, something of no account, fluttered the sheet of paper.

'I must sit down,' she said to Polly who was dusting the shelves. Who in this house had ever needed a Latin grammar? she wondered. She imagined Ralph interrupted or suddenly called away, casting about for a safe hiding place. It had been early summer, the grates cleaned and cold. There had only been the books, three walls of books . . . Perhaps he forgot which one he put it in, Harriet thought. We shall never know. We can never know what really happened in the past.

Eventually she got up and went into the garden. She walked purposefully. 'She always strode out,' said Paget. She could feel the letter in her pocket through the thickness of two petticoats and her drawers – burning my skin, she thought. She came to rest in the rose garden, newly made and still rather naked, though the young roses had put out brave leaves and small virginal buds. There Paddy found her, a Paddy confined in blue serge and thick stockings and the inevitable wobbly hat. What clothes for summer, thought Harriet! I shall have to speak to Deb.

'Can we say poems?' said Paddy, taking Harriet's bony liver-spotted hand. 'Curry says poems.'

'Curry? Who's Curry?' And then enlightenment. 'You mean Mrs Murray?'

'She knows lots of poems.'

'How extraordinary! How she has kept her many lights under bushels all these years. She came here when she was twelve, a very quiet skinny child.'

'Did you teach her poems?'

'No,' said Harriet, smiling briefly.

There were lots of poetry books in the nursery that Curry might have read, though except when Paddy threw the egg she had rarely crossed the nursery threshold. Who, anyway, had taught her to read? Harriet reached down for Paddy's smooth plump hand.

'We'll walk back to the house and you shall say one of Curry's poems. Your favourite.'

They walked slowly, unusual for both of them. Paddy recited in a high sing-song. Harriet did not hear the words. She felt a weight on her heart. Lies, deception, old injustices – 'Such a weight,' said Harriet. Ralph's letter and the key, the key on which she had tied that blank label twenty-five years ago, were like lead in her pocket.

To Deborah she said, 'When I'm dead go to my desk in the blue dressing room and in the secret drawer you'll find an envelope for Edward.' Since Deborah did not ask 'Why?' or 'What is it for?' Harriet felt compelled to add, 'Inside is a letter for him. From me. And a letter of his father's. And a key.'

After the stroke that left her speechless and immobile

Harriet lay in her bed three days 'suspended' said Curry. It was Curry who did all the necessary things for her and others, less necessary but kindly, like rubbing her cold feet or reading to her from the Bible. Deborah, pregnant with Tom, was sick every morning and often through the day as well. She tried to be brave, to be cheerful. When once Harriet tried to speak and failed, arching herself up in bed with the effort, Deborah wiped her brow and murmured soothing nonsense while all the time inside her own head a voice was clamouring: Don't die. I need you. Don't leave me here alone.

Harriet died at dawn, holding Curry's hand.

Deborah, waking to the news, went into what young Dr Ward called 'paroxysms of grief' so that he was obliged to sit with her, soothing her, holding her cold hands. Edward would not hear of giving her anything to make her sleep in case the baby was harmed.

You have no heart, thought Dr Ward, who only lived, he sometimes felt, to cherish her in dreams.

The envelope, the letters and the key were forgotten.

'How very exciting,' said Miss Hartley who had called on parish business and found Bretton open to the sun and apparently deserted by everyone but Etta. 'My dear, have you tried it in all the locks?'

'No,' said Etta. She took Miss Hartley's bird-like hand. 'Can we try them now?'

In spite of the 'ravages' – Paddy's periodic sales of furniture – Bretton was still blessed with many keyholes. 'Too big,' cried Etta or 'Too small' and sometimes 'There's no point, it wouldn't fit in *there*.' After a while Miss Hartley began to flag, for though her heart was in the hunt she had had a long walk from the village in the heat. 'My dear, I must rest,' she said as they reached the back landing on the third floor. There were only the maids' rooms left, which now meant Curry and Mrs

Prince in this part of the house. Etta was not allowed in those.

'Everywhere else is empty,' said Etta sadly.

But everywhere was not empty. In a small room at the top of the stairs was a remarkable assortment of luggage: leather cases, iron-bound trunks, one with cow hair on the outside, brown and white. The cases were empty but the trunks . . .

'Ball gowns!' exclaimed Miss Hartley, revived. 'Riding hats, habits, gloves, veils.'

Miss Hartley was romantic. 'Single women often are,' Harriet would have said. She spent her life in the shoes of her heroines. She stooped, fingering the melton cloth. In her mind's eye she was cantering charmingly beneath the Bretton oaks. 'I don't think we should pry, dear,' she said to Etta, but when she lowered the lid of the trunk she was smiling, as she might have smiled to a young gentleman who swept off his hat and gave her good morning, admiring her seat on the horse.

'Good heavens,' said Paddy, meeting them in the hall. 'You're all cobwebs.'

'We've searched and searched,' Etta said.

'I'm sorry. So much has been sold. It might have fitted a writing box or a lady's desk.'

'We've tried everything.' Etta drooped visibly.

'Never mind,' said Paddy. 'We'll just have to keep trying till we find it.'

How dare he send such a note, thought Harriet! She threw it on her dressing table and went to the window. It was August. Another August. I am thirty-nine, she told herself. Time passes.

'Tell Johnnie to saddle the mare,' she told Webb, the parlourmaid. 'But I won't need him, I'll ride alone.'

No lady rode alone. 'Nonsense!' exclaimed Harriet. 'I'm only going in the park.'

Under the oaks she halted, pulled the note from her pocket.

'We'll raise the rents,' Ralph had said the week before.

'I don't think that would be wise.'

'Don't you?' It was unlike him to be so aggressive. These days he was hardly ever at home, he spent his time hunting, or at race meetings, or with other disaffected husbands and idle bachelors. He did not interfere with the running of Bretton. 'Don't you? Well, this time it's I who will make the decision. Shipley can deal with it before Michaelmas.'

'Meredrew may not be able to pay a large increase.'

'Then he can make way for someone who can. The Chances can pay. They could pay double and never notice.'

Ralph was in Frilton when the note came up to the house and Harriet intercepted it. Its tone and content worried her. She crumpled it and dug it deep in the pocket of her riding skirt.

'It is up to me, I suppose,' she said to the brown mare.

The yard at Roman Hill was deserted. The door stood wide open. As an old woman Harriet would be able to recall every moment of those few times she crossed that forbidden ground. Each time the door stood open as if she was expected. In spite of this she was at a disadvantage – there was no one to hold her horse and where should she tie it? There was a stone mounting block by the chestnut tree but no ring in the wall. The brown mare, whatever her virtues, was unreliable if left loose and now, in old age, had grown cunning. Harriet, dismounting, gazed about helplessly.

Why no women? The house was silent except for the sparrows, the martins, the doves on the roof. Several casements were flung wide open and she could see the curtains moving, but that was the light wind not human hands. It would be undignified to call out. Let somebody come soon, thought Harriet, preparing to mount again.

He was coming across the yard, a tall fair man. Always when she met him he gave her a shock, as if she was meeting him for the first time.

'Mrs Bretton. What an unexpected honour!'

'There is no one in,' she said foolishly, still holding her stirrup.

'They're all at the fair.' He saw her puzzled look. 'In Frilton.'

It was an eight-mile walk to Frilton, an eight-mile walk home. Or had they taken a waggon? For a moment Harriet pondered the wisdom of allowing a gaggle of servants and farm boys loose in Frilton with all its temptations. William's hand reached out for the mare's reins. 'I'll put her up,' he said. 'Please step into the house. The parlour is the room at the end of the passage. But perhaps you remember?'

She remembered counting the coins on to the little mahogany table. She remembered Joseph's face, the proud nose, the glint of amusement in his eyes. 'If your husband knew,' he had said. 'He'll never know,' replied Harriet.

Now she retrieved the crushed note, smoothed it out and dropped it on the same table. 'My husband hasn't seen this,' she told William. 'I suggest you forget whatever it is Mr Shipley has advised you. The rents will not go up.'

William looked at her. It was a long hard look. Like a man judging a horse, thought Harriet, or a cow. He made no move to offer her refreshment or even a chair. He asked abruptly, 'Why have you come?'

There was no sensible reply to this. She did not know herself. But his note: 'I won't pay. You know why. William Chance.' Her gloved hand touched the corner of it. She sensed his hostility and as well a sort of pitying amusement that a proud woman should be so reduced.

'Mrs Bretton, I assure you I understand your husband's desire to increase the rents – he has heavy debts again, no doubt. But they are already high for this part of the world and another increase would bring down old Meredrew and maybe Crawley too. That would be a cruel thing. They love their land and farm it well. Enough that the times are against them without Bretton squeezing them too. I thought if I refused to pay he would think again. I would take some pleasure in causing a scandal and he knows it.'

Harriet stared. Her hand clutched at the paper and crushed it in her palm. 'I don't know what you mean,' she said. 'What scandal?'

'Of course you know. It's you who runs Bretton, every square inch of it. You know all your husband's weaknesses, his . . . shall we say history of weaknesses? Surely after so many years nothing remains secret between you? Or how do you manage his business so well?'

I should never have come, thought Harriet, it was a whim, an impulse, a girl's foolishness. But I'm no longer a girl, I'm nearly an old woman. Does he hate me? Why does he hate me? What happened between Bretton and Roman Hill, and when, and why will no one tell me? She strode to the door, brushing past him with a set face, her skirts belling out to sweep the walls of the passage. But of course in the yard there was no horse and she did not know where William had taken her.

'So I stood there looking foolish,' remembered Harriet, 'until he followed me out of the house and fetched the mare.'

He said, 'You ought not to come here, Mrs Bretton. Your husband wouldn't like it.'

'Why?' demanded Harriet. She felt stronger in the saddle, courage seeping back.

'But you know.'

'I don't know. I've never known. And if no one tells me I shall run mad.'

His hand was still on the mare's neck. He was looking Harriet in the face. 'Full in the face,' said Harriet. 'To see if I was lying.' Then he gave a short laugh and turned away.

'Won't you tell me?' she asked.

'You ought to ask your husband.'

'He won't say anything.'

'Won't he? Ask him about Clarissa.'

As she rode out of the gate he called after her. 'Look in the churchyard first, if you want.'

Paget arranged for agents to look over Bretton and put a price on it. They did so with all the solemnity of men pricing a pig at market, prodding and poking. When they asked Bushey pertinent questions he took them as impertinent and snarled at them so horribly that they retreated to the flower garden, less inclined now to be generous in their assessments. 'In any case,' said Curry, whose demeanour of the day was that of the Ice Queen, 'we all know what they're assessing it *for*.' They spent the morning pacing about with estate maps and note-books and shattering disdain and only grew excited once, in the Great Plantation that ran along the Frilton road.

Hugh, eating his solitary dinner that evening, was interrupted by Paget, puffing and apologetic, to tell him the outcome.

'I suppose it was inevitable. We all know the timber's worth money,' Hugh said. 'But would anyone get permission for forty houses along there? Forty?'

'I fear they might.'

'You mean it's been talked of before?'

'Mr Tom ... Mr Bretton, I mean ... was always interested in selling that piece for development. He often suggested it as the means to mend the fortunes of the estate.'

Hugh thought for a moment. He refilled his wine glass and poured one for Paget without asking. 'Would it? Would it be enough?'

'Oh, I doubt it. I doubt it very much.'

'But of course there would never be enough to save Bretton and keep up his place in Italy.'

'Quite so.'

'But who would buy such a house?' Hugh asked, and he waved his glass gently at the ornate plaster ceiling, the tall bare walls.

'Oh, people don't want big houses any more – the cost, the difficulties with staff . . . But the fireplaces, the panelling from the library, bricks, slates, lead, there's a market for such things. It reminds me, I'm afraid, of the corpses that were so valuable once to students of anatomy. Oh, there'll be great quarrelling over the bones once life's out of the body, Mr Haley.'

Hugh thought of Bretton with the life out of it. His life for one, he thought; Etta's, Curry's. For the first time he thought of the house not as four walls and a roof but as a place people had inhabited, liking, disliking, loving, surviving. Up and down its passages, in and out of its rooms, here at this very table voices had called, demanded, cried out, discussed Waterloo, Alma, Grootewald, rhubarb jam, gout, nurserymaids, legacies, debts, broken necks. 'Well, I'm not a Bretton, they had nothing to do with me,' he might have said once. His historical consciousness was rudimentary. But in these last few weeks he had come to feel involved, both with Bretton's past and its precarious future. Was it because of the fountain? It had been broken on the order of a grieving man. Hugh, who felt he could never make such a gesture, still

213

appreciated its romantic appeal. How many more such gestures had been made here, by whom and why? Bretton took on another dimension. It was no longer fireplaces, panelling, bricks, slates, lead.

'Mr Paget, come and drink your wine in the library and give me a little advice.'

'Advice?'

'Perhaps I shouldn't ask you for advice. But figures. You could give me some figures.'

'I'm not sure,' began Paget, rising awkwardly.

'I need figures,' said Hugh with a new firmness. 'How can I come to any decision without figures?'

Curry sent Lily to bed and Mrs Prince had retired with her cocoa long ago. Dack's boy – who was not a boy but a shambling large man of thirty-five with ganglions – had fetched the last hod of coke to pacify the kitchener. The back regions of Bretton grew quiet. In the Piggery passage the empty dog baskets were lined up, in the Piggery itself the leads still hung on their pegs, but there were no dogs now nor had been since the war. In the nursery Etta slept. The only sound was mice in the wainscot.

The men were still in the library.

That old Paget has never stayed so late, thought Curry. At eleven she entered and trimmed a smoking lamp. Hugh was poring over papers covered in numbers, Paget sitting back smoking. The clock ticked. Time passed. At midnight Curry walked again to the library door and knocked.

'Is there anything else you want, sir?'

Hugh looked up, blinking. 'I thought you'd gone to bed, Mrs Murray. No, thank you. I'll see Mr Paget out and lock up.' He smiled at her. It was his lazy, good-natured smile. Once it had attracted Laura, who was susceptible to such things. Probably he had forgotten who Curry was, or he had never looked at her before, only thought of her in Laura's terms: the old harridan. 'Goodnight,' he said amiably, still smiling.

'Goodnight, sir.'

'My God,' said Paget as the door closed, 'that woman has an inscrutable face.'

Mrs Prince found a snail in the hall and ejected it, outraged. No snail had ever dared invade the house in Kensington. 'I suppose in this place it's only to be expected,' she said darkly to Curry half an hour later, grappling with the kitchener which would not toast and with Hugh's kedgeree which threatened to congeal.

Hugh was always prepared for a good breakfast. Even in the trenches, had they known it, he had made something of it. 'Sometimes not very much,' he would have admitted. But: 'A good breakfast starts the day well,' he was fond of saying. It was probably what Nanny Peterson had told him in the white nursery at Luccombe before he had been sent away to school. It had become a habit now, his exaggerated enjoyment of the first meal of the day: toast, bacon, kidneys, kedgeree. He seldom had lunch but made these last him all day until dinner. He was usually up at six when he was home from London, and he tried to read or walk in the garden until Lily called him at half past eight. 'Leading the life of a country gentleman,' he called it.

This morning he met Paddy.

He could not think of anything original to say, so stood watching her cut down some drooping plants in the border. She had strong workmanlike hands. Was seven in the morning an ideal time to be gardening? He knew next to nothing about it – or about gardeners. 'Oh, Miss Bretton is more than a *gardener*,' Miss Hartley had said to him so that he had an absurd vision of gardeners in distinct hierarchies like Thrones and Powers.

'I think you ought to know,' he remarked after a while, as Paddy snipped on. 'I shall try to buy Bretton from your brother if I can.'

The snipping stopped. Her look was amused. What was amusing? Shouldn't she be pleased? How dark her eyes always seemed from a distance, yet when one drew close they were grey, quite clearly grey, startlingly so between such inky lashes. Taken alone those eyes were not how a man – an unimaginative man – might expect the eyes of a forty-year-old woman to seem. The face was bony, brown, lined, experienced – but the eyes ... He remembered how, at Laura's dinner party, he had once or twice seen them blazing across the table.

'I wish you luck,' she said suddenly, without conviction. She pulled off a glove and rubbed her hot forehead.

'Do you?'

'Yes, I do. I'm sorry if I sound doubtful. You don't know my brother very well. He's set on demolition.'

'I don't see demolition's necessary.'

'Nor do I. Nor does anyone but Tom. I think he wants to make a point, that's all.'

'What sort of point?'

'I'm not sure I understand. I wonder if he does. To make sure he never has to come back? Who knows.'

From the direction of the house came a thin noise, someone hallooing. Hugh looked at his watch. It was eight fifteen. Etta? Since Laura had been away Etta had been allowed to breakfast in the dining room. Explaining this to Paddy as they walked slowly up the lawn he said, 'Of course, it makes me feel less solitary. As it is we sit side by side at a table that can seat twelve comfortably. It's ridiculous.'

They were in sight of the house. Paddy looked up at it as Hugh had looked at Laura the morning she had left, with regret and a valedictory sadness. She, like Hugh, was relinquishing the burden of responsibility.

'You care for it,' he said and touched her arm, drawing her to a stop. 'You do.'

She shook her head. 'I don't think so.'

'Father,' admonished Etta, panting up. 'We've been looking everywhere and calling and calling. Breakfast's ready. Good morning, Miss Bretton.'

'I'm glad you sometimes remember your manners,' said Hugh.

'But you must come. The kedgeree's going to bits or something. Mrs Prince is having a turn.'

'A what?' She's too much with the servants, he thought. Certainly she had always been left too much to her own devices. 'Why don't you take Henrietta in the park yourself?' he had said to Laura in the Kensington days. 'I employ a nurserymaid to do that.' 'Well, I think you should take her occasionally.'

For a while then, on the maids' afternoon off, Laura had walked to the park. She was so bored that she felt oppressed, as if she carried a great weight with her. If she met friends by chance they invariably expressed surprise that she had a child so old, so sturdy or so utterly unlike her. She thought she detected a subtle change of tone in their conversation. She was a mother now, it implied, she could no longer be counted among the young and frivolous. 'I might be already middle-aged,' she complained to Hugh, who could not understand. 'She's your daughter, you must bring her up,' he told her pitilessly.

She was his daughter now, and he could see the pitfalls of bringing her up without guidance. In the last two weeks he had often wished his mother was still alive. Who looked after you? he wanted to ask Paddy. Who kept you in hand? How is it done?

Paddy watched them go into the house together. They were certainly more together than she had seen them before, she thought. She walked on to the vegetable garden, counting her own blessings carefully.

She could not remember having done this for years.

'Whenever you're unhappy, count your blessings,' Harriet had encouraged her.

'Do you count yours?' the young Paddy demanded.

'Sometimes.'

'What are they?'

Harriet had hesitated. 'All this,' she had said, moving her hand vaguely, looking about. 'Good food, shelter, my children, your mother, Mrs Murray, you.'

'Do I have to come at the end?'

'Oh, it's not in order of importance.'

In the vegetable garden Paddy paused to lob a clod of earth at the inevitable pigeons. I should have so many blessings, she thought despairingly. How ungracious she had been when Hugh Haley had said he hoped to buy Bretton! Miss Hartley could not have dreamed up a more fitting solution. And yet . . . I don't believe it will happen, thought Paddy. He will have to choose between his wife and the house and in the end, being the man he is, he must choose his wife. She hurried towards the green door, stepped out into the lane, walked down it a little, reached the gate.

'I always know where to find you,' Philip had said.

'Where?'

'In Hobeys, sitting and dreaming.'

'And weeping,' she had added with a sudden premonition. But he had laughed.

'You never cry.'

The day Grace had walked up to break the news of Philip's death Paddy had been at the Lodge, clearing and cleaning it for a new tenant, and no, she had not cried. She had walked to Hobeys and sat and sat with her arms round her knees until she was too stiff to get up. She felt empty, light-headed. Only the hard earth and the grass stems were real, and the shifting branches of the trees. Even Jack Chance was unreal for a moment, hauling her to her feet.

'It's growing dark. They raised the hue and cry hours ago. You must go back.'

She clutched his lapels. 'Don't send me back.'

He had bent to kiss her forehead. He knew, as well as she, that if he had embraced her she would have sobbed and sobbed. 'You must go home, Pat. They'll be sending for the police next. Come on. Put up your chin. Damn them all.'

'He killed himself,' she whispered.

'It was an accident. He fell with the gun.'

'He's dead and it's my fault.'

'It isn't anyone's fault. Paddy, go home.'

She had stepped away from him. The night air was cold. It was a long way to the gate. She walked steadily, her head up.

It was what Harriet had done, hurrying through the heavy dew, her skirts bunched up, her heart pounding. At the gate she had wrestled with the chain. As she did so she wondered if the back of her dress was all leaves, or grass stains. I don't care if it is, she thought. I shall say I fell over. But up at the house there was no need of explanations, no one questioned her. No one would dare, she realized thankfully.

Seeing her face when she came in, no one questioned Paddy either. It had been a terrible shock. Even Edward, momentarily, had been touched by it. He let them put his daughter to bed and was relieved when Curry told him she was sleeping.

Waking in the night, Paddy found Curry in the armchair by the window. 'Watching,' said Curry.

'Did he kill himself?' asked Paddy.

'I shouldn't think so, should you?' was the sensible reply.

'But he was always so careful. How could he have had an accident?'

Her bare feet made no sound on the boards. Curry gathered her to her flat chest and rocked her, smoothing down the loose mass of her hair.

18

~

E TTA KNEW NOTHING of Hugh's momentous plans.
She was full of anxiety these days, took hours to go
to sleep and woke early. She was beginning to understand that she did, after all, have Hugh's affection and
so was growing more assertive and confident, but still
the worm of doubt turned. Lily, hearing her crying in
the night, thought she was missing Laura. 'Mothers are
important,' she told Mrs Prince in the morning, going
down for the hot-water cans.

'I don't want to go away,' Etta confided to Pen,
sitting in the barn at Home Farm combing her hair.
They often sat on the sacks at this task, though Pen's
hair was black and greasy – 'Full of lice,' said Mrs Dack
– and Etta's was thick and electric.

'*I'd* like to go away,' said Pen. She would never have
tolerated anyone else scraping her hair into a pigtail.
She bit her lip against the pain.

'You wouldn't really.'

'I would.'

'Away from your mother and sisters and brothers?' It
seemed inconceivable to Etta, always alone, to wish to
leave such a family. But she was learning that an inability to be content was a condition of life. She was sure
her father had disliked Bretton when he had first come
but now he adored it, now, when he was about to give it

up. She scowled, taking some time over the bow at the end of the pigtail.

'There. Now you look quite different.'

Pen's grumpy little face, revealed by the new hair-style, showed a tentative delight. She looked nothing like Babs. None of the Potters bore any strong resemblance to the others though now and then a mannerism of Mrs Potter united them. Pen's father might have been a gipsy or a circus performer, someone at any rate dark and supple. She twisted effortlessly over the horse trough, judging the effect of the pigtail. 'It's all right,' she conceded at last. Then, dipping her fingers in the water: 'You'd go back to London, wouldn't you? Don't you like London?'

'No,' said Etta firmly.

'*I* would.'

'Well, I like it here. I want to stay at Bretton.'

Pen laughed, skipping away. She wore no shoes and there were smudged imprints of her long feet in the dust. 'Takes all sorts,' she told Etta over her shoulder.

Sometimes when Etta woke early there was a mist in the park and the smell of autumn. 'What is it?' she had asked Curry, sniffing. 'The year dying,' said Curry. It seemed impossible after such fine weather, but morning and evening there was this tang of damp stubble and brown grasses and earth. Often now the owl hooted, coming down past the cedars to his hunting grounds beyond the stables. Etta, hanging out of the nursery window, heard him and shivered with delight. But autumn meant the end of Bretton. She was sure it would mean the end of Bretton.

'Well?' asked Pen, up on the corn sacks.

'They're going to cut down the trees in the Plantation,' said Etta, repeating kitchen gossip.

'Our Babs says they'll pull down the house.'

Etta, running back to it, stopped to marvel at its

solidity. It was unbelievable anyone should even try to pull it down. She found Bushey in among the vegetables and questioned him till he grew irritable. At bedtime she begged Lily to say it was not true.

'Of course it isn't true,' declared Lily cheerfully.

'But Babs says . . .'

'Babs! Just remember, it's not natural for a Potter to tell the truth.'

'You mean she tells lies?'

'I mean she gabbles about things that don't concern her.'

'But are they going to pull it down?'

'Not in a hundred years,' said Lily.

In the morning, looking out at the mist and catching that whiff of decay, a sense of impermanence gripped Etta. She felt afraid.

'They won't pull it down, will they?' she asked Curry.

'Only over my bones,' said Curry.

That weekend Hugh heard from Laura. France was too enchanting, Madge 'remarkable', the weather 'divine'. She did not speak of returning. The tone of every sentence was that of someone newly arrived in paradise. 'She'll come home at the end of the month with Madge,' said Hugh to Etta, as one grown-up to another. Etta herself had received a postcard which said nothing but 'Love Mother' and which she conscientiously propped on her mantelshelf and stared at for some time before she fell asleep. It was perhaps significant it did not go beneath her pillow with her other treasures: the stone with the hole through it, the green pheasant's feather, the mysterious key. Or maybe it was not in the least significant but only practical: postcards were meant to be looked at.

Hugh, wrestling with the fountain, wrestling too with his new worries over Bretton, found he did not have to wrestle with his conscience over Laura. For the first time in years he was not oppressed by that nagging sense of responsibility. It was a terrible thing feeling so responsible for another person's happiness. And how often he had failed Laura! He had scarcely succeeded with anything in their marriage. He had been wrong to be jealous, then wrong to acknowledge her several lovers, wrong to show self-restraint, wrong to desire her, especially wrong to force her to have a child. He had grown rather wild and uncontrolled over that, had frightened her, or she would never have allowed it. 'It's my body,' she had cried, growing alarmed. 'I don't want it bloated and torn apart.'

He had seen she was terribly afraid but had mistaken the object of her fear. 'You mustn't look at it like that,' he told her helplessly. 'It's the most natural thing in the world.'

'A man would say that.'

It was not pregnancy and childbirth she could not face, it was what they augured for the future. 'I'll grow fat and complacent,' she confided to Madge, 'and after one he'll want another and I shall be . . . changed. Completely changed.'

Madge did not say: but change is life and life is change. She was not given to such triteness. She simply put her arm round Laura and murmured regretfully, 'And your bosom will be absolutely ruined, darling.'

I suppose I will get used to this, Harriet thought, clasping her hands round her belly. She stood in front of the great cheval mirror in her room, looking enormously tall in her nightgown, and pressed the material back until the swelling was clearly visible. A bursting joy and a dreadful nagging fear combined in her and made her frown, biting her lip. 'It's bound to be a boy,' Ralph had said when she told him.

'A girl would be as good,' she said quietly.

'Not for Bretton,' he had retorted.

Girls are good for Bretton, she might have argued, even at this early stage understanding how things had been, how things were, but she said no more, simply getting on with life and every morning standing by the mirror with her hands cupped about her belly, half joyful, half afraid.

'Motherhood made me less angular,' she told Deborah. It also unleashed all her pent-up capacity for love. 'If I'd loved my children as much as I wanted I'd have smothered them,' she said. After Edward was born and she locked her door to Ralph she turned her attention to the estate and the village. She went forth to 'terrorize' said Curry. She terrorized the villagers into clean water and sanitary conditions. The parson and the churchwardens fled at her approach. But though many had a great deal to thank her for she received no gratitude, only that grudging country respect which conceals burning resentment.

'No reformer is popular,' said Harriet. And once, more angrily: 'They'd rather keep their old wells and die of typhoid than sink a new one and be healthy.' When the parson rashly said he knew of no 'deserving poor' in the village in need of charitable coals she cried, 'I could find you a dozen,' and did so immediately.

'Mama, you are a terrible old woman,' Fan told her, on a visit from the Devon parsonage.

'So I am. But I get things done.'

Getting things done was what Harriet was remembered for long after her death. Often Paddy, involved in some village wrangle, some deadlocked committee meeting, heard, 'Old Mrs Bretton would have got things done.' 'If only they knew,' Harriet could have said, 'what things have been done and left undone by me.'

In 1862 Ralph was ill. 'It's nothing,' the doctors told Harriet. 'His heart isn't strong. He must take life more easily, that's all.' With unconscious irony they assured her Ralph would benefit from being relieved of the responsibility for the estate. Could he not employ a bailiff? 'Bailiff!' exploded Harriet later while dressing for dinner. 'I've been the bailiff of this place for twenty years.' It was November and cold. She wore two shawls in the dining room and Ralph asked, 'What's happening to women's clothes? You used to show off your shoulders when you were young.'

'Not in this house,' she retorted.

'Do you remember . . .' He was inclined to reminisce since they had begun to treat him as an invalid, but only, she thought, to goad her into flying out at him, like a small boy stirring the water with a stick.

'I remember everything,' she told him.

After dinner she went out into the garden, swathed in a rain-cape as large as a horseblanket. A thin drizzle fell, bitterly cold. In the rose garden she turned at bay for Ralph had followed her with a lantern.

'How can you see? It's pitch dark.'

'I don't need to see. I know this place too well to want eyes.'

'You must come in. What will the servants think?'

'They're paid to work,' said Harriet, 'not think.'

She could sense his anger as surely as she could feel the warmth of the lantern as he raised it. For years, she thought, he had been indifferent to what she did. She managed Bretton and she never disgraced him – that had always been sufficient. Now, for apparently no reason, he was all rage. He's too cold for rage, she told herself. He has never lost his temper, not even when I locked the door.

'I command you . . .' he began.

'I shouldn't have laughed,' Harriet said afterwards, 'but it struck me as so melodramatic.' She had not laughed unkindly. 'I was astonished really,' she remembered.

Ralph cried, 'My God, you never . . .' and choked,

and dropped the lantern and fell over on to the stone path.

Harriet ran to the house. She ran as fast as she could with her great skirts and the tarpaulin draped over her shoulders. She threw that off under the cedars and grabbed up whole armfuls of dress and ran and ran. She still rode every day. She was fit. Forty-five and fit. She ran to the side door by the shrubbery and into the library passage and then the hall and she could hardly breathe. When Bragg came she had to lean against the wall. She said, 'Mr Bretton is lying in the rose garden. He's ill. Tell Sam to run for one of the men and fetch him to the house. And send Johnnie Dack for the doctor.' After that she was aware of noise and lamps being lit and the fact that her hair was coming down, all her hair, a sodden dark mass of it steaming into frizzy curls. She went upstairs, gathering her wits, and ordered the fire to be poked up in Ralph's room and bottles and warming pans, more pillows, water, basins, gruel.

The doctor arrived from Frilton in just over an hour. His hat and cape and the rug from his gig were set to dry by the kitchen fire. He said Ralph had had a seizure. 'I know that,' said Harriet. Warmth, rest, beef tea she was told, and absolute quiet, no excitement, no stimulation. The following day he was no better and the day after worse, his temperature rising. Two doctors conferring pronounced pneumonia and shook their heads. 'His heart will not stand it,' they told each other sagely.

At the end of the week Ralph died.

The day he was buried the rain fell mixed with sleet. The village women turned out to stand on the road side of the churchyard wall with their children clinging to their skirts but only to see the hearse arrive, the horses nodding their dripping plumes. Harriet was at Bretton, feeling hideous in black, looking over the account books. It was a 'lonely' funeral – or so said Curry who had been two at the time and playing in the hovel by the sheepwash. She could not say how she knew, but atmospheres and attitudes and feelings passed down through the Bretton servants like 'butter through muslin' said Curry. It came to be known that Ralph's was a lonely funeral, only the parson, Shipley, a couple of raffish friends and Sir George Brocket in attendance. Even Sir George was of little account, a 'poor lame old thing' said the village. Though the farm men had time off they kept a respectful distance and went home quickly, cursing the wet.

'It was so wet, so cold,' Harriet told Curry years later. 'I shall never forget it. The rain rattled all the windows in the house and none of the fires would draw. The girls and Edward stayed in the nursery all day though they'd grown out of it and had rooms near mine. Edward was fourteen.'

'Lonely,' said Curry.

'The dead aren't lonely. Only the living,' said Harriet.

In Harriet's day there was a routine for the mistress of the house that 'defied belief' said Harriet. Beginning with the settling of the menus for the day or week, menus for upstairs, downstairs and the nursery, and going on to arrangements for guests, letter writing, children's lessons, new staff interviewed, old staff pacified, village duties, gardening, accounts, farm business, haysel, harvest, Christmas ... 'It was never done,' Harriet asserted.

And always the problem of lack of money.

'Nobody looking at Bretton would think we were poor,' said Fan miserably.

'Oh Mother, you can't!' wailed Mary when Harriet resolved to sell the carriage horses.

'But we never use the carriage,' said Harriet.

'We do on Sunday.'

'Now your father's dead we'll use the dogcart.'

'The dogcart! But . . .'

'The horses will pay for your ball.'

The carriage horses, the expensive London greys, were sold. The hunters went. The riding ponies went, all except Edward's. The brown mare was very old and when she died was buried in the orchard in what Ralph would have considered an inexcusable show of sentiment. 'She was a good servant and a good friend,' was Harriet's comment. The men laboured all day at the hole. It was hard work burying a horse. The mare had been a link to Joseph Chance, a symbol of Harriet's first rebellion. On the new mounting block was inscribed: Josephine. 1840–1864.

Mary had her ball and danced with as many young men as Harriet could 'scrape up' across the county, but none of them proposed. The bay trotter was replaced by a staid cob who pulled Harriet in the dogcart and then took Edward hunting. The grass-cutting pony and a donkey were the only other inhabitants of the vast stables. Johnnie Dack had gone to Lord Irstead as coachman. There was only a boy, Morris, who burnished the bits and turned the handle of the monstrous chaff cutter.

'So what will pay for *my* ball?' asked Fan.

Harriet sold her jewels to pay for it, but no one knew that except old Shipley. 'They weren't Bretton jewels,' said Harriet. 'They were my own.' She had never cared much for them but they had been Sophie's and might one day have passed to the girls. But: 'Fan must have what Mary had,' insisted Harriet. Later, of course, there was Edward.

Edward did not have a ball, he had horses. 'Hunters again,' said Harriet with pleasure, for now the stables did not seem so desolate. After them would come Tom's ponies, then some young Irish half breds, then all Paddy's troublesome chargers and finally old Croaker, who was taken by the Army in 1914 and died in Flanders.

'I wasn't allowed to ride as a child,' Paddy said. She was forbidden even to take down Harriet's old saddle and exercise the pony when Tom was at school. Instead she took it to Roman Hill and Jack Chance let her try anything on four legs and so the legend of Paddy as a latter-day Boadicea was born, galloping the local gentry into the ground the way that lady had galloped the Romans. 'You should see her go,' said Philip proudly to his father. 'It's as if . . . as if she gets the devil in her.'

'Well, she comes of a long line of proud and devilish people,' Deborah could have told him, recalling that sprawling and ancient house inhabited perhaps six hundred years. After all she had not created Paddy unaided.

Harriet spent her last day before the stroke that was to kill her out of doors. 'In our garden,' she said to Deborah. In the late afternoon she walked round to the stables and came to rest on the mounting block, dirtying her fine black skirts. Josephine. Poor Joey. What a wretch she had always been at the ford, trampling the water, threatening to lie down. 'If I'd had any sense,' said Harriet aloud, 'I'd have ridden her away and never come back.'

The doves came to peck near her feet. She could hear Morris whistling. A horse blew affectionately through its nose, anticipating titbits.

William, thought Harriet. William.

If she closed her eyes she could feel his kisses on her face.

Etta sat on the mounting block in an attitude of doom. It seemed to her that change, which she so much dreaded, was come upon them again. The tentative little roots she had put down would be torn up. She would have to go back to London and the regularities of a different kind of life, a life she might once have learned to tolerate before she had lived at Bretton. She drew her feet up under her and gripped her knees hard and looked across the stableyard to where the wall below the dovecot was stained with droppings and the few birds pecked and crooned. There were weeds between the cobblestones, and the three great doors, one in the middle of each of the long ranges, opening on to ten empty stalls apiece, looked shabby and unused.

'We will stay here, won't we?' she had asked Hugh at breakfast.

'I don't know, Hetty. Pass me the salt, would you?'

'But we will, won't we?'

'I can't say,' said Hugh.

This morning the air was vibrant. 'Lord, something's up,' Lily informed Mrs Prince, running in for more toast. Father's upset, Etta had said to herself as she entered the room. She sat neatly, her napkin over her flat chest and tucked in the top of her pinafore.

'Do you have to wear that like a bib?' Hugh asked.

She removed it, laid it decorously on her lap. Silently she absorbed the current of his frustration and despair. By his plate was a letter with a French stamp. She knew it was a French stamp although it was a long way from her and upside down. Mother, she thought. Was Mother the cause of Hugh's distress?

'We will stay here, won't we?'

'I don't know . . .'

This conversation had been repeated, with variations, for four breakfasts in a row. Hugh, having taken a week off from the bank, had to face interrogation every morning over his bacon and kidneys. He knew he disappointed her with his evasions. He thought her clear blue gaze intimidating. He knew he must fall short of her ideal for he had always, or so he had been led to believe, fallen short of Laura's. He had not even lived up to his mother's expectations, too shy to do her credit in company, too cautious to be a hero, too ordinary.

In Etta's eyes Hugh was the rock and the provider. Laura had always trusted his integrity, his willingness. 'Oh, Hugh will pay,' she would exclaim and with such certainty that Etta never doubted he would, and presumably did, take on himself all those accounts for gloves, hats, pictures, jewellery, *objets d'art*. He also paid for the alarming motor car Laura desired, and drove, for all of three months; for the parties, the dinners and the moves: Hampstead to Kensington to remotest Bretton. While he was in the Army bills must have piled up relentlessly but they had never seemed a source of conflict. Laura said Hugh would pay and he did, though how much of his once-considerable inheritance he used up in the process was between him and his bank. As an only son he had received all his parents had to leave, including the stately old house where he had grown up and which he sold, regretfully, just before the outbreak of war. For a while, he knew, he could afford an extravagant wife.

What he had not suspected was that in affording Laura he might not be able to afford anything more for himself.

'I can't meet his price,' he told Paget in Paget's office, turning his hat between his blunt fingers and staring down at the market square. 'If I did I'd have nothing left to do repairs or put by something for Henrietta.'

Paget said he was sorry. He was especially sorry for Bretton; there was no hope for it now, no hope that is that it might remain intact.

'I can't match speculators' prices,' Hugh said. He seemed to have said this before. He had rehearsed so much to say to Paget after receiving the letter of polite rejection but none of it, he thought now, would be of any use. 'I expect it's for the best. Nonsense, really, a man and a small child in a house as big as that.'

'Miss Paddy will be disappointed.'

'Oh, I don't know. Will she? She might have written to her brother and put in a good word for me.'

'Perhaps she did,' said Paget diplomatically.

'I doubt it.' Hugh resumed his watch from the window. It was not a market day and the square was quiet. 'You know, when I was in France I used to think I'd like to buy a place in the country again if I got home alive. I had to sell up when my parents died because . . . because it seemed the best thing to do at the time. I suppose it wasn't a real country house, it was on the edge of the town, but you wouldn't have known it. It was only when I went away to school that I realized real country was more than a few acres of garden.'

He had sold the house because he had known it was the only way he could afford Laura. He had thought then that it was not much of a sacrifice for he was in love and no sacrifice could be enough.

Paget grunted sympathetically and shook his pen above the blotter, watching the ink spread reassuringly in two large blobs.

'Is there any trouble over Roman Hill?' asked Hugh unexpectedly. He had caught a glimpse of a tall man in a riding coat, boots, a cap. The cap lifted. The grey day was illuminated by that garnet-coloured head.

'Trouble?' Paget looked up quickly. 'I was not aware of any. I believe Mr Chance has a right to look cheerful. Will you take a glass of sherry before you go, Mr Haley?'

'No, thank you,' said Hugh. 'I have another appointment.'

He ran down to the square and raised his hat to Johnny Chance. 'Have you half an hour to spare?'

'If you don't mind the Black Horse. I have to meet a dealer there at twelve.'

Back at Bretton there was Etta waiting to ambush him with questions. She was wearing a grey jumper and it looked too small. Hugh said, 'You've grown out of that. We'll have to get you another one.'

'I've almost grown out of everything. We are staying here, aren't we?'

'As long as we can. Come on, let's watch Bushey turn on the fountain.'

She recognized it as an appeal. He too was suffering then.

'All right. I'll run and get my hat.'

How extraordinary, thought Hugh, that she should bother with a hat! He remembered Laura telling her she must always wear one out of doors. 'Why?' from Etta. 'Because it's the proper thing to do.'

'It will work, won't it?' Etta asked as they made their way to the rose garden. The hat, a troublesome article, was a sort of woollen tam-o'-shanter that slanted drunkenly on one side of her head.

'The fountain? I hope so.'

There was an appropriate gurgle, a gout of mud, and then the water ran clear and fast into the bowl, falling in silvery ribbons over the edge to the channel below.

'Hooray!' cried Etta, swinging on Hugh's hand.

'Hooray indeed,' said Bushey, clinking spanners in the shrubs above. He sounded grumpy and his face, peering crossly down at them, was surrounded by leaves like Jack-in-the-green.

'It's lovely,' said Etta. 'It makes a lovely noise.'

They listened. 'Too fast,' said Hugh.

Bushey disappeared and tinkered with the stop-cock. The flow steadied.

'Yes,' said Hugh.

He felt satisfied. He had had an interesting talk with Johnny Chance, he had overcome Bushey's resistance and he had pleased his daughter. He looked boyishly complacent. 'What do you think?' he asked Bushey genially.

'That warn't meant to run again,' announced the face

234

between the leaves. Then as Etta bent over to dip her fingers in the moving water it added, 'Mrs Deborah would be pleased do she see it.'

Johnny Chance took Etta out in the pony trap. He drove with unconscious expertise and much faster than Laura. Etta clung to the seat beneath the cushion, consumed by terror and delight. There was hardly any water in the ford in the village street but she felt the drops fly up, wetting her bare legs. The pony, in Laura's charge, had always hesitated here. Now he went forward willingly, dust and stones spurting from under his quick hooves.

'He knows,' said Johnny, amused.

'What does he know?'

'Who's master.'

At the top of the rise he put the reins in her hands. They felt heavy between her small fingers. 'Go on,' he said. 'You're in charge.'

They came home over the stubbles of Home Farm, bumping and straining, weaving between the shocks on the Twenty Acre. 'It should have been carted,' said Johnny, shading his eyes and looking about. 'I thought all their corn was in the stack.'

'Miss Bretton's going to London.'

'London, is it? There's a rumour in the village she's off to Italy to sort out that brother of hers.'

Etta watched his hands on the reins. They were big hands, rough, the nails cut short. She liked them. She liked everything about him, his red hair, his tanned skin, his old clothes smelling of tobacco and horse, his direct stare. He asked suddenly, 'When's your mother coming home?'

'I don't know. Father's had two letters. I've had a postcard.' She felt she ought to let him know she had been remembered.

'She must be enjoying herself.'

'Yes. It's all new.'

'What is?'

'France. The people. Where she is. She likes new things.'

'And when they're not new any more?'

'Oh, she finds something else,' replied Etta cheerfully. It seemed quite natural to her. She had never known Laura content for long, knew intimately the prickly descent from first rapture to snappish endurance. 'Must I endure this any longer?' Laura was fond of demanding.

'No,' Hugh had said, again and again. 'But what is it you really want?' He would once, like the poets, have plucked down the moon and stars for her. She would have tired of those, he now knew, as quickly as everything else.

The question Johnny Chance sensitively avoided asking was answered anyway.

'Mother always comes back,' said Etta as if she felt it was Johnny who needed reassurance.

'I see.'

'She sometimes goes away for a few weeks. I miss her but . . .' She saw his frown. 'I don't worry.'

Johnny set the pony into a trot as they reached the lane. The thick brown mane lifted and fell to the rhythm. They turned up the back drive in the shade of the trees and came triumphantly into the weedy stable-yard.

'You've caught the sun,' said Hugh as Etta ran in.

'My hat blew off. I didn't put it back.'

'I don't need to ask if you had a good time.'

'I drove the pony.' Her face was flushed and damp. At any moment, he thought, she might ignite. 'I drove all the way to Roman Hill and then through a gate and into a field and round and up to Home Farm.'

Her happiness was infectious. Hurrying from the kitchen Curry could hear them laughing.

'Oh, Mrs Murray,' said Hugh, 'could you ask Mrs Prince to put our tea in a basket? We'll eat it in the rose garden.'

19

PADDY REBELLED.

'You arrange it,' she told Paget who called at the Lodge on some business to do with Home Farm. 'It's nothing to do with me any more.'

She was 'stubborn' Paget reported to his wife, and worse: he saw the old devilish spark in her eye. 'I don't know what she's up to,' he complained. She was going to London to stay with an old friend, a woman she had met during the war. 'But why now?' asked Paget. 'With everything so uncertain. If she has to go anywhere why not to Italy to talk Mr Tom into selling out to Haley?'

There was not enough money for Italy. There was barely enough for London.

'I have nothing to wear,' said Paddy, surveying the wreck of her wardrobe strewn across the bed.

'Who has since the war?' remarked Grace consolingly.

'There's only tweeds, riding habits and ten-year-old tea gowns.' Before the war Paddy had been known to wear a tea gown and a formal suit for visiting Paget, neighbours and the village. Those things were all old-fashioned now. 'Too long, too shaped, too fussy,' she told Grace. 'Anyone would know they were ten years old.'

Or twenty, thought Grace.

At Bretton only Fan and Deborah had been fashionable, Fan by force of personality and Deborah 'because of Edward' said Harriet. Edward took delight in seeing his wife well dressed. A great part of the money Harriet had laboriously saved disappeared into the pockets of London tailors. Harriet said staunchly, 'It gives him pleasure,' when even Deborah protested at some new extravagance, but she compressed her lips and looked away to where the park fence sagged in disrepair. 'You're so practical, Mother,' Edward told her that night she was moved at last to open protest. 'What a life it would be if all the money went on hedge cutting and ditch digging!'

The young Harriet of the forties might have agreed with him, but the old Harriet of the eighties knew that the ditches must be dug before a hundred guineas could go on a dress. 'I could buy three good farm horses for that,' she said. She had kept Bretton going only by making such choices – and by 'skulduggery' said Curry. Sometimes her only weapon had been her character: she had simply overawed her creditors. But 'It gives him pleasure' she said and settled with the dressmaker, the milliner, all the rest. Ambivalent as always towards her difficult son, she felt compelled to indulge him and restrain him at the same time. 'He never understood restraint,' she said. Now, so astonishingly in love, he would not even acknowledge the word. 'It's so romantic,' said the servants. 'It's unnatural,' said Harriet.

After Deborah's death the frocks and hats and exquisite underwear were put away in the great trunks in the attic where Miss Hartley was to find them thirty years later. Nothing was cut up or cut down for Paddy except once, though her clothes were always in a desperate state. Often there was little to distinguish her from the Potters whose rags were expected to last for three generations before they went for floor cloths.

'I was never interested in clothes,' Paddy told Grace.

Tall, 'oblong' as she called it and ignored – who was there to encourage her?

'If you really mean to go to London,' said Grace, 'we ought to see Miss Squires. And go to Frilton.' She was dubious about what Frilton might have to offer but anything was better than this.

'I expect Webster's will still give me credit,' was Paddy's bleak offering.

Webster's had given credit to Harriet but she had only bought calico aprons and bolts of cloth. Everything she wore had been stitched at Bretton. Everything except the ball dress which she wore only once, and tore. It was folded away in muslin and tissue paper 'and forgotten' lied Harriet. For her daughters' balls she wore the proper black of widowhood and middle age with a lace cap that made her look 'hideous' said Fan. As for the rest: 'I expect a suit to last twenty years,' said Harriet, 'and then do another ten in the garden.' 'I should think that's obvious to the whole county,' said Mary.

Mary was the one who felt impelled to keep up appearances. Fan did not 'give a biscuit' Edward complained and any shortcomings in Harriet were put down to the eccentricity of a strong character. 'Mother, I wish you'd remember who you are,' Mary said frequently. 'I do,' said Harriet. 'I never forget it.' In church, in the village, at home, she was conscious of this forthright domineering Mrs Bretton. I have made her, she thought, I've made her as a disguise. Behind the hard shell she knew another Harriet, not the Harriet Harcourt that had been, or Harriet Bretton of the now and the future, or Harriet the mother, the bailiff, the overseer. 'Just Harriet' said Harriet. Of the children only Fan had discerned her, called her, to herself, Harriet-in-the-garden. 'My mother's happiest in her garden,' she told her husband. In the garden she was 'different' said Fan, groping for truthful adjectives, 'warm, open'. Though she and Harriet stormed at each other – 'tooth and claw' said Edward – there were no wounds. 'I know she loves me,' said Fan.

Mary knew no such thing. She deplored Harriet's attitude.

'What attitude?' asked Harriet, alarmed.

'You're always concerned with outward things: clean faces, clean clothes, food, markets, columns of figures.'

'I suppose I am,' said Harriet.

Where Harriet bludgeoned the village into a proper appreciation of drains, Mary's concern was its moral welfare. She craved a spiritual fulfilment and in seeking it brought pious platitudes and 'dread' said Harriet to every cottage in Stenton.

'The least we can do,' said Mary, 'is to make sure they understand the Commandments.'

'Are they so difficult to understand?' asked Harriet.

'Mother, you know what I mean.'

Harriet thought: I believe I've given birth to a missionary. She said firmly, 'A shilling is much more use than a sermon.'

When Mary left for Brighton and Cousin Lizzie Harriet missed her long pale fervent face. 'I think I ought to go. The poor woman needs me,' Mary had said, as if certain Harriet did not. She wrote copious happy letters to Bretton full of praise for sea air, Cousin Lizzie and a curate. Perhaps she has found what she was looking for, thought Harriet. When she came home she grew restless within twenty-four hours as if Bretton could not satisfy her, there was nothing there worthy of her reforming zeal. 'I'm a hopeless case,' said Harriet. 'She gave me up long ago.' With her gently greying hair and ugly spectacles Mary seemed no one she recognized, surely not the woman who had grown out of the golden-haired little girl in the portrait in the yellow drawing room.

'It's always so nice to see you,' she said with genuine warmth though she knew the visit would be fraught with difficulty, with unspoken censure, with the re-examination of old sins.

'It's strange,' and Mary looked about with 'myopic disdain' said Harriet. 'I don't really feel I belong here at all. I don't think I ever did.'

The train plunged into a tunnel. I look indescribably old, thought Paddy, looking at her reflection in the window. Her Frilton hat looked soberly rustic, a market-day hat for a nice plain middle-aged woman. The last time she had caught sight of herself like this she had been travelling in the opposite direction, going home to Bretton in the last year of the war. Beside her Tom had sat, in uniform, asleep or pretending to be.

'I'm lucky to have any leave at all,' he said when he met her outside the hospital.

'You must go down to see Father. Tom, you must. Look, I'll come with you if I can change my time off.'

She had thought his face oddly stiff and grey. His eyes avoided hers. She felt that often he simply withdrew as if into some private inner world.

'If I get out of this alive,' he said, 'I'm going abroad. Italy perhaps. Why not? Mother used to live there.'

'But what about Bretton?'

'I don't give a damn about Bretton.'

I don't give a damn about Bretton, thought Paddy. The thin drizzle of early autumn was misting the carriage window. The woman opposite had closed her book. They were clanking through the suburbs. The war is over, thought Paddy. Tom is in Italy where he wanted to be. And I . . .

She removed her hat in the taxi and arrived on Sylvia's doorstep looking somehow wild and bewildered, draggled by rain.

'Why have I come?' she demanded.

'Because I asked you,' Sylvia replied, holding open the door.

*

She found herself unexpectedly popular. She moved with such elastic grace, wore her slightly eccentric clothes with such indifference, spoke with such delightful honesty, admitted so readily she had not seen the latest art nor read the latest books nor had the least idea of the latest fashions, that the consensus was she had newly arrived from abroad, perhaps India. Paddy said nothing to contradict. 'Perhaps Bretton is abroad,' she said to Sylvia. 'Think of it. So far away in spirit it might be another continent.'

Sylvia had never been to Bretton but she had seen several photographs, one very old of Paddy as a child with a severe old lady in black holding a croquet mallet. In all of them Bretton looked vast and romantic.

'I can't think what you ever had in common with that woman,' was Sylvia's husband's unsympathetic comment.

'The war,' said Sylvia. 'Gas, gangrene, blood, filthy dressings, death.'

'I wish you wouldn't speak of such things.'

'I wish you wouldn't refer to my friend as "that woman"!'

All the same, the first few days were perilous. She wondered if she had opened a box on a dragon. Besides, the dragon had no money, or very little, which meant theatre tickets and taxis and afternoon tea were a constant source of friction. Sylvia's husband Harry said Paddy looked as if she should be striding into the African interior driving the natives before her with an umbrella. 'She's infernally tall,' he added, 'and she answers back.'

She had always answered back. 'Answered up for myself,' she would have said. As a child she had been punished for it, standing in the corner for an hour, deprived of jam for tea. 'That Miss Paddy's a handful,' said the nurserymaids, coming and going.

'Do you remember . . .' Sylvia would begin as they

sat by the fire before going to bed, but her memories were of the hospital, of Paddy resolute behind a starched bib, 'taking a stand'.

'Where's Harry?'

'At the Club.'

He was often out or in his study. 'I don't care for that woman,' he would say and after dinner he would excuse himself and disappear. If they were not going out the women would sit by the fire and talk. He would come in late and find them still there, perhaps one in a chair and one on the floor. Like girls, he thought. Often they were laughing.

'He resents my being here,' Paddy said.

'Of course not. He's just never met anyone like you.'

He walked warily, like a man in sight of a strange animal. She had forthright opinions. Such energy, such defiance, seemed to him masculine and he deplored it in a woman.

'He's afraid of me,' Paddy said, 'because he suspects I can think for myself.'

'Poor Harry,' said Sylvia, smiling.

The dress had been made out of one of Harriet's ball gowns, peach silk, heavily embroidered. 'How it has lasted,' exclaimed Miss Squires, smoothing it out. Paddy wondered where Harriet had worn such delicate stuff – surely not at Bretton? Why not Bretton? There must have been balls at Bretton – Aunt Mary's, Aunt Fan's. The peach silk belonged, however, to another decade. 'To another Harriet,' Harriet would have said. Tight in the waist and full in the skirt – 'There ought to be a hoop, a crinoline,' said Miss Squires. 'It must be fifty, sixty years old.' She was busy tucking pins in her blouse. 'It does seem such a shame to cut it.' But she cut it quite savagely into a 1920s tube. 'It might be by Worth,' said Grace, present at the trying-on. It was a masterpiece, a creation. 'I feel naked,' said Paddy.

'My dear, that's the fashion.'

'You'd die of a fashion like this at Bretton.'

In London Sylvia said, 'My God, where did you find such a lovely thing?'

Where did you wear it? Paddy silently asked Harriet. The hem was torn. Why was it never mended? Such a dress, expensive, exquisite – the little of it Paddy now wore was still beautiful and the rich embroidery trickled between her breasts.

'She's quite different tonight,' Harry reported to Sylvia. She could hardly frighten the natives dressed in such splendour. 'She's more . . .' He cast about, frowning. 'More human.'

'I told you,' said Sylvia. 'You should have watched her nursing those boys.'

His reservations were under assault, but they held out. She was tall enough to look him in the eye, which he found unnerving. Though she was warm and tender in his stiff arms as they danced he still felt irrationally anxious, as if she were explosive.

'They never take me to dances,' she had complained to Jack Chance. It had been a foggy October evening and the lamps were lit at Roman Hill. She had been schooling the grey filly behind the stackyard and she had come indoors to thaw her hands and face before going home. Jack was at the table in the parlour, writing. How the conversation came round to dances was a mystery but it did and she said, 'They never take me. I've never been to one. I'm almost eighteen and I've never been to one!'

'Aren't the Paulleys having one for that boy Philip? He's twenty-one in the spring, isn't he?'

'Yes, I suppose so.'

'Well, you'll be invited to that.'

'I've been asked out before. Not to dances: tennis, tea, staying a weekend. But I'm not allowed to go.'

'You'll go to that one. Grace Paulley will see to it.'

Paddy had turned away, putting up both hands to repin her slippery hair. 'I don't even know how to dance,' she said.

She had danced the polka with Maudie in the nursery and cantered self-consciously round the maypole with Philip when she was twelve, but nothing could have prepared her for dancing with Jack Chance in the old parlour, snatching the skirt of her habit out of the way, hairpins sliding out at every turn. After a while he began to hum the tune of an old waltz, his mother's favourite, and suddenly she grasped what it was about and they moved together easily, happily, up and down between the table and the chairs.

Where was Meg? she wondered afterwards. No one came to ask what they were doing. The house was silent. They danced until she had no breath left and a long loop of hair was falling down her back. Then he let her go, quite abruptly, and said, 'So now you can waltz. There's nothing to it,' and went back to his writing.

Before April the next year when the invitation arrived she had persuaded Curry to teach her the steps of half a dozen dances. 'Curry?' asked Grace when she found out. 'Curry dancing?' 'There was no one else,' said Paddy. After this all that was needed was a dress. Edward expressed no interest. He felt he was doing the Paulleys an honour by going. He told Paddy Curry must see to it; he knew nothing about women's clothes, women's fancies. Curry looked grim. 'He said that, did he?' she asked. She went up to the attics and opened the trunks one after the other and then bore away an armful of finery to Miss Moy, the charming new dressmaker in Frilton. Miss Moy obediently transformed what she was given to a ball dress of white silk and lace.

'Good God!' Edward could not believe his eyes when Paddy came downstairs on the night of Philip's birthday.

'It's just the thing for a young girl,' Curry said.

'Girls should be modest,' said Edward.

Paddy's eyes were clear winter grey between their black lashes. The piled-up hair amazed him. He had never noticed her tiny waist before, her breasts.

'What a fuss for a birthday party,' he grumbled, watching her put on her cape. He would never guess the dress had been made out of one of Deborah's. 'And we shall never tell him,' Curry had warned. It was, after all, the first and only time. 'I shall probably never be allowed out again,' said Paddy.

'Bring me some cake, Pat,' howled Tom from the stairs.

'I'll try.'

She could see his face between the banister rails. It looked tired and rebellious. He was acutely conscious of being abandoned. Usually he had all the treats and Paddy stayed behind.

In the hall she saw herself in the great gilded mirror, a tall slender figure with soft black hair above a frightened white face. 'Goodness,' said Curry, hurrying with wraps. 'Pinch your cheeks. You look like a ghost.'

Brook Court was all lights, flowers and music. I don't know what to do, thought Paddy, paralysed. I can't ask Father. She did not hear the introductions, she was not aware of Grace's cheek pressed to her own, or Philip's hand in hers. Was it Philip who stared at her in amazement, or Mr Paulley, or the whole room? Her cheeks were colourless. Girls and young men she only vaguely knew or did not know at all were speaking or gazing at her, at her height, her proud nose, her dress. 'Save me all the waltzes,' said Philip. Or did he?

She did not know what to write on her card. Her hands in her gloves felt hot. Had Philip really meant her to save him the waltzes? Other young men approached, seeing her alone and vulnerable. They all seemed to know she hunted, had seen her, had heard of her. Dance after dance was taken.

'They'll tell Father I go to Roman Hill,' she whispered to Philip when he came to claim her.

'No, they won't. Why should they?'

She craned to see Edward, talking earnestly to someone unknown. 'I *know* someone will tell him. And the Chances are here.'

The Chances often dined at Brook Court. It was one of the unspoken reasons why Philip was only just tolerated at Bretton. Tonight Grace felt the responsibility of keeping the families apart. 'It's all so ridiculous,' she said. 'Whatever it was that happened happened fifty years ago.' Later, exhausted, she added: 'Jack Chance makes me blush.'

'There isn't a woman for twenty miles he hasn't made blush before now,' replied Frank cheerfully. 'Remember when he was young? Seventeen, eighteen. He should have been whipped but his father was dead and no one else dared do it.'

There was supper, more dancing, then speeches, Philip contorted with embarrassment like a small boy. Afterwards there was clapping, laughter, congratulations. Paddy found herself waltzing again.

'You look so beautiful,' said Philip. It was not an original remark but he said it with devotion. 'They all want to dance with you. I'm jealous.'

Paddy's legs felt strange and her head was swimming. She seemed to have been dancing for ever. The supper had not soaked up the unaccustomed wine and she was still in a state of nerves, parrying questions from young men who had admired her on a horse, a Chance horse. Safe in Philip's arms she recounted the evening's surprises: the women's compliments, the girls' confidences, the young men's admiration. 'Well, you *are* charming,' said Philip. 'Why shouldn't they say so if it's the truth?'

Then at the corner as they turned: 'I love you, Pat.'

Her arms felt as weak as her legs. The lights blurred and flickered. There was an overpowering smell of perfume, flowers, champagne.

'Say something. Pat?'

She had nothing to say. She was numb. They turned and turned and she did not look up at him. 'No one has ever said that to me before,' she said almost inaudibly, thinking back down years and years.

'I should hope not. I hope I'm the first. And I hope no one else will ever say it because I'm going to marry you.'

The music ended. She slipped trembling from his hands. He could not tell if she were secretly pleased or merely stunned. Her face was as white as it had been when she first entered the room. stealing herself for the ordeal ahead.

A gallop, the lancers, the last waltz – 'I kept all the waltzes for you,' Paddy said afterwards when Philip expressed surprise at her daring. 'Yes, but what a way to draw attention to yourself, *and* after you'd been so worried someone might tell your father!'

'Look at that,' someone had murmured to Grace. 'Jack Chance asking the Bretton girl to dance as cool as you like.'

The Bretton girl had been casting about for Philip. She had refused three ardent boys to give him this last waltz. When she saw him she was struck motionless, at a loss. He was leading out Isabel Lord whose mother had made sure of him by determined effrontery, and the music was already starting. She turned to Jack with resentment, scarcely hearing him, and he saw and understood, mocking her gently. 'Don't worry. He only has eyes for you.'

She accepted his hand as she had accepted it all her life since she had first gone down to Roman Hill. She had never once hesitated when he held it out to her:

climbing on a horse, over a fence, up a stack, in and out of the trap, or learning the steps of the waltz in the old parlour. As they came slightly closer together in the crowd on the floor she said softly, 'Philip asked me to marry him.'

Jack's hand tightened on hers, but perhaps it was simply to steer her out of harm's way. He said brusquely, 'You're far too young,' and they moved down the long side of the room in perfect accord – no one watching would have known there was anything wrong. But what was wrong? 'He loves me,' whispered Paddy, pretending to smile as they neared Grace and the little knot of matrons sitting out. Jack made no reply.

'Nobody has ever loved me before,' Paddy's voice came, lower and lower.

'You're a silly child,' Jack told her. 'How do you know? Just because no one's said it aloud.'

'But it should be said aloud,' asserted Paddy. They went round again in their formal embrace. She was thinking: How could anyone ever have thought a waltz shocking?

'This is the only ball I shall ever go to,' she said suddenly. 'It will have to do as a coming-out dance.'

'It seems to have been a success then.' They were somewhere in the middle of the room and still, even in such a crowd, he held her decorously from him.

'He loves me,' she repeated, lost in the wonder of it. She raised her face to look up at Jack. His brown eyes were staring away, away to where the orchestra were working up to the last few bars. His face was hard.

'Well,' he said at last. 'It had to happen sooner or later. Nature takes its course.'

The music ended on an exaggerated note. There was loud and prolonged clapping.

'Thank you, Miss Bretton,' said Jack Chance.

Edward, by the door, pretended not to see.

Grace's neighbour, behind her fan, said with amusement, 'I've never seen Mr Chance so serious. And dancing with that lovely girl too.'

20

Laura's latest letter was remarkably full and remarkably affectionate. 'My darlings . . .' she began.

Hugh and Etta were not taken in.

'When is Mother coming home?' asked Etta.

'She doesn't say.'

'I think she should have come back by now.'

'Do you? I think she ought to come back when she's ready.'

Etta considered. 'She might never be ready,' she announced solemnly.

Hugh put down the letter carefully. 'D'you miss her, Hetty?'

'Yes,' said Etta, and 'No, I don't think so,' and then 'Only sometimes.'

Sometimes she went to Laura's bedroom and sniffed at her pillows and inside the great wardrobe that had been Harriet's. The elusive fading scent reminded her. It made her think for a moment, eyes tightly shut, that if she turned and looked Laura would be seated on the edge of the bed polishing her nails or brushing her glossy cap of hair. Sometimes she hung over Laura's writing box or sat in Laura's accustomed place on the drawing-room sofa and sometimes she stood under the cedars and heard, quite distinctly, Laura's high delighted voice wafting from the tennis court. But she did not yet feel herself abandoned. Laura had come and gone all her short life. Only Hugh was constant.

It was Hugh who should have gone to the hotels and boarding houses by the bleak wind-driven sea. 'What could *I* do with a sick child?' asked Laura. 'There was nothing to do there, nothing.' She implied that doing nothing might come easily to Hugh, so steadfast, so unadventurous. She did not understand constancy, the dogged keeping of appointments or promises.

Since Hugh could not, in this case, relieve her of her responsibility, she had submitted to what she called 'trial by sea air'. She had walked the fronts of two south-coast resorts and one, from which she thought she might never recover, in the bitter east. To right and left were the elderly, the tubercular and the young crippled. 'Such sights,' she wrote wildly to Hugh. 'If you had any heart you'd snatch us away from this place. I've never been so cold.' Hugh pointed out that as a partner in the business he had 'commitments'. He did not mention snatching her away. 'He has no heart at all,' Laura complained to a fellow guest, 'or how could he insist we stay in such a place?' and her wide childlike gaze swept the window through which could be seen the grey heaving sea angered again today by that piercing wind.

'I'm better,' said Etta to the doctors, aware by instinct of her mother's restlessness. 'I think I want to go home.' Medical opinion, unsympathetically, came down on the side of the arctic wind. Another fortnight, they said but cautiously, as if preparing the way for a change of mind. 'In a fortnight,' said Laura, 'they'll say we must stay another fortnight, and another. Think how many guineas they could get out of us in all those weeks.' As if to avoid parting with a shilling she immediately vanished for four days.

'Don't tell your father, darling,' she said to Etta, 'but

I really must have a little holiday all to myself. You'll be quite all right with nurse.'

'Of course I shall,' said Etta.

She was more than quite all right, she had a delightful time. Once, on being made to read the Bible during one of Laura's pious periods which often followed her throwing-over of a lover, Etta had come across, 'Take up thy bed and walk.' 'That's what I did,' she said afterwards. 'At the hotel.'

'I won't go in the carriage,' she told the nurse the first morning of Laura's absence. She hated being wheeled along in that Victorian basket contraption like the crippled children and the old men. 'I can walk,' she declared.

She walked stoutly every morning into the tearing wind. Then if she was quiet and docile she would be allowed fifteen minutes on the damp sands, picking up shells and stones and going as close to the furious water as she dared.

'Where has your mother gone, dear?' asked the invalids at the hotel, eager for gossip to sustain their pointless lives.

'Away,' Etta would reply enigmatically. She was used to Laura being away and this time she was enjoying the freedom. Only on the fourth day did she grow anxious. The nurse too was agitated. 'Mrs Haley will be returning shortly,' she told the hotel management, detecting growing alarm in that quarter also. She was a competent and highly qualified young woman and she was underemployed. She would have been happier bringing order and cleanliness to real illness. She knew Etta was perfectly healthy. 'Perfectly,' she told her fellow nurses on the promenade. She lost face, she felt, by being unable to hold up her patient as a medical catastrophe, only alive by being in her knowledgeable hands. Besides, Etta was not only well, she was 'eccentric' said the nurse. Obedient and polite, still she could be . . . 'Precocious,' said the arthritic old ladies in the hotel. The constant companionship of adults combined with a natural solidity and pragmatism produced 'little Miss Hoity Toity' said the nurse, folding her mouth tightly. Etta was like no child she had ever met. She did not refuse to wear her cumbersome outdoor clothes, she put them on of her own accord 'because it's cold and I don't want pneumonia.' 'A child that age shouldn't know about pneumonia,' said the nurse, appalled. It was unnatural. She thought Laura unnatural too but in a different way. 'As to that,' she told eager ears on the promenade, 'my lips are sealed.'

On the evening of the fourth day Laura returned.

'You look nice,' said Etta, sitting up in bed at her step.

'I'm recharged,' said Laura. She was all joy and light, laughing and girlish.

'I like your hat. Is it new?'

'Shhh,' said Laura. 'It's a terrible extravagance.'

'It's a nice one.'

At moments like these their fragile contact mended and held. In this lovely mood Laura charmed as naturally as birds charm, coming to feed on an outstretched hand. To make the most of it Etta begged a story and listened, rigid, as Laura told it, afraid even to move in case Laura took fright, said, 'Well, if you're going to fidget . . .' and ran lightly away. Laura made the stories up, never hesitating, never at a loss. They were 'plucked from the air' she said. Etta would always remember this magical story-telling Laura as the real one, and the petulant, dissatisfied, hard, selfish, estranged woman who was more usually there as someone else, a stranger who did not belong.

'I want to go home,' said Etta as the story ended.

'My poor darling. Of course we'll go home.'

'In the morning?'

'I don't see why not.'

'Can you kiss me goodnight?'

'What a funny question!'

'Other people's mothers kiss them goodnight.'

Laura stooped, pecked the offered cheek without interest. The magic was already fading. 'How do you know?'

'I just know,' said Etta.

Though Hugh was a rock he was 'a jagged rock' said Etta later. To the best of her knowledge he had never kissed her, perfunctorily or otherwise. She felt he did not like her, might even resent her. He was the solid foundation where Laura was sand but that was all he ever seemed to be, something fundamental on which she might come to rest when all around was chaos. He would not nurture her though, encourage her green shoots. She was aware of him downstairs when she was in bed or in his study when she plunged into the Kensington drawing room to Laura at the appointed hour, but she hardly ever spoke to him, hardly saw him. As time passed she came to see his silence, his absence, as disapproval. Perhaps he wished she was not his daughter or that she had been different. 'He might wish I'd been a boy,' she said once to the nurserymaid. 'Why should he?' asked the girl, amazed.

Who could say what he wished? Etta knew grown-ups as mysterious, inconsistent. She learned that parents are difficult. On the rare occasions she played with other children she looked attentively at theirs, apparently so ordinary, so united. It was as if she alone had to cope with her two wayward adults. Other offspring were spared such responsibility.

'I'm sure your mother will be back for your birthday,' Hugh said, tucking Laura's passionate scrawl back into the envelope.

'I hope so,' said Etta. There had been other birthdays dishonoured; she knew how to temper such a hope.

'Hetty,' and he hesitated. So, something was coming. She had sensed it before he had begun to read her

Laura's letter and now she felt something happen in her chest, a sort of clutching feeling. 'Hetty, after Christmas I thought perhaps you ought to go to school.'

She let out her breath. A new horizon then – and change, change. Had there been too much change? 'Do I have to?'

'I don't want you growing up completely ignorant.'

'I'm not completely ignorant.'

'You haven't many books. You ought to do music,' said Hugh feebly.

'Is that being ignorant, not having books?'

Once, thought Hugh, I was the only man in my trench with a book but they all knew more than I did, how to dig, shoot, crack jokes, survive. He closed his eyes. The cadences of country voices came back to him, arguing about latrines, scarce cigarettes. They had known how to endure and no book had taught them that.

'Where shall we be?' asked Etta in a small voice.

'Where?' Hugh returned from a far place, a little shaken.

'After Christmas. When I have to go to school.'

'Oh, then . . .' He rubbed his chin. 'I've no idea, Hetty.'

There were no certainties at all then, they were adrift with the current. Etta finished her toast carefully, leaving no crumbs.

'Will we go back to London?'

'No.'

One certainty? Etta knew how adults changed their minds. 'Oh darling, I didn't *promise*,' Laura would say.

'Are you really absolutely sure?'

'Really absolutely.'

Hugh had walked to the window and was looking out. When Etta grew up she would always remember him like that, standing looking out. 'What did you see?' she would ask the memory. But: 'What are you looking at?' the child Etta demanded.

'The cedars,' said Hugh.

Curry came in to clear the breakfast. She seemed more starched than usual as if she had been delivered only that very moment, clean and stiff, from the industrious Mrs Potter. She shot dark glances at Etta, noting the dribbles of butter down her pinafore, the thick hair struggling already from its ribbon.

'That Pen Potter's on the back step wanting Miss Etta,' she said disapprovingly.

'May I go, Father?'

'Do what you like,' said Hugh, 'but don't get into mischief.' At the closing of the door he added apologetically to Curry, 'She has no one else, has she?'

He wished suddenly that he could give her more of what he felt she ought to have: friends, attention, outings, protection from the ugliness of life. Momentarily he was overwhelmed. A daughter . . . A daughter to keep safe, to guide, to give away. His mind shied from the possible disasters. A son might have been easier, he thought. He would not have had to worry so much about a son. Since he did not have one he could not guess that the burden might be equal, though different.

'I suppose young Pen's all right,' he said vaguely.

Curry did not care to reply. She went on putting plates on to a tray.

'Who did Miss Bretton play with when she was small?' Hugh demanded abruptly, just before she had finished. 'I suppose she knew other children?'

'A few.'

'But most of the time she was alone.'

'Later on there was Mr Philip from Brook Court.'

'The one she nearly married?'

Curry picked up the tray. 'Yes, sir.'

There might be hope, after all, Hugh thought. If Paddy had survived, so could Etta.

★

'Father says I might have to go to school after Christmas,' Etta informed Curry. Wind and rain had made her glowing pink. She smelled of pigs.

'Where *have* you been? You'd like school, wouldn't you?'

'I don't think so.'

Since Hugh said nothing more about their leaving Bretton she did not think about it, though she still cried in the night and had worrying dreams. The future was an imponderable blank so with a child's natural capacity for living in the now she did not ponder on it. In any case, it seemed she could not be spared for school or anything else. Hugh needed her as a companion. At nights before she went to bed she sat with him in the blue room playing spillikins or Old Maid. Sometimes he read aloud but he was always solemn and self-conscious; Etta preferred to read to him. Used to playing alone, to acting every part in imaginary dramas, she was good at voices, tackled difficult prose headlong. Hugh would listen with his eyes closed, smiling gently.

The blue room was their retreat. Unused by Laura it held no memories of her. 'Unused altogether,' said Curry, 'since Mrs Harriet died.' It had been Harriet's sitting room. Edward had never entered it after reading the letter she had left him in her desk, a letter he had found only by chance. 'Keep it locked up,' he had said to Curry. 'It was my mother's private room. I don't want anything changed.' Curry did as she was told and added the key, thoughtfully, to her chatelaine. From then on the room was spring-cleaned once a year and nothing more.

'Why don't Mr Bretton go in?' the kitchenmaid asked over the greasy dishes. 'Old Mrs B was always that good to him.'

'Guilt,' said Mrs Meikeljon. 'He never showed her affection while she was alive. Now she's dead he'd rather forget.'

Even during the war the room remained unused. The Matron assumed Edward had private possessions stacked within, that it was part of the arrangements. She passed the door almost without seeing it, accepting it as forbidden ground. When Curry was forced to give up her keys she slipped that one from the bunch and kept it along with some others, duplicates, under her pillow. 'Curry has the keys,' Harriet had always said. 'They could not be in safer hands.'

There were great iron keys and small fancy ones, keys to front doors and back doors and larders and meat safes, to the cabinet of rare books in the library and the linen press on the back landing, to store cupboards and clothes cupboards and medicine cupboards. 'I can open them all,' Curry told Paddy, who had ventured for the first time into her room and seen the neatly labelled board over the chest of drawers where other women might have hung a mirror. Those were the keys that would not fit on the chatelaine, the lesser keys. 'I'll always know you've got a key to everywhere,' said the child Paddy.

'And sometimes two,' said Curry.

The day after Philip Paulley set off for a distant cousin in Hereford and Paddy understood, finally, bitterly, that he would never marry her, she shut herself up in her room.

'Come out,' thundered Edward. 'You must eat.'

'No,' said Paddy.

'Your father may come round,' Philip had told her, but without hope. In the passion of her own feelings Paddy never wondered if his heart might be broken too. She thought his words senseless and pathetic. When he declared he loved her she no longer believed him – where were the actions to prove it? For nearly four years she had been waiting for him to do what he had promised.

'You said you were going to marry me,' she cried. Small birds in the hedge behind her fluttered in alarm.

'Don't shout,' said Philip, glancing across Hobeys half furtive, half defiant. 'They'll hear you at Roman Hill.'

'You don't love me at all,' and then, because even when most tempestuous she was always just: 'You do. I know you do. But you don't love me enough.'

His white face, a moment ago so stricken, was now colouring with fury. 'How can you say that? How can you?'

'Because if you loved me enough you would marry me. Whatever anybody thought or said or did. You'd marry me.'

'You give that boy a hard time,' Jack had said.

'I don't. I love him.'

'You overwhelm him.'

'I want to marry him.'

'You want to escape from Bretton.'

'So you don't believe I love him at all.'

'When you were eighteen you loved him. Remember that summer? Kissing in the long grass up on Hobeys. Perhaps I should have put a stop to it. Now you want to get away from Bretton as much as you want Philip Paulley. You may still love him – but it's not the same.'

How cruel he was, thought Paddy, telling her truths she never wanted to hear. Until now she had not thought of love as changeable, nor was she experienced enough to know that change did not necessarily mean decline. 'I was in love,' she told Jack, 'and now I love.' With stubborn decision she repeated, 'I love him.'

She thought of this often during the long hours in her room, refusing comfort, refusing food, refusing to unlock her door. 'I won't come out,' she told Ellen who brought up the trays, and Mrs Meikeljon who puffed up the stairs secretly to whisper coaxingly through the keyhole. Only Curry did not come near. 'You had to get it out of your system,' she said afterwards. 'It had been coming on for years. I knew that when the hysteria wore off you'd come to yourself.' But the hysteria wore off to leave a limp and apathetic Paddy, slightly dizzy from lack of food. There was silence from the bedroom. Edward said, 'Break down the door,' meaning: Fetch the men to do it. But Curry walked upstairs and simply fitted the key in the lock and opened it.

'I thought there was only one key to this door,' said Paddy.

'Did you?' and Curry had hung her own back on the board above the chest of drawers.

Edward thought Paddy had come out of her own accord. He was even mildly sympathetic. He told her bluntly she was a fool but that no more would be said. He was appalled by her appearance, wasted, unsteady, face puffed and blotched with weeping. It confirmed him in his belief that women were outside men's comprehension. 'All girls have moods,' Sarah had told him in those difficult days when Paddy had been fourteen, fifteen, growing up. For all her 'old-stickness' as Paddy called it, she had been staunch in Paddy's defence. 'Patricia has too many moods,' said Edward, whose own prevailing one since Deborah's death had been unremitting gloom. Sometimes, though she was always quiet, even meek in his presence, he would look at Paddy with loathing. This child with Deborah's eyes was nothing to do with him. But whose was she? Who had bequeathed all the attributes not Deborah's? The face, the black hair, the 'moods'. Since he did not know about her childish escapades with Philip, the forbidden familiarity with Roman Hill, he found her no trouble, except when she gave in to these occasional tantrums. She was reasonably tidy, she was punctual to meals. What else she was, what else she did, he gave no thought to at all. Only who she was worried him, because she was not his.

In the blue room, apparently shut up for ever, Curry put vases of the spring flowers Harriet had loved. Though her heart had been Deborah's, her gratitude went to Harriet who had given her most, who had given her Bretton. The portrait of the young woman whose demure smile was so at variance with her stubborn chin looked down on her secret ministrations from above the cold fireplace. It was not the true Harriet. 'It isn't me at all,' she had told Sophie when it was finished, but it was part of Sophie's wedding present to Ralph and Sophie was absurdly pleased with it. It depicted, perhaps, a Harriet she had long hoped existed.

Hugh, teaching Etta to play chess, occasionally looked up and wondered who she was. He liked the blowy fullness of her skirts, the flowers in her lap and hair, the freshness. He thought all women must look like that at one moment in their lives, if one could catch them before such touching innocence was lost. Etta, face puckered by some enormous mental problem, square little hand poised over one piece after another and then withdrawing, said without looking up, 'Her name was Harriet Harcourt and she married Ralph Bretton in 1843.'

'Good Lord! The things you know,' said Hugh, startled.

There had once been two portraits of Deborah in this room, pictures of some quality. Both had been taken down. In one she had been a girl of sixteen, neither child nor woman, smiling the secret smile of adolescence. She had been seated on a low garden wall against a background of blue hills and cypresses. In the other, painted the year before Tom was born, she had seemed a formal, melancholy woman, looking older than twenty-seven. These, and all the photographs he could find, Edward had destroyed. Her bedroom, next to his own, had been cleared out. Having no shrine therefore, Curry filled no special vases, but all the flowers about the house were for her. Once, when Paddy was thrusting roses into a pot, she said, 'Your mother used to put them everywhere, seven, eight vases to a room.'

'I remember,' said Paddy, who never thought of Deborah without pain.

Hugh wrote a long restrained letter to Tom Bretton and then hoped he had struck the right note. He had taken such care not to offend that perhaps each paragraph was more insipid than the last. He looked it over critically but saw nothing he could usefully change. Between deference and aggression there seemed no middle way.

Since it was a morning for tackling the more disagreeable things of life he wrote next to Laura.

This too was a masterpiece of self-effacement. He put down line after stilted line, hoping she was well, asking politely whether she knew when she might be coming back, mentioning Etta's rude health and the gradual deterioration of the gardens without Paddy's attention. Most of it, he knew, would not interest her in the least. He wondered if, were he not to write at all, he might shake what he thought of as her complacency. He was sure she was happiest away from him and in such a state his prosaic communications would only be intrusions, reminding her of the unbearable. Nevertheless, he wrote on. He had no other means of communication. This, though imperfect, must suffice.

At last he signed his name. The cloud lifted. He sat back in his chair and examined his hands, tense and slightly inky. From somewhere far away he heard the closing of a door, footsteps, a female voice. There was nothing unfamiliar in this and he knew, as the clock struck, that Curry was carrying the china and cutlery to the dining room for his lunch, that Mrs Prince was at the stove, that Lily was making Etta wash her hands, that all the shrivelled ritual of the great house was in motion.

Such a house is nothing, he thought, without its family.

Bricks, glass and flagstones did not make Bretton; the

young woman with the lapful of flowers, the unknown Ralph, the partly known Edward, Paddy, the errant Tom – these had made Bretton. The gentleman on the landing wall in the grey silk suit and the up-to-the-minute wig – he had made Bretton.

Why did I ever think I wanted this place? he wondered.

He looked at the letter to Tom Bretton. He could always put it on the fire. Curry lit a fire in the blue room now the evenings were misted and chill.

A knock. 'Are you coming, Father?'

Hugh found himself looking keenly at his daughter, as if assessing her chances of coping with this house and the sort of life she might expect to lead here. She stood at the door, an ordinary child, not obviously destined for either prettiness or intellectual triumph.

She said, seeing his frown, 'You must come. Else it'll go cold. Curry's waiting.'

'She should blow a trumpet,' Hugh said light-heartedly, making an effort. His brow had cleared. 'How did they summon the family to the table in the old days?'

He got up from the desk and stood for a moment, gazing intently at the two letters.

'My hands are dirty. But tell Mrs Murray I'm on my way,' and he snatched up the envelopes and thrust them in his pocket, smiling.

21

'SHE WANTS TO leave the day after tomorrow,' said
Sylvia. 'She says she must.'

'What an incomprehensible woman!' said her husband, but he said it more kindly than he might have
done the week before. He had hoped to see her in that
peach-coloured frock again, the feather in her soft hair.
Only dressed like that and in that buoyant mood had
she declared herself ordinarily and satisfactorily female.
With sudden dread he asked, 'You aren't going to beg
her to stay?'

'It wouldn't do any good if I did,' said Sylvia. 'Paddy
is never easily turned from the direction she's chosen.'

She had not easily been turned from Philip but one
could not out-argue death, nor, by persistence, defeat
it. After Philip had shot himself walking out after rabbits
in far-off Hereford she had been kept close at Bretton.
Edward demanded her devotion to his comfort and,
while disapproving of the horse dealing, did not seriously discourage it for fear boredom would make her
restless.

All the same, she had escaped. She escaped to Roman
Hill.

'Be careful,' Jack had warned her as he had so many
times. 'All those hot young bloods in the hunting field.
Mind you don't land on your back.'

She had blushed. 'What do you think I am?'

'A sadly neglected child who mistakes flirting for affection. And grief can make us act strangely.'

'You've no right to give me moral lectures.'

'Lending you my horses gives me the right.'

'It doesn't!'

'Then pay me for their hire and you can have a rest from the lectures.'

'What are you thinking?' asked Sylvia.

'Oh, something someone said ... years ago. He was afraid of what foolishness I might get up to in pursuit of love.'

'And what did you get up to?'

'Nothing at all.'

Paddy was looking at her face in Sylvia's mirror. 'Use what you like,' said Sylvia. 'Powder. Perfume. I don't know why we're going out at all. It's your last evening. Do you want to go?'

'I thought you did. Anyway, we're already dressed for it. What would Harry say if we suddenly appeared in nightgowns and said we'd changed our minds?'

'We did once at the hospital. D'you remember? Appeared in nightgowns, I mean.'

'Only in the middle of a raid. I call that a legitimate excuse.'

Encased in unbecoming uniforms, they had once been photographed, solemn as undertakers. Sylvia had framed hers and sometimes looked at it, wondering. Had such a world ever existed? She had been two weeks on the ward before Paddy had arrived, chill miserable weeks, lonely beyond belief. 'Do you think yourself above such tasks?' the iron-faced sister had demanded once, and once: 'Have you no common sense, girl, none at all?' Sylvia, treated with contempt, had grown clumsier and more stupid by the day. Then Paddy had come. 'Just in time,' said Sylvia.

'What did I do?' asked Paddy.

'I don't know exactly. You just were.'

'Nurse Clements seems to have improved since you arrived,' said the sister to Paddy.

'You gave me courage,' said Sylvia. Confidence, flooding back, made her a capable nurse. She thought Paddy was like a flame in a dark place, shedding light and warmth. Too much warmth sometimes – there had been tempestuous scenes with authority. 'They won't bully me,' said Paddy. The men adored her.

'I needed you there when Harry proposed,' said Sylvia.

'Good God! Why?'

'To give me the strength to say no.'

The London interlude was over. Paddy did not consider it had been a success. She had ached to be away from Bretton and now ached to return. She decided, rather nonsensically, that it had something to do with the peach-coloured frock. It was as if Harriet was brought closer by her wearing it, so that now, putting it on for the last time by the gaslight of another age, she could imagine Harriet speaking and breathing beside her.

'Skirts will be even shorter next year,' Sylvia predicted happily as they descended to the waiting taxi.

What we had to put up with at the turn of the century, thought Paddy, stays and bloomers and layers of this and that. How did we manage? Philip and I in a mazurka headlong down Hobeys . . .

'Dance with me,' she had commanded, and Philip had rushed her down the tumbling slopes, half laughing, half embarrassed. 'Say you love me again. Say you're going to marry me.' At that he had pulled her gently into the shadows under the elms and kissed her. His were shy kisses, ticklish and clumsy.

'Oh, I so enjoyed your birthday,' she said, leaning back in the circle of his arms. 'Let's dance again.'

'What have you been doing?' asked Jack when she went to Roman Hill. 'Sporting under hedges?'

'How dare you!' She stuck out her chin, Miss Bretton of Bretton. Love had made her thin-skinned. She could not bear his familiar mockery, his genial teasing.

'That's right. Brazen it out.'

'It's none of your business. You're not my father.'

'No, thank God.'

They were in the parlour. A dog was curled asleep in the wing chair, another on the rug. A clock ticked. The sound of clashing dishes came from the kitchen, the length of the passage away. Someone was singing.

Paddy said disarmingly, 'He makes me so happy.'

'Good.' Jack spoke after an age, stirring his long frame. 'Good. I'm glad.'

She knew him too well, knew that oblique sober look. 'Are you? Are you? You do wish us well, don't you?'

He had been sitting at the desk. Now he stood up and came to her – all fierce movements. For a moment she swayed, stepped back. Then his large hands cupped her head, all the straying black hair. He bent his head and kissed her on the cheek.

'That's my answer,' he said.

The action and the words were enigmatic. She gazed up at him trying to gauge his mood, his opinion. She willed him to be on her side. She had no one else but Curry to confide in. Though Grace had smiled on her at the ball she could not confide in Grace. Never, never, she thought. Instinct told her Grace might be shocked by such emotion.

'What should I do?' she asked suddenly, a little frightened.

The spaniel on the rug stretched and yawned. Instead of singing the extraordinary muted echo of raucous laughter reached them, and a momentary draught as if somewhere in the house an outside door had been opened and closed.

'Do?' Jack stooped over the desk. He seemed to have lost interest. 'There's nothing you can do. These things run their course.'

It was a cruel way, she thought afterwards, to speak of such coruscating love.

'Philip. Philip,' she cried, running up Hobeys and turning circles, throwing out her arms. 'Philip, Philip, Philip.'

Harriet never went to *her* ball, the ball for which the peach silk dress had been made. At least, she set out – but never arrived.

'I can't possibly go without you,' she had said to Ralph the day before. 'It would be unthinkable.'

'Of course you must go. It would be more unthinkable to cry off now.' He was in bed with a head cold, swathed in towels and blankets, propped among hot-water jars. 'Morley's one of my oldest friends, he's Lord Lieutenant, and half the county will be there.'

'But alone . . .' began Harriet again.

'You must take Frome.' Frome was one of Curry's predecessors, an anxious vacillating creature much under Harriet's thumb.

'But think how strange it will look.'

Ralph had only one thought, that Bretton should be represented at the biggest ball of the year, the county occasion. So the dress was taken from its wrappings and hung in Harriet's dressing room, shimmering in the candlelight. Bragg touched it reverently. It would break her heart not to see Harriet in it, her hair carefully arranged. 'I could put the back hair into a bun under that little lace square, all done up with fresh flowers, madam, and then the sides in ringlets . . .' she could hear herself saying. She was aware she had the ability to transform Harriet and she longed to do so. 'Ringlets are frivolous,' she knew Harriet would say, but: 'Ringlets are the fashion, madam,' she would reply firmly, setting to work. Harriet did not follow fashion – what was the point in this remote place? On the other hand the peach dress was undeniably the latest cut: the neck, the sleeves, the tiny pinched-in waist.

'Bretton must be represented,' Ralph had said. 'I think I do Bretton justice,' said Harriet to her reflection, descending the stairs. The ringlets swung against her cheek. Frome, standing holding her evening cloak, blinked at her, astonished.

The carriage was at the door.

It was a dream, Harriet thought afterwards. When she looked back she saw only moments caught in a skein of darkness: Frome's hunted expression, her jet brooch like a carbuncle; light from the house spilling down the skirts of the peach dress before the carriage door was closed; her own hands in her lap holding the nosegay of roses.

Four miles from their destination some country cart held to the middle of the road on a blind bend and forced them over. The front nearside wheel hit a milestone and splintered, the horses lost their heads, Andrews was flung off the box and all was pandemonium. Harriet was the first into the road, climbing out before the carriage had quite turned on its side. Frome's screams continued behind her, all on one note.

'Andrews, get up. Where's Johnnie?' Harriet had an imperious manner in times of crisis.

Johnnie Dack had sensibly released the traces. The horses were away. 'Mr Andrews hev a bump on the head,' he said, and Harriet fetched one of the carriage lamps to make sure.

There was a cottage down the road. Harriet roused out the frightened old man who lived in it. Andrews was unconscious and Frome hysterical. Johnnie Dack commandeered the country cart to fetch a doctor.

'It was the strangest evening I ever spent,' Harriet said afterwards. She sat in her beautiful dress in that hovel of a kitchen, the only room downstairs, brewing tea at a fitful fire she had made herself while Andrews snored on a filthy bed in the far corner. Frome, white and whimpering, nursed her bruises in the only decent chair, and the old man stood bemused, staring at them. In an hour – 'the longest hour of my life' said Harriet – the doctor was there, a brusque young competent sort of man. By then Andrews was coming to himself and sat up with a dish of tea, his eyes watering.

'Better to leave him here till morning,' said the doctor. He could not quite believe in Harriet, in the dress, the cloak, the long ringlets reddened by the firelight. 'May I drive you home, madam? You and your companion.'

But Frome grew hysterical again; she would not step into another carriage as long as she lived. Her weeping was so violent that Harriet wondered her body could withstand it.

'I believe it's the effect of shock,' said the young doctor, a little at a loss, and hurried Harriet out into the warm night.

'But what am I to do with her?' asked Harriet.

There was the sound of wheels. The lights of a gig advanced like small wavering stars. The doctor said, 'Perhaps we shall be lucky,' and stepped out, calling.

'Are you going to Stenton? Frilton?'

The horse was pulled up reluctantly. It rolled its eyes at the doctor behind its winkers, throwing its head up.

'Stenton certainly.'

'Then I would be obliged, sir, if you would deliver a message to Mr Bretton of Bretton Hall.'

William Chance leaned forward. In the fitful light of the moon and his lamps he could see Harriet only indistinctly. She had put up her hood and her face was obscured by a mass of crushed ringlets.

'Mrs Bretton?' and then, looking away down the road: 'Is that your carriage? Has there been an accident?'

'There's no harm done,' said Harriet calmly.

'Except that the horses are away,' the doctor told him, 'and the coachman has a knock on the head, and Mrs Bretton's companion is hysterical. Perhaps . . . Could I ask you . . . It is Mr Chance, is it not?'

'I really think,' began Harriet, seeing what was coming.

'There is no need for you to stay. I shall persuade Mrs . . . Frome? . . . to walk to the next cottage. There's a young woman there who will make her comfortable. Your man will do very well where he is until tomorrow.'

William gave her the rug to put over the peach silk. After that he was fully occupied with the horse, a typical Chance tearaway. They passed the wrecked carriage at a tremendous pace and the road stretched away white in the moonlight.

'How did it happen?' William asked after a while.

Harriet told him.

'Your husband thinks you're dancing and dining with the Lord Lieutenant,' said William cheerfully. 'What a sorry end to your evening!'

Harriet said nothing.

He did not drive through Stenton but took the back lane to Roman Hill. 'You can drive to the door,' she pointed out. 'To Bretton. Since you've been so good to me, how can my husband object?'

'If I'd snatched you from highway robbers he'd object. Guilty consciences make irrational men.'

'I don't understand.'

There were no lights at the house. The stableyard was deserted. 'Will you come in?' asked William. 'My wife . . .'

'No,' said Harriet in a low hoarse voice. 'No, I won't come in. I must go home.'

She sprang down from the gig, her skirts bunched up. He left the horse and followed, crossing the shadowy stockyard in her wake.

'Mrs Bretton . . .'

She had skirted the orchard and was by the beck. There was no bridge in those days and only stepping stones near the ford. The trees hid her from the house, hid him. It scarcely mattered. No one had waited up for him, he had not been expected. He had driven forty miles to a horse sale but had bought nothing and decided to come home.

'Mrs Bretton . . .' and he set off after Harriet with a rising temper. How dare she run away from him like a frightened child? How dare she refuse to enter his house. How dare she, her shoulder touching his, have sat so remote and proud down all those miles of empty lanes?

'You have dirt on your face. Or a bruise,' he had said at some point, looking at her solemn profile. She had put up a hand and felt with her fingertips.

'It's a bruise, I think.'

From under the rug billows of silk escaped. 'The hem is torn,' he remarked. 'I'm sorry. It never occurred to me you might have been hurt.'

'I'm perfectly all right.'

She was far from perfectly all right. She was tearing away from him over Lower Bit like a deer. Her cloak blew back and the moonlight bleached the colour from her dress. At the stile into Hobeys she stopped. A woman in an 1850s ball gown could not negotiate it without help, not even Harriet.

'If you must get over it,' said William, catching her up. 'Here, give me your hand. You're making an exhibition of yourself, you know.' His temper had cooled but still his grip was painful.

'I can manage from here,' she said. 'I'm grateful for your kindness.'

'You sound like a child,' he exclaimed.

'I'm not a child.' She was thirty-nine. She was completely at a loss.

'I know you're beautiful,' he said. It was the last thing she had expected. She gave a strange nervous laugh, gathering up her skirts.

He reached out to touch her cheek and then his hand slid warmly under the curve of her jaw and he leaned forward and down and kissed her on the mouth.

I had never wanted any man but him and I didn't know what wanting was until he kissed me, thought Harriet later. The strength of that desire still astonished her as an old woman. At the time it astonished William. So this was why she was behaving so strangely.

He had so grudgingly admired her since she had come so boldly and so secretly to pay for the brown mare. He remembered her ardent young face breaking into laughter as his father had kissed her hand. Since then he had told himself she was everything he hated in a woman: narrowly reared to be decorative and dutiful, repressed, restricted, delicate, a perpetrator of good works. And yet . . . he knew she managed the estate, omni-competent, full of energy. It had been a great struggle for him to be unjust to her and now, relieved, he gave it up.

I was vulnerable in that dress, thought Harriet; vulnerable because it made me enchanting to him and because it offered no protection: no high neck, no buttons, no 'layers' said Harriet. His lips and hands were very sure, experienced from so many conquests.

'I love you,' he said.

She did not believe him. What woman should? But she gave herself up gladly to the lie.

In the 1850s Bretton was always full of people: eight servants in, six out and plenty of daily and casual labour. There were curious eyes everywhere. At Roman Hill William's young wife was busy with her young son. Guilt and lack of privacy were as good as a chastity belt. Harriet did not see William again for months.

She rode the brown mare a great deal but the mare was old and a little stiff. Once or twice she took the grey cob. She felt such a deluge of relief when she was away from Bretton but she was drawn back willy-nilly 'because they can't get on without me' she said. Every time she passed the gate to Hobeys she turned her face resolutely away.

'The trouble with that,' said Harriet, 'is that it's a coward's way out.' She had never been a coward. She fretted, wrestling with moral implications and absolutes. Gradually she grew harsh and demanding, a more temperamental mistress than of old. The labourers shook their heads and smiled knowingly and said it was her time of life, poor woman. Besides which, they reasoned, the account books might conjure that frown between her eyes: prices falling, markets difficult, Mr Ralph extravagant. But each day as she looked up the track to the farm buildings and away from the gate to Hobeys Harriet thought: Ralph finds his pleasure elsewhere, why shouldn't I? Other women do it. And: What about his wife, his child? William has no cause to look elsewhere even if I do. And inevitably: You can't do such things in a village and hope to keep them secret.

In February one of the men cut himself badly in the root chopper and was laid out on the floor of the barn to die.

'What is all this?' asked Harriet, stalking through the door. She had been summoned in the middle of dinner, there was snow falling and Ralph was away.

'He be dyin', mum,' said someone, standing back to let her look.

'Have you sent for the doctor?' They had, they assured her, but he was not expected to be in time. The blood was everywhere, too much, too red.

Harriet bent down and looked for what had to be done, if anything. These men, who were all used to pig killings, castrations, great cuts with scythe and sickle –

they all stood back, aghast, watching her dabble about. 'Yes, dabble,' Harriet told Deborah. 'He had nearly severed his arm. But there was still blood in him. Whether it was enough I couldn't tell.' She did what she could, much as she might have attended to the brown mare on the long-ago hunting field. When she had finished she felt suddenly sick but it seemed undignified to show it. She rose, looked about. 'Is the doctor coming?'

Someone went to listen and returned to report hoofbeats on the sleety wind.

It was William Chance. He had brought the doctor at the gallop. 'At the gallop and on a night like this!' the doctor protested, trembling as he climbed down. Why William? Had he been near when the accident happened? How could he have been? Harriet shrank, feeling the cold strike through her. The doctor said he must have light and looked at her crossly, seeing her pale and bloodstained. Would she faint on him? After an interminable time he gave orders for the man to be moved to the farmhouse. William sent two boys for a hurdle and did what he could to trim the stable lamps. He did not look at Harriet.

As in all crises, time passed slowly. There was a silent procession to the house, the pale body hurried along in a flicker of light. Most of the men went home. It was beginning to snow in earnest. After an age – 'Oh, it seemed an age,' said Harriet – William said, 'I'll see Mrs Bretton home,' and put a man's oiled cape round her shoulders with impersonal politeness. 'So I came back to Bretton,' said Harriet. But even to Deborah she never told the whole story.

There was blood on her skirt, on the good tweed of her coat, but William made no comment, simply put the waterproof round her and led her out into the snow. He had a lantern but it simply lit a thick white swirling mist into which they ventured blindly, steadily, knowing their own territory. At the gate to Hobeys William stopped. He stopped abruptly and said harshly, 'Harriet.'

It was not a question, it was just her name, as if he had been compelled to speak it. She made to go past him but he caught her arm, doused the lantern, dropped it, gathered her to him. How could he do all that at once? was her last coherent thought.

His mouth was cold. 'Harry,' he said. 'Harriet.' There was soft wet snow on their faces, on her closed eyes.

Then the sound of wheels, of jingling harness, made William reach for the lantern and begin to try to light it. This is what it will always come to, Harriet thought, guilt and pretence. The waggon, late home from taking corn to the mill, struggled by them, and by its cyclops light old Jerry Plant peered down and then touched his cap under his sacking shawl.

'That's a cruel night,' he said. 'You should be safe at home, mum.'

I should, thought Harriet. I should be safe in Bretton, caged, inviolate. The waggon slewed on towards the farm. She crossed to the green door into the garden and put her hand on the latch, leaning her forehead on the cold wood.

'Harriet,' said William gently. His hand brushed her shoulder.

'I don't belong with you,' said Harriet.

22

PADDY CAME DOWN the long drive at Bretton on the chestnut mare and vanished among the rhododendrons. Etta, watching from the steps, saw them emerge, sideways, with terrific speed, hop over the park fence and run seriously away in a westerly direction.

'Who is that?' Hugh asked Bushey. They had been admiring the stone newly raised over Edward's grave.

'Miss B.,' said Bushey sourly. 'Larkin' about fit to break her bones. She should be past all that.'

It seemed for a moment she soon would be. The mare had been bought the other side of Frilton and obviously intended to return there. Streaking beneath the oaks, intent on her mischief, she did not see the men or even the stone until the last moment, and then, swerving violently, slipped somehow and turned over.

'I was ready for that,' said Paddy brightly, picking herself up from some yards away and walking towards her stricken transport.

'My God, I thought you'd been killed,' said Hugh.

'I must say,' and Paddy picked up the trailing reins and made encouraging noises, 'I don't think I've ever surpassed that for a dramatic entrance. It might have been more effective, of course, if you'd caught me as I flew off.'

'Perhaps in future,' said Hugh, slapping the rump of

the reclining chestnut mare, 'you could give me a minute's warning and I'll do what I can.'

The mare blew loudly but did not stir, Paddy said, 'If she's broken the saddle tree . . .' and gave a snort of laughter. 'Mr Johnny Chance owes me thirty guineas already. Five for a buck, I think I said. We haven't covered a hundred yards without a mishap yet and now she's winded herself, the young fool, and will lie here all night unless we put a firework under her tail.'

Hugh said, 'Bushey could fetch a pail of water.'

The thought of Bushey staggering from the house and dousing the mare's smouldering temper with the contents of his bucket made Paddy laugh. She said, between choking noises, that she preferred the idea of the firework.

'I see you enjoyed London,' said Hugh, refusing to join in the merriment.

'Why on earth should you think so? I didn't at all. Have you heard from my brother?' This last was shot at him as she walked round to wallop the mare on her glossy flank.

'No.'

'We may never hear from him again. I understand he's given orders to Paget to sell for the best price.'

'That won't be mine then.'

The mare gave a heave and came to her feet. She looked sadder and wiser. Hugh remarked on it. 'Don't put your faith in fickle females,' said Paddy. 'Will you give me a leg up?'

'Ought you to ride her after this?'

For answer she gave another snort of laughter and held out a booted leg. The mare danced a little, recovered. By the time they had reached the park railings she was giving an imitation of an angry rocking horse, and she jumped when asked with a sort of suppressed fury, disappearing up the drive with her tail whirling.

'That horse isn't safe,' said Hugh, who knew nothing about horses.

'Oh, that take a bit to shift Miss B.,' said the philosophical Bushey.

What would it take to shift Tom? Hugh wondered. He had had no reply to his letter. Hearing Paddy had returned early from London he hoped she might have news. In the long evenings after Etta had gone to bed he had made lists of the improvements he would make – and then had screwed them up and burnt them. Bretton would never be his. Every day when he looked at the weeds, the leaking gutters, the damp, he told himself he should rejoice at his deliverance.

'Miss Paddy had a horse once . . .' Bushey was saying, involved in circuitous reminiscence. Hugh walked beside him, nodding, but not hearing. As they crossed the last of the rough grass and came from under the sweet chestnut by the fence, the soft dull afternoon was lit for a moment by a watery sun. In front, its many windows shining, stood the house.

'. . . and that was what she said, blow me,' concluded Bushey, climbing over the railing.

'Yes,' said Hugh, prompted by the silence, but he was gazing at the house between its guardian trees, and his smile was loving.

'I've lost count of what you owe me,' said Paddy. 'She behaved abominably.'

'I'm sorry. She's been a lamb these last few days.'

They were watching the chestnut mare making short work of her oats, dropping half of them, snorting the rest into the air, impatient in all she did. Johnny sighed. 'Perhaps she'll go quietly in harness,' was all he said as they crossed the yard again.

In the parlour he counted ten guineas on to the little mahogany table.

'I'm afraid you'll have to wait for the rest.'

She laughed, but gathered it up. 'Did you think I'd let you off?'

'Never. Besides, from the quantity of mud on your back it seems I should be grateful I haven't to pay for a broken neck. What are you looking at?'

'Who is this?' She had picked up a photograph in a gilt frame.

'My grandfather, William.'

'I've never seen it before.'

'My grandmother left him. She was his second wife and very young, a doctor's daughter. She lost her first two children as babies and when the third was three she took him home to her parents. Of course, William wasn't dedicated to monogamy, I understand. And he was a difficult man, an autocrat and rising in society. Still, he wanted more than a decorative wife and one who gave in tamely when he bullied her. And my mother told me Rebecca hated the farm and all that therein was, poor woman, besides losing the children and not having William's undivided attention. No wonder she ran away.'

'But she came back,' Paddy said, looking at William's uncompromising face. 'She came back and ran the farm. Jack was only ten. He told me.'

'My grandmother couldn't have run a jumble sale,' said Johnny affectionately. 'She made an art of indolence. But if she thought something was right she would not be moved. She thought leaving William was right, though it caused something of a scandal, I imagine; and she thought coming back was right so she came. She was lucky, she found a good man to keep the farm going – well, someone found him – until my father was old enough to cope by himself. He was sent away to school "to put some polish on him" as it was phrased to me, but that didn't last long: he was back and out in the fields and learning how to buy and sell horses before he was seventeen. Too much like his father for Rebecca probably. She'd inherited her parents' house and went to live there when he married. I only saw her once and she seemed an old old woman. She sat on a sofa all day or played the piano, my mother said.'

Paddy picked up the small terrier who had been waiting patiently at her feet for attention. She was encumbered by her bowler hat, in which she had put the ten guineas. Johnny came to take it from her and, close to, saw the fine lines on her skin, the hairpins slipping from the net that held her hair, the extraordinary clear grey of her eyes. The dog was trying to lick her chin.

'You remind me of someone,' he said impulsively.

'Good heavens!' Her eyes widened. She struggled with the dog, smiling. 'Curry said that to me once. "He reminds me of someone," she said. It was a rather fat young man with curly moustaches and a yachting cap. It turned out he was the image of one of the porters at Frilton station.'

Johnny said, 'Give me that rascal. He's a terrible ladies' man. No, it's not a lady porter you remind me of, it's your grandmother.'

He set down the dog and rummaged in a drawer. The small photograph he produced barely did justice to its subject, dogeared and faded as it was. It was Harriet certainly, but at a distance, standing on a Bretton lawn with her two small daughters and an assortment of spaniels. She was recognizable more than anything by her stance, head up, ready for action and that suspicion of latent humour well-repressed.

'I found it when I was turning out,' said Johnny. 'I found William too. My grandmother wouldn't allow him to be on show, my father said. But where this comes from, your guess is as good as mine.'

The sense of loss overwhelmed her again. It was like, Paddy thought, being flung into a void. This woman she had loved, this stronghold of her childhood, did not belong to her at all.

'It's not my grandmother,' she said.

When she had wearily explained he remained silent, looking at her. Then: 'She loved you. She always treated you as her granddaughter.'

'Perhaps she didn't know.'

Johnny laughed. His laughter was heartening, catching her up as she sank so that she felt solid ground again. She looked down at Harriet on the lawn with a new strength.

'If you ask me, from what I've heard,' said Johnny, 'your grandmother knew everything.'

'Early Victorian,' said Paget, sucking the end of his pencil. 'Wouldn't you think so, Miss Paddy?'

'I think Harriet brought it into the family when she married,' Paddy was looking, not at the table, but at the two things it displayed: a very fine Chinese vase and a silhouette in a silver frame. 'I think that was my great-grandmother,' she said doubtfully. 'Sophie Harcourt.' Paget's eye was bland. We both know, she thought, that I can't truthfully name anyone in this house as my relation. Except Deborah.

There was nothing of Deborah left at Bretton.

The silhouette of Sophie, Harriet's birthday present, we a continual reproach. Harriet felt, when in the room with it, under observation. 'One day,' Sophie had said, 'you'll know what it's like to be a mother yourself.' Was being a mother so terrible then? Harriet had not thought so until this moment. She was not aware of ever having done anything to cause her parents anxiety. Indeed, she had often hung back, conscious of her height and nose and stubborn chin. Then she had been grumbled at for being so 'retiring'. 'I'm not retiring in company I like,' she told Sophie apologetically. Still, if that was being troublesome she could not see it. Her cousin Edith had let men kiss her – several undistinguished and unattractive men – and had once tried to run away with a schoolmaster. If one could not fall between two extremes surely it was better to be slow rather than fast?

'It's only that I don't . . .' she would begin. 'I don't know.'

She spent the years between fifteen and twenty-five in this fretful state of indecision. The longer marriage eluded her the less she understood its purpose. She had no hope of financial independence though she longed for it, recognizing it as the true escape from this uncongenial life. Her relationship with Sophie scorched and chilled in turn. Ralph Bretton's frantic wooing, his rash assault, broke down all her half-erected barriers. A conventional courtship would not have touched her, but she was not yet proof against romance.

Still: 'I don't know, Mama,' she said.

But in a blaze of satisfaction, decision and acquisitiveness, Sophie drove the marriage through. In settling her children in life she always showed this furious organizing ability. The rest of the time she was indolent and dissatisfied like most of the other women she knew.

'You said yourself you're fond of him,' she told Harriet over the packing of the bridal underwear, the day dresses, afternoon dresses, skirts, blouses, habits, belts, collars, caps, hats and travelling coats.

Harriet wished she had not been so foolish as to confide anything. 'I think I am. But . . .'

There was always a but with Harriet, Sophie had found. All her life. And the small child refusing to wear new shoes might easily turn into the grown woman refusing an advantageous marriage. 'Once she says "no" and sets her mind on it we'll never get her to the altar,' Sophie told her husband.

'But she's always been so tractable,' he replied. He had never had to wrestle with Harriet's 'buts', not as Sophie had, and only Sophie knew what it had cost to overcome them.

'She is not always tractable,' said Sophie darkly.

'She'll do as she is told.'

'She won't do anything at all if she's frightened into being stubborn. You must remember, it's only six weeks since she first met Ralph Bretton.'

'And lucky to get him. Why doesn't she see it?'

What Harriet saw was difficult to guess.

'No girl would think of turning down such an excellent offer,' one of the aunts told her.

'Why not?' asked Harriet. It was one of her mulish days. Sophie had tried her too hard all morning with measuring for the wedding dress.

'Why not? Good gracious, child, what are you saying?'

'Yes. Why not?'

The question was never answered, and before Harriet could think of an answer for herself they drowned her in tissue paper, tea sets and lace-encrusted nightgowns, so that it was only coming out of the church into the clash of bells that she thought with a dreadful constriction of her heart: What have I done?

'What have I done?' she asked Sophie at the wedding breakfast.

'Every bride feels nervous,' said Sophie soothingly.

'I think I can love him but . . .'

Here we go again, thought Sophie. 'My dear, you are married now. You must do your best to please your husband.'

So Harriet and the furniture, pictures, china, linen, the silhouette of Sophie, came to Bretton. The sidetables in the dining room had been hers and the Georgian knifeboxes on them, the elegant sofa table in the blue room, the lady's desk at which she had struggled with the Bretton accounts.

'There is some good stuff left, you know,' Paget said consolingly eighty years later. 'I believe we may clear the death duties without being too hard-pressed.'

'We'll be left with the shell, you mean?' asked Paddy.

They passed up the wide stairs. Paget was a little unnerved. He would have given anything to know what Paddy was thinking. He had put off this necessary inventory until he could put it off no longer, and he had hoped, pointlessly he now found, that her two weeks in London would have restored her good humour. Instead he found her in a brittle, incendiary mood. He knew it of old – and was afraid. He had heard she had been seen riding a horse of Johnny Chance's. He could scarcely credit it. And yet . . . she might do anything, he thought, anything.

The rain spattered against the windows. The dim landing was in deeper shadow than usual, the mirrors dulled, the great pictures practically invisible. Bedroom after bedroom opened one from another. Paget shook his head. So much had already gone. Stopping to catch his breath and sharpen his pencil he said, 'I never thought I'd live to see this day, Miss Paddy,'

In front of him, in what had been her own bedroom once, was the rosewood cabinet with the Chelsea figures. He did not care for Chelsea figures. He noted the cabinet, putting a tentative date against it in his list and wondering if it too had arrived with Harriet.

'It was my mother's,' said Paddy coldly. 'Father missed it when he scoured the house after she died.'

'I'm sorry . . . Old memories best left . . . Now, what about the china?'

'I don't know. There used to be a tea set, no, a chocolate set in it. Very old. A pinkish colour.'

'And where is it now?'

'I sold it,' said Paddy. 'It will be in one or other of the books.'

'You have no heart,' Edward had said. 'That was my grandmother's set. Precious stuff.'

'I know, Father. That's why I sold it. We must eat.'

It was 1919 and Bretton was a ruin of green paint, flimsy partitioning and the lingering whiff of carbolic.

The gardens had run wild for four years. There were marks on every wall downstairs where the iron bed-frames had scraped. 'We must eat,' said Paddy and packed up the exquisite little chocolate dishes and carried them away. Beggars can be choosers, she told herself, if they stand out for a choice.

'I remember doing an inventory during the war,' Paget said, mopping his brow. 'Before the nurses moved in. Your father spent a very anxious week while things were packed up. All the portraits went into the attics. The men had only just finished when he took it into his head the doctors or patients might set the place on fire and was all for taking them down and putting them in the Lodge. Sixty big pictures! I told him: they'll be as safe up there as anywhere.'

The boule cabinet had gone, the pair of regency card tables, a great deal of the early walnut, two clocks. The bedrooms were scarcely better furnished than when the Matron had shared one with her Sisters, only a screen marking the lines of seniority and privilege. Laura's bedroom was luxurious because it was full of Laura's furniture from the house in Kensington. Paget looked round it, smiling. 'Such a charming woman,' he said.

Later: 'Do you remember how they put lino down in the hall and the stairs were bare? What a clatter it all was!'

Paddy remembered. She remembered how she has stood in the doorway, horrified, her hands clenched in her damp gloves. Her father, in the Lodge, had been shaking with anger. 'They've no right, Pat, no right. Damn them all. The house is ruined.'

It had been spring and there had been young men under the cedars on crutches. The stables were full of noise, for the orderlies had been banished to the grooms' lofts and besides that, the ambulances came there, delivering the batches of young men. 'One batch after another,' said Curry who still controlled the kitchens.

Some walked, some hopped, some came on stretchers, some spoke and some 'gibbered' said Curry's anxious minions. One ran naked into the midst of their dinner preparations and hid himself in the larders. Curry locked the door on the doctors and coaxed him out, wrapping him in a bicycling cape of Fan's she found in the Piggery. Even so she did not think he heard her voice, or only as a distant murmur beyond the sound of guns. 'One batch after another and none of them convalescent,' she said. They were all bad cases sent to 'vegetate' said Curry scornfully. They came to Bretton for their difficult wounds to mend a little and to grow strong enough for another operation. 'We got the flotsam and jetsam,' said Bushey, but he said it soberly, afraid he might one day find there had been a thousand such houses full of equally ruined young men. He disliked the nurses: they came to smoke in his garden out of sight of their superiors. Though his own grandmother had smoked a pipe he thought them shocking. Curry found them shocking for other reasons. Where she was practical and unsentimental they were practical and callous.

'Not all of them,' said Paddy. 'Surely not all of them?'

'I wouldn't set them to tend pigs,' said Curry. 'And the VADs are worse, turning up their noses at everything and anything.' Buckets of disinfectant, old dressings, enemas – they could not face anything.

'But I'm a VAD,' said Paddy.

'You've got sense.'

And sensibilities unfortunately. The boys at Bretton made Paddy's heart ache. Her heart ached far more at Bretton than at her London hospital with its continuous stream of acute cases. There she had no time to think or was too tired. Here she felt real despair for the first time. In such a mood she entered the ward that had once been the yellow drawing room. 'I am Miss

Bretton.' The Sister in charge had goggled at such effrontery. Someone had stifled a laugh. The nurses had paused in whatever they were doing and had looked up, scarcely breathing. 'I am Miss Bretton,' she had said. Her hat had been awful, old and shapeless, her uniform coat covered in smuts from the train. She had not eaten since London and she had a headache. Her eyes had been like flints. 'She had that look on her face when she threw the egg out of the window,' said Curry.

Now the lino had gone from the hall. The flagstones had been scrubbed and covered by the threadbare Baluchi rugs. But the hospital lingered. Something of its stark utilitarian character had invaded Bretton. So much had been sold to 'pay for things' that some rooms were almost empty.

There were always things to pay for: plastering, pointing, gutters, burst pipes, boilers, flues, broken locks, servants. The Bretton servants fled from the hospital, the hospital servants fled from Curry. 'We started here and here we shall finish,' Curry told the kitchener. 'The latest thing,' Harriet had said happily, watching it installed. It had remained the latest thing at Bretton until the tennis court, and then the crippled boys in their iron cots, the latest thing for 1916.

'And this was your grandmother's room,' said Paget, opening the door.

It was Hugh's room now but had once been Harriet's exclusive territory. As a child Paddy had called it 'the red room' because the curtains at the tall windows looking out on the cedars had been dark wine velvet. Put away during the war they had been lost or forgotten and pale blue silk, thin and shabby, now hung in their place. The silk would have suited Harriet better, Paddy thought. Red had not been her colour. Blue, strong and cool, was more like Harriet.

'Strong but not passionate,' she had once described

her grandmother to Curry. 'Determined, yes. But not passionate.'

'People can be passionate without having hysterics,' retorted Curry. It was something she often said to the young Paddy, always in scrapes.

Harriet never had hysterics. 'Thank God,' she said, 'I've never fainted in my life.' There were times she might have liked to but 'I can't' she said. With no means of escape she coped with life as it happened. Not much happens, she thought, shut away in this rural retreat.

Then she found the book.

'To my dear Ralph from his own Clarissa.' It was a schoolroom hand, well taught. The book was Keats. Harriet would never have believed her husband knew a word of Keats.

'Who is Clarissa?' she asked.

'Clarissa? Nobody.'

'The girl you loved who refused you. Was that Clarissa?'

'There was no such person. No one refused me.'

'But you married me. Why did you marry me?'

There was something . . . There was something. She did not know what it was. Ralph . . . Clarissa . . . Roman Hill. She still walked to Home Farm past the gate to Hobeys but now she stopped and stared away down the frolicking green. 'I should be ashamed,' she thought. But she had no shame. If William had asked, if there had been somewhere safe, she would have gone to him.

He did not ask. There was nowhere safe. She was not a willing girl he could take under a stack in two minutes' happy coupling. A year had passed already, more years would pass, and still she would not be his. She would remain at Bretton while he inhabited the valley, all Hobeys between them. Conditioning, convention, a moral code like armour was between them.

'Do you know anyone called Clarissa?' Harriet asked her housekeeper, writing on and on, not looking up.

'No, madam.'

'But you've heard something?'

'I heard say there was a Miss Clarissa Chance, madam.'

Harriet dressed with great care and went secretly down Hobeys to Roman Hill. 'Who's to say how secret anything is in the country?' she said afterwards. She spoke to Rebecca in loud commanding tones – 'my most hateful' she admitted – and was put to wait in the best parlour.

'How dare you come here?' were William's first words. She was shaken by them. She had come with no expectations of any sort but she had not dreamed of outright hostility.

'I came to ask . . . I have no one else I can ask . . . Who is, who was Clarissa?'

The silence had a particular quality; she could not tell what it was. William had his back against the door but she felt he might fling it open at any moment, dismiss her harshly. She twisted her hands together without thinking. It was a strange thing for her to do and the helplessness of it touched him.

'I had a sister Clarissa.'

'A sister.'

'I always thought you knew. Everyone knows.'

'I don't know,' cried Harriet. 'I don't know anything.'

He was breathing quickly, but he was not angry. She sank into the wing chair, gripping the arms. He was not angry. He was afraid to tell her whatever it was, the thing everyone else knew, the whole village knew, Bretton knew . . . 'But I can only guess,' said Harriet.

'My sister had a child by your husband and died. That is all there is,' said William.

'All? All!'

'It was a long time ago.'

'It was the year Ralph married me.'

'It may have been.'

'You know it was.'

'It could never be proved it was his child. You know that.'

She rose. 'Thank you,' she said. 'There was no one else I could ask.' She took a step towards the door.

'Harriet,' he said.

It was a long time since the snowstorm, his cold mouth warming against hers. She looked up and met his eyes and dignity fled, her hands shook.

'Never come here again,' he said, and as he opened the door for her: 'You and I should only meet on neutral ground.'

Another spring came. There were cuckoos shouting in the hazel woods and the swallows returned to the Bretton stables. The young green ran up the side of Hobeys and every leaf was shiny with new life. Harriet walked under the cedars in the moonlight, like a bitch, she thought, like the bulling heifers. And why not? It was only natural. I was caged till I was twenty-five and then I did my 'duty', thought Harriet. There had been nothing natural in that. She paced up and down, up and down under the cedars. Was William waiting in Hobeys? Neutral ground, suspended between two worlds. I cannot go, thought Harriet. I dare not.

Soon the days began and ended in mist. The cock pheasants battled in the drive. Harriet looked in her mirror and saw grey hairs. Ralph was ill, short of breath, at home more than he had ever been because journeys tired him. He spent days in the library, sometimes with Shipley, looking over old documents, old maps, old accounts. He looked frail and aged. Harriet put Keats back on the obscure shelf where she had found it and said nothing about Clarissa.

The days wore on. Harriet was in 'low spirits' said Bragg who found her more and more difficult to please. She was often sharp with the servants, a thing they naturally resented, but what was worse, she was often silent. She rose early and walked in the park alone. She came in to eat breakfast without speaking. She sat with the account books late into the night. 'I don't know what we're coming to,' said the housekeeper, Mrs Pretty. 'The master shut up all day with those old books and the mistress looking to die of melancholy.'

At last, at last, driven to it, Harriet went down to Roman Hill.

It took all her courage. 'But I wanted to know,' she said. The wind was stripping the leaves from the elms in Hobeys. If William had once waited for her he was not waiting now. She stumbled a little over the sour trodden turf. She had dressed carefully in sober grey. Hooked into it she was Mrs Ralph Bretton, not the Harriet who had walked under the cedars in the moonlight. At the farm the hens were scratching round the chestnuts and there was a smell of new bread.

'I'm afraid he's not home yet,' said Rebecca. She was not the shy young girl whose bridecake Harriet had carried away and still kept. She looked older, tired, a little untidy. Her small son had died in the spring diphtheria epidemic.

'It was really not important.' Harriet struggled for a plausible excuse. She had not come prepared. 'I'm sure Shipley will explain it to me. It's nothing. I'm sorry to have disturbed you.'

Rebecca moved to hold the door wider and Harriet saw she was expecting another child. 'Will you step in, Mrs Bretton?'

'No, thank you,' Harriet heard herself say.

'We're sorry to hear Mr Bretton is unwell.'

'He must be careful,' said Harriet. 'His heart is weak.'

'I'll tell my husband you called.'

'There is no need.'

The dusk smelled of the coming winter. Harriet let her expensive skirts brush among the wet leaves. She walked slowly, stopping once to catch her breath. She felt as if she had been running. Never had the climb to the summit seemed so long. A blackbird singing late in the tossing elms broke off and flew away at her approach, giving the alarm.

Behind her, feet were brushing through the grass – a long heavy stride, half running. Harriet knew it was William without turning round but even so his first words came as a shock.

'I told you never to go to the farm.'

'Ralph is very ill,' she said irrelevantly, as if trying to deflect his anger.

'I'm sorry for that. But why did you come?'

'I came because I need to know about Clarissa.'

'There's nothing to know. She died the year after you were married. The new year. '44.'

'And the baby?'

'Was fostered and died too.'

He stood in front of her. In all the greyness only her face was distinct, a long pale oval, thinning now with age so that the strong bones were more prominent.

'I thought . . . I thought there might be more to it. I wanted to know what she was like. All these years and I never knew why I may not come to Roman Hill,' and she stood with her hands at her sides, her head bowed. 'I feel so tired,' she said.

When he kissed her forehead and her cheek he thought it was like kissing a statue, but the statue trembled. Her mouth was warm, and welcomed him.

23

GRACE PAULLEY BICYCLED up from the village.
'My dear, I was nearly demolished by the doctor on the bend near Sweet's cottage. He drives all over the road.'

'It's that car. He has to tackle so many things simultaneously to make it go that it's a wonder he has enough arms and legs. Or perhaps he's hoping to increase business. He must be bored in Stenton. Mrs Potter can cure most things with elderberries or castor oil.'

Grace leaned the bicycle against the wall. 'I never liked the Lodge much,' she remarked. 'Why not come and stay with us?'

She had no great hopes but she felt a faint stirring of relief when Paddy refused and immediately felt guilty. 'Well, if you want to invite a tiger into the house . . .' Frank had said.

'Have you heard anything?' She had intended to strike out into new calm waters but Paddy's look showed her the rocks ahead.

'From Tom? I had two lines yesterday.'

'Only two?'

'I'm beginning to think two is his limit. He simply said he'd make a decision in his own time.'

The letter had read, 'I shall do what I want. You

cannot make me sorry for you or for Curry or that outdated barracks of a house.'

Grace scrutinized Paddy minutely. London had not done anything to lighten the dark shadows beneath her eyes or give a more optimistic shape to her long mouth. It had not restored her pleasure in life. Grace sighed, feeling the old fondness – an irritating and irritable fondness – rise up as she looked. 'I longed for a daughter,' she had said once, and Fate had thrust Paddy at her. She felt that her own daughter would have been pretty and biddable, a great comfort, whereas Paddy was emotional and 'wild' said Grace, trying not to shudder. 'But I did what I could,' she might have added truthfully.

It had been Grace, after all, who took Paddy away after the accident.

'Oh, I wish we knew . . .' she began. She broke off as her eye wandered about the room, noting its unusual tidiness, the absence of pictures – sent back to Bretton? – and the strange cold uninhabited feel of the place, as if nobody lived there and as soon as she and Paddy had finished this conversation it would be locked up and abandoned. 'There's nothing worse than indecision,' she continued, rallying. 'I dread turning in at the gate and finding men at work in the park, chopping and felling. My dear, you have a terrible bruise on your chin. I didn't notice it before. What have you been doing?'

'Oh that,' and Paddy touched it lingeringly, smiling. 'I fell off Johnny Chance's mare. It's nothing. I've had far worse in my time.'

'I know,' said Grace with feeling.

Seared by grief and shock, Paddy was an automaton. It was the only time a horse had died under her.

'It wasn't your fault,' said Jack, lifting her sobbing into the gig.

'But I asked him to jump. I felt him hesitate. I asked him.' The words were gulped out. She could hardly breathe from crying.

'Pull yourself together. Things happen. Death happens. The horse broke his neck. It's over and done. If you go on making that noise I'll push you out and you can walk home. They'll all find out what you've been up to then.'

A February dusk, dank, cold, sleety. The racy bay between the shafts covered the ground at an alarming rate, a true Chance-bred mare. The cold mists were thickening and the mud under her hooves was freezing fast.

'Look at me,' said Paddy. Her habit was mud from neck to hem, her hair down, her face smeared with dirt and blood. Someone had picked her up. Who? One of her many admirers? She had had eyes for nothing but the horse, kicking once then lying still. 'I shall never hunt again,' she said. They were only ten miles from Bretton. The mare wanted her stable, her rug, her oats. Little flints and great gouts of cold mud flew up from her hooves. 'Steady,' said Jack reprovingly. In another half a mile he had to stop to light the lamps.

Paddy was cold inside and out. She was too numb to care if Edward found out she had spent the last seven years riding Jack Chance's horses as well as her own. Nothing could be worse than knowing Showman was dead. 'It could happen to anyone,' a voice had said, looking at the corpse, but the sidesaddle at her feet rebuked her: it happened to you. A mile from Stenton when Jack handed her his large handkerchief and suggested she wipe some of the mud off her face she sat holding it. 'It isn't any good,' she said. 'There's so much.'

She was a strange nervous creature, Jack thought, sometimes a paragon of unbridled selfishness. Yet underneath there was always this lost innocent child struggling about. When the news had come, borne over the miles of field and wood in that remarkable swift way of the country, he had harnessed the mare with dread, only too conscious of the possible repercussions. What if someone had already been sent to Bretton? He could imagine Edward's astonishment, Edward's rage. He had imagined it for years, a great strain for any man with a conscience. 'Thank God I have no conscience then,' said Jack to himself, none at least in deceiving Edward Bretton. 'If he can't see what's going on under his own nose he's more of a fool than I thought,' was his verdict. He drove through the gathering gloom of the afternoon with a furious concentration though, hoping to salvage what he could of Paddy and Paddy's reputation.

'For God's sake,' he said roughly. Though she had ceased to sob the tears fell inexorably, silently, patterning the dirt on her cheeks. Of all the horses she had ever ridden Showman had been closest to her heart. 'I didn't have much close to my heart,' she said later.

'What will you say? He doesn't know you've been hunting, does he?' Jack demanded, drawing up in the lane a hundred yards before Roman Hill.

'He'll think I was riding my own.'

'Can you get in without being seen?'

'Probably.' She was haughty again. Her overpowering relief at seeing him drive out of the mist, taking charge, had evaporated. Now she could be hard, be in control. 'I put on my armour,' she said. 'It was the only way I could face what might come at Bretton.'

He understood. He knew her in all her moods. He took back his handkerchief without a word, raised his whip in salute and let the mare jog on.

She got in through the pantry window and crept up the backstairs like a felon. She could hear Mrs Meikeljon in the kitchen and the flustered giggling voice of the new housemaid. 'Of course, I might easily have met Curry on the stairs,' she said. But Curry knew all about

Roman Hill. Nothing was concealed from Curry. In her room she used three basinfuls of water getting her face clean, and then . . .

Then a closing in, a shrivelling. For a month she did not want to ride, could not contemplate going out. She grew shrewish and 'sluttish' said Curry, finding her with her hair uncombed, clothes dropped on the floor. 'It was as if I were dying,' said Paddy. It snowed. A great cold set in. The familiar was transformed: house, stables, barns. The cedar trees were weighted with white, the lawns unsullied sparkling sheets. 'What sort of life is this?' Paddy asked Curry over and over. 'Hiding, lying, coming and going like a thief. Why do I have to do it? I hate it. Why can't I lead a normal life? I'm twenty-three. I never go anywhere but horse sales or hunting fields. Curry, Curry, what happened at Roman Hill that Father won't even speak the name of the place?'

'I don't know,' said Curry. 'It was all so long ago.'

'But you know something?'

'I only know what they say in the village.'

In this bitter, introspective mood there was nothing to be done with her, Curry thought. The thaw might bring an improvement. The death of the horse had touched off some deep anguish, a life-long resentment bound to fester in such confinement. But when the thaw set in Paddy's despair only deepened. Used to activity to conquer these depressions, she had brooded too long. Edward did not help by forbidding her a party at the Brockets' because of her 'continuing sullenness'. Fathers were gods in those days. Still, even so spring must come. 'We must hope for the best,' said Curry earnestly, for the past was punctuated with shattering outbursts of rebellion following on Paddy's 'muley-grubs'.

It was Grace who took her away to stay with her sister in the New Forest. She was wary of Edward now but she circumnavigated him, putting her plan to Curry first. Curry was not afraid of anybody. In the end Edward raised no objections whatsoever, only hoping that it wasn't the beginning of a lot of gadding about. Young girls did too much of it these days and often met unsuitable people. He meant, Paddy divined, that she was not to give her heart to any young man who might seriously consider it worth keeping.

The New Forest was beautiful, the young men adequately charming, the life delightfully idle. Grace was amazed how tractable Paddy could be, how tennis and boat trips and carriage drives could please her. Before her eyes Paddy lost her skeletal drawn look, bloomed noticeably, grew plumper. 'I tried, I tried quite hard,' Grace told her husband on their return. 'And I think I might have done some good.'

'You're over it then?' said Jack, meeting Paddy in Hobeys.

She raised haunted eyes to his face. 'I want to run away.'

'Poor Pat.' He touched her cheek with his hardened hand. 'And the only man who'd ever have the nerve to run away with you will never ask.'

She jerked up her chin. 'Who?'

He would not tell her. Instead he took her to see the new ram he had installed to harness the spring water where it bubbled from the far side of the hill. His conversation was technical and informative, like a schoolmaster.

'Who, Jack?'

But he never told her.

The gravestone was on the north side of the church. 'I would never have looked there,' Harriet said. It seemed so much alone in a waste of frosted grass. 'Clarissa daughter of Joseph and Anne Chance. 1824–1844.'

Well, I have looked, thought Harriet. What was there

to see? She walked back to the path out of the shade of the trees and the sun was like a blessing. A little further on she stood looking over the low wall across the glebe field to the parsonage garden. The child died too, she thought. Where is the child buried? They should be together. Such humane actions ought to bring no harm.

It was not certain if the village knew about the child. There had been plenty of earthy speculation, that was natural. It was common knowledge that Ralph Bretton had jilted a girl expecting to be his wife. A few weeks before he brought home Harriet, the wealthy substitute, Clarissa had gone to stay with relatives. She was not in the best of health, Mrs Chance told her neighbours. There was a great deal of sympathy. Pregnancy was never mentioned. After all, bedding before wedding was normal in Stenton, however much the parson fulminated, but there always *was* a wedding, however long delayed. Since there was no way Joseph could force a Bretton to the altar without a court order and a scandal that would divide his family as well as Ralph's, he pretended to be deaf to his wife's weeping. He must be hard or his heart would break, he said to William. The child was to be born elsewhere and fostered and Clarissa come home as if nothing had happened.

Clarissa came home to lie on the north side of the church.

Who had decided she should lie so far from her family? Harriet wondered nearly twenty years later, an outcast in the shadow of the tower and the trees.

'Ha,' said Nobby Fowler, coming up the path with his spade over his shoulder. 'Good day, Mrs Bretton. That was a powerful frost in the night.'

'Yes,' said Harriet.

'The Tucker youngest died yesterday.'

'I know.'

'It makes hard digging, this frost.'

★

302

I shall speak to him, thought Harriet. I shall ask him if he cared for her, if he could have brought himself to marry her, if he knew about the child. She did not think the answers to these questions really mattered but felt compelled to ask them. It was quite likely he would lie, she knew. But in the tone of his voice she might hear the real reason for her bitter marriage, the reason he had wooed her so urgently, used her so insensitively, neglected her so entirely.

'I want to know about Clarissa . . .' she would begin.

But Ralph died.

Now the millstone is entirely mine, thought Harriet, and Clarissa was pushed out and down, far down. 'I never thought of her for years after that,' said Harriet. There were debts and debts, some she knew nothing about. Furniture had to be sold, and land. William Chance bought the land and began to quarry it. I could have done that, thought Harriet, if I had known. She felt cheated. Then she saw it was an angry gesture made to hurt her, much as she had refused to buy the carriage horses from him the only time Ralph had softened towards Roman Hill. Black accentuated her pale strong face, the grey in her hair. Her clothes were so plain that she always gave the impression of being stripped for action, of being on the point of departure.

After a year William walked up to Bretton.

Harriet retreated at once to the library, so much Ralph's room that she considered herself safe there. When William came in and the door closed behind him she knew she was not safe anywhere; she felt dizzy and for a moment she could not look at him. She heard his footsteps on the boards, even his breathing, but when he spoke it seemed to be into a profound silence.

'I think I've starved for you long enough.'

And I for you, answered the voice in her brain. But she could not speak. Her throat contracted and contracted with the heavy beating of her heart. She saw him through a mist. If he touches me I'm lost, she thought. She moved towards the window and now her hearing seemed affected, the pounding of her heart filled her ears.

'There's no help for it,' she thought she said. 'You will have to starve.'

'I will not.'

'You must. I have my children and this house. You have Rebecca and a new son.'

He was standing in the middle of the room by the great globe. He was motionless. From Paddy she was to learn that stillness for a mercurial spirit is a sign of even greater passion, but she only guessed it now. Then he reached out in a violent, uncontrolled gesture and set the globe spinning, so violent, so uncontrolled that it rocked dangerously, the wooden stand groaning.

'I love you,' he said. 'I have never loved anyone like this,' and then, as if once released his anger must rise and rise to engulf them both: 'He's dead. He's been dead a year. I've waited, counting the days.'

'But nothing has changed,' and she covered her face with her hands.

'We can meet.'

'In the village, yes. You can raise your hat to me. In church, in Frilton. But I can't make you free of this house, coming and going as you please. It is not mine, it is my son's, and he's too young to manage it alone. And what effect would it have on my daughters to see their mother's lover on the stair?'

'I didn't mean . . .'

'But there is nowhere. There is nowhere we can meet and be happy, knowing we hurt no one.'

'Rebecca doesn't care for me, only for children.'

Harriet was afraid that if he did not leave she might suffocate. 'We're caught in the same net then, she and I,' she said. 'We're mothers before anything. You're too late. You should have asked me years ago, in the hayfield. Do you remember the hayfield? No. But if you'd asked me then I'd have come with you, I'd have run away, I'd have left everything, even the children.'

William put a hand on the globe and it came to rest. He said wearily, 'No, you'd never have done that. It was always too late.'

I hung on to the library table as he left, remembered Harriet, to stop myself running after him.

'You are breaking my heart,' he wrote. 'Let me see you. Just once.'

Harriet had been a widow for four years. She put the letter in the fire. She told herself she was too old for such foolery, she would soon be a grandmother. Never again would she walk down under the elms and give herself up to his kisses. In church she turned her head so that she did not see him and her temper and her hats grew monstrous. There were bad harvests. There was the cattle plague. Somehow she kept going. She gave the balls for her daughters, transforming Bretton with massed palms and ferns, London chefs, an orchestra, a string quartet for the supper room, ribbons, hot-house flowers, a thousand candles. 'If we're going to do it we must do it properly,' said Harriet. For the first time in seventy years there were footmen to open the great front door.

There were no more letters from William Chance.

Rebecca had left Roman Hill with her young son, her only living child. The general opinion in Stenton was that she had never been herself since the diphtheria had taken the first of her babies, besides which her husband was reputed to visit a woman in Frilton and was known the county over as a lady's man. Visiting Shipley Harriet was told, 'I hear Chance is drinking himself to an early grave. He's taken the loss of his wife rather badly.'

'One usually hears a lot of nonsense,' remarked Harriet robustly.

On the way home she drove erratically, thinking of William old and lonely and drunk. Not William, she told herself; not William drunk.

'Mother,' said Mary, 'you'll have us in the ditch. Let me have the reins.'

'Take your hand away,' said Harriet coldly.

'But Mother . . .'

She took not the avenue to Bretton, but the lane to Home Farm, setting Mary down at the green door. 'I have to see Dack,' she said.

'But Mother . . .'

Harriet drove on.

She drove as far as the gate to Hobeys. There she left the horse and dogcart, wrestling with the chains and the unwieldy hook. She hurried down the slopes, skirts held up, head held up. The young cattle stared and moved uneasily. There was smoke rising from the chimneys below among the trees. The rooks were making a racket in the rookery in Upper Bit. The October sun was warm on Harriet's face.

The door was open.

She did not touch the bell. She did not knock. She walked in. I suppose there were servants in the kitchen, she thought afterwards. She walked silently down the passage to the door of the old parlour and opened it and he was there.

Not drunk, was Harriet's first thought. There was a general untidiness. She knew for certain it was a room no one ever dusted. William was standing by his desk sharpening a pencil with his pocket knife. He dropped both.

'I had heard you were ill,' she said.

'Have you run all the way from Bretton to see if I'm dying? Did you hope I was?'

'Of course not. How could you be so ridiculous?'

'But you came down the hill. Your skirts are wet.'

'It's my hill.' It was a childish response but she was

losing her way. All these words, she thought, and no meaning, no sense.

'But I pay you for it. I believe I can call it my own.'

She stood tall and straight in front of him. 'Thank God for my stays,' Harriet had often cried. Thank God too for a severe upbringing, long training in self-denial. She only had to step forward, touch him. But how absurd it would be! Here she was in her widow's black, her grand bonnet. What would she look like, a woman of fifty behaving like some romantic girl? After all, she was nearly as tall as he was.

Thus real life admitted the absurdities Miss Hartley's romantic fiction would affect not to know about: Harriet standing in front of the only man she had ever loved thinking: I'm nearly as tall as he is. He looks old, tired. I must turn round somehow and walk away.

'Harriet.' He held out his hand palm upward, a suppliant and a forgiving gesture.

She laid her own in it briefly and then left him.

24

PADDY HAD BEEN dividing the plants in the border. 'There's nothing like grubbing in the earth,' she had once said to Grace. 'It's a comforting occupation.' Happiness bloomed slowly inside her. After two back-breaking hours she straightened, brushed the dirt from her hands down her tweed skirt and set off on a tour of the gardens, walking slowly, often stopping to pull out some weed or push aside some branch. She noted the signs of ruin, but without the old anguish. One person could not be equal to such a struggle. 'This place needs an army of gardeners,' Harriet had said to Deborah, a Harriet in leather gloves and carrying a wicked pruning knife.

'We're an army of two then,' said Deborah.

In truth they had been an army of five, for there had been three gardeners in Edward's early days. 'Great ignorant lumps,' Harriet had said scornfully, but they had dug and cleared and trimmed and cut the grass. Disliking the prevailing fashion for bedding plants, Harriet designed a peony border. It had reached away down the lawn from the lily pool. During the war it was destroyed and grassed over. 'I suppose war is a reasonable excuse,' Paddy imagined Harriet saying. Careless of her uniform skirts, she had rescued what she could from the rubbish heap and planted them at the Lodge.

'What *are* you doing?' asked Edward, hearing the spade and coming out.

'They were Grandmother's.'

'Peonies,' said Edward with disfavour. 'They won't like being moved.'

'They'll be all right,' said Paddy. And they were.

Now, skirting the cedars and going down the grass path to the tennis court her heart lifted. Though the gardens were under sentence of death they were still beautiful and she had helped make them so, adding her little to the rest. The tennis court itself had been for Aunt Fan: 'But everyone has tennis parties nowadays,' she had told Harriet. She was a striving, athletic girl, equally passionate about the game and the hearty tea that followed. She did not grace a court, Harriet noticed, she dominated it. The more belligerent young men clamoured to partner her and congratulated her often on her winning serve. 'Aggression doesn't get husbands,' said Harriet grimly. She would have discouraged both girls from marriage – but what else was there for them? Ralph had spent nothing on their education and what Harriet had scraped together had gone on all the county had to offer genteel young ladies: poetry, dance and needlework, a sketchy grasp of the order of kings and queens. 'There is nothing wrong with any of those,' Harriet sighed, 'but they are not enough.'

'What *is* enough?' Mary demanded. She liked Miss Avebury's undemanding music classes and could occupy herself for hours with scrapbooks and indifferent watercolours and the reproduction of religious texts.

'Nothing is enough, but there are mathematics and philosophy for a start,' said Harriet, whose own education had been so deficient. 'There are languages.'

'I speak a little French, Mama.'

'Not to be understood in France,' was Harriet's dampening reply.

'Oh, Mother!' It seemed they were always saying it in

those days. 'Mama' was reserved for compliance, 'Mother' for protest. Harriet wondered what pain she had caused Sophie, knowing only too well what pain Sophie had caused her.

Mary would have been happy to marry and relish Sophie's enervating domesticity if anyone had asked her. It would have suited her. 'And I suppose we must do what suits us,' said Harriet wearily. But no one did ask. Mary was too 'holy' said Fan. 'It would be like living with a moral tract,' one young man commented unkindly.

'You're always so practical,' Mary accused Harriet. She meant that Harriet did not think deeply about the condition of the world. 'I feel deeply,' Harriet would have said.

'We'll just have to accept each other as we are,' she stated with gentle firmness. 'Mary and Martha.'

Then Fan met John Arlington Roach on a Devon holiday. He pursued her along the sands and the promenade. He wrote to Harriet to ask if he might . . . 'He might, but he shan't,' said Harriet. 'He hasn't a penny – and he's a parson.' Fan, who enjoyed a drama, slipped out at midnight and bicycled to the station, waiting in delightful trepidation for the milk train with one small carpet bag and a hatbox. 'Of course they'd have been suspicious if I'd had a trunk,' she explained afterwards to Harriet who went down to Devon for the wedding. Edward and Mary stayed at Bretton. 'They would,' said Fan without rancour. She had been staying with John's mother until the banns were called and Harriet was summoned. 'I suppose clergymen ought not to elope,' she said gravely, but her eyes were full of light. Old Mrs Roach, having reluctantly countenanced Fan's escape, secretly worried over her suitability for parsonage life. She was reassured by Harriet, so severe, so stately. 'Mama, you are like the Queen,' Fan said admiringly, allowing Harriet to be the first to kiss her after the ceremony. Harriet said she hoped not and inclined her cheek so that her son-in-law might peck it. 'There's a deal too much kissing at weddings,' said old Mrs Roach crossly, introducing wave upon wave of her clerical family, deans, deacons, wealthy and portly men in gaiters. 'You see,' said the irrepressible Fan, catching Harriet's arm. 'John will have rather a lot of money when she dies. Do you forgive us?'

Without Fan the tennis parties stopped. Bushey, a young man then and an under-gardener, mowed the court only three or four times during the summer. Then Deborah came. Young, lithe, quick, she was the physical antithesis of Fan, but her serve was as devilish and she too had more partners than she could do with, laughingly distributing the surplus among the shyer girls sitting out. She hated parties but she loved games: rounders, cricket, croquet. With her came Paddy and great changes. 'There'll always be changes when a man is in love,' said Curry. Edward was dangerous in love, spending immoderately. He built the lily pool, the fountain. He cost Bretton dear. 'And me,' said Deborah, frightened by his unabating passion. Harriet and Curry were her props. 'But it was as if my womb was closed to him. Is that possible?' said Deborah.

All through those years the tennis court was in use again, shaved to perfection, marked up with the messy old marking machine with the squeaky wheel. Tea was laid out on whiteclothed tables under the cedars. The new lily pool was charming, the fish tame enough to feed by hand. 'I should be happy,' said Deborah. She was never happy in the house, only in the garden. In the garden she found peace, bent over the border flowers, pruning the roses, feeding the carp. On long summer evenings she stayed out until dark, sometimes alone, more usually with Harriet, sometimes in silence, often talking. What did they talk about? 'Everything,' said Deborah. 'Everything that interests women.'

Edward would have thought this pitifully little, too little to have kept them engrossed hours at a stretch. He watched them from his dressing-room window, walking about in the mothy dusk, trowels in hand, or baskets, or even forks. He could not send the servants to order his wife to bed. He had to wait.

Paddy passed the tennis court and went down the yew hedge to the gate to the vegetable garden. The hothouses looked less desolate today, and the hedges were cut, the ground already turned over for the winter crops. In the far corner was the smoke of a bonfire rising straight up, blue on the cold air. Hugh's bonfire. We are all marking time, thought Paddy. She could see him, a stocky figure, bare-headed, feeding something to the flames. As she reached the green door he saw her, raised his hand.

'You wouldn't credit the amount of debris in the hothouses,' he said, strolling over.

'Is that what you're doing?'

'I'm supposed to be on holiday.'

'I used to hide in there,' Paddy said.

'Whatever for?'

The figs and vines had been glorious in those days. Paddy had often lurked amid the foliage until she could get into the house unobserved. Once she had been trying a new mare of Jack's and was hot and dishevelled. 'You're always in here,' the young Tom had accused. 'You're stealing grapes. I shall tell.'

'If you do I'll creep into your room in the night and kill you,' she told him.

Perhaps he believed she might do it. She was certainly capable of it, he decided. He kept silent until he was seventeen, a sullen discontented seventeen, and then he betrayed her in panic, caught out in some misdemeanour of his own.

'My God, I'd take a whip to you if you were younger,' Edward had cried. 'You're no better than . . .' Paddy saw him begin to shake, to lose the last of his control. 'Get out. Go upstairs. Go. Go!'

But he had needed her. The war snatched Tom away, took Bretton from him, but though Paddy volunteered and vanished to new worlds she wrote every week and reappeared to battle some order into his miserable existence at the Lodge. If he was proud of her in any way he did not say so. If he missed her in her absences only Curry could have detected it. But he needed her and only felt his life steady and resume its decent normal course when she came home.

Hugh poked his bonfire. Laura's last letter was in the ashes. It had been a tearful thing, full of recrimination: 'You never loved me, you never wanted me . . .' She was coming back soon but could never stay at Bretton. 'Never, never,' she had written, underlined. She hasn't found anyone to love her in France, thought Hugh, and he felt a sudden pity and, which was new, a gentle amusement.

'I don't understand you,' he had told her time after time.

'You never will.'

'But I love you.'

'Poor Hugh.'

He stirred the embers. He thought of the reply he had posted that morning. 'What about Etta?' he had demanded. He had not even put 'Love Hugh'. His usually neat writing had dashed across the page. He had written again to Tom too. 'I don't know what put me in such a temper,' he said to Paddy. He had struck out like this once or twice in the war, acting before thinking. 'It was too noisy to think,' he said. They had given him the MC anyway, as if his actions had been coolly deliberated. 'To encourage the others to be fools, I suppose,' said Hugh, who was seldom cynical.

They watched the smoke suddenly flatten and then stream sideways across the garden.

'There might be a storm,' said Paddy, looking up at the sky.

'I want to stay here,' Hugh said. 'I want to make a proper home for Etta.'

'It's a big house.'

'For two? Perhaps I could let half. A whole family could camp in the ballroom. I think . . .' and he grinned, pushing the toe of his boot into the ashes so that hot red sparks flew about them. 'I think I've just fallen in love with it.'

Paddy stuffed her hands in her pockets. There was smoke wreathing round her hair.

'Man is born to trouble,' she said, smiling, watching the sparks.

'Is that what old Maycroft would say?'

'No. It's what Bushey would say.'

'A Mrs Talbot has called,' said Lily when he came back to the house. 'I showed her into the yellow drawing room, sir. I hope I did right.'

Hugh opened the door.

'Hello, Madge.'

'I know it's a quite dreadful time to call but I meant to come yesterday and . . .' she paused, looking up 'through her lashes' thought Hugh, amused. 'And I was too cowardly. I parked the motor in the stableyard. Is that all right? That was another piece of cowardice. I hated the thought of it sitting on the gravel by those immense steps letting you know I was here. I thought I'd hide it round the back and creep in through the kitchens.'

The thought of Madge using anything but the front door was difficult to believe. Hugh said, 'Did you think I'd eat you or something?'

'I thought you might be furious. You have a right to be.'

'With you?'

'Why not with me? I invited Laura to France.'

'And you think I blame you for it?'

'Darling, you should.'

He was in flannels and a tweed jacket. 'Countrified' Laura would have called it. He smelled of bonfire. His fair hair was on end. Madge sat uneasily, an unlit cigarette between her fingers, and all the false soothing phrases fled away and left her speechless. She had always thought Hugh a bit of a dull fool, had even thought it up to the moment she had turned the nose of the car through the Bretton gates. 'He's such a boy,' Laura had always said. 'So sweet. He'd do anything for me, absolutely anything.' 'Darling, he's so boring,' Madge had replied. 'He does hate parties so, and dancing. How could you marry a man who hates dancing? Rennie always calls him the spectre at the feast.'

Once during the war Madge had seen him in uniform. 'All men look better in uniform,' she said sagely, but this time, instead of puckering her lips at air, she left the imprint of them on his cheek. 'Well, I might never see him again,' she said to herself. He had had a 'good' war. Laura meant by this that not only had he survived but had been rapidly promoted as well as being awarded the MC. Madge thought privately he had had a hell of a time. In public and to Laura she said lightly, 'My dear, he behaves as if he's a hundred and ten at least. What are you going to do with the man?' But: 'Major and Mrs Haley,' said Laura happily. 'I do so like it.'

'I'm not Major anything any more,' said Hugh.

'But all those crusty old men at Eastbourne still call themselves Major this or that – and heaven knows what wars they all fought in.'

'They were regular officers.'

'But darling Hugh, who cares?' and on seeing his stubborn look, his compressed mouth: 'You spoil everything,' she cried.

Madge thought: The Major's still there underneath.

Looking at him with this new wariness she could see his appeal. A nice man, kind, dependable. It was the word they had always used for him: dependable. We were fools to make fun of it, she thought. She saw him strike the match to light her cigarette and leaned forward to meet the flame. Though his cuffs were spotless his hands were very slightly dirty, ingrained about the nails.

'You've been gardening,' she said.

'Odd-jobbing might describe it better.'

'I thought you looked well. A sort of outdoor glow.' She laughed self-consciously. 'How ridiculous that sounds. Hugh, I wanted . . .' She raised her head, inhaled, watched the smoke as it thinned about her. 'I've come about Laura.'

'I thought you had. Did she ask you to?'

'No.'

'Then why?'

'I'm not sure. At least, I was sure until I turned in at your gates. Then I wasn't certain of anything any more. Hugh, do you really want to buy this vast heap? Oh, don't answer that. Don't take any notice. I've had what you might call a crisis of conscience. I've come to . . . explain myself.'

'Good God, don't attempt it.' Hugh reached over to ring the bell. 'Oh, Lily, lay another place at lunch for Mrs Talbot. And where's Etta? She'd better eat downstairs today.'

'Please, sir, I think Mrs Prince has done shepherd's pie and rice for the nursery.'

'Never mind,' said Hugh amiably. 'Send it to the dining room.'

'My God,' said Madge as the door closed. 'It's years and years since I had rice pudding.'

'I'm sure Etta won't mind sharing.'

Was he laughing at her? His smile, she remembered, had always been slow and shy, and he had never smiled at all at people he did not like. He's not a hypocrite, she thought.

'Do you really want me to stay to lunch?'

'I can hardly send you from my door fainting with hunger. Lily will be sounding the gong in ten minutes. Have a drink.'

'Hugh. Hugh, I must speak to you about Laura.'

'I think I'd rather you didn't.'

'Are you going to divorce her?'

'I don't know. Perhaps that's up to her.'

'Look, she met a man called Boyd in France but . . . well, it went wrong, fizzled out. I wanted to say . . . Perhaps I wanted to say sorry. She behaved very badly in France, all furious happiness one minute and absolute doldrums the next. You know how she can be. She said nobody gave a fig for her, even you. I said nonsense, you'd always been wild about her, look what you'd given her, done for her, moving out here on one of her whims, letting her hold open house, money no object. But she said you didn't want her any more and showed me your letter about buying the house. "He prefers the house to me," she said.' He did not speak. A little unnerved Madge fiddled with the cigarette, crossed and re-crossed her legs. 'She's at Larter House if you want to know.'

'I thought she might be.'

'I was sure she hadn't let you know. I thought you might be worried.'

He bent forwards and removed the cigarette stub from between her fingers. His touch was cool and impersonal, but kind. 'You're afraid you'll have her at Larter for life,' he said softly.

'Hugh!'

The gong sounded. In the hall Etta was jumping the last three stairs, pink and excited. 'Paddy's going to teach me to ride. Mr Chance is going to lend us his pony.'

317

'It's the first I've heard of it,' said Hugh. 'And I think you should call her Miss Bretton.'

'But she wants to be called Paddy. She said so. Hello, Mrs Talbot.'

'I wouldn't have recognized you,' said Madge.

'I'm ten on Sunday.'

'Many happy returns of Sunday.' They're both solid, uncomplaining people, she thought. They'll survive Laura. They have more strength than most people. More than me.

Hugh offered her his arm.

'Come on,' he said. 'There's rice pudding, remember?'

25

Downstairs Mrs Prince asked Lily, 'What are they going through all that lot for? I thought Miss Bretton had been all over the house with Mr Paget.'

'I think Miss Bretton's looking for something,' said Lily.

'In the trunks in the attics?'

In the cellars, in the nursery, in every cupboard. 'Houses keep many secrets,' said Curry to Etta, as they bobbed in her wake.

'You mean, we'll never find it?' asked Etta, deflated. She had begun the day in a torrent of excitement. Hugh had gone to London and promised to bring back her birthday present. The first riding lesson was promised for the afternoon. Paddy, bringing a great basket of chrysanthemums to the house, had stayed to help her search.

'Search for what?' demanded Mrs Prince, who had hoped for a quiet hour to read the paper and the tea leaves.

'Whatever my key fits.'

'Whatever what?'

'The lock for my key. The right lock.'

Mrs Prince had pursed her mouth up. 'You've looked and looked, dear. I think it's just a little key that got lost when someone was visiting. Think how many people must have come and gone all the years this great old house stood here.'

'Will you look in the tea leaves?'

'There won't be anything in there.'

'There might be,' said Etta. 'Please.'

The tea leaves were non-committal. Mrs Prince confessed herself baffled. They made 'strange shapes' she said: 'Muddled.' After an hour Etta was a bundle of suppressed anxiety. There was surely not a lock they had not tried? Climbing the stairs behind Paddy she thought she heard the voices. They were always faint and they did not frighten her.

'How could you, in bloomers . . .'

'I've starved for you long enough.'

'A shilling is much more use than a sermon.'

'I am Miss Bretton.'

'Mama, you are a terrible old woman.'

'Inside is a letter for him. And a letter of his father's. And a key.'

'Harriet. Harriet.'

Outside was a still, gold October day. In the corner of the house facing south one might believe it was still summer except for the autumn scents of wet grass and rotting apples, of dead leaves and Hugh's bonfire. Paddy had come to rest on the stone seat looking down on the lily pool and the slight humps and depressions that had been the peony border.

'Have you found it? Have you found it?' Etta flew up the terrace steps breathing white smoke and with leaves caught in her woollen tam-o'-shanter.

'No,' said Paddy.

'I've been to the farm.' She had to gabble to hide her disappointment. 'I saw the timber drag. There are six horses pulling it and they're going to bring back a whole oak. Mr Dack says the oak's five hundred years old. He says I can go and watch it come back from the

Plantation.' She came to sit companionably on the stone seat. It was hard on her bottom so she sat on her hands. 'Where is it?'

'Here,' and Paddy opened her hand. There on the palm lay the small key from the Piggery.

'I expect it only opened something empty,' Etta said philosophically.

'Probably. So much is sold. So much was moved and lost during the war. My father burned boxes of papers, letters . . . It looks like the key to a writing box.' She turned it in her hand. 'Only I'm sure I've seen it before.'

'Where?'

Paddy shook her head. 'I'm sorry, Etta. I really can't remember.'

In Harriet's day there had been a bearskin rug in the blue dressing room. Paddy had longed and longed to touch his massive grey head, but the dressing room, at the end of the passage by the guest bedrooms, was where Harriet always did the accounts after Ralph died. Bookshelves were put up and the great ledgers brought up from the library. The little French desk that had once been Sophie's and had come to Harriet at her death stood in the window.

'Little children have no business in there,' said the current nurserymaid, catching Paddy toddling fast in that direction.

Then one day she had been invited in.

The window had overlooked the front porch and had been partly obscured by wisteria. The sunlight filtering through the leaves dappled Harriet's dreary black, her high collar, the lace over her silver hair.

'I must finish this letter. Sit down and don't wriggle,' came her voice, calm, full-bodied, authoritarian.

'Yes, Grandmother.'

The bear's head was domed, hard, strange, with

fearsome teeth. The red and blue carpet beneath had a lozenge pattern. Perhaps the walls had been blue. Was that why it had been called the blue dressing room? From the floor Harriet had seemed hugely tall. She wrote on and on for a long time, the pen scratching. At last she sighed; the paper rustled as she folded it. 'There. Now we can go into the garden.'

She had opened a drawer in the desk. Paddy watched her drop the letter into it. There was already another letter there and a small key.

'Aren't we going to post it?' asked Paddy, who enjoyed walking to the Bretton postbox at the back gate.

'This isn't a letter to post, it's a letter for someone to read when . . . For someone in this house.'

It seemed mysterious. Grown-ups were often mysterious. Paddy stooped to caress the bear again. Through the open window came the sound of pigeons calling, of the softer liquid notes of the white doves, of feet crunching the gravel.

'I like the bear,' said Paddy.

'So do I,' said Harriet.

The letter Harriet had found in the library had been enclosed in a single sheet of paper. There was writing on the paper, a round childish hand. 'Sir,' it read. 'I am sorry to inform you your daughter died Wednesday last, 12 October, of a fever. It was very peaceful.' The pen had scored the p twice and a little unsteadily as if the writer was disturbed at telling this kindly lie. 'She spoke of you often while she was ill. She has been buried in Dalborough with my own family which I thought best. I remain your,' and there was a gap as if he could not find the word to qualify himself. 'I remain your servant James Drewett.'

Ralph's letter began, 'My dearest Linnet.'

Her name was Caroline and he called her Linnet. For sixteen years he had written to her, obviously often

visited her, given her money. So that was where it
went, thought Harriet. 'So that was where *he* went.'
For sixteen years he had been a generous and attentive
father to the daughter Clarissa Chance had borne him,
the daughter the Chances thought had died as a child.
Had he found out where she had been sent and taken
her away, paying the Drewetts to bring her up as their
own? Drewett's hand was painstaking though ill-edu-
cated: a conscientious man then, serious. 'My dearest
Linnet, your old father hopes his last little gift made
you happy. I have another. I shall tell you about it first
before I go on to lighter things. I have a picnic planned
– now that is a lighter thing, isn't it? But this present is
serious, you must listen seriously.

'I have written a new will. I have left you the farm of
Roman Hill where your mother was brought up . . .'

On and on: Roman Hill, his plans for her when she
grew up, dresses he would buy, foreign journeys they
might make, drives, rides, picnics, singing lessons. Such
generosity was nothing, he loved her. His love shone
out of every line, every word.

But what lies might he have to tell? He had let the
Chances think that she was dead. Out of spite? Who
could say? When he died she would inherit the farm, by
which time she might be a married woman, middle-
aged. How could he justify keeping her from the rest of
her family? He meant to tell them soon, he said, soon.
She would have an uncle, aunts. As Harriet read she
knew this was the first false note.

'He would have died,' she said to herself, 'rather than
go down to Roman Hill to explain such ages-old deceit.'

'Your loving Papa,' wrote Ralph. It was his hand,
positive sloping strokes, neat and unhurried. 'Your
loving Papa.' No wonder Harriet had felt faint in the
library, had sat down heavily, her hand to her side. 'I
never feel faint,' she would have said, but her legs
would not hold her up. Shock and bitterness, a sense of

betrayal, of total loss, swept over her. 'It's old age,' she said to Curry. This must be secret even from Curry. When she felt strong enough she went upstairs to lock the letter in her desk.

In the same drawer was the mysterious key.

Later, to Edward, she wrote, 'You must do as you think best, I know, but it seems to me some reparation should be made. Your father intended Caroline to inherit Roman Hill. This could never have come about without great division in the family, dreadful quarrels, and all the old scandal raked over anew. Now perhaps you could bequeath Roman Hill to Jack Chance for a nominal sum. I feel it should be done.' She had felt it deeply, deeply. She could not forget Clarissa had been William's sister. 'I believe this key,' she wrote, 'may open the place where your father kept the will. It may not. He may, of course, have destroyed it after Caroline's death.'

She was tired when she came to write the last few words. She was conscious of Paddy's patient gaze on her slowly moving hand.

'There,' she said. 'Now we can go into the garden.'

Curry had always known the baby was not Edward's. She knew more about Deborah than anybody, though all that passed between them were the polite conventional phrases of mistress and servant. Her knowledge was an inner knowledge, inexplicable, instinctive, sharpened by love. It did not matter to her whose baby it was; she was not interested in the provenance of babies. They were conceived, they were born, they grew, sometimes they died. Often they died. Twelve years in the hovel by the sheepwash had taught her the relative unimportance of the 'how'. Harriet's moral code was not her own though she paid lip-service to it in the kitchen; she had her own, widely differing, perhaps harsher.

But at some point she became aware that Harriet also knew the baby was not Edward's, and that she did not mind. It was to Harriet Paddy ran unsteadily across the lawns, it was with Harriet she first dug fat fingers into garden soil, planting her own seeds with breathy concentration. 'She's more Harriet's than mine,' Deborah said, and smiled to see them, the one with the real watering can, the other with a toy. How I love them both, she thought!

'I wish she were your real granddaughter,' she said.

'She *is* my real granddaughter,' said Harriet.

The day Edward emptied Harriet's desk and found the letter addressed to himself, and Ralph's letter, and the key, was the day Deborah went into labour. He felt he needed occupation; there was nothing he could do with the house full of doctors, midwives, nurses, maids going up and down with water and tea and objects under cloths. He walked round the park with the dogs but a thin drizzle was falling; he felt damp and anxious. He did not want to go far from the house. At last he took himself to the blue dressing room and sat down at the desk and opened it and went methodically through every paper, bill, note, letter and receipt.

'You must do as you think best . . .'

'My dearest Linnet.'

'Your loving Papa.'

He was never loving, thought Edward. 'I know you will always try to do what is right,' Harriet had said to him as a child, as a young man, as a husband. Always, as he jibbed, her hand plucked him on. Now her vigorous script leapt at him from the page. What is right in this case? he wondered. Why should she think it right to give away Roman Hill? He was intensely moved: by anger pure and simple, by the bitter thought of signing away any part of his estate even after death, by jealousy, self-pity, irrational resolution. As Harriet had said

325

'reparation should be made' so he with his whole being cried 'No! Never!' Already he had been forced to give up so much. Roman Hill was the last of the tenant farms. The Chances did not know this child had lived, nor that Ralph, enchanted, had brought her up. Enchanted. The word came to Edward as he stood looking out between the wisteria branches. Ralph had not been enchanted with his own children, he thought, his legitimate children.

There was another carriage coming up the drive. Another doctor? That young one should be here, he thought. She likes him. She trusts him. I can't do with these pompous old fools. He thought he would stay here in Harriet's room until it was over, until they came to tell him he had a son, but when he looked down he saw the tremor in his hands and felt he must sit down again. So all this explained some of Ralph's long absences, that frequent total disregard for his family even when he was in this same house. He was not capable, Edward thought, of loving more than one human being. Once he had thought that being was Ralph himself, now he saw he had been mistaken. How hard he had tried for his father's attention! His father, tall, handsome, mysterious by virtue of being so remote, had seemed to Edward as a boy to be the only person whose praise might be worth having. Unable to come to peaceful terms with Harriet, who was as baffled by him as he by her, he had sought refuge in the idealization of Ralph.

'Your loving Papa,' he read for the last time, his eyes drawn irresistibly. He felt a terrible weight in his chest. With care he built a little pyre in the small hearth: the old bills, the receipts, lists of linen, pages of scribbled sums. He lit them, watching the flames lick up, rising at last to a merry crackling. He put Ralph's letter on top, Harriet's on top of that. He saw for a moment 'I am sorry to inform you . . .' and he poked viciously, watching the ashes soften into little heaps.

'I have made a mess in the grate, Mrs Murray,' he said when he went down at the gong.

'I'll see to it, sir.'

'Is there any news?'

He did not feel like eating. He felt oppressed by too much conflicting emotion. He heard her: 'No, sir. I'm sure they would tell you at once if there was,' but could make no reply, could only glance up the wide sweep of stairs with a look Curry interpreted as pitiful longing and which he, had he seen himself in the mirror, would not have been able to interpret at all. I will give my son everything, he thought.

Later, when there was still no word from upstairs, he took the key Harriet had left him and went round the house to find where it fitted. He knew Harriet had done this and had discovered nothing but he felt he would surely find the lock, the cabinet, the drawer, and within it the will. His determination to destroy it took him over. Nothing, nothing would be left to remind him of that ill-considered love of Ralph's, or to cause complications: this had been Ralph's last testament. 'And so revokes all previous wills,' Paget would tell him gravely.

He destroyed it himself, thought Edward. His hunt grew a little feverish. Of course he destroyed it after he learned of her death. The key fitted no lock, opened no cabinets, no drawers, no doors, boxes or even clocks.

'Mr Bretton,' said the nurse, knocking timidly. 'Mr Bretton, would you come up. The doctor is waiting.'

'Is he born?'

She nodded. Her smile was tremulous but he did not notice. He felt joy springing up, overcoming all bitterness. A son. He had a son.

He would look for the will another time, he thought, and if he did not find it would throw the key away. He wanted there to be no memory to ambush his future happiness. He forced himself to control the spreading grin of delight, to follow the nurse calmly, but as he climbed the stairs he felt healed and blessed and his heart was singing.

Etta was climbing over the gate from Hobeys. She snagged her stockings into a hole.

Johnny had said, 'So it's your birthday tomorrow,' as he had lifted her from the pony. His eyes had met Paddy's over her head. 'Perhaps I'll stroll up and wish you many happy returns.'

The pony had behaved 'like a saint' said Johnny, winking. Etta had never imagined such live and quivering power. Nothing would induce her to cry out that she was afraid. She sat up, white-faced, her hands clenched. 'This won't do,' said Paddy. 'Put your hands on your hips, look up at the sky and recite me a poem.'

In half an hour they were trotting.

'It's all down to poetry,' Paddy said, dropping in to the house.

'Confidence,' said Johnny. 'It's all a trick.'

'The power of the bones,' she answered. 'Etta knows all about that. Bonniman even explained to her. I told her this was the power of poetry.' As an afterthought, smiling, she added: 'Thank God the pony behaved.'

Etta ran up Hobeys, panting. Never before had she managed the whole climb without stopping. Bonniman, clearing the ditch where the hedge sloped down to Upper Bit, saw her flash past, her sturdy legs in their black stockings and boots making light work of the tussocks. 'What it is to be young,' he said.

Over the gate, seeing the hole, seeing the pink flesh. Lily would grumble. Lily would have to sit and darn it by the light of the pink-shaded oil lamp on the nursery table. All she could think was that Hugh would be home and she must tell him about her day, about the long fruitless but exciting hunt with the key, the great straining timber drag, her favourite lunch, Mrs Prince's more hopeful afternoon tea leaves, and now the pony, the ride, the heady sensation of achievement.

'Hoi, where you tearin' to, Miss Hurry-go-by?' shouted Bushey, pulling parsnips. For once she could not stop for him; she waved and gave a jump in the air and laughed, but she kept running. Through the gate, along the yew hedge, past the tennis court, round the border, and there were the cedars, the long stretch of lawn, the lily pool, the steps. She had a stitch in her side, her hand pressed to it, willing it away. The pain caught her breath but she ran on, gasping. Joy flooded her whole being, drove out past and future, loneliness, Laura, leaving Bretton.

'Do you leave footprints I'll scalp you,' cried Lily in the hall.

'Where's Father? Is Father home?'

'No. He's coming from the station, I 'spect. Take them dratted boots to the kitchen. Look at the mud! What'll Mrs Murray say when she see all this?'

'I need a button-hook,' said Etta as she burst into the kitchen.

'You need a box on the ear,' said Babs Potter, but when she saw the state of Etta's boots she hurried her to the boot room before Mrs Prince could see the damage done to her spotless bricks. 'You know muddy feet come in the back,' she admonished, unbuttoning both the boots and Etta's coat.

'And don't you go on about tea leaves,' Mrs Prince warned as they made a reappearance. 'I've got the dinner to prepare.'

Etta fled up to the nursery but nothing could hold her attention. She ran down to the yellow drawing room from where she would see Hugh turn down the avenue. 'Come out of there,' said Lily. 'Mr Paget's coming this evening. I want everything just so.'

'But where can I go?' Etta wailed. It had been too much excitement to contain. She felt it ebbing inexorably. Father do come, she prayed.

'Go in the library. No one'll mind you reading them old books.'

From the library she could still see Hugh arrive.

Horrible books, thought Etta. They were in long ranks floor to ceiling, dull red spines, dull brown ones, faded gold lettering. She could not understand the titles of the ones at eye level. She climbed the library steps and, because they moved, shunted herself about for a while pretending she was in the doctor's unreliable motor car. The afternoon was closing in. Leaves blew by the window. She made the globe revolve, a considerable feat for it had grown stiff after a century of neglect. It seemed to Etta a miserable undistinguished brown, even the oceans. Some parts of the continents looked oddly shaped. I could draw a map like that, she thought, sort of blobbing in the bits I don't know. It intrigued her to think some erudite grown-up had been ignorant of the true shape of Australia and had 'blobbed' it so fantastically.

The keyhole was somewhere in Africa, another unknown.

Etta's searching fingers, running lightly from Greenland to Japan, felt the small hole. She looked at it for a long time before she realized what it was, it was so cunningly concealed. What would anyone keep in a globe? she wondered. But the man who had filled Africa with such strange geographical features, such scores of imagined mountain ranges, would be the sort of man to conceive a keyhole there, just to make things more interesting. Or perhaps the mountains were to disguise the keyhole.

'Oh,' said Etta.

She drew the small key from her pocket.

Hugh came in the front door because he felt a front door should be used. He was not abashed by its grandeur. He was scarcely inside when a small figure flew at him out of the gloom crying out something about keys and holes and Africa and riding lessons and poetry.

'Hetty, do calm down,' he said, catching her arms.

'Oh, Mr Haley. There is a cup of tea in the drawing room,' said Curry, emerging silently from the back regions, her white collar standing out in the greyness.

'Thank you, Mrs Murray. Etta, do stop hanging on my hand and pulling. What on earth is it?'

'The globe. The globe,' said Etta.

Hugh grinned at Curry. 'What on earth did she have for lunch?' he asked.

'Come and see,' said Etta.

The globe was open. 'Like an egg,' said Etta, darting to show them. Inside were papers, a Bible, a pair of gloves, a small jewel box. Hugh leaned over, intrigued. The gloves had belonged to a man. The small box opened on a woman's ring set with rubies. 'Rubies!' breathed Etta, hanging over his elbow. He pushed aside some of the papers and saw 'Last will and testament'. 'I think,' he said, 'we must ask Miss Bretton to come up and sort these out.'

'But rubies,' said Etta. 'I knew there'd be treasure. Does it mean Paddy will have some money?'

Hugh ruffled her hair. 'Probably not. Still, we can hope. Perhaps she would rather keep the ring if she could. It might have belonged to someone she knew. Let's shut it up now and go and have tea.'

He locked the globe again.

'I think we should let Mrs Murray guard the key until Miss Bretton needs it, don't you?' and he put it into Curry's worn hand.

'Thank you, sir.' He caught a glimpse of dark satisfaction as if now, with this last small discovery, she had the whole of Bretton safely in her keeping. As he went out, his arm round Etta's shoulders, she said, 'I have put your post on the tea tray, sir.'

There it lay, a letter addressed in a cramped unhappy

hand, a hand only partially familiar and yet a hand he knew and recognized before he fully took in the significance of the stamp.

'I hope it's from Mother,' said Etta cheerfully, carefully arranging his cup. 'She must come home for my birthday.'

'It's from Italy,' said Hugh.

26

THE KITCHENER HAD misbehaved all morning. The wind, Mrs Prince told Hugh, was in the north-west. Later the beast grew rageful, its dampers stuck open, and Bushey had to be summoned to close them by brute force, raging himself. 'And all on Miss Etta's birthday,' said Lily.

It was a day of wind and sunshine. The grass in the park, undergrazed all summer, rippled across shining acres like spring barley. Curry, stepping outside the smoky fug of the kitchen, was taken aback by the keen tearing air, the brightness. They seemed to pierce her ancient defences, the immaculate black, the corsets, the tough white skin, her careful heart.

Paddy walked up from the Lodge early to find Etta wobbling all over the drive on the bicycle Hugh had given her. She had been struggling with it since break-fast and was almost ready to take flight through the rhododendrons, her stockings torn into holes, a great bruise on one cheek. She had been in the kitchen, she said breathlessly, and they were cooking her birthday cake.

'Well, Johnny Chance is bringing my present,' announced Paddy mysteriously.

For a moment she stood on the steps looking back across the park. As if at her silent command a small moving shape appeared. Etta gripped her bicycle and stared. It was a pony and trap, coming at a canter. The pony's mane was plaited with red and silver ribbon, there were red rosettes on his winkers, red velvet on his browband. When Johnny swept off his hat and raised his whip in salute all Etta's freckles started with delight.

'Many happy returns,' he said.

The pony drew up with a flourish on the gravel sweep where carriages had once waited, where Harriet's dogcart had stood, where the funeral horses had shaken their black plumes. Etta left the bicycle and ran across. The pony snorted and threw his head up.

'Steady,' said Johnny. 'You ought to know better than to run under his nose. Here, this is for you.' There was a basket in the well of the trap, the picnic basket tied with more of the red ribbon.

'From me,' said Paddy, lifting it out.

'It's a puppy!' shrieked Etta as a small white fat slug bundled itself into her arms.

'You must ask Paget,' said Paddy, 'but I'm sure it's valid.'

'Was valid,' retorted Johnny Chance. He was leafing through one of Harriet's botanical volumes, struck by the fineness of the illustrations.

'It's dated 1860. The will that was proved was dated 1846. I know. I had to look it up. Years ago, I had something . . . I don't remember. Paget queried some plan of Tom's.' She spoke softly, almost as if to herself. Her fingers folded and refolded the paper. This, she thought, not that other, contained Ralph's last, lost instructions.

'It was all a long time ago,' said Johnny bluntly. 'Does it matter?'

'But he meant Caroline to have Roman Hill. If she had had children . . .'

334

'She died. She died when she was fifteen or sixteen. There were no children.'

Paddy's head was bowed. 'We never knew,' she said. 'How could we never have known?'

'My father found out. About Caroline. Not, of course, about the will.'

Harriet, Paddy cried silently. Harriet, did *you* know? She looked up suddenly as if she might surprise her grandmother sitting at the library table where Johnny stood with her book. 'You may kneel on a chair to look at the pictures,' Harriet had said. How strong and deft her fingers had been, with their boyishly short nails, always a suggestion of earth deeply ingrained in the skin. Those had been the days when a lady was expected to have perfect hands, soft, white, perfumed. 'I have gardener's hands,' said Harriet proudly.

Paddy felt the tears scorch along her lids between the lashes. She closed her eyes more tightly but they spilled over, running down her cheeks to the corners of her mouth.

Johnny put down the book, astonished. Then he came and crouched awkwardly by her chair, putting his arms about her. He did not know what had made her weep, nor did he guess how privileged he was to behold such a phenomenon. He was conscious only of her long slender bones, the dead weight of her head on his shoulder, unimaginable grief.

'I loved her so much,' said the strained, muffled voice.

'I know you did.' He had no idea whom she meant.

'And Mother. And Jack.'

'I know. I know.' He must calm her somehow. His encircling arms tightened. He said the first thing that came into his head. 'My mother always said Father was in love with you.' As he spoke he was aware he should have used 'loved' or 'adored', ambiguous terms that

335

might apply to mothers, daughters, friends. But 'in love'? He remembered how the whole district had whispered about the nature of their relationship, how sometimes unguarded remarks had crackled with sexual innuendo.

'In love!' cried Paddy, brushing at her wet face. Already she was straightening, resolution flowing through her. 'With himself perhaps. Have you a handkerchief?'

Johnny removed himself to a polite distance. She was brisk with the handkerchief. He would never have thought such dignity could be restored so quickly.

'What will you do about the will?' she asked.

'Nothing.'

'But Roman Hill . . .'

'This,' he said, picking it up, 'was sixty years ago.'

There were shrieks from the hall, Lily's voice: 'Lord, Miss Etta, get that puppy out to the Piggery and find it a basket. There's Mr Paget outside and a puddle on the clean flags.'

Paddy stood up. 'I think you should show Paget the will,' she said firmly.

'You sound like a schoolmistress. Or like Mrs Murray.'

'That will . . .'

'You and I and Hugh Haley are the only ones who know about . . .' and he folded it and put it in his pocket, 'this will.'

'Oh, Miss Paddy,' cried Paget, entering without knocking. 'Have you any idea of what's going on? I'm so sorry, am I intruding? I had no inkling it was young Henrietta's birthday. Mr Chance, good morning. I should have been over here last night but business kept me late in Frilton.'

'I think you ought to sit down,' said Paddy.

'No. No, my dear. I shall be quite all right in a moment when I have my breath. I must see Mr Haley

336

as soon as I can. But what do you make of this,' and he handed her the telegram.

Paddy read: 'Let the fool have the house and Home Farm. Chance can have the rest. Tell Pat.'

'I believe by "fool" he means poor young Haley,' murmured Paget.

The door opened. Etta came in with the puppy asleep in her arms, Hugh behind her. '. . . out of the blue,' they heard Paget say tremulously.

'I think the house is yours,' said Paddy, holding out the paper.

'Does that mean we can stay?' Etta's freckles paled with anxiety.

'Yes,' said Hugh. He put a hand on her head. 'Run along and put that puppy in a basket. Mr Paget, perhaps you'd like to look at the letter I received. It's somewhat less abrupt and a little more explicit.'

'There's a taxi in the avenue,' said Paddy, having seen the windscreen glint between the rhododendrons.

Etta gave a start. Flooded with joy already she could scarcely accommodate this new one. She saw the stupefied faces of the grown-ups, their kind but puzzled faces.

'It's Mother,' she told them fiercely, for she knew, she knew. The absolute certainty filled her along with the barely containable happiness. She turned and plunged through the door and they heard her calling for Curry and Lily and Laura all in one high-pitched ecstatic note.

The front door was open. There were figures there, a rush of cold air, the smell of dead leaves, voices. Hugh started forward and then, drawing level with Paddy, put a hand briefly on her arm.

'We must talk later. There's something I want to put to you. An idea. A solution.'

He did not look at her. His eyes were fixed on the doorway. He had the expression of a man who has steeled himself to a desert and found gardens.

'Darlings,' said Laura.

She did not open her arms to embrace them, her husband and her daughter. She simply stood there smiling, the fur collar of her coat turned up to the tips of her small ears, her perfume gradually filling the hall, her eyes soft and bright. She knew, as well as they did, that she broke promises easily, but this one she had kept. She had remembered Etta's birthday. She had come. Her triumph was almost tangible. Her smile was the smile of victory.

Hugh did not stoop to kiss her, but neither did he hang back awkwardly like an uncertain boy. All that, he felt, was past. He took her arm confidently, leading her in, while Lily closed the door behind her and Curry, Etta and the puppy stood to one side, waiting.

'You're in time to hear the news,' Hugh said. 'Tom Bretton's agreed to sell me the house.'

'How lovely,' exclaimed Laura bravely.

Johnny Chance had found his way to the Piggery where, in the flower room, he found a pair of great old scissors. With these he cut Ralph's last will and testament in quarters. Then he went into the kitchen and fed the quarters carefully to the kitchener.

'Why, Mr Chance,' said Mrs Prince, flustered, 'there's no call for you to poke the fire up.' Lily had just told her of Laura's arrival and she had been mysteriously upset by it. 'The only good thing is, she won't stay long,' had been her final comment. 'My tea leaves have let me down,' she told Johnny confidentially. 'Oh, what a day for excitement.'

'And how's the cake?'

'Look for yourself.' She bore it forth for inspection, a pink and white masterpiece.

Birthday cake, bride cake, funeral cake . . . Time marches on, Johnny thought. He put a large brown finger to the sugary pink roses.

'I hope it tastes as good as it looks,' he said.

Paddy said, taking Paget by the arm – 'To coerce me,' he told his wife later – 'I want you to do this. I'll explain it to Tom. You don't have to worry that he'll be difficult.'

'Hobeys a gift!' He had grown very pink and breathed heavily with indignation. 'I've never heard of such a thing.'

'It's only a rough hill, low grade pasture . . .'

'It's no such thing, Miss Paddy.'

'Call it a gift from my father. The Chances have been such good tenants after all. You must know how it can be done.'

'But Miss Paddy . . .'

'There are reasons.'

Paget pursed his mouth. 'Old scandals are best forgotten. Old wounds. Young Mr Chance . . .'

'Loves Hobeys as they all did.'

'Hobeys!' cried Paget. 'Why Hobeys?'

Paddy gave him an arch look, a Harriet look. Laughter pulled at her mouth and glittered in her eye.

'Let's just say I'd rather it didn't go to strangers,' she said sweetly.

Paddy and Etta walked down Hobeys in the dusk. They walked close together and above them, all down the edge of the field, the branches of the trees creaked back and forth in the wind. At some point, looking up at the stripped elms, Paddy removed her hat, and at some other Etta had to stop for a stone in her boot.

'Your father wants me to live at Home Farm.'

'With Mr Dack?'

'Mr Dack's going to live in a cottage in the village. He's too old to manage.'

'Can't you live at Bretton? It's ever so big.'

'No, I can't.'

'Then I s'pose Home Farm would do. Do you want to live there?'

'I don't know. I've never had to think about it till now.'

'But you will.' Etta grasped her hand suddenly, moved to such presumption by sudden fright, by the thought that there was nowhere else, that if Paddy refused Home Farm she would leave Bretton for ever. 'You will, won't you?'

Disconcertingly, Paddy made no reply. They went on down, the last leaves blown in their faces, all about them the grass flattened by the wind and shadowed by the coming night. Etta's ears had turned bright red and her nose was running. She still clung to Paddy's hand.

In Lower Bit she asked, 'Why are we going to Roman Hill?'

'Because I want to tell Mr Chance Hobeys belongs to him now. He left so soon after your birthday tea I didn't manage to do it then.'

'Really belongs to him?'

'Yes, really.'

They had reached the beck. 'May I tell him?' asked Etta.

The mulberry had dropped its fruits, dark and bloody. The hens had retreated to some corner out of the wind. The yard by the house was thick with chestnut leaves, their pungent smell filling all the air. Etta came to a standstill, her feet covered by them.

'Well, Hettyetta?'

Light from the doorway spilled towards her. She had known how he would look, laughter in his brown eyes, the red hair springing up. She opened her mouth to tell him the good news but she was so tired suddenly, tired with so much joy, such heady excitement, the long walk down in the rising wind. For a moment all pleasure drained away and left only the one last spreading anxiety.

'Please make Paddy stay at Home Farm,' she said in a small and shaky voice.

He came forward and swept her up. She saw that under the red brows his eyes were serious. He would try then, she thought, and because Paddy liked him he would succeed.

Paddy had come round the corner of the house. They heard her feet in the leaves.

'Have you told him?' she asked.

'Told me what?' demanded Johnny.

Etta, half asleep, made no protest when he carried her like a baby back towards the doorway. 'You tell him,' she said. She was so tired and besides, in her bones she felt this news about Hobeys was Paddy's news, Paddy's gift.

'Well, whatever it is, you'd better come inside to tell me. It's dark out here and there's a gale blowing up.'

He went in, still carrying the child.

Paddy stood for a moment, her hand on the trunk of the tree, braced, irresolute. She felt, as she had felt long ago, that once beyond that door she was committed to another life. Then it had been hunting, breaking, horse-dealing, dancing up and down the parlour in Jack's arms. This time it would bring her Home Farm, another twenty years of toil and struggle.

As she stepped across the threshold the wind snatched the heavy door from her grasp and shut it, firmly, behind her.